Biblioteca do Convento de Mafra - Ã.F. Nikolic

INDEPENDENT
BIMONTHLY
LITERARY
MAGAZINE

REVISTA
LITERÁRIA
INDEPENDENTE
BIMENSAL

ADELAIDE
Independent Bimonthly Literary Magazine
Revista Literária Independente Bimensal
Year III, Number 10, November 2017
Ano III, Número 10, novembro de 2017

ISBN-13: 978-0-9995164-6-1
ISBN-10: 0-9995164-6-9

Adelaide Literary Magazine is an independent international bimonthly publication, based in New York and Lisbon. Founded by Stevan V. Nikolic and Adelaide Franco Nikolic in 2015, the magazine's aim is to publish quality poetry, fiction, nonfiction, artwork, and photography, as well as interviews, articles, and book reviews, written in English and Portuguese. We seek to publish outstanding literary fiction, nonfiction, and poetry, and to promote the writers we publish, helping both new, emerging, and established authors reach a wider literary audience. We publish print and digital editions of our magazine six times a year, in September, November, January, March, May, and July. Online edition is updated continuously. There are no charges for reading the magazine online.

A Revista Literária Adelaide é uma publicação bimensal internacional e independente, localizada em Nova Iorque e Lisboa. Fundada por Stevan V. Nikolic e Adelaide Franco Nikolic em 2015, o objectivo da revista é publicar poesia, ficção, não-ficção, arte e fotografia de qualidade assim como entrevistas, artigos e críticas literárias, escritas em inglês e português. Pretendemos publicar ficção, não-ficção e poesia excepcionais assim como promover os escritores que publicamos, ajudando os autores novos e emergentes a atingir uma audiência literária mais vasta. Publicamos edições impressas e digitais da nossa revista seis vezes por ano: em setembro, novembro, janeiro, março, maio e julho. A edição online é actualizada regularmente. Não há qualquer custo associado à leitura da revista online.

(http://adelaidemagazine.org)

Published by: Adelaide Books, New York
e-mail: info@adelaidebooks.org
phone: +351 918 635 457

FOUNDERS / FUNDADORES
Stevan V. Nikolic & Adelaide Franco Nikolic

EDITOR IN CHIEF / EDITOR-CHEFE
Stevan V. Nikolic
editor@adelaidemagazine.org

MANAGING DIRECTOR / DIRECTORA EXECUTIVA
Adelaide Franco Nikolic

GRAPHIC & WEB DESIGN
Istina Group DBA

PORTUGUESE LANGUAGE EDITOR / EDITORA PORTUGUESA
Adelaide Franco Nikolic

BOOK REVIEWS
Heena Rathore
Jack Messenger
Ana Sofia Pereira
Scott Morris

CONTRIBUTING AUTHORS IN THIS ISSUE

Grant Segall, Dan Howard, Santino DeFranco, Debra Leigh Scott, Patricia Trentacoste, Jeffrey Kass, Michael Hetherton, Shirley A Guldimann, Tinka Harvard, Richard Bentley, Vera Lúcia Gonçalves, Bill Schillaci, Charlotte Freccia, Lily Wright, David Heath, Adrian Encomienda, Jonathan Ferrini, Ben Orlando, Michael LeBlanc, Michael Washburn, David Cairns, Ronald Kovach, Mark Gunther, John Bliss, Alicia Marie Devers, Gracjan Kraszewski, Andy Tu, Raymond Arcangel, Saul Hernandez, Dennis J. Dymek, Terry Sanville, Michael Warren, Mark Hannon, Emily Peña Murphey, Robert Cardullo, Gina Miller-Meinema, Pamela Carter, Doug Weaver, David Boyl, David Heath, Pam Munter, Holley Hyler, Angela Yurchenko, Lowell Jaeger, Gary Beck, Timothy Robbins, Pierre Sotér, Richard Weaver, Seth Jani, Mark Young, Susie Gharib, Kennie Romero, Jacquelyne Nemeth, Thomas Locicero, Omar Alexandre, William Ruleman, Glen Sorestad, Adrian Slonaker, Jean Berrett, George Gad Economou, Francisco Mejia, Katie Predick, Sara Pridmore Bailey, Leslie Philibert, Dianne Moritz, Eduardo Escalante, Mather Schneider, Steven Pelcman, Michelle Cacho-Negrete, Anders M. Svenning, Janet Mason, Nina Wilson, Richard Schmitt, Steven McBrearty, Pierre Sotér, A.F. Nikolic.

CONTENTS / CONTEÚDOS

INTERVIEWS / ENTREVISTAS

BOOK REVIEWS / CRITÍCAS LITERÁRIAS

NEW TITLES

ART & PHOTOGRAPHY / ARTE & FOTOGRAFIA

Front cover photo:
Biblioteca do Convento de Mafra - Ã.F. Nikolic

Biblioteca do Convento de Mafra - Ã.F. Nikolic

Editor's Notes

Stevan V. Nikolic

THE RIGHT TIME TO PUBLISH

What is the best time to publish your book? This is the most often asked question and the biggest dilemma both aspiring and established authors have.

There are two aspects of the answer to this question. One relates to the author's (and editor's) satisfaction with the manuscript submitted for publishing and the second to the commercial effect the story presented may have with readers at the particular time of the book release.

Mark Twain once said that the best time to start writing an article is when you are completely satisfied with what you wrote. In other words, applied to creative writing, the best time to start writing a novel is once you are completely satisfied with the novel you wrote. Indeed, there are many examples of writers going back and re-writing and republishing already published works of fiction. Personally, I think that the best method of perfecting a piece of literary work is, once you complete your manuscript, to give yourself some "time and mental" distance before going back to the final reading of your manuscript. You should not go back to your manuscript until your mind is completely "clean" from any thoughts related to it. Only then, you'll be able to go through your writings with the "fresh eye" and clean understanding of potentially needed changes or corrections.

However, don't forget that any piece of literary work, once it is published and accepted by readers, receives a life of its own, its own integrity, and doesn't belong completely to you anymore. It matures and becomes an "adult." So, instead of going back and rewriting your story, it would be more beneficial for you and your readers to let it go and put your mind to writing a new book.

When it comes to the best time to launch your book with reference to commercial effect it may have, in general terms, there is no such a thing as the best time. Any time is good, as long as the launch of your book if accompanied with the adequate marketing program. When it comes to trade, the best release time is the beginning of the year (January to March), which enable publishers to present published title to at all major trade shows during the year (London Book Fair, Book Expo US, Frankfurt etc.).

Talking about sales, most of us would assume – Christmas. Of course, the holiday season is important for every retailer (including booksellers). However, according to industry sources, last year, there were over $3.4 billion in sales over the long hot summer, compared to about $2.9 billion spent for holiday gift giving. And we certainly should not forget the fact often mentioned by many publishers: "Book promotion and sales is not a "sprint", it is more like a "marathon."

As a publisher, I always advise authors not to worry about the "right time" to publish. Sometimes, the best way to teach "your baby to swim" is to throw it into the water. Let it go. Readers will decide. And you will write a new book.

Biblioteca do Convento de Mafra - Ã.F. Nikolic

WORKING THE EDGE
Grant Segall

Stefan picked his way down the driveway, skirting a pothole with the season's first ice, trying to save what was left of his hip for what was left of the countryside.

A faint rustling stopped. He turned and scanned the back yard, the chicken-wire fence, the last of the woods beyond. At night lately, he'd caught a couple of crackles and flickers back there. But now, a little after dawn, he could just make out the poplars shimmering.

No, Marta — closer. Standing over your hydrangeas. Staring back. Something we haven't seen in the Ridge for decades. A deer. A buck. With three, four, five points.

He glanced down the driveway again. Nobody there but the beggar across the street, looking too hungry for human prey to bother the buck.

Stefan crept toward the lawn, hugging his bathrobe. He'd forgotten how delicate deer looked, big as they were. The buck's long eyelashes were blinking. His spindly legs were flexed, ready to flee. His antlers looked too scrawny and velvety to duel for a doe any time soon. He seemed to hover over the flowers like a hummingbird.

Sure, along the highway, from the countryside. But why bother in 1995? I'm stuck in the Ridge a few more months, meeting those silly new codes, then trying to sell our sturdy house in a rickety neighborhood. But what's here for a buck anymore?

Back in '48, when Stefan built the first home here, the restocked deer were surging. Marta, coaxed up from Canalside, tried to drive them from her garden with dried blood. He stalked them deep in the woods, beyond her earshot. Still, the boys needed more than venison, so he helped build other homes, the school, the church, the shopping center, and a highway to fill them all. Soon the swelling Ridge merged with Canalside, where hunting was banned. No matter. The deer had already fled to higher hills.

Now the buck finally bent his head and began to chew the hydrangeas. Sorry, Marta, but they'll come back next year, and who knows if the buck ever will?

Like the boys, the highway kept on growing. Soon it was taking neighbors with any money to newer, fancier places and chasing the deer further out. But Marta dug in here with a few new friends who'd bought in low and a few old ones who couldn't afford to sell out low. So he and the boys saw the deer just once a year, camping near them the Sunday night after Thanksgiving, hunting them the Monday at dawn.

The buck threw him another look. Still though he'd been, Stefan froze all over again. The buck returned to the flowers. Magenta again, your favorite, after what, five, six years of periwinkle? It figures. Stick around long enough, and things change and change again.

They changed when the boys moved west for bigger game. And changed again when Marta, for all she denied it, grew too frail to spare him for the hunts. And again last April, when she spared him too much. His hip willing, he'd revisit the deer next month and fix up a cabin among them in the spring.

The buck swiveled his ears. Next door, halfway across his deck, Lamont froze, briefcase bag on shoulder, nostrils extra wide.

Then the buck swiveled his whole head the other way. Eileen was working her way down her stoop in curlers, holding out an apple. "Oh," she wheezed, "you're a beauty."

The buck promptly cleared the fence and vanished. The woods were still thick enough for cover, it seemed. The yard fell quiet again, just the way Stefan usually liked it. But the neighbors kept staring, and so did he, as if the buck would make the same mistake twice.

"Well," Lamont finally said, "I shouldn't be surprised. We hear they've taken over the bigger towns already: Columbus, Canton...."

"Why?" Eileen asked the bureaucrat instead of the hunter.

Lamont cocked the case toward a glassy roof on the next hill out. "We're getting in the deer's space, so they're getting in ours."

Fighting a shiver, Stefan counted the days to a yard too wide and wooded for the neighbors to chat across.

"They do all right here?" asked Eileen.

"Sure, at first. Especially in edge neighborhoods like this. They raid the gardens and hide in the parks, alleys, ravines...."

"Then what?"

"Then they clear out, if they're lucky. Before getting run over, infected, whatever." Lamont chuckled. "Like they used to say, different kinds don't mix."

Stefan turned from two kinds of neighbors and shuffled to the curb. His paper was in a dry spot and theirs in puddles again. No, I sure haven't raised the tip. Maybe the Ridge is trying to fool me into staying.

"So you met the buck at last."

"At last?" Stefan blurted, forgetting this once to keep quiet.

"Certainly." The beggar pushed back his silver mane. "He's been enjoying our hospitality for a week now. As the homies would say, we've got hooves in the 'hood."

We? Stefan bent for the paper in silence. For maybe a month now, the beggar had been coming who knew how early from who knew where, hogging the planter by Our Lady's soup kitchen, ignoring the bums from the underpass, cozying up to the rightful residents. Stefan would have admired the hard work, if begging had counted.

"We've got a fox too, a couple of herons in the lagoon, a coyote in the ravine." The beggar cocked his coffee can toward the underpass. "Let's just hope the riffraff leave them alone."

Stefan turned up the driveway, unbagging the paper. What makes the guy think he isn't riffraff himself? His fancy patter? Fancy hair? Private hideout?

Stefan sank into the couch in the Florida room, beneath the family photos and the old buckhead (a 3 2/3-pointer, really, since he hadn't let the taxidermist fake a tip lost in the chase). Sipping coffee, adjusting his glasses, he reread a letter from Steve's new printer and tried skimming a book from Walt about Washington's trip on the Ohio. But he mostly listened to the church bells mark time and watched the sun turn the leaves red and gold. He saw just the usual creatures out there: pigeons mobbing Eileen's feeder, a Cooper's hawk scouting the highway, a squirrel scurrying nowhere.

That night, he rolled around the queen bed more than usual. In the morning, he slid open the glass door as quietly as he used to part the bamboo in Guadalcanal. No buck this time, no fresh wounds in the hydrangeas, no prints in the frost. Sure, the buck belongs in the countryside, especially near hunting season, when he'll need a mate and I'll need prey. Admit it, though: For one day, he made the Ridge seem new and wild again.

Soon Eileen brought a whole basket of apples down her sagging stoop, which Marta had wanted him to shore up. The squirrels helped themselves. The buck stayed away. Still, Eileen started refilling the basket daily. It just drew more squirrels, who scattered the leaf piles and trampled the garden.

Early Saturday morning, Stefan climbed a ladder in back and started rehanging a few shingles. Soon he'd drawn a crowd. Desiree was sweeping the deck and Brianna prancing across it, her hands overhead like antlers. "You're kind to try feeding them," Lamont told Eileen, "but..."

"Now, you know I feed anyone: the bingo players, the homeless, little girls with sweet teeth..." She glanced at Stefan, whose Army jacket was getting baggy lately. "Anyone who lets me, that is."

Stefan banged a rusty nail. It snapped. His hip twinged. Marta, enviably free of envy, had hinted about Eileen toward the end. But the last thing he wanted was another old lady to share lame help and thanks with.

"You OK up there?" Lamont called.

"'Course." It seemed the buck was a new excuse for people to mind each other's business.

"Heard about our fix-up loans? You could hire a little help."

Stefan drove home what was left of the nail, remembering when he'd been worth the hire himself.

One morning, he saw hoof prints in the mud. Starting that night, he quit climbing upstairs and spread his bedroll on the couch in the Florida room instead. With the space heater crackling, the buckhead standing guard, the poplars rustling outside, and the live buck lurking somewhere, he almost felt like a hunter again.

A week later, he caught the buck a second time, or more the other way around. After a moment, the buck started gobbling the fallen nuts again, looking up once or twice a minute, surprising Stefan every time. Full at last, he slipped through a gap in Eileen's pickets.

Stefan fetched the paper. "There's a timely story this morning," said the beggar, "about birth control for deer." Where was the guy's copy? "I read it at home, of course." Could the homeless get home delivery?

The morning after Halloween, the buck nosed some Twix wrappers on the driveway, glancing now and then at Stefan hammering a siding cap. Near Election Day, he nosed a bag of handbills by Lamont's garage, hardly glancing at Stefan boxing up ancient metal roller skates for the grandkids.

One tease of a mild day, the buck relieved himself against the back of an ankle. "Ewww!" Brianna squealed from a swirl of chalk on her driveway.

Eileen pinkened and raked the other way.

"He's just spreading his musk," Stefan mumbled, explaining a fact of life to a girl too young and a woman almost his age. "Marking his territory."

The rake paused. "Well, it beats graffiti, I guess."

The buck began to rub his cheek against a branch of the chestnut. Eileen drank him in. Brianna tittered and rubbed her cheek against her chalk stick.

Then a motorbike revved past the driveway. "Vroom vroom!" cried Brianna, steering the chalk like a handlebar.

"Too bad there's no doe around," whispered Eileen.

"Just as well," said Stefan. "Tough place here for fawns."

The next afternoon, when it was nearing 60 out, Stefan headed toward the Ridge's last real barbershop. From the alley, someone whispered, "Closer." Stefan hunched his shoulders and started to hurry past. But the man was facing the other way, toward the rubble from the old depot, and brandishing something at the buck.

"Hey!" Stefan cried.

The buck fled through the rubble. The stalker spun. "Oh, you!" It was the beggar again, with one of Our Lady's triangle sandwiches. "Guess I'm not hungry today," he mumbled, maybe shyer about his kindness than his usual greed.

Stefan steadied his breath. "Really, we should let the buck fend for itself." Those "we's" were contagious, it seemed.

"Let's save that for tougher creatures, like yourself."

That night, the warm spell gave way to swirls of fat snow. Stefan was dragging the garbage to the curb when an ambulance swung into Eileen's driveway, and paramedics who looked barely old enough to work hauled her out. She raised an eyebrow, asking him to what — save her? the buck? the Ridge? He'd ridden along with Marta, holding her clammy hand, mumbling "It's all right." Now he hung back with something between a wave and a shrug. Eileen rolled her eyes and vanished.

In the morning, his paper lay on top of a little snowbank and Eileen's beneath it. He scooped up both, so hers wouldn't get soaked. "Good idea," said the beggar, "keeping her absence secret from the riffraff."

Safe from her thanks now, Stefan started clearing Eileen's papers and mail daily. But he drew the line at propping her stoop or filling her basket. The first few mornings, the buck nosed the basket awhile. Stefan finally stowed it in his basement. The next time, the buck nosed the foundation.

That afternoon, Stefan was oiling the garage lock when his hip seized up — his good hip, no less. He spun. There was the buck, nosing the sliding glass, stamping the grass, cocking his antlers, daring the old buckhead to fight.

"Scram!" someone shouted. The buck obeyed at once. "Oh, didn't see you," said Lamont. "Just trying to save your door."

"Thanks, but we don't really have to worry about him charging," said Stefan, drowning in "we's" by now. "Not without a doe around."

Lamont cocked a thumb at the woods, where a few stubborn old leaves were hanging on. "It's been sounding lately like a whole harem's back there."

On Thanksgiving, Stefan nibbled a boxed turkey dinner from Rzepka's. Eileen used to bring colcannon with too many onions, and Marta to give thanks for family and friends. This time, Stefan gave silent thanks for escaping a dinner alone with Eileen.

Afterwards, he walked a potted kale to the cemetery and cleared Marta's stone of snow and litter. Two punks watched from the mausoleum steps, smoking who knew what, snickering who knew why, killing time.

He made it back home by dusk, both hips creaking. The buck never looked up from the chestnut. All right, all right, no hunting this season, at least. Thank the early winter, the sneaky years, our trusting guest.

Stefan spent Monday puttering, dozing, and reading about Washington's call for the canal. The next morning, he couldn't find Eileen's paper. "Someone must have cancelled it," said the beggar. In the afternoon, her daughter showed up

for once, waving stiffly, leading around a woman with a clipboard and a camera. The next day, two men hammered a For Sale sign into the dingy snow and propped up the stoop at last. Sorry, Marta. Eileen must have gone to a nursing home or a grave. Giving her place the jump on ours.

That night, he was dozing over the book when the Florida room burst open. The coffee table bounced off the wall. The buck bounded away. The cold blew in.

Stefan managed to rise. Chunks of glass slid onto the old buckhead below. The brow was gored and the coat flecked with blood. Not enough blood to weaken the live buck, just to rile him up all the more.

Stefan bagged the head, hauled it to the garage, and dumped it in the trash. Then he called a glazier's hotline and got Muzak awhile. Face it, Lamont's right: There must be a doe or two around, hoping to make new life in a dying neighborhood.

A dispatcher finally gave out two prices: a fortune for next-day service or two fortunes for overnight. Either way, Stefan would have to crawl to Lamont for that loan and put off the cabin. "Forget it," he said. For tonight, anyway, he'd just strengthen his guard against two-legged intruders.

He eased his way down to the basement and unlocked the gun case. He wiped down the knife, resheathed it, and strapped it to his hip (still good for that much, at least). He inspected the rifle: tarnished but not warped. He squeezed the trigger a few times and worked it loose. Then he took aim at the dartboard. It froze in his sights. No old-age shakes yet, at least.

Stefan loaded the rifle and set it beside the bedroll. The temperature rose just enough for rain, some of it blowing inside. Could he shoot burglars like deer? On Guadalcanal, he'd scattered some silhouettes on a bluff, but never faced anyone up close.

It was still dark when he gave up trying to sleep and opened the side door. The newspaper truck rumbled past. His copy landed with a splash. Talk about things changing again. Then someone came from across the street. The beggar, on duty already. Stefan hung back. The man rescued the paper, slipped off the bag, shook everything dry, leaned against a streetlight, and began to read calmly, routinely. Now what? Do I call the cops or give him a tip? Eileen would have loved sharing her copy back when. But maybe it was more fun to sneak Stefan's.

Later that morning, Stefan was boarding up the door when the realtor pulled up and a big family followed: a stringy black woman, a dumpy white man, and kids of all shapes and shades in between. Soon the brood was scampering from one muddy yard to another, with Brianna in tow. Lamont came out chuckling. Then he saw the boards and spun inside.

That afternoon, the doorbell rang. It was a wildlife agent, with those shoulder patches of animals more from Disney than nature.

"Yeah?" asked Stefan, a shiver slipping loose.

"Just stay inside, please, while we catch the deer."

It figured that the law would bust the deer and spare the bums. "How?"

"With tranquilizer darts."

"Then what?"

The agent lowered his voice. "We dispose of them privately."

"Why not let them loose in the country?"

"Hunters might eat the tranquilizer."

For an hour or so, Stefan read about land barons plotting the canal and daydreamed about tranquilizing the agent. Near dusk, the bell rang again. "Smart deer," said the agent, his breath steaming like the buck's. "We'll try again tomorrow. For now, you can come back out."

"Thanks." Stefan shut the door. As if old-timers could brave the Ridge at night. Or could I, just this once — hunt near home again, and help the deer die right?

When the last light was gone, he slipped his jacket on, belted the knife, shouldered the rifle, and went outside. He'd forgotten how private the dark was. Brianna was gazing out a window without seeing him. In a minute, though, he made out the gap in the pickets and started down the deer path beyond. The woods were still thick enough

to muffle the street's clatter and the highway's whirr. They seemed like the woods of old almost, except for a slightly smoky smell.

The path sank toward the stream. He knelt on the bank, in a tangle of vines. In seconds, his pants had soaked through. He fought a shiver one minute and a yawn the next. Orion was rising, the ancient hunter as strong and upright as ever. Stefan would shoot whichever came along first: the buck or a doe. Then the rest of the herd might finally have the sense to give up on the Ridge.

He blinked. The buck was lapping the stream. Stefan sprang up and swung the rifle. The buck kept drinking slowly, as if he had all the time in the world. Stefan steadied his breath. Was the water still OK around here? In the hospital, he'd given Marta sip after sip, not knowing what else to do for her. But he could do more for the buck: a neighbor by now, and the best one, really, not shoving loans or colcannon or coffee cans at him, just keeping him quiet company, keeping the Ridge alive.

The buck looked up calmly, knowingly. Stefan fingered the trigger. The sights were wobbling. In the clutch, he had the shakes after all.

The buck turned away. Before Stefan knew it, he'd fired. The buck lurched and fled, his hoofbeats jerky but fast. Stefan had done the worst thing a hunter could — wounded his prey too lightly, leaving him living in pain.

Another shot sounded. From another gun. Stefan dove with young speed. The hoofbeats stopped with a crash.

"Freeze," someone whispered, as if Stefan would have dared to move anyway. A hawthorn parted. A pistol poked out. In the beggar's hand.

"You again." The man holstered his gun and offered a hand up.

"You too." Stefan managed to stand on his own.

"Oh, I was just taking my evening constitutional." Around a wiener roast, from the smell of him. "Until you turned it into work. Now come."

The beggar led him down the path briskly, surely. Off to the side a ways, Stefan caught a tarp and the last of a campfire. He should have known.

Despite the silver hair, the man was still young and strong enough to live in the wild.

"Keep it quiet, please."

"I keep everything quiet."

They found the buck sprawled on an old tire, panting, steaming, quivering, a leg oozing, a flank gushing. One eye was shut, but the other was watching them blurrily. Without a by-your-leave, the beggar breathed and aimed. The buck just kept watching. Near the end, Marta had tried to comfort Stefan more than the other way around. "Rest up," he whispered, "like the doctor said." Soon she rested too well.

The beggar finally fired. The buck heaved and shuddered. The eyelid fell. Stefan's own eyes blurred foolishly, when death was the surest way to be shut of the Ridge.

The beggar took out a pocket knife and started skinning the buck deftly. Stefan drew his hunting knife and fumbled with a foreleg. A siren came down the block. It figured the cops would be prompt for once. The siren stopped. A door slammed. Footsteps followed but stopped short of the woods.

Unruffled, the beggar said, "I suppose Our Lady couldn't take the meat. But the riffraff could roast it at the carhop."

Stefan didn't know which would be a sorrier fate for the buck: to feed the buzzards here or the bums there. "They know it needs to age first?"

"Of course. Somewhere safe and dry. Like your garage."

Stefan shrugged. The way things were going, he might as well give them the whole house.

"You could try some meat yourself," the beggar said. "Fill out a little." Stefan had hit a new low: a beggar worrying about him.

More footsteps, another slam, and the cops pulled away. The beggar wiped his knife and sheathed it. Stefan did likewise. Leaving the head behind, they hauled the torso to the yard. Someone chuckled — Lamont, by his side door. "Lucky I know the cops."

"Much obliged," said the beggar.

Stefan nodded, though jail would have put off his housing problem awhile.

They hung the buck from a beam, over a bucket and some newspapers. Then they wiped off their hands on rags, while Stefan ignored his hips. "Well," the beggar murmured, "later, let's say." He crossed the yard and slipped through Eileen's gap as quietly as the buck used to do.

Stefan shuffled inside with the rifle. He'd gotten even more years from it than from Marta. Now it was just a menace all around. He tossed it in the fireplace and lit the tinder. He spent the rest of the night in the armchair, watching the stock blacken and the barrel glow.

A blink or two later, he woke to the bells. He glanced out back before remembering and trudging to the curb. A crowd was lined up by Our Lady already, but the planter was free. The beggar must have been sleeping late for once, after a long night's work with a buck and a geezer.

"Hey," someone cried, "it's the rifleman!"

"Tell us when the meat's ready," called someone else.

Stefan retreated with the paper, his privacy just a memory. By the garage was the new buckhead, the antlers perfect, the coat still silky. He'd have to put a stop to all these favors. But the beggar had beaten him to it again. Stuck on an antler was a torn envelope with flowery script: "Take care of the Ridge for me."

Stefan stared at the woods. Just another vacant property now. Another occupant had turned out to be too soft for the Ridge.

Stefan called the glazier again. "Oh, no emergency, I guess." Then he bagged the head for the taxidermist's. If I'm stuck here a little longer, I'd better hang this one in the basement, safe from any other fool buck who might come around.

About the Author:

Grant Segall, a Harvard grad and a Cleveland Plain Dealer reporter and columnist, won three national prizes and many statewide ones. His articles have been published in Time, The Washington Post, The Boston Globe, Philadelphia Magazine, American Education, and more. His short stories have been published in five college reviews and two independent zines, earning honorable mention in Whiskey Island's yearly contest at Cleveland State. He is the author of the well-received John D. Rockefeller: Anointed with Oil (Oxford University Press, 2001), which Booklist called "fascinating" and "first-rate." "Rockefeller" has been published in the U.S., Korea, and China.

SPANKING

Earl Javorsky

Herb Baumgartner considered the idea of getting spanked. It was worth it, bearing a little pain—in theory at least—if his wife really could then be over it, get off it, forget about whatever new infraction she had invented for him, and just allow them to be free of it.

To be precise, it had been Doctor Hofflinger's theory. Herb remembered the session when the Good Doctor had first brought it up:

"What do you mean, let her spank me?" Herb had said, astonished. Even Janice's jaw had dropped for a second, a look quickly transformed into an expression of somber consideration, a funny sideways nod, as though the idea wasn't really that far out.

"Spank," said Hofflinger, smacking his hand on his fat thigh, his head bald with a fringe, smooth pink face and a squinty left eye. "Spank you like the naughty child she thinks you are."

"Why the hell would I let her do that?" Herb looked at his watch, thinking about how many more sessions were covered by the insurance, aware that Annie had caught his time-check and now had a fresh excuse to be pissed.

"Because your surrender to it will win the trust she needs to develop in order to breakthrough to a new relationship paradigm." Stanley Hofflinger, PhD, beamed at Janice, laced his fingers together and stretched his arms over his head, then turned back to Herb.

Herb drummed his fingers on the armrest of the leather sofa he lounged in, his wife sitting straight up at the other end, and considered just closing his eyes and tuning out. Tempting, it was, to just nod off for a bit and let the witch break through on her own.

"Herbert?"

That night they had dinner at Sabatino's. Janice let Herb eat his veal and angel hair pasta without mentioning their session. They shared a bottle of Valpolicella and discussed his work—"Why, as partner, can't you vote yourself a raise?"—his clothes— "You know, there's a Barney's outlet in the Valley now. You could get rid of some of those antique suits you wear"—and their daughter—"She lives in a dorm on campus, for God's sake; she doesn't need a damned car." Herb chewed and sipped; he nodded his head occasionally. There were no adequate responses, and Janice was quite used to talking to herself.

They ordered dessert and coffee. Herb liked to spoon vanilla ice cream into his coffee and then eat it; the rich, sweet flavor and the combination of hot and cold pleased him immensely, and he closed his eyes to savor the effect. From across the table, Janice merely said, "Well?"

Now, on the way home in the car, Janice was telling him the details of what they were going to do. She had obviously spent some time thinking about it—perhaps even been given specific coaching from Hofflinger, whom she had called by cell phone and chatted with as they drove to the restaurant.

So she enumerated the stations of his cross: They would bathe; they would have a drink (just one); they would proceed to the bedroom; Herb would stand at the end of the bed, facing the head-board; he would bend over and place his hands on the bed . . .

Just one drink turned into three, but otherwise Herb faithfully followed the script. The first drink got him to the bathtub; the second—on top of the wine at dinner—put him in a dreamy state where he was quite content to go along with the show. Janice actually looked quite lovely in the candlelight. She washed his feet and moved her soapy hands up his legs, stopping just short of a more satisfying contact and telling him to turn around. She then scrubbed his back with a loofah. Her manner was brisk and businesslike; she was in charge now and it suited her perfectly.

They rinsed and then stepped out onto the bath-room mat. Janice wrapped a towel around her-self, cinched it, and used a second towel to dry Herb. She had never done this before; except for when they first dated in college, they had never bathed together. Now she was drying his chest, under his arms, his face, then down between his legs, her hands strong behind the fabric. Herb pointed to the bottle of Remy on the counter. Janice shrugged, so he poured his third and downed it as she led him to the bedroom.

More candles, scented with a touch of vanilla, the bedspread pulled back, the sheets brand new Egyptian cotton. Janice walked him to the side of the bed and touched his hand to the sheet before releasing it. Herb stood awkwardly, bent at the waist, allowing his weight to rest on both hands against the fabric.

The first stroke came as a surprise, as if he hadn't really expected her to go through with it, or at least thought there might be some further prepa-ration, but no, there it was, a sharp, resounding smack that stung and made him jerk forward with a slight, involuntary grunt. There was no script for what they would do next, so he waited, his bent shadow huge against the bedroom wall. He heard labored breathing from the foot of the bed and looked back just in time to see Janice cock her arm back and bring it down for a second blast on his backside—the same spot exactly—and then a

third, upon which she suddenly bellowed "Hoohaw!" and rested herself against him, hands on his hips, her pubic hair tickling his sore ass. Janice had never said "Hoohaw" in her entire life, and had always been subdued and prim, especial-ly in the sack.

It was getting fucking irritating now, but just as Herb was about to say, "Enough, already," Janice reached from behind and cupped his balls with a hand hot as fresh toast.

Hot, Janice thought. This was hot like when she and Herb were new, like sex in his car, hot now even with their loose skin and flabby middle-age flesh. Herb had drifted into his own orbit so long ago, and she into hers, and now there was this spark that could bring their orbits into synch again, or at least to a moment's intersection. Janice bent over and kissed Herb on the shoulder blade, the wild hair on his back, curly and brown, tickling her lip, while she caressed him with her left hand. She turned him around and took him eagerly.

Three weeks later, Herb was playing golf with his best friend Barry Crandall, a stockbroker who had been cheating on his wife since she got pregnant with their first child. After the third hole, Herb noticed that Barry was walking oddly. At the fifth, he decided to ask about it.

"Knee bothering you again?"

Barry, who had been remarkably cheerful even though his game was off, stared down at his ball and said, "Nope. Knee's fine."

When Barry started lining up his next shot, Herb said, "Well, you're walking funny."

Barry let his club swing like a pendulum over the ball as he looked out over the fairway. He finally looked up at Herb and said, "I've got a sore ass."

"Hemorrhoids?" Herb was beginning to wish he hadn't pressed the issue.

Now Barry took a step forward, close up to Herb, then looked around before fixing his eyes on Herb's and saying, "Strictly private now, right?"

"Absolutely. One hundred per cent."

"Ellen got us into therapy. Some goofball that your wife told her about. He came up with this fucking wild idea . . ." Barry paused. His mouth closed, then opened again, his eyes desperate now, committed but clearly wanting to get off the hook.

"Spanking?" Herb volunteered. He hoped his sympathetic smile wouldn't morph into a smirk.

Barry shook his head. "Where in the world would you get that idea? I mean, how did you guess? Oh my God, you've got to be kidding."

They proceeded in silence, playing badly and not caring.

Over beers in the clubhouse, Barry finally brought it up again. "I hate it, but it's worth it. Unbelievable, really."

Herb nodded and said, "Hey, I know. I haven't had this much fun in years."

"Fun?" Barry drained his Heineken. "Twenty years of legal secretaries, lady lawyers, and law students—none of them holds a candle to Ellen. It's like we're on a fucking honeymoon."

Herb raised his bottle in a toast: "Here's to fucking honeymoons!"

Janice drove home from the market and started dinner. Salmon, scalloped potatoes, creamed broccoli, salad with garlic bread. Dessert, even. They had started going to the gym together; she wanted to firm up, be more attractive to him. Herb had even bought two new suits—they had shopped together at Nordstrom—and looked quite handsome in them. She, in turn, had agreed that their daughter should have a car. Well, why not? What had her resistance been? She couldn't remember. That Dr. Hofflinger was a genius.

Later, after dinner, after the ritual bath, the three drinks, the drying him off, they caressed by the bed. Herb nuzzled her freshly shampooed hair, then sighed and, turning to the bed, assumed the position.

Janice stood gazing fondly at her husband's hairy back. They had, at Dr. Hofflinger's suggestion, taken it up a notch and added a riding crop, which she now flicked through the air

several times, marveling at the whirring sound it made, the promise it offered. The phone rang, but she ignored it. On the fourth ring, the answering machine picked up. After listening to her own voice on the outgoing message, Janice heard Ellen Crandall saying, "Pick up, for God's sake, you've got to see this!"

Janice sighed. The spell was broken, but the mood could be revived; she went to the phone and picked it up.

"Hi, Ellen, can I get back to you in a bit?"

Ellen's voice was breathless. "You've got to turn on the television. I can't believe what I'm seeing."

Janice shook her head. "I can't do that right now. What the hell is going on?" She watched Herb pour himself a fourth drink.

A shriek came from the phone. "There he is again, look at him, for Christ's sake. Janice? It's on the news. Dr. Hofflinger is getting busted at some S&M parlor in the Valley. He's wearing mesh nylons and a fuzzy pink sweater that says, 'I'm a naughty little boy.' Can you fucking believe it? They're pushing him into a police car!"

Janice told Ellen she would call her back later. She turned to Herb, who raised his eyebrows questioningly, and led him back to the bed. She would have to tell him eventually, but not at this particular moment.

About the Author:

Dan Howard was born Daniel Earl Javorsky in Berlin and immigrated to the US. He has been, among other things, a delivery boy, musician, product rep in the chemical entertainment industry, university music teacher, software salesman, copy editor, proofreader, and novelist. His novels include *Down Solo* and *Trust Me*, and a sequel to *Down Solo* has just been released.

BIG BOY

Santino DeFranco

He was a real big son of a bitch. But I'm not talking about the son of a bitch part, but the big part. He was almost six and a half feet tall and around two-hundred and fifty pounds. Not a fat two-fifty, either. Like a shredded-I-can-see-every-striation-in-your-body two-fifty. He had this long blonde hair when he first came in—he looked like Thor from the movies or comic books. But a goofy, less Mjolnir, more basketball, wielding one. Cindy walked him through the main door. The door with the big locks. He had Thor by the arm—pushed the back of his elbow and guided him in like a toddler. He didn't resist either, just fumbled forward, one foot in front of the other. I think it was the dope. The drugs. He must have been juiced up, like almost all the intakes. Cindy walked him in and sat him down next to me in the fun room and he just sat there staring at me like he was waiting for my response. Mouth pursed, breathing through his nose like a dragon. All that was missing was the bifurcated smoke.

You think you can watch him for a second, Jules? Cindy asked. But Jules isn't my real name, see. He just calls me that. My real name's Julian, but I haven't been called that since, well, I can't remember. Well, in court and hearings and real stuff, real places...they call me Julian, but not here. Bank tellers and money collectors call me that too, and telemarketers. Yes, is Mr. Julian Bennett home? Or I'd like to speak with Julian please. They'd say trying to make it seem like they knew me and we were old pals or something. Julian please! Ha, jokes on them. Nobody calls me that. Unless, well, except when the jokes on me, when they're taking my money or putting me in places like this.

Sure thing, I said to Cindy. But you're wearing someone else's nametag again. Who's Sandy? I asked. But I knew who Sandy was. He was Sandy, but I'd always called him Cindy. I think I misheard him or misread his tag or something and just kept up with it. Pretended like I thought it was his name. You can do that when you're in here. It's like a kid hitting when his toy gets taken away. When you're two, you can get away with that. Parents say don't do that, Bobby. We don't hit, do we? Or they ignore it or laugh. Probably not the good parents, though. They probably don't laugh, but there's plenty of bad parents out there. But Cindy thought I thought he really had a girl name, and I liked it that way. Gave me some sort of an upper hand on him. I knew something he didn't, even if it was just my perception of him—not tangible, but real, nonetheless. Hell, time's not tangible, but many damn people think that's real. They probably don't stay in places like this too often, though, or they'd probably think differently—about time, that is.

When Cindy walked away, his hips shook a bit and his arms stretched out toward the ground with his wrists arched upward. Maybe that's why I started calling him a girl name? He was a bit of a queen, but that's okay, but still made me think he's a girl, or at least a bit girlish, or maybe just slightly more girlish than the other guys here. So now he's Cindy, but now he's not here cause he walked away, and Lorne sat staring at me like he wanted to eat my babies, which I don't have, but he didn't know that at the time.

I didn't think much else about him except that he scared me and that he smelled. His hygiene might have been what got him in this place to begin with. He never showered. Well, I can't back that fully. I should say I don't think he ever showered. There are a lot of hours in a day—some say 24, but who really knows how long it takes to spin this big ball around in the universe—and out of those hours I didn't spend every single one of them with him, but maybe much less. Probably only one or two hours a day, but sometimes more. Sometimes, throughout most of the day, we'd be together when we weren't doing other things like sleeping or seeing Dr. Mitchell, but even then, he'd be away from me here or there. So I suppose he could have showered in there somewhere, but if I was a betting man—which I'm not. Tried it a few times, but always ended in me losing much more than my money. But if I was a man that'd like to throw down a wager, I'd put my money on him not showering much, if at all, outside what they forced him to in here. I suppose, though, that he could have showered on the regular, but then just shit his pants or something or was always really gassy and sneaking out stinkys round the clock or his sweat rotted quickly to omit the smell that he always reeked of. And those crusted boogers hanging from those long nose hairs just happened to grow so fast. So, I guess it is possible his hygiene wasn't all that bad, but he just had the misfortune of a bad body make up. But he wasn't weird about the smell or snot or earwax. I just don't think he even thought of it. One time, I handed him some tissues and he asked what they were for and I told him his nose was spewing molten lava snot all over the place and it was sticking to his facial hair where a mustache would have been if he cut the rest of his whiskers around his face, just leaving that above his lip. And he didn't even get mad. He just shrugged and wiped it and said thanks like it was just a thing and was the thing to do. But Cindy walked out of sight, Lorne didn't growl in hunger for babies, but he did put his hand in his coat pocket like he was about to pull out a gun. But he didn't pull one out—a gun that is, he did pull his hand out, or otherwise it'd be stuck in his coat for all of eternity and I don't think that would serve anyone too much good. When his hand did come out of that coat, he had a wad of crumpled papers in it, which turned out to be wax paper, and more specifically, the little wax wrappers that hold taffy. All sorts of different colored and flavored taffy. Here, take one, he said. I like the blue ones the best. They're cotton candy. I told him that

we're not supposed to have candy in here. Say it's contraband. Like we're prisoners, but I guess we kind of are, huh? But he didn't listen much and told me take one. Matter of fact, take 'em all, and that he had more.

And he shoved the whole lot into my sweaty hands, though they weren't sweaty before, but they began to sweat when I started to think about having to hide contraband and all the trouble that went along with it. Lorne then told me that we were friends. You know that, right? he said. Yeah, I suppose it did.

After a few days they finally cut his hair. Thank God they cut his hair. The short hair made him look slightly less menacing. Just slightly, though. I found out he was a footballer in high school. American, not world. Football, that is. Which made a bit of sense. Then he said he was a wrestler. The strangle you and throw your ass down on a mat type while wearing super tight, stretchy singlets type, not the ones on TV in the ring with the girls and the chairs. He was good, too. Said he was some sort of high school champion, but they wouldn't let him wrestle in college for whatever reason. His parents wouldn't, not the state or school or anything. Said they wanted to keep an eye out for him and make sure he was okay, but he wasn't. He was sitting with me in the fun room, so he was anything but okay. His parents needed their vision tested, cause that eye, whichever one was on the lookout, wasn't working much.

The third day he was in during his first stay, he pulled me to the side while I was watching a daytime talk show, which really made me mad 'cause I really wanted to know who was the father of the child they were fighting about on the TV up on the wall. He took me to the side where the games were and told me he wanted to show me something. Share something with me. He trusted me.

I'm a rapper, he said. Which I was offended by. I didn't want to be racist, but he was white and rappers are black and it didn't make sense. Not that white people can't rap, like they're not allowed to, but they can't rap. I told him he should stick to country or something, and leave rap and basketball to the blacks. When he gets rhythm and an extra tendon or ligament or muscle—whatever it is—in his leg so he can jump higher, he can go back to rap. But he didn't listen to me. He didn't really even acknowledge my advice, and insisted on rapping for me.

He didn't have a beat, so first, he beat-boxed as his hand cupped around his whiskers to set the tone. That's what the beat would sound like if I had a stereo, but I don't, he said. He kept the beat up for a while, which wasn't so bad, except when the spray of saliva escaped through his hand and landed on my face and lips. That was unpleasant and I wondered if I'd get leprosy if he had it. One day he took his shoes off and itched the heel of his foot on the carpet and clumps of skin remained on the floor—like a snake shedding its skin or something—but I haven't felt any signs of leprosy or any other fatal disease, so I think I'm off the hook for the time being.

That beat would go on for about fifteen seconds, then I'd come in and start with this, Lorne said.

He then rapped for nearly the rest of the show. I missed the reveal of the paternity test of the couple that was on the screen and two others. I think he must have rapped for at least an entire night. It was fretful, but when a large, human weapon raps, you listen. At least I do. I am not large, or any sort of weapon. And I didn't have other friends or music. So I sat there listening to Lorne white rap about so much stuff. It didn't make too much sense to me and I don't know if he'd ever rehearsed it before, to anyone or even out loud because it didn't seem to blend together like the rap I was used to hearing. And I thought it probably sounded differently in his head than it did aloud to my ears. I'm not one-hundred on this, but I think he was talking about the president and then segued into stars and cars and bars. But Cindy had come over and given me some red pills mid cypher, which started to fuzz my brain up pretty quickly.

The next day, he was gone and I didn't see him for a while. Juliett, the slow talker, said Lorne's parents had come and picked him up.

Then, a few weeks later, with no warning at all or announcement, he was back in the fun room. I walked out after my shower and there he was, just sitting in one of the chairs with drool running down his mouth. I didn't wipe it up. I wanted to. I thought about it. Thought I'd be parental and caring. Show some compassion for an old friend,

but I couldn't get myself to do it. I sat next to him, watching him. Staring at him. Studying him while I could when he couldn't stare back. Get a bead on him. His chest heaved up and down every few breaths and a spasm struck his arm every eight seconds, but sometimes it wasn't eight but every three seconds, and other times it'd even wait about a minute in between twitches.

He finally opened his eyes and the fog of drugs was mostly evaporated. He smiled and pulled out a piece of blue taffy and slid it over to me. I never knew how he got those things in. Nobody got anything into this place. But he somehow did. So I guess some people did get some things in here, and I wondered what else other people got in here. Want to hear my new rap, he asked. Of course I do, I responded without hesitation, more out of reaction than thought. This time the rap was worse. Less coherent, but the more he rapped, the more excited he got. He stood and bobbed his head and began white dancing—very jagged, stiff, as smooth as a piece of broken glass, but he didn't care. He was zoning and spitting his words and his spit all over the white chairs and white floor and white coffee tables. There was so much nonsense—it was fantastic! Until he kicked the chair and Cindy ran in with Rob, the new guy, and a needle. They stood a few chairs distance away and asked Lorne to calm down. They asked him to sit down so they could give him a shot. He obliged, but not before feinting toward them and yelling BOO! Which gave them quite the fright, and they jumped like kangaroos back two steps, but then shot him full of something. His steady flow of drool continued immediately. I didn't wipe it up. Eventually, some of it found its way to the floor and formed a tiny puddle.

I walked over to the stuffed animals and grabbed an orange cat and put it under Lorne's heavy arm. It looked like a cat I once knew when I used to run with them. Not like we ran the town hustling, or like they were a bad influence on me or anything. I mean, I used to run with them: one-foot-in-front-of-the-other in quick successive motions, run. I understood the cats. I really did. And I thought, since I understood them, we had a kinship of sorts, and they would feel that kinship, too, and run with me. I envisioned a hoard of feral cats jogging behind me—their leader—marching on wherever I went, supporting me in my adventures. They would be my soldiers, and I their general. For whatever reason, though, they did-n't follow me right away. I brought milk, and cheese—I know they're not mice, but who doesn't like cheese? I brought tuna and even catnip. I left everything in the alley behind our house and waited for their arrival. I'd coax them for a minute with meows of my own, so they knew I was one of them—that I understood them. They would eventually come to me and eat my offerings. But they wouldn't run with me.

That went on for weeks until, one day, I decided I needed to show them what they were missing. An orange cat I called Mister Toxic, because he reminded me of a villain who somehow survived a toxic chemical waste spill only to come back to the streets and continue his nefarious ways, ate a can of tuna I left for my troops. After he was full, he wanted to leave me alone in the alley with the roaches, so I scooped him up and started jogging with him in my arms. Immediately, he felt a bit sea sick, or airsick, or maybe even land sick, I sup-pose—I don't really know— and he started heav-ing and clawing at my face, but I continued in stride. I wasn't concerned with the scratches too much, or even the bites, but when he pissed his toxic waste on my face, and into my open-gasping -for-air mouth, it broke my concentration, and I dropped my soldier to the ground. I was not the greatest leader. He ran off before I could reach for him again. I think he was beginning to come around to the running thing, but when you gotta go, you gotta go. Who can really blame him for that? I can't. I repeated this process for days with a new cat in tow. Mother put an end to it, thought, after the fifth day when I came home and one of the cats, Senorita Chiclet, leaned in for a kiss, but out of inexperience she applied too much pressure and punctured a hole in my bottom lip. I didn't think it was that bad, but mother took me to the emergency room and they did end up putting eight stitches in my mouth.

When the doctor heard the story of how my lip opened, he told her that that was very weird for a child of my age to be doing, and urged her to send me to a psychologist for treatment. On my eleventh birthday, mother sent me to see my first therapist. She says that's how everything began... with the cats.

But the cat under Lorne's arm was different. They said it was never alive and it wasn't shot and stuffed like the deer heads on the walls of the fancy restaurants or rich people's cabins like in the movies.

That night, at dinner, Lorne told me about his mother. She was nuts. But that's to be expected. Or at least for him so say she was nuts. For all I know she wasn't nuts at all. But he said so. He said she'd taken him to the doctor after his dad died and put him on all sorts of drugs. That she was trying to keep him dumb and his mind from expanding. I don't want my mind to expand, though. My skull seems pretty structurally sound and if my mind expands I'm pretty sure that will create some internal issues. But he wanted a big-ger mind, and who am I to judge? Lorne had start-ed to communicate with the spirits and she didn't like that—couldn't handle that. They talked in tongues and he was the only one that understood them. Voices from the past, he said, were helping guide him through the future and beyond the physical real world of this life. Metaphysics or something. He said none of this is real, just our perception of reality that we see through the lens of our own senses. And he knew the way to break free from the tangible reality. She seemed a bit off to me. If my son was able to transcend the physical world, I wouldn't want to keep him from that. Boo to her. But boo to a lot of people that tell others what they can think and do and what-not. She could have easily just left Lorne alone to his own devises and let him live his own life. If they're not hurting themselves or anyone else, I say let them be. Lorne certainly wasn't doing ei-ther, so I say let him be.

Four days now, he said to me, as he bit into his buttered roll. It looked dry, and I wanted him to put more butter on it, or pour some water in his mouth as he chewed it. Choking hazards are real and I'm not good at the Heimlich maneuver—I've never performed said maneuver—but who's good at something the first time around? I'm a slow learner, anyway.

Four days of what? I asked.

The meds. I haven't been taking them. I'm feeling so good without them. Clarity. There's so much clarity.

You have butter on your chin, I replied.

I've been chewing gum and sticking it on the side of my mouth, between my teeth and gums. The pill sticks to it and then I open up and they think I swallowed it.

I wouldn't lick it off, though. Maybe use a napkin and wipe it. When's the last time you washed your face? I asked. The butter's not worth it for the risk.

Want me to show you how to fake the swallow? He asked. Are you paying attention?

Seems like a lot of work. Too much work.

Too much work to get your fucking mind back?! He yelled and stood up.

I really don't want my skull to crack. I don't think my bone structure is built quite like yours and if my mind expanded. I think even the slightest, I'd be done. My head would crack right open.

He picked up my milk and threw it on my face. I wasn't going to say anything about it. He didn't look happy with me. But sometimes a lot of people don't look happy with me. They usually don't throw milk on me. But milk doesn't hurt much, so I don't know what the big deal was. If it was a brick or chair, I could see tackling him to the floor and stabbing him with the needles, but milk? Maybe Cindy could have just asked him to apologize or something. But I wouldn't have accepted it. We're friends and we don't need to apologize. Sometimes we say things. Sometimes we do things. I know he didn't mean anything by it.

They said he was in the scare room for a week before his mother and step-father came and got him. Clarence told me that. Kind of barked it at me while I was going to the toilet to take a dump. Threw me off a bit and took me a minute to process before I regained my train of thought and what I was doing in front of the shitter.

Big boy's gone! Big boy's gone, indeed. They took him in the night, Clarence said. But I don't think he was one-hundred on that. Nobody does anything during the night. That's a time for sleep. Cindy tells me that. Night Time is sleep time. Why would he go and be about during the night? Hell, why would anyone be out meddling with Lorne or any other "Big Boy" during the night, when Night Time is sleep time?

When I was done with my business, which I thought smelled just slightly better than Lorne on most days, I walked by his room and saw it was empty. The bed was stripped and there wasn't

even the slightest trace of anyone ever having slept in there, let alone Lorne. I went back to my room and sat on my bed. On my magazine stand, on top of my Popular Mechanics pile, was a carton of milk with a sticky note on it.

Lorne asked me to bring this to you—Cindy.

I threw the milk in the garbage in a fit of violent rage. But not like Lorne's fit of violent rage. I just set it in the garbage, and thought about how I wasn't happy about the milk being in my room. He didn't need to apologize. I was furious. Friends don't need to apologize for things like that. I, mean, it wasn't a brick, or something that could have hurt.

The last time I saw Lorne, I didn't really see him. I saw him. But I didn't see him in person. He was on Jorge's phone. But he pronounces it like George. With an American "G" instead of a Mexican "H" with a "hay" at the end. He was Mexican. I think he was Mexican. But he'd always tell me I aint no hay eating whore! But I don't think whores eat hay. They say it's for horses, but I'm not any sort of equestrian scholar or veterinarian. And after he told me that about eating hay and whores he showed me a video from some local news site, but we had to keep the volume off since we're not supposed to have phones and music machines and the such in the house, but we were in the fun room and it was making it more fun, so I don't know if they'd have minded so much, since it kind of made sense.

Jorge said, Hey! Psst! In kind of a whisper holler sort of way and got my attention. Jules! Come here and take a look at your big boy, he said. And so I did, but I didn't know he was talking about Lorne at the time, since I'd never watched Lorne through a screen before—unless you consider the Thor movies, but that wasn't really him, just looked like him

It was a news cast. The subtitles were on, so we got a little information that way, but we didn't need them to tell us what was going on. We could see it, better than Lorne's parents could see and our eyes were watchful on our friend. The title said, STOLEN CAR LEADS TO POLICE CHASE AND SHOOTING. It was a red four-door car that looked too small for Lorne to get in and out of, so I immediately thought Jorge was mistaken, and this big boy wasn't so big and he wasn't our boy. But when the car stopped and the door opened and a head emerged from the car, I knew it sure was our boy. And it didn't matter too much that I couldn't see his face because of the bird's eye view from the chopper camera. His head slid back out of view into the car, but the door remained open.

The subtitled words on the screen read:

POLICE: Exit the vehicle with your hands up!

POLICE: Get out of the car!

Lorne's head popped back out, and I thought, way to go 'ol boy! Don't take no shit from the man! He got out of the car! Don't do it, I thought. Don't do what they tell you to.

When he did fully emerge, his hands were tucked inside of his long brown jacket—just like in a strait jacket on his way to the scare room. But he didn't look scared now or doped. He looked happy and when he looked up his eyes were big and sunny like he knew something we didn't. Which, maybe he did, since he'd always talked about knowing things that the rest of us didn't.

POLICE: Take your hands out of your jacket!

POLICE: Sir, slowly take your hands out of your jacket! We will shoot!

Lorne turned left and right and seemed like he was going to make a break for it, but he didn't. He pulled his hands out of his jacket. FAST. He pulled them out fast! I'd have been so scared if I was one of those cops, I'd have run away. Having Lorne rap to me with those dark blue eyes staring at me and it was all the fear I could take, but guns? No way! I'd have been running with a stream coming down my leg. And what do ya know! He pointed those guns at those cops and started shooting! Good for him! Good for you, Lorne! Go out on your terms. You don't need to listen to them! And he opened fire and his hands and arms moved so rapidly and he looked like a gunslinger from the movies. Not one of those cowboy westerns where the guys are reloading their six-shooters, but the action movies where they have endless bullets before they have to reload and the good guy is killing bad guys left and right and all the bullets flying at the good guy are just an inch off as they whizz by the good-guys head. But the bullets from the cops didn't whizz by Lorne's head. Duck and roll! I thought. That's what they do in the movies.

The cops' bullets hit 'ol Lorne in the chest and the face and what seemed like everywhere, and if Lorne's fingers had held one of them shooting guns instead of those two fingers in each hand, I bet he'd have shot every one of those damn cops. But I still think those fingers might have sprayed out a few bullets, because it was Lorne and he knew something the rest of us didn't and he looked like Thor and, I don't know, but he just might have had some type of hammer like that Mjolnir too. I bet he did.

All I know is he was my friend and he wasn't that great of a rapper, but what white guy is? Can't fault him for that. And his mom was always trying to get him to think and be someone he didn't want to be and he never did hurt me with that milk, but I sure wish he didn't need to apologize to me for it.

About the Author:

Santino DeFranco is a former professional Mixed Martial Arts fighter and has fought in the UFC, as well as appeared on the reality TV show The Ultimate Fighter. After a brain aneurysm and subsequent surgery, he retired from professional competition and has been writing ever since. His memoir was a finalist for the "Books for Film" competition, and is currently being considered for publication. His feature length screenplay was a semifinalist in the Marquee Screen Writing Competition, and his fiction and non-fiction has appeared in Bourbon Penn Press, Vice.com, Curios Literary Journal, and Foliate Oak Literary Journal. Santino holds an MFA from Northern Arizona, and he is married with two children. He currently trains UFC fighters for a living, and he also teaches English at Glendale Community College in Glendale, Arizona.

DO IT YOURSELF FINISHING SCHOOL
by Debra Leigh Scott

It started because I couldn't abide crudeness in my life.

All around me I see crude and rude behavior, like our high school football players in their old pickups, blasting music in the middle of the night, waking up babies or old people who need their sleep. Or like the men using foul language in public places, even when they haven't been drinking. Or worse than that, in my opinion, are the girls using the f-word everywhere and laughing like hyenas with their mouths open clear to their tonsils. Why can't people eat without gulping big bites or making loud noises? Why is it so hard to walk without slouching? Nobody seems to care about how much crudeness has taken over our world.

On TV, I watch people pushing and shoving each other at those Black Friday store sales, like they're running away from Godzilla. I'd say we act like a pack of wild animals, except that I watch a lot of animal videos on youtube and they all act way better than us. That's why I want to spend my life working with animals. In their own quiet way, they've got a lot to teach us.

We aren't polite enough. We aren't kind. At least not from what I can see here in Horn Lake. Too much low living, and not much by way of class, except for maybe the Elvis Ranch, called the Circle G, where every year they're supposed to be working to fix it back up. People would like that, if there were better places to picnic, and maybe some rides, or new boats for rental on the lake. It might give everybody a wanting to be more genteel, having things nice like that.

Anyway, there didn't seem to be a reason to wait for Horn Lake to get much better in the area of general crudeness, so I started small to improve myself alone, by always saying please and thank you, practicing that every day, and always holding doors for people, or helping moms with their baby strollers in revolving doors. I try not to curse ever, except once in a while I will say foul words inside my own head when I am very, very mad. If you ask me, even the most upright souls at the New Prospect Missionary Baptist Church couldn't take offense at that. And, in my experience, they are pretty easy to take offense.

I bought a steam iron over at Benzer Pharmacy and keep my clothes pressed – even the plain old jeans and t-shirts. I only have a few dresses, and none of them fit very well, but I still iron them before I put them on, even though I never wear them anywhere but my bedroom, since they were my mother's and I haven't grown into them yet. I bought some shoe polish at Publix and polish all my shoes, even the sneakers, just trying to keep myself orderly. It seems only right that when people have to look at a person, you give them something pleasant to look at.

Then all of a sudden on this one night, it was like a whole new way of seeing the world opened up to me. Like usual, I was hunkered down on my bed, searching around youtube for more animal videos, and I found some clips of Jackie Kennedy riding a horse, making jumps around a ring. It was beautiful to behold. My uncle Trey told me a few years back that I was plenty strong enough to work at his stables, mucking them out, wiping down the horses. So, that's what I do every chance I get, and he pays me pretty fair. I love horses probably more than any of the other animals I love. My favorite is Bright Star, a really beautiful black stallion who's taken some of the blue ribbons on the horse show circuit. Sometimes I even get to go with Uncle Trey to the Eastern Tennessee horse shows, where we'd help the owners get their animals ready, and I'd watch from below the bleachers when they competed. So I could tell when I watched the video that Jackie was a great rider, and that she and her horse loved each other.

Up until then, though, the only thing I'd ever seen of Jackie Kennedy was that video clip of her in her pink suit, climbing onto the trunk of the car to get the skull and brains that got blown out of her husband's head.

But now I knew she was elegant in a way I'd never seen in my life before. So I kept watching more videos about her, and found one I liked best called "A Tour of the White House". And that video changed the way I thought a person could be, because Mrs. Jacqueline Bouvier Kennedy was the very opposite of crude.

I watched that video over and over and over again, studying how she made her voice so soft, with all that good pronouncing. I'd practice speaking along with her, almost like I was learning a foreign language. Pretty soon, I'd memorized nearly all of her speech, even though I didn't know what words like Smithsonian or Staffordshire meant, until I looked them up. I knew then that I wanted to live in a world with people who knew about those things, and maybe even had some of the kinds of things that Mrs. Kennedy cared so much about. Maybe when you live with Staffordshire on your mantel, even those teeny tiny black and white dog figurines, you are not the kind of person to be rude or rough, or who would break things when you get drunk, which is what my father used to do all the time right before he finally went away for good.

Not that I blame him for leaving. He and my mom both worked at the Newly Weds plant where they make seasonings, and what they call "coatings" to put on factory-processed foods. Their website calls it "creating one of a kind flavor experiences." I call it making fake flavors to put into fake food to trick people into eating it. Which is, of course, another crude thing to do to people, if you ask

me. But that's where they both worked, since Newly Weds employs most of the people around here. My mom was in the office, and my dad worked 12-hour shifts as a supervisor in the plant. That is, until the day my dad brought an official complaint that said the handling of food was being done by workers with bare hands, and that maybe the company would want to reconsider its sanitary policies. Right after that, management told him that the line he supervised was being shipped to the Chicago plant. He tried to get reassigned, but the only thing they offered was working at the shipping dock lifting all day long, even though HR knew my daddy's back had been bad for over ten years. So when he turned that down, he was denied unemployment. Then, matters got even worse since everybody on his line who lost their job blamed him for stirring up trouble. So he lost most of his friends, even some from way back to his high school days. People hold grudges really long here in Horn Lake, too. It was hard on him, and that's the truth. He never broke a single thing in our home before that, but after, with him never finding work, and losing his friends, he'd sometimes just get to busting up on a rampage. And I guess that's where I got to feeling so strong about being polite, because I just couldn't stand all the busting up and crying and mean talk in my home.

It came as no surprise that people made fun of me trying to be so genteel, and I tried not to care. I wasn't ever popular anywhere in Horn Lake anyway. In fact, I'd say I was the opposite of popular, where people would turn their backs when I walked by. So, anyway, I began to say "yes" instead of "yeah" or "yep", and I tried to remember to always stand up straight, to hold my hands folded in front of me, and to keep my head at an elegant angle. And, even when people made faces behind my back, I tried to be the way I thought an aristocrat would behave. "Aristocrat" was another word I had to look up at first. I'd heard it before, but never really knew exactly what it meant.

I spent some time looking at books about Jackie in our library – I guess she became a kind of obsession -- and I learned that she went to Miss Porter's School in Connecticut where she was given her excellent education, and was also trained in speaking and moving with beauty, in standing straight, and in knowing how to place her knife and fork just right, how to lift a tea cup like a proper person, how to choose the best china. I knew from looking at the pictures of the students and reading about the kind of people who sent their children there that Miss Porter's would never take on somebody like me. But that didn't stop me. I searched the internet and found advice, and made a kind of at-home course of the sorts of things they taught at a finishing school:

Good Manners

Table Manners

Etiquette

How to be Charming

Entertaining v. Hospitality

Flower Etiquette

Comportment and Deportment

The Importance of a Pleasant Voice

I printed out a saying from one of the online Etiquette sites and hung it over my desk:

"Respect for ourselves guides our morals, respect for others guides our manners."

I had a scholarship to University of Memphis, to work on the BA requirements before I apply to Veterinary School, up at UTC in Knoxville. But I was thinking that if I didn't get all this finishing school work done by end of summer, I could always take a gap year to work on it. No sense showing up on campus before I was totally transformed. Why just be my same old half-finished, unpopular self when I could turn this into a whole new time for me?

When my daddy was doing his rampaging, mama packed up our most valuable breakables and moved them up to the attic. So, one day, I went up searching for Great-Grandma Baylis's Parisian china. Those dishes were probably our greatest treasures, since the Baylis family was wealthier back then, and we are nowhere near what anybody would call wealthy now. I found the china packed in a big double-thick cardboard box, wrapped in old newsprint. I was sitting there holding one of the teacups, just sort of practicing the correct way to pinch your fingers around the teeny handle, when my mother nearly stunned me into dropping and breaking it, showing up like a bolt of lightning.

"Lee Avinger, what are you doing in this attic?"

I had to grab onto the cup with both hands to hold it steady, I was so taken back. Her hair was flying all around her head with a bunch of static, too, which just a little bit of conditioner would have set right.

"Just looking, mama," I said, holding the cup up for her to see. "Can't we bring them back downstairs now?"

Mama just shook her head. "I packed them up so careful, they may as well just stay up here. I never used them anyway. We don't know one person could be trusted not to harm them."

"Well, just for us, then," I said. It was only the two of us now that daddy was gone, anyway, except sometimes Uncle Trey would stop by for dinner now that Aunt Berta passed away.

"I packed them for you," mama said. "For when you get married. Same as my mama did for me, and her mama did for her. You're my only child, and I want you to have them."

"What makes you think I'm gonna get married, mama?"

I never had one date my whole life, for reasons of being the opposite of popular. And those football players are about the only thing this town offers by way of boys. Most of them have very low foreheads and a kind of beady-eyed stupidity.

"You're the last of my line, Lee. Uncle Trey and Aunt Berta never had children. I don't want us dying out."

It seemed unfair of her to put all the responsibility of an entire line of ancestors on me at that moment, when all I wanted was to bring some old china back to the dining room. But it would have been impolite to be contrary, since she seemed to feel things in such a strong way just then.

"Maybe we can just bring the tea set down," I said.

We could have tea time on the weekend afternoons, something my online classes talked about in great detail. It could be just mama and me, and I'd buy some of those little teacakes with the pastel icing at The Cake Lady Bakery. No china smashers would be invited.

I turned the cup over, to show her. "See that name?' Johann Haviland, Bavaria'? That's the name of the china makers, and where they made the china."

My mother leaned over and squinted since she didn't have her reading glasses on.

"Your greatgrandmother Baylis told me she bought them on her wedding trip in Paris, France."

"Well, she may have bought them there, but they were made in Bavaria," I said. "It's very elegant."

My mother squinted at me.

"Bavaria. That's part of Germany," I said. "And see here? "Rajah"? That's the name of the pattern....the design."

My mother kept squinting. "Okay," she said. "Maybe just the tea set."

Senior "Famous Person Day" was coming up, as one of the last big events before graduation from Horn Lake High School. It was clear there was no one else I was called to be but Mrs. Jackie Kennedy. I didn't say anything to mama because she already told me this fixation on Jackie Kennedy was giving her the willies.

"It's gotta mean something, though," I said to her. "Jacqueline Lee Bouvier. That was her name."

"So?"

"And her sister was Caroline Lee Bouvier, but she was called Lee," I said. "Caroline, like you, and Lee, like me."

My mother just squinched up her lips.

"And their mother's last name was Lee," I finished. "Don't you think that's gotta mean something? All those "Lee" names, and me being "Lee"?"

Mama just shook her head. "Honey, you are always looking for signs and symbols and secret meanings. There just aren't any, and that's the truth. Things just are what they are."

"If I thought that was true, I'd want to die," I said.

But I knew better than to bring up Jackie Kennedy again, even though it didn't stop my plans.

I'd already practiced enough of her speaking from the videos, and if I wrote a small speech, I could use some of what she herself said. I knew it was

risky with so many....shall we call them "Republicans".....in Horn Lake. And I know there are still families around these parts who believe that the country would have been set right forever if only Mr. George Wallace had been elected president.

Of course, I didn't look anything like her. Jackie, I mean. I was overly thin, with wheat-colored hair I pulled back in a pony-tail. But I had a bunch of pictures I took off the internet that I stuffed into my backpack, and ditched school so I could take the bus bright and early up to Memphis, since I figured a bigger city with some thrift stores might be the place to get help with the clothes and maybe even find a pillbox hat. And the best thing? Mrs. Jackie Bouvier Kennedy wore gloves all the time. That is what made it the most perfect. All elegant women wore gloves back then. And I know mama says there are no signs, but almost right off the bat, I found the Junior League Repeat Shop on Summer Avenue. It was run by the Ladies of the Junior League in Memphis, so I felt it was a good time to practice some of my finishing school manners. Standing up straight and using my best speaking voice, I went up to one of the ladies and said, "Excuse me, ma'am, my name is Lee, and I'm from Horn Lake, Mississippi."

She looked at little surprised, and I think it was because she wasn't used to anyone with manners anymore. She smiled at me and said, "Well hello, Lee from Horn Lake. My name is Miss Ella. What brings you all the way up to Memphis?"

I told her all about Senior Famous Person Day and how I needed to find something like Jackie Kennedy's pink suit and pillbox hat, and some white leather gloves.

"Do you also know, ma'am, where I might be able to find a wig that would look like the hairstyle she had in Dallas?"

Miss Ella didn't speak right away, and I could see she was sizing me up. "Did your teacher assign you this character, Lee?" she asked me. "This is an awfully big project."

"I know, ma'am," I said, hoping she wasn't Republican. "But I came to it on my own. I think Mrs. Kennedy is a very important figure in our history, and that she was brave and elegant and strong in a way we all need to be again."

Miss Ella didn't answer.

"And she lived in the south," I added, just for good measure. "In Virginia."

I handed her some of my internet photos.

Miss Ella nodded her head. "Okay," she said. "Well, we will have to improvise."

She led me to a back room of things not for sale, where, she said, some of the better clothes were held not to be put out all at once. She told me that Jackie's suit was a fabric called boucle, and after searching around a little, she found a suit made of boucle in a kind of light grey color. Some more searching found us a light blue pill box hat with a few scraggly feathers sticking out of a big leopard print button on the right hand side.

"No worries about that," Miss Ella said. "They can be removed no problem."

We found shoes – black leather pumps with a small princess heel that fit only a little snug. And gloves. Not white, though. We had to settle for black. But Miss Ella said it would match the shoes and that would be just fine.

"You're going to have to dye the fabric, honey, if you want it to be pink," she said. "Rit dye has a hot pink that should work."

I guess my face must have showed it because I panicked. Where would I be able to do that without making a mess and calling attention? I didn't want another give-up-on-Jackie conversation with my mother.

Miss Ella stood there, holding the boucle suit and pill box hat, looking at me. She sighed one of those long sighs the way older women sometimes do, because they've been through so much in their life and now here's one more trial standing in front of them they have to go through.

"I guess Jesus brought you to me for a reason," she said. "Come on."

She rang me out and put my purchases in a big white plastic bag with handles. She made a private call on her cell phone, and we walked a few blocks to a hair salon where she introduced me to her cousin's son, Wade.

He sat me down on one of his salon chairs, and told me to put the bag near his hostess desk.

"I hear you need a wig," he said.

We told him what my project was, and I talked to him a little about the not-wanting to be crude thing that got me to this point. He was nodding, not saying much.

"So you're pretty sure this is the perfect project?" he said. "Jackie Kennedy's a pretty dramatic choice for these parts."

I nodded. "I already bought the clothes," I said.

"Which reminds me," Miss Ella said. "I'm going to run over to the hardware store and pick up some Rit dye, and a few other things before they close up."

She promised to be right back, and left me alone with Wade, which I figured was probably safe enough, seeing as how he was the cousin of someone in the Junior League.

I showed him some of my photos of Jackie on that day in Dallas. "It was a flip all the way around," I said.

Wade went into the back and brought out a few synthetic wigs in dark brown all on Styrofoam heads.

"I know people will make fun of me," I said, as I looked them over. "People make fun of me all the time."

"Well, sometimes that's enough to stop us from doing what we're led to do," he said. "And sometimes it isn't. You just need to pick which time is which."

We picked a wig that looked closest to the color in the pictures, and Wade plugged in a curling iron and started flipping the ends up all around the bottom.

"You might need to hit this with a little more curling iron the day of the presentation," he said.

I told him I didn't have one, and he said he'd lend one of his to me from the shop. "Why don't I just lend you the wig, too," he said, "seeing as how you'll probably never wear it again after this, right?"

He told me I could just get it all back to him after Famous Person Day and we'd call it square.

I know that my mama would disagree, but all this

kindness just seemed like too much of a miracle to be anything but a sign.

"When is this Famous Person Day, anyway?" he asked. He tried to sound casual, I could tell.

"Next Monday," I said.

"Mondays are my days off," he said, handing me his card out of a little holder on the ledge. "That's my cell phone. You need some help, or need advice you call that number right there."

Miss Ella came back in, a little out of breath. She got the hot pink dye, she said, and a big Rubbermaid tub. "I know her suit was strawberry pink," she said, "but we have to cover the other colors in the fabric, so it needs to be bolder."

I nodded, just believing her.

"But I'm afraid you're going to have to do this yourself, Lee," she said. "Because the dying is going to need to soak a good while. I can sit right here and take the feathers and button off the hat while Wade finishes up, but I don't think we can help you with the dying."

I figured I might be able to do it in the tool shed. Mama never went in there, since it was always filled with daddy's saws and hammers and levelers. I could make a mess and nobody but me would know. It was a dank old place that still smelled of man sweat something terrible.

"How do I dry it?" I asked.

"No dryer, 'cause it's wool. You soak it, like the directions say, at least overnight," Miss Ella said, "and then you put it on a plastic hanger – that's important because you don't want rust marks from a metal hanger – and let it air dry. You'll have to try and clip the hat up with a clothespin so that the air can circulate around it and dry it evenly."

Mrs. Ella drove me home, not because I asked. She insisted that it was a long way to have to go on the bus with all the things I was carrying. I worried the whole way that she would want to introduce herself to my mama, or that mama would be on the front porch, like she was sometimes having a beer after work, and see us. But we got home before work at the Newly Weds plant was over for the day, so nobody was there. Miss Ella patted me on the back and said good luck.

"I suspect this isn't the last time we'll meet," she said. "I just have a feeling."

I nodded because it seemed like she was right. Sometimes people just appear in your life and you know they'll be there a long time. Besides, I'd be at the university in Memphis, so it would be my home for a while. Maybe I could even volunteer at the Junior League store a few days a month.

She backed out of the driveway and waved goodbye. I got busy right away with setting up the tool shed and soaking the suit and hat, trying to get it all done before mama got home. The wig I hid in my closet, so bugs from the shed wouldn't get into the hairspray Wade had doused it with, and the shoes and gloves I put in my underwear drawer, but then, on second thought moved them to under my computer desk, since mama does my laundry.

I had it figured out that I'd ask permission to stay home from church on Sunday to finish up homework, and that's when I'd get the outfit all set up in my backpack, and practice my speech. I felt bad keeping this from mama, but she worries about people thinking I'm a weirdo, and thinks I take things too far sometimes. Mama never likes to call attention.

It all worked out, though. The pillbox hat was a little deeper pink than the suit, but I figured it wouldn't show since it was all the way on the top of my head. By Sunday morning, after mama left for the 10 am service, I brought everything in from the shed and packed it into a brand new plastic bag from under the sink, before putting it all in my backpack. I already knew my speech by heart, but repeated it in my head anyway.

When the day of the presentation came, I dressed in the ladies' room, down from the old gym that isn't used except during adult night class square dancing. I did my best with the wig, trying to get the flip just right, and to balance the pill box hat, which was trickier than I realized, and probably should have practiced. I put my regular clothes in my backpack in the locker. Nobody else was anywhere around, so it wasn't until I walked into the auditorium for my speech time that people started to laugh.

Mrs. Benson hurried over to me. "Lee, is this some kind of joke?"

I know the clothes didn't fit perfectly, but I thought I looked as good as any of the others in their dress up costumes.

"No ma'am," I said. "I think Jackie Kennedy is about the best First Lady we ever had, and I practiced my speech really hard."

She nodded her head kinda slow, biting her lip, because people were still laughing at me. But she hurried to the podium and gave them all her famous side-eye.

"You all are being very rude. One more squeak from any of you and you'll all get an F on your participation grade," she said.

So things got real quiet and I gave my speech. I'd practiced so much that I think I sounded pretty much like Jackie, and I talked to them all about that horrible day in Dallas when I had to hold my husband's brains in my hands, and I talked to them about how life is too crude and mean and nasty and vicious, and how we need to practice being more polite and polished with each other. Kindness is a kind of art, I said, as I finished up the speech.

Nobody clapped at first, until Mrs. B's side-eye got them putting their hands together, but only barely.

"That was excellent, Lee. And I think we should be treating each other with kindness," she said. "Most people in here could take that lesson to heart."

Mine was the last presentation, so after it ended, we all filed out of the auditorium.

I went to my locker to get my backpack. No way I could wear my Jackie outfit home on the bus. But Buddy Jakins, captain of the football team, grabbed me by the arm and pulled me into the old gym hallway where a bunch of his football player thugs were waiting, and there they started pulling at my wig and my suit and stomping on my high heeled shoes. I was trying to protect myself, but the boys were shoving and pulling at me, and somebody hit my nose real hard and blood was gushing everywhere. Somebody stuck their hand up my skirt and tore my stockings down. By the time they left me alone, there was blood on my suit, and the heel of one of my shoes was broken off. My wig got pulled off my head and was

thrown to the floor and stomped on. I think somebody even peed on it, 'cause it was lying in a yellow puddle.

Everybody was gone, escaped so they wouldn't get caught. Except for Buddy. He stood at the end of the hallway watching me trying to pull myself together.

"How's that for kindness, faggot?" he said.

I pulled myself up, leaning on the wall to stop the dizziness.

"Fucking faggot," he said again. "You ever set foot in this school again and I'll go all the way to killing your fairie ass."

I left out the cafeteria kitchen door, walking slow in my bare feet. There was nobody there this time of day, since lunch time was hours ago and things were all cleaned and closed up until tomorrow. There was a path that led down past the baseball field into the woods, near the creek. There was an old fort there that nobody knew about but me and a few of my Avinger cousins. That's where I finally sat down and cried. After a while, I stood up and pulled the suit off, got my old t-shirt and jeans back on. I put these Jackie Kennedy clothes, folded neat, into my back pack. The wig still smelled of pee, so I found an old plastic bag stuck to a tree, and wrapped it in that, trying to keep the smell off everything else.

I wouldn't be able to go home. Somebody was sure to have called mama by now. So, I figured it was time for the plan I'd been making since I turned 13. I'd go to the stables to say goodbye to Bright Star, and get the stash of money I'd been saving there in that floorboard hole ever since I started working for Uncle Trey. It should be enough to get me out of here. I'd call Wade's number from the card and tell him what happened. He'd know what to do about the suit and wig – and maybe he'd help me get the blood out of the fabric. Or maybe, like Jackie, I could just decide to keep it bloody. My nose was swelling up pretty bad, and the crying made it hurt more. But some ice once I got to the bus stop market would be enough to keep the swelling from getting any worse.

When I got to the stables, though, my plans crumbled. Mama's car was there. She and Uncle Trey were standing in the drive, and when she saw me, she ran up to me and trapped me in a bear hug.

"God-damn it, Lee! You scared us to death!"

Uncle Trey sidled up beside us, saying nothing.

"What were you thinking? Why would you ever do such a thing?"

I hated to see mama crying most of the time, but at that moment, I felt like I just wouldn't explain myself to anybody. I was too tired of trying for so long and not even knowing what I was trying for. Trying to be like everybody else? Trying to be someone Horn Lake could be comfortable with? Well, I guess I blew a great big hole in all that "trying" today, didn't I?

Maybe, for me, that was what finishing school was for: to help me be finished with all that trying.

Mama was still hugging me. She was whispering so Trey wouldn't hear, "I knew about the dresses you took from me, Lee. The ones in the back of your closet. I never cared about that, I swear to Jesus. But a pink suit and black heels, in front of a whole auditorium of people, a week before graduation?"

"Maybe I was running out of time," I said.

That felt like it might be true. And I understood something, just then. Mama had been counting the days until she could pack me off to Memphis, where I might have a better chance at things. But I'd been feeling the days going by without me ever getting to stand up brave and true, to dare those people who always hated me anyway to deal with this. To deal with me.

"Mrs. Benson called," mama said. "Principal Walker wanted to suspend you."

"I told your mama there'd be trouble if they tried to do that, because I would make sure of it," Uncle Trey said. "Not sure how, but I'd think of something."

"Well, Mrs. Benson told Principal Walker there was no difference between what you did and the All-Girl Football Team charity event every fall that the fathers like to dress up for, stealing clothes from their wives' closets and acting like idiots. She reminded Principal Walker that he was one of those in a dress, out there making women out to

be a pack of morons, and that she had pictures. At least you were being respectful of a woman from our history."

"And that shut him up real good," Uncle Trey said.

I couldn't help myself. I started laughing, picturing Mrs. Benson squaring off against 300-lb Principal Walker, and beating him down.

"Deal is, though, they're not suspending anybody else either," mama said, "even though they know sure as shooting who all was guilty of jumping you in that old hallway. Word spread like wildfire about that."

I never expected that any of those boys would get into any kind of trouble. They've been my torturers all my life in Horn Lake. People always turned a blind eye.

Mama said Mrs. Benson named me the winner of the Best Famous Person competition, and there'd be a plaque and a money prize at graduation. She also said that they were giving me an excused absence for the last two days of school so I could get to a doctor and make sure my face swelling went down.

"I'm not crazy about the whole dress-wearing thing, Lee," my uncle Trey said. "And I don't feel all the way right about you maybe liking boys instead of girls, or whatever else all this means, I can't lie."

My mother was looking sideways at her brother, like she was waiting to see if she needed to hit him upside the head or not. "Where's this going, Trey?" she said.

"All I'm saying, Caroline, is that Lee is my blood. And I got his back anybody comes at him ever again." He looked down at the ground for a second or two, and bent down to wipe some dust off his Frye boots. "And, Lee, I'm sorry if I never stepped up before, after your father left," he said. "That was wrong, and I take responsibility."

The two of them standing there like that, showing with all their hearts that they had some mighty strong love for me, no matter what I just did, well, that was about the best thing that ever happened to me. I never expected it, not in a thousand years. My heart felt like it might explode. I figured I could talk to them later about how we who act more genteel won't stoop to brawling with the likes of the Buddy Jakins of the world. We rise above to show who we are.

I don't know that I needed a plaque, really, because things already felt like they were right in a whole new kind of way. I was beat up and bloody with a pissed-on wig in my backpack, but I did what I'd set out to do. And I learned how to be dignified and brave and crazy all at the same time and face whatever might be the consequences. So after that, there wasn't much else left to do. Mama and Uncle Trey and I headed home to put ice on my face, unpack the tea set, and celebrate the way refined people do.

Tomorrow, we'll drive up to Memphis where they can meet Miss Ella and Wade, and maybe we'll even take them to Corky's BBQ for pulled pork sandwiches and banana pudding. We can visit the campus at UofM and I might even start imagining my future, since, even though my eyes are swollen pretty bad right now, my vision's more clear than ever before.

About the Author:

Debra Leigh Scott (www.debraleighscott.com) is a multi-discipline artist – a singer, writer, playwright, documentary filmmaker as well as an activist whose work focuses largely in areas of education rights and economic justice.

She is the Founding Director of Hidden River Arts (www.hiddenriverarts.com) Her fiction has appeared in such literary journals as The Oxford American, The Chattahoochee Review, River City, Words of Wisdom, TPQ, The Abiko Quarterly (Japan), Purnev (Portugal) and The Ashen Eye (Thailand). Her collection of short stories, Other Likely Stories, was published by Sowilo Press in 2010. She has since been at work on a series of plays about women's lives in a dying American empire, a documentary/book project called 'Junct: The Trashing of Higher Ed. in America, and has been performing with her singing partner, Jean Brooks, as "Cabaret Divas".

INDIA LAKE

Patricia Trentacoste

Marnie's cottage rises out of a stand of aspens on a hillock over India Lake. The slope is a gentle one, with long grasses, stony footholds, purple tea-root, and poisonous vines. Those, she allows to grow wild, because too much beauty makes her jumpy. Three years ago, when she inherited the place, it was a deep-hued plum full of lucky juice, but it rolled uphill to her on the cracked heels of her parents' accidental deaths. A faulty choke line and too many on-board fireworks took their lives, the same month she'd graduated from Penn State, in astrophysics, of all things, as her mom used to add, to disguise her shameless pride.

One minute, Marnie was applying for a job at the Hayden Planetarium in New York. The next, she was waking up in her old room, alone, paralyzed with grief, but flush with cash and real estate. There'd been a year of boozing, weeping and mis-managing her inheritance, before she landed a job as an online editor for an astronomy organiza-tion: cosmical dot org. She works from home now, where the cottage, the lake, the morning crow who comes to check on her, the bees who work goo into the gabled beam-wood, the rise of the moon, and the slope of the sun, all comfort her. She loves the house and the house loves her.

Hoping to borrow Marnie's kitchen for a day, her best friend Ava left several messages in a row. After the fifth ring, Marnie stroked the old land line's receiver and picked up, humidity crackling along the old mouse-chewed lines.

Tomatoes," Ava said, stretching out the long a in the middle. "Straight from my garden. The best Roma's and Black Krim's you can raise in Michi-gan. We'll put up a dozen quarts each. Crimson treasure, darlin'. I wouldn't ask but I need your stove." Her voice was effusive, rushing into Marnie's ear as if she'd forgotten what week it was for them both—death week. Or maybe she remembered and this was her way of coping.

"Canning, here?" Marnie took a gulp of coffee. "I'm barely awake. Give me a minute." She scuffed across the floor in her flip-flops to prop the porch door with a rock and sniff the air. That's when the heat quickened inside her, like an egg wanting to hatch or dozens of them ready to burst into a spawn stream. How odd. Over can-ning? "It's going to be a scorcher, Ava. Have you been outside? Wouldn't you rather go to the lake?"

"Oh, come on, Ben promised to help."

Marnie quieted and placed the phone on her chest. Ben was Ava's late husband's only broth-er—the surviving twin. He was also the eternal spawn stream in Marnie's gut. She parted the branches of her mother's Ficus tree and looked down to where the lake was a hazy, golden mirror of the Michigan sky. "Why not?" she heard her-self saying. "Bring your mess and bring that brother-in-law of yours. Let's boil and smash some fruit!" the taste of panic already in her mouth.

Pinging gravel drew her running down the steps. They'd arrived mid-morning. With lots of babble about the alchemy of Mason jars—how you can make one thing out of something else entirely—Ava offered a quick cheek for a kiss, no eye-contact. Setting down a box, Ben gave her a shy hug. "Hi, Marn, how've you been?"

She bit her lip and shrugged, noticing the thin scar under his chin from that time he fell off the dock when they were kids.

Bushels of tomatoes, two canners, jars, strainers, lids and seals, bags of sweet basil and papery garlic swept inside with them. Ava shook out stiff white aprons and passed them around with a flourish in her wrists. Ben set the fans in place, carefully moving cords out of tripping reach. He inspected a bit of corner-round under one of the cupboards.

"Your work?" Marnie asked him.

"Was it done right?" He cocked his mouth.

"I suppose so," she teased.

"Then, yeah, it's my work," grinning now. It was good to see that wide-open smile coming right at her.

"Ben?" Ava called him over to the sink for help with a canner.

Marnie could have predicted it, the way Ava seeks and gets his attention. This time it made her want to toss a tomato at a wall, just one for effect. Would it make the room look like a crime scene? Splat, blood-spray, a living thing transmogrified? You're an awful person, she said to herself. Really awful, today of all days. Be nice to her.

Ava saw her looking at the thermometer on the pantry door, eighty-one degrees, already. Quickly, she flipped it over. They labored through the long tide of the day until quarts of scarlet puree rose in columns, popping their seals like good little soldiers. By nightfall, the walls dripped with steam, and Marnie, from the strain of behaving herself. Through all their talk of pot wars and permaculture, she had not once invoked the dead brother to win a point. She'd let the praises of clean food and green medicine flow until every word and surface had a seed stuck to it, including the underside of Ben's jaw. Both brothers had that jaw, like they stored tobacco in their cheeks or chewed gum till their face muscles were legible.

She considered licking it off his face. Ben wiped his chin, missing the seed entirely, making the fish inside Marnie's belly wriggle a second time.

Just then Ava slipped and Ben leapt from his chair

to catch her in his arms. Laughing, they looked at the tile for the culprit. A small tangle of garlic skins, that's what it was.

Marnie wilted. Look here, aren't all the tomatoes red, round and luscious, the promise of alchemy in our perfect little bodies? When a drubbing noise started up out back, thud-ping, thud-ping, she cocked her ear toward the windows. Giant beetle bugs were banging against the screens and buzzing in fits as they skittered off the metal weave. It was exactly what she wanted to do, flip onto her back and spin a while. It wasn't only them. She felt wildly overheated, inside her mind and in her extremities, reckless and unopposable.

When a leaf fell in a slow drift to the window-sill, she glanced over at the tomato-people. They were shoulder-to-shoulder at the sink now, de-seeding, with heads bent like gourds on wilted vines, so she slipped outside and worked herself through some picker bushes to retrieve the leaf. After tucking it inside her pocket, she rubbed her thumb over its leathery seams. Why had she done such a screwy thing? She knew why. There was too much Ava in the house. Not enough Zachary. He was too absent, too dead. Thinking such thoughts made her a bad person again.

"What's up?" Ben asked when she came back inside.

"There's a hoot-y owl..." trailing off, pointing toward the lake and glancing up at the clock. Her face felt scarlet, the leaf, supple between her fingers.

Ava set her strainer with its pulpy undertow onto a spoon rest. "You're miserable, Marn. I've taken this too far. Sorry, kiddo. I really am," smiling guiltily. "What a Saturday, eh?" As she leaned forward to mop her midriff with the limp hem of her apron, her hair tumbled around her shoulders. Twisting it into a braid, which fell apart instantly, she sighed with the failure. This was Ava's signature gesture, twirling her hair into place without combs or clips or any idea of how needy or sensual she could be.

"No worries," Marnie assured her. "We're coming to the end of it." She dripped the last of the Sangria into their glasses while rolling an ice cube up and down her neck.

Eyeballing her, Ben pushed a bowl of cashews away and turned in his chair. The cowlick in the back of his head whorled opposite to Zac's. "Anyone else getting a headache from this stuff?" For a second, his face darkened and he looked rather ragged. Maybe the headache was real.

"It's Sangria," Marnie explained, "it's supposed to be sweet-ish."

"Swedish? Now, why should a Spanish wine be Swedish?"

Fine. She and Ava laughed at his joke and repeated the word Swedish like a couple of flirts until Marnie moved the pitcher to the sink-top for good. She didn't mean to make a show of it, but her hands were wet.

"Cutting us off, Marn?" Ava asked. "You know best. I can always count on you to know best." But she wasn't looking at Marnie, she was looking at Ben.

"Can you?" Marnie felt her lips tighten. "Maybe you shouldn't."

Ava frowned. "What's going on with you, Marnie? You're so, you're so pensive."

At first Marnie waved her hand around the room at the mess in her kitchen, at the glaringly obvious imposition, but what came out of her mouth surprised even her. Deeper and drier all the sudden, her voice sounded like someone else's. "He is gone, you know. Zac. He's gone. He chose his time and place—that day, that wide open Tennessee sky," her voice now like scraped bark. "When are we going to let him get on with it?"

They stared at her.

Pulling the leaf out of her pocket, she slapped it hard on the table. An empty jar wobbled. "I wonder what he thought about on his way down? Don't you ever? Wonder, that is? I mean, we never speak of it. Why shouldn't we? Now, tonight." She grabbed her own chest with both hands, wrist over wrist and hung on. "I want to talk about it. Let's talk about it—."

Ava cried instantly and Ben stood up so fast he sent a jar of juice crashing to the floor. "Marnie!" Red and sparkling glass spread over the tiles and seeped into the grout.

She kept talking. "At least the man died the way

he lived, our Zachary—higher than most." A bitter laugh shot out of her. "The damn fool. Damn fools, the lot of them. My parents. Fireworks? Are you kidding me?"

There! At last. Those few essential words. She'd been the one to say them and in the saying of them disrespected the dead, though not much, because Zac, for one, would have approved of her stupid joke. He would have knocked his fist on her shoulder, put his forehead against hers and made her look back at him cross-eyed, because he was also the keeper of their clan's merriment, the dispeller of their illusions. She may not have been his wife or his sister, or his twin like Ben, but she loved him too, she loved him like a…, like a what? Like a friend would love a friend. How she missed him. As for her parents. Well, they forgave her every fault all her life, out of love.

Ava pushed her chair from the table and gracefully walked down the hall to the bathroom, trailing her fingers along the wall, while Ben stood over Marnie, confused. It was like a horrific noise had resounded in the distance, an explosion too deafening to be heard, an undefinable letting loose. Someone had spoken of letting Zachary be once and for all in the place where he was. For two years, they had not spoken of the awful way he died. Not the three of them like this—boozy, irreverent, unclear about what happened on the day their risky master gardener fell to his cartoonish death.

The truth was, Zac knew better than anyone what he gambled every time he plied his trade, as he called it, buying and selling huge quantities of medicinal marijuana, dispensing the product personally to chemo and epilepsy patients, escalating risk for himself. Divvying and free-trading was how he made his living decent, he'd said. But he hadn't lived. According to the pilot he unbuckled his seatbelt while cloud-cruising a grower's field over an Appalachian bluff. It was a mistake. He was reaching for something when the helicopter lurched. That's what the pilot said. For all any of them knew, he might have plummeted on purpose. Or been pushed.

A bead of sweat trickled down Marnie's spine and cooled inside her waistband. Then another and another. Finally, she kneeled down and began to sop up the mess on the tile, picking glass out of the grout lines and dropping it into the bowl of her stiff apron, the blood of tomatoes on her hands, swearing she could smell cannabis burning out where the beetles gathered. Oh, Zachary, I hurt them. That wasn't the plan.

Ava returned quietly and reclaimed her chair. Her face was washed, her nose still red.

As he slumped into his, Ben patted Ava's shoulder while wrenching his apron off and tossing it into the sink. "There are days," he began, "when I think he knew exactly what he was doing." His two hands flicked open and trailed almost delicately down through the hot kitchen air. "Free-falling—like that ... right out of existence ... obliterated by a single false move."

The fact that Ava didn't flinch, told Marnie, she'd considered this herself, that her husband on some level volunteered for death. They'd all considered it.

Ben continued, "I try to tell myself, he dodged something worse. But what could be worse? Implosion of the Ozone? Jail time?" He softened his voice and looked at his hands. "He could have been having a bad day. Been off his game." When his eyebrows arched upward, his face flushed, not the way Zac's would, from the ears forward, but like a rising ventricular tide. He shook his head, "They say we shared brainwaves. So, I should have known, right? ... that he was headed in the wrong direction, addicting himself to danger?

"What's worse is, I'll never know. Did he get out just in time or not in time? Out of his life, I mean. Even if I did, if we knew, would it be any easier? I want a new story. A lie will do." He looked at Ava. He looked at Marnie. "Sorry, Marnie. We shouldn't have come here, today of all days."

But before Marnie could respond, Ava uncoiled and arched forward, her voice breaking open, "Whatever!" she snapped in as sarcastic a tone as Marnie had ever heard her use. "Here's what I know. When he fell out of that thing he took me with him. I am no longer me. I am someone else. I hate everything about my life," her voice broke again. It was so final, this pronouncement. Marnie wanted her to do so much more, say more. She wanted her to take her grief by the throat and deprive it of oxygen. But Ava merely did something she'd seen her do often, though

she hadn't understood it. She stared at Benjamin who was now trying to insert two jar rims inside each other. A startling came over Ava then an intake of breath.

She's looking for him! Marnie realized. Looking for Zac. And she's found him in the still-living man.

Ben rose to his full height as if every bone in his body was made of something sharp, took the reddened cloth from Marnie's hands and untied her apron, catching a shard in his knuckle which he removed with his teeth. He pulled her off her knees and gentled her into a chair, then went out back to shake his brother out of the towel.

Silence, staring, sweating tomatoes, the swiff-swiff of the fans, the insect frenzy on the patio. Grief and loss gone awry. Ava reaching aggressively across the table toward Marnie, Marnie not drawing back or moving forward. Eyes suddenly wild, Ava clutched a strand of Marnie's hair and twirled it into a tight coil, tugged on it till it pinched, till she drew tears and even then, did not let go. Ben was too far away to see that after Ava loosened her grip, a painful tuft of Marnie's brown-black hair was curling in and around Ava's fingers. She rose to deposit the strand in the waste basket, looking at it almost hostilely, then absently, as if she didn't know where it came from.

When Ben stepped back inside, Ava, in a clear bright voice said, "Let's go swimming." It was a few minutes after midnight.

Ben headed for the tall grass in a shoreline thicket where he stripped off his clothes in pieces. Unclasping her sandals nonchalantly, Marnie watched him. First, his T-shirt, hung on a branch. Then his Bermuda's. He draped his boxers over a craggy, low-limbed tree crotch and set his shoes one at a time at its feet. Being raw, being himself inside his body as if his skin clothed him and he wasn't naked at all. Deep in black wavy grasses with mosquitoes and robber flies, he waited as Marnie laced her arm in Ava's and lead her to the water's edge. She didn't hold Ava's violence against her. She was glad for it. It was honest.

In one clean motion, Ben leapt from the shadows and swam hard until his head emerged as a dark sphere in the small lake, his silhouette moving in and out of the moonlight. When he reared and let out a whoop, a spray haloed his mane. He was as alive as any man could be. Ava dove in and caught up to him, a willing fish on his line. Together they headed for the far shore, four arms rising and dipping in even rotation.

But when Marnie thrust out her arms to push off, an owl screamed. It was low-flying and close. She lost her footing and skidded on her heels, stumbling rather than diving into the black water below. Kicking hard, she swam for the top, coughing and spanking the surface to upright herself. Did they see? She spun around. No, they were off in the shadows. She began paddling more smoothly until the water glided past her like a thin mead. Her breathing evened—this was her swimming hole, her India Lake. She belonged there, if anyone did.

Out of nowhere Ava surfaced. With an innocent giggle, she splashed Marnie then sank into the warm steam above the lake. But no matter how Marnie moved, back-stroking with her gaze on the stars or paddling in circles so the tiny lights shining from cottages danced like a ring of flickering candles, Ben was no farther than a body's-length away. The lake became a whale and she lounged on its wet skin as she pleased.

Ava returned to cup Marnie's fingers into a handle. They were going to play Zachary's game. The forget-everything-else game they'd been playing since teenagers. She hooked her free hand around Ben's as Ava towed them in a circle. On their backs, they floated arms out straight, eyes on the constellations, their arc a wide, slow moving swirl through wet silk. Then Ben took a turn. Around and around he drew his eager swans in an eddy of moonlight, all soft wind and long throats being swallowed by the night. A sweet calm slid into her.

"I see him now," Ava gestured toward a star inside a faint curl of the Milky Way. "He's up there! Is that Perseus, Marnie?"

Ben stared and stared at the trajectory of Ava's finger then grasped Ava's hand and tugged his women into another rotation.

At last, Marnie broke away. Immersed in the night and brandied in a wet place as warm as her own blood, she tried to accept a new possibility—

that Ben was truly, not reactively or out of displaced grief, brotherly duty, but actually, in love with Ava. Such love is opium. She scanned the water. There they were, floating like children far from shore in the hollow of a deep lake, adrift but together. Had it always been so? Did the gods pluck Zac from the sky only to give Ava the other brother?

When Ben dove under Ava, she sprang from his hands in a stunning dive, her hair plastered down her back and her torso arced in a flawless arabesque, a calligrapher's stroke of ebony against the sky and Marnie loved her completely, would grant her anything, except what she wanted most, Zac's replica.

Ben came for Marnie next, groping for her knees then her ankles. He clasped them tightly and vaulted her out of the water in the same fashion. She rose like Minerva and descended through the vortex without losing her shape, sleek, amphibious, laughing.

"Please," she begged.

He looked baffled, then grinned. "It's your night."

He dropped like an anchor, feet first, eyes wide open, deeper and deeper till she could no longer see the flash of his teeth. His hands found her ankles as before and he thrust her skyward. This time she held her body tauter, kept her arms at her sides, fingers pointed like flippers. Water ran rivulets down her eyelashes and the curves of her lips, over her chin, her shoulders, her breasts, slicking her gym shorts to her hips, rushing up the middle of her like hot honey.

As she dropped through the swirl between his palms, he read her body like wet brail, then surfaced quietly and swam languorous circles around her. She twirled within his orbit and felt a rush of immaculate courage. A small cry came out of her which she disguised by coughing.

He swam closer. "All right, Marnie?"

They were so near each other she could smell the cologne of the lake warming in the air between their faces. "I'd like you to come over for dinner on Thursday. Just you. No tomatoes."

His lips parted in surprise. He did not look across the seas of sorrow for Ava. He grew serious. "I'm for it," he said. "I have been for a long time, Marn."

Below them lingered a lone slippery fish. I-t bore Zachary's face including his cornflower blue eyes. She smiled at it and it snaked away leaving an electric tracer in the dark green.

About the Author:

Patricia Trentacoste, a Detroit-born, retired, philosophy instructor, (Wayne State University and Oakland University), she is returning to fiction-writing and now live in the Sleeping Bear Dunes area of northern Michigan. Patricia is a member of Michigan Writers. Otherwise, she makes mobiles in her art shed and volunteers in the Benzie County Juvenile Court System.

Previous publications include monographs on aesthetics and moral psychology; a "true-life" piece for Women's Day Magazine; a by-weekly feature column for The Voice, (Macomb and St. Clair counties); and a bit of ghost-writing for an international essayist. A recent short story is coming out this month, "Pug and Woolie," in the Dunes Review, October, 2017.

DO YOU KNOW HOW FAST YOU WERE GOING?

Jeffrey Kass

"Freeze boy!" the officer shouted as he drew his 9 mm handgun and pointed it right at the kid's head.

The white plain clothed police officer dressed in blue jeans and a black polo raced his unmarked navy blue Dodge Charger to a screeching halt right behind the Chevy Camaro rental car I had just parallel parked along the west side of South Boyle Avenue, off Manchester Road. I was in St. Louis for work and was headed to eat at one of my favorite local dinner spots, Sanctuaria. Their version of "Fish n'Chips" is a corn cake breaded Mahi Mahi with jicama fries. But my growling stomach was no longer on my mind.

A second plain clothed cop dressed in beige khaki pants, a blue polo shirt and Kevin Durant Nike tennis shoes, emerged from the Charger.

"Turn around, boy!" he said in a stern voice. He patted down and searched the 19 or 20-year-old black kid. His groin. His legs. Arms. Everywhere.

I stayed in my car, partially out of fear, partially to make sure nothing awful went down.

By this time, I had cracked the window on the passenger's side of my rental car, the side closest to the sidewalk where the two cops and young man were standing. In the subtlest way I could, I aimed my iPhone video camera at the passenger side mirror of my car. The side mirror was pointed directly at the cops and kid. I wasn't looking to make the 6:00 news, but I thought it would be a good idea to document what was taking place, even though I wasn't quite sure what that was yet.

"I'm going to handcuff you while we ask you a few questions, okay?" The officer didn't wait for a response. Instead, he took a pair of handcuffs stuffed in some pouch on his waist and closed them on the boy's hands. They weren't the metal silver looking kind of handcuffs you see in older movies. They were clear plastic and tied tight like those nylon cable ties I use on my flagpole in my front yard to make sure my flag doesn't blow away.

"Ouch, that hurts!" the boy complained.

"That's what happens when you cross us. Did you have a gun?" the officer asked in an increasingly harsh voice.

"No," the kid responded, almost in a fuck-you tone.

"We saw you throw a gun into the bushes when you spotted us watching you."

"Man, I didn't even know ya'll were watchin' me and don't even own a gun." The boy had started raising his voice at this point.

The second officer left to search the shrubs, grass and areas at least for an entire block south down Boyle. Scoured the place.

"I can't find anything, Jo Jo," he shouted to his partner in a disappointed tone. On his return, obviously coming up empty, he returned to take over the questioning. "You have two choices. We can sit here all day with you in handcuffs until you come clean about what the hell you're up to, or you can cooperate and make this easy. Sounds like an easy decision if ya ask me."

"Why you trippin'? Just on my way to the convenience store to buy some snacks and joe's." The kid had stopped his sarcasm and his tone turned to frightened.

The kid was about 5'10", thin, had a medium dark brown complexion with a few tiny black moles on the side of his face and a short disheveled afro. Probably hadn't shaved in two to three days. Striking green eyes. He wore baggy jeans--you know the kind that droop almost down to the back of the knees. The kind I always thought looked ridiculous on people. He had a white t-shirt and a dark bomber type jacket. Slightly worn white Adidas tennis shoes with three black stripes on each side. The shoes were the newest looking article of clothing on his body.

It was a bit of a cold day for St. Louis for late May. Fifty-five degrees and almost no humidity. I may have never moved away from St. Louis had most days been that pleasant. Usually by May it was so hot and humid a person would sweat profusely just walking a block. "Looks like I brought you our beautiful Colorado weather," I told my friend Aaron hours earlier. Amazing how a couple years in Colorado changed my level of tolerance from the brutal humidity of the Midwest. If you can call St. Louis and its southern mentality, the Midwest.

"Let me see your driver's license, boy!"

I didn't understand why only now they were interested in who this kid was.

"Man, I told you, I was just walking to the convenience store to buy some cookies and smokes."

The kid reached into his pocket. "Here," and handed the cop his ID.

The first officer took the license back to his car. Within a few minutes, he came back with a look of increased disappointment on his face. "You lucky bastard. No record." He paused for a few seconds. "Yet. But you're gonna get a record if you don't come clean about what you're up to."

The boy didn't answer. Just gave the officers a "what's the use in repeating myself" kind of look.

Another several minutes went by with the two cops chatting about their next move.

"Unlock him, Lance," his partner Jo Jo said in a resigned voice.

Officer Lance fumbled through his coat jacket and pouch. "I can't find the damn keys. Shit!"

The other officer went back to the car, and after a few more minutes, finally returned with a set of keys. "I found 'em!" They mumbled something else to the boy as he left headed in the same direction he was before his detention. "We'll be watching you," was the cop's departing words to the kid.

The officers also left the scene, but I stayed in the car, my heart beating nervously. While I probably was never in any danger myself, I'm pretty sure the cops wouldn't have been too happy if they knew I had recorded the whole thing. It took a few more minutes but my breathing and heartbeat finally slowed, as my nerves quickly turned to anger. I called my friend Ryan in Denver. Then Joe in Atlanta. Reggie in New York. I always had more black friends than the typical white guy, and felt like I had to share what had transpired. "You're not going to believe what I just witnessed," I started out each call. Of course, none of my friends responded with surprise, but still, I felt like I had to share.

Just as I was wrapping up my last call and preparing to finally go to dinner, the black kid started walking past my car, heading back towards direction from which he originally came. Only this time he had a cigarette in his hand and he was carrying a plastic bag. "N&M Mart" it said on the side.

I decided to approach him.

"Hey, kid, may I ask you what happened twenty minutes ago? Are you okay?"

"Man, same ole shit, different day. Fourth time this damn month they stopped me," he said in a forfeited tone.

"Why were they questioning you?" I curiously asked, genuinely wanting to get to the bottom of things. I only was able to make out part of the interaction while it was happening.

"They said they saw me throw a gun into the bushes. Total bullshit. I told 'em I don't even own a damn gun. My brother used to own one, but he's in jail now and I didn't want to end up like that. Ty don't even get to see his baby. The whole thing is fucked up. They arrested him walking after some neighbors called the police, saying they saw some black kid walking around. That shit coulda been me."

As I was driving back after dinner, still in deep thought from what had transpired earlier, I got pulled over by the cops for speeding down Skinker Boulevard. I've been known to have a heavy foot. The red Camaro I rented probably hadn't helped my cause.

"Do you know how fast you were going," the officer asked me after I rolled down my window.

"I was just flowing with traffic," I annoyingly said to the officer. I already was running late to meet my friend Aaron and his wife for a drink and the thought of spending twenty minutes parked on the side of the road was starting to bother me.

"Registration, license and insurance, please."

"It's a rental car, but here's my license and insurance card." I unlatched my seat belt and reached into my front pocket to grab the license and insurance card from my wallet as the officer stood outside the window patiently waiting. Then I handed them to the cop. "Here you go. I'm just visiting St. Louis and really didn't know I was speeding, officer."

"Stay in your car. I'll be back in a few minutes," he responded.

As promised, he returned with my license and insurance. "Do me a favor, slow down. I'm just going to give you warning this time. Enjoy your stay in St. Louis."

"Thank you, officer. I'll be more careful." And then I drove off.

About the Author:

Jeffrey Kass is a writer and lawyer in the U.S., in Denver, Colorado. He has published over 100 political and professional articles over the past 20 years on the Middle East, race, intellectual property law and issues facing entrepreneurs. In 2016, he shifted his writing focus to the memoir and fiction genres. He just finished his first book, Sheldon & Irene – A Traumedy, which is currently under consideration for representation by an agent. Professionally, Jeffrey was recognized by the National Law Journal as one of the top 50 trailblazing Intellectual Property trial lawyers in 2016. Small Business Monthly also named him one of the top 10 lawyers for entrepreneurs. He also was named a SuperLawyer, an award given to less than 5% of lawyers. Jeffrey focuses his practice on trademark, patent and copyright law and disputes, as well as technology law, business litigation, and business planning matters. He is general counsel to over 40 startup and emerging companies. Most importantly, Jeffrey is the father of three children, with whom he enjoys a myriad of activities.

RISING

Michael Hetherton

The old man looked out over the sandhills. A cool wind waved the tall grass, pale from fall frost. Blue and grey clouds moved across the sky. The sun broke through, lighting the grass, sage, green juniper, and dark chokecherry. A flock of grouse burst loudly from the grass and sage, their wings flashing white and grey, fighting to rise-—then they caught the wind, drifting quickly away in the early morning light.

The old man lay in his warm bed believing that he was really there, in the Miller ranch pasture looking over the grassy sandhills, the birds gliding away into the blue horizon. Since they had told him, the old man had felt a monotonous fear at times creeping in at night when sleep wouldn't come. But he'd slept well this night, and for the first time in months, the pain was gone. He felt good—he would hunt today.

Pulling himself up he put on trousers, an old plaid shirt and wool sweater. He ignored the medications lined up on the dresser.

In the kitchen he filled the coffee pot and set a pan on the stove. This morning, he will have bacon and eggs and coffee.

With coffee started the old man went to the living room and looked out the front window. Grey clouds moved above the bare treetops in the yard. Copper and red leaves from the apple tree dappled the garden dirt. A picture of his late wife, Betty, hung on the wall above the old box TV. Another photo, of their small family, sat on an end table. Jack, their only child, was just five then, small, and sweet looking, his hair short and slicked-back.

A big poplar in the yard had gone down from heavy snows, the old house and garage badly needed paint, but not much had changed-—he'd lived there going on sixty years, now, since selling off his father's small farm and going to work for the prairie town. Farming did not provide a decent living then and Betty wanted to be closer to the school, and town facilities, for Jack's sake. He took a deep breath, remembering his son as a small boy. He'd not seen Jack, nor his wife Cindy, in almost five years. The last few Christmases he'd not even gotten a card from them.

Betty left him in 1975. It was only years later that he realised she'd been unhappy a long time. He'd been blind to it, had become set and narrow in his ways, silent, and distant. Earl, the town foreman called him, old grumpy. Eventually, Betty moved in with Frank McGivney, a widower who owned a small oilfield service company. Betty wanted Jack to live with her and Frank; Jack was thirteen. He got along well with Frank's kids who were near his age; he fit in there, and seemed happy being part of a large family. Jack would visit him at the house once and awhile, but he always seemed excited to go home to the McGivney's. Through Jack's school years he went to watch him play ball, attended his school events once and awhile, but did not ever seem to develop much in common with his son.

As Jack, and the McGivney kids left home, and the oil patch picked up, Betty and Frank did pretty well. They had friends, went out allot, and traveled some. In '94 Tom sold out, they bought a home in Kelowna, and spent winters near Scottsdale. Jack, married to Cindy now, often spent

Christmas with the McGivney's. Frank and Betty came back occasionally to see Frank's family, attend a town homecoming, an anniversary, or funeral. Betty was happy, he could see. She worked at staying slim, wore nice clothes, and had her hair done a new way every time he saw her. Then she died, suddenly, in '98. Her service was at Grace United in town, with a gathering after at the hall. He did not attend. He had not seen much of his son Jack, since.

He'd stayed on with the town past retirement age, as much to give himself something to do. He was reliable so they were glad to keep him on all those years. He'd lived alone in the house, now, for over forty years. After the diagnosis he visited the lawyer, Ibrahim. What little he had would go to Jack and Cindy.

He'd not hunted yet this season, had not been able to. It was a cold, windy fall, with many rainy days. The wind was up again today, but he would hunt anyway.

Smelling the coffee he went to the kitchen, poured a steaming cup, took out a few strips of bacon from the fridge and set them in the smoking pan. The bacon sizzled and spattered—as it began to bubble and crisp-up he cracked two eggs. He put bread in the toaster, and basted the eggs with bacon fat until they went white on top, the edges curling and turning brown, then buttered the hot toast. He ate, slowly, and sipped the hot coffee in the quiet kitchen. "Oh…God damnit, that's good," he mumbled to himself.

After breakfast, from a basement cedar closet he took out his brown canvas hunting jacket, worn and faded, and blotched with old bloodstains, smelling of sage from sprigs left in the game pockets. He pulled out his Winchester model-12 pump shotgun and a full shell belt; the meat getter, he used to call the gun when Jack was a boy. He took the gear upstairs, struggling a little on the steep steps, put on boots, an old blue neckerchief with white polka dots, and a wool cap, then went out.

The old garage smelled of spilled oil, and dust. On the wall was a mount of a large sandhills mule deer buck he'd killed on the Elkink ranch way back in 1967. He loaded his hunting gear, backed the truck out carefully and let it idle awhile to warm.

He'd tried to stay in contact with Jack over the years, had tried in his way to tell him he loved him, but Jack, though always polite, seldom responded. He missed him—had not ever stopped missing him all these years. A dull aching that never really left. And he still worried about him, though Jack was over fifty, now. On coffee row not so long ago Bill Harder let him know that he'd bumped into Jack in Medicine Hat, where he and Cindy had settled after buying into a tire shop years back. "Your boy looks good. Sounded happy," Bill told him. He just nodded, unable to say or ask anything.

On the road north through rolling harvested grain fields the old man could see the lights from pump jacks and compressor stations dotting the country. There'd been a boom in the Saskatchewan oil fields. He hoped the development would not bother the birds and wildlife. By the time he turned west on Christopher Road the cloudy morning had brightened a little. At a cross roads near a big, dry, alkali lake in the shortgrass cattle pastures the country began to change. Upland from the bright, blue-white alkali, the Miller pasture started, running west, mile after mile of low grassy hills.

Further on the dusty road he passed broke-up rows of old caragana hedges lined out like an abandoned orchard running up a pale, grassy slope into the sandhills. He'd hunted these hedgerows going back to the 1950's; sharp-tail grouse, and fast flying Hungarian partridge. A few weathered wooden buildings tilted from constant wind stood in fields. Men like his father had broken this land and farmed it—but it was sandy land that drifted badly in dry years and most of them abandoned their farms. His father had stayed, married his mother, and made a go of it.

He turned in along the edge of the old caraganna rows and drove slowly along the trail below the open slope. After a mile or so he turned into the ungrazed pasture onto an almost overgrown car trail. He came to some tangled barbwire and fallen over fence posts. Some grey weathered planks, that were once an outbuilding, lay scattered in the grass. Beyond that, a few stubby caraganas and trees marked where the house had stood. The old man stopped the truck, opened the window, and looked out at where he had once lived. Only the rusted shell of a coal burning stove, half buried and covered by grass, remained. He understood it had been for the best, to sell out, but had always deeply regretted letting go the homestead ten acres with the rest of the farm.

Back on the main road, past the Branson ranch yard he came to the approach into the Miller's east pasture. Over a Texas gate he drove slowly along the sandy trail. Up a gentle rise, to the south, lay an open valley of brushy sandhills, sage flats, and small stands of aspen, many of the trees still with bright yellow leaves dangling on them. The trail curved, then flattened out near a long esker of grassy dunes. Near a high point he stopped, looking out over the hunting lands.

Jack had sometimes come hunting with him when he was little. In the field the boy would look at the shot birds, admire and stroke their patterned feathers, but he'd never shown much interest in hunting or shooting. He mostly stayed quiet in the truck cab, satisfied just to sleep in the sun shining through the windshield. As Jack got older it became obvious he did not want to hunt, so he stopped asking him to come with him.

In the 60's and 70's he'd hunted with locals, for geese in the morning, and "chicken" in the afternoon. Some of the men mixed drinking with hunting and he drifted away from them. Others moved out of the country, some died, many had just quit. Eventually he only hunted alone. He wondered why he hadn't got a hunting dog, maybe a pair of Springer's and trained them for upland? And he could not understand why he could not connect with his son, or how to change to make it easier. He'd never asked why he and Cindy had not had children of their own. When they were married he remembered he'd felt tears rise, seeing them so young, a little apprehensive and nervous, but smiling and happy as they looked into each other's eyes. At the wedding Betty had told him he was a stubborn son-of-a-bitch. On coffee row at the café, not so long ago, Ed Bass told him he was an old stubborn son-of-a-bitch.

The old man opened the truck's center counsel, took out a small silver flask and shook it. There was a splash of brandy left—he put the flask in the chest pocket of his jacket. He pulled three #6's from the belt, stepped out of the truck with the old shotgun and slid the red and copper shells

into the chamber. A year or so after Betty left he indulged, buying a semi-auto Berretta, but then seldom used it, still preferring the feel of the Winchester. His desire to kill birds fell off over the years, he took fewer and fewer. But he still walked the sandhills and fields with the old model 12, the flask, and a small lunch, learning how game birds lived, where they danced fed and roosted, the population ebbing or falling, after good and bad winters. He eventually sold the Beretta to young David Campbell.

He started out now, breathing in the sharp October air smelling of sage, juniper, and damp grass. The wind made his eyes water. He walked slowly, toward the long, lumpy string of dunes thickly covered with black-branched chokecherry, tilted grass, and green juniper on some slopes. He'd walked that stretch of dunes maybe a hundred times over the years.

The grass in the flats came to his hips, the sagebrush bright and thick there, too. He slowed more as he neared the grass dunes, stepping into a brown patch of rosebush as a break in the streaming clouds let through sunlight. He stood in the quiet awhile, puffing, using the old shotgun for support, the grass waving in the wind around him. Cloud shadows drifted over the land. The rhythm of his breath came back and he was calm inside.

… Then, six grouse broke from the grass, cluck-cluck-cluck, flashing white and grey in the new morning sun as they fought to rise against the wind. He instinctively raised the shotgun-—then lowered it, and watched the birds gain height and speed as they went with the wind, wildly beating their wings, then gliding away into the dark horizon clouds. He was a little surprised, having expected only a single or two, thinking most of the birds would be feeding in the grain fields in the morning¾as he relaxed, four more grouse burst from the grass, followed quickly by a single from the nearby sage, then three more lifting loudly, wings flashing, from the chokecherry bushes. A familiar feeling of excitement came, from so many birds rising—and he felt that old, lingering worry dissipate, from thinking that one fall it could all be over, the birds gone forever—and it was always good when he found them again, even after a tough winter or wet spring. He always found them again in the fall.

The old man watched the last grouse glide away and disappear.

He took out the flask, opened it, tipped it to his mouth and swallowed the last of the brandy, then threw the flask into the grass-—he'd never use it again. He'd known it was over, felt it deep in his bones and heart and it released all the fear and pain that had been there. As he looked out at the sandhills more grouse began to lift, from all around him, across all the grassland, singles, small flocks and large, all of them rising, rising into the air, loudly beating their wings; hundreds of birds; thousands of them, lifting, lifting, filling the air and sky above the grass. And they kept rising; rising, rising, rising, without end.

Early that morning, Earl, the town foreman stopped by the old man's house. He had not seen him in awhile and was worried about him. He knocked at the door, but he did not answer. He slipped into the house, turned on the kitchen light, and yelled his name. The old man still did not answer, so he walked through the quiet rooms. He found him in bed. He had been dead, he thought, for a some time.

About the Author:

Michael Hetherton's short story collection, Grass-lands, won a Saskatchewan Book Award for best first book, and was runner-up, best short fiction collection, Independent Publisher's Book Awards. In past years his stories have appeared in Greens-boro Review, Grain, South Dakota Review, and many others. He lives in Saskatchewan, Cana-da.

KIOKU

Shirley A Guldimann

The old woman paints a cone-shaped green mountain onto heavy white paper, and in front of the mountain, a small kimono-clad figure, one triangle for a body and an inverted one for a face, onto which she draws eyes, nose, mouth, creating a ningyo, a doll, to delight any child. Her brush wavers as she streaks thinned cerulean blue across the remaining white expanse.

The young teacher approaches her: "a lovely picture," she says.

"My hand used to be so steady," the old woman laments, thinking of the fine calligraphic strokes that once had been hers.

"Look," the teacher says, "the white you've left visible is like a bank of clouds sailing across the blue sky."

"I don't remember how the sky behind the mountain really appeared," the old woman says.

"Maybe your hand has remembered for you," the teacher says.

The old woman's husband wouldn't have anything to do with the Senior Center. He passed a year ago, and now the old woman finds the center not an unpleasant place to spend a morning once a week. Today, it is sunny, and the seniors sit outside at two picnic tables in the faint spring breeze under the flickering shade of a sycamore. Still, the old woman wears a knit vest under her heavy sweater. She is no longer the atsugari, warm-blooded one, she was in her youth.

"Today," the young teacher says firmly as though to stop time, as if today didn't flow inexorably from yesterday into tomorrow, "we'll work on portraits. Pair up and draw each other. For my demo, I'd like a volunteer."

The Turkish lady volunteers. Doubtless a beauty in her youth. You can see it in her fine high cheekbones. The old woman identifies everyone by nationality because names elude her. There is the Italian lady, the Hispanic lady, and the Irish gentleman. And there is a cluster she thinks of as the American ladies, because they claim no other origin than where they are, here, in Los Angeles. The old woman is called "Mimi" by the Americans and others who cannot manage the syllables in Miyeko, her Japanese first name. That is fine with her. For her part, she is adept at sidestepping the use of names.

The Turkish lady reminds the old woman of the bijin, the great beauty, of Tamana where the old woman grew up. LIke the bijin, the Turkish lady is tall. Her carriage is upright, so rare among the center's seniors, men as well as women. It makes her seem invulnerable to adversity. That was how the village viewed the bijin of Tamana too. But when the bijin lost her husband in the war against the United States, she caved in to grief, and her family, embarrassed by her public displays of emotion, married her off to her departed husband's younger brother.

The old woman, reminiscing, has missed the teacher's demonstration. No matter. She and the other students generally do what they want with the paints, brushes, pencils, paper that the Center provides. Some do practically nothing at all but chat, and that's fine too. The sun filtering through the sycamore splatters the old woman's sheet of paper with shadows of leaves. It would be nice to trace and color them.

"Would you like me to be your partner," the young teacher asks the old woman. "I'm afraid the others have already paired up and we're an odd number today."

The old woman, confused, squints up at the teacher. "You can draw me," the teacher explains.

"I cannot draw people," the old woman says. Staring into another's face, attempting to see into their thoughts, strikes her as offensive.

"If you change your mind, I'm here for you."

The old woman thanks the teacher, knowing it must be frustrating for her to work with seniors who can be as uncooperative as children.

The old woman traces leaf patterns in green pencil while the others attempt drawing each other. She then paints in watercolor translucent triangles of pink on top of the leaf design in the form of a kimono-clad doll. The leaf design works as a kimono pattern. The Turkish lady breaks from her drawing to exclaim over the old woman's artwork: "How beautiful it is!" Others join in praising the result. One of the American ladies says, "Mimi, show me how it's done." The old woman, embarrassed, says, "Nothing, it is nothing." What pleases her is not her doll but the goodwill of her fellow seniors. This is what she will recall of her morning and recount to her daughter-in-law, who will drive her home from the center.

That evening the old woman dreams of her husband, and wakes with a start. She has not thought of him in several days. She rises from bed and walks over to her husband's photo, which hangs on the wall opposite.

"Warukatta ne, that was wrong of me," she says. "I'm sorry."

Even so, she cannot resist the next day putting on a dab of perfume that he had not cared for but that she likes. She does this before their grandson, now a young man, picks her up at her apartment to take her out to lunch. She enjoys his cheerful company, and his good looks bring back to her his grandfather.

Four months later the seniors at the center are making dolls to decorate a nearby center for children at risk. "Play, enjoy!" the young teacher tells them.

"I want to make a doll for a boy," says one of the men.

"Do it!" the teacher says with a smile.

This project stymies the old woman. She admires the Hispanic lady who is making dolls out of multicolored yarn.

"Your son said you'd been ill. How are you feeling today?" the teacher asks the old woman.

"Fine, thank you," the old woman says. She had suffered a mild heart attack and was briefly hospitalized, but does not want to go into that. She is glad to be back in class.

"Do you need help getting started?" the teacher asks.

"Thank you," the old woman says.

"Here are some supplies." The teacher sets paper, yarn and scissors in front of the old woman. "Do something fun, easy. See, like those ladies."

The old woman glances over at the American ladies. They are making strings of paper dolls out of colorful wrapping paper.

The old woman's hands, not used to being idle, reach for several sheets of paper, which she cuts into squares, and folds and unfolds, folds and unfolds, and fits together. She creates a flat, kimono-clad doll, about five inches long. When was the last time she had seen something like this?

A boy's thin, smiling face comes into focus. But his name is not in her kioku, her memory. Nonetheless, she can see he wears a khaki school uniform and rides his bicycle back and forth, back and forth, across the street in front of her home as she, a youngster herself, studies history on the veranda. Watching him from a distance is like watching a movie, only in color before there was color in movies.

"I don't know why he rides back and forth like that," she said to a friend at school.

"Don't you?" her friend said. "He likes you."

"Masaka, that can't be. He doesn't know me."

"But it is true. I heard it from his sister."

During the war, along with so many in the neighborhood, the boy who rode the bicycle was inducted. The old woman recalls how the boy's sister implored her to write to him. High school boys and girls went to separate schools in those days. The old woman's parents disapproved of the request, but she secretly wrote the bicycle boy a note wishing him well and made for him, yes, a paper doll, like the one she folded today. It was the custom, done for good luck.

The old woman struggles to recall the name for those flat paper dolls.

The boy wrote back to her. She read his letter in an air raid shelter near the Kumamoto factory where she had been sent to sew military uniforms. He was training to become a pilot. When he flew his plane into battle her doll, he said, would be with him. Eventually, news came that he would not be returning from the war.

"Shinjirarenai, I can't comprehend it," the old woman now mutters to herself, repeating what she said many years ago on learning of the bicycle boy's death. She suddenly unfolds the doll she created, smoothing the pieces of paper as flat as

possible. She runs her hand over and over them, but cannot rid them of the creases she so precisely made.

A year after Japan's surrender the old woman, then nineteen, sailed to California. It was a rough passage. She had left her hometown to avoid the marriage her parents were arranging for her with an older man. "Iya, I don't want to," she had told them in a burst of flagrant disobedience. In Los Angeles, she stayed with a cousin already living there. She later married a Japanese-American man who had been interned in the Heart Mountain camp during the war. She bore him a son, and her son had a son. Looking after three generations she grew old as each day folded inexorably from yesterday into today and tomorrow.

 "What happened to the lovely doll you were working on?" the teacher says.

The old woman starts, looks up. "It was no good," she says.

"There's lots more paper. Why not try something new then?" the teacher says, smiling.

The old woman reaches for a fresh sheet of paper and runs her hand over the smooth surface, memories stirring, her heart beating hard.

About the Author:

Shirley Asano is a Southern California writer who is currently working on a collection of linked short stories. Focusing on the immigrant experience she explores in her fiction the intersections of cultures and the transformation of interior lives that consequently occurs. Her fiction has appeared in various literary journals, and her nonfiction in the Los Angeles Times and the News-Press. Shirley holds a B.A. in English from the University of California, Los Angeles; M.A. in theology from Fuller Theological Seminary; and, J.D. from the University of Southern California.

THE HUNTED

Tinka Harvard

Daniel lifted his head from Thieme's Atlas of Anatomy and slid his glasses off, turning his ear toward the door. Being inside warm and cozy during rain storms was one of his favorite things to do. He wondered, Is that the doorbell? Who would be out in this rain?

His grandmother constantly reminds him that he spends too much time inside. "Go out some time," she tells him. "You gotta work hard and play hard in this life," was one of her mantras.

But today would not be ideal. At the sound of the doorbell he wondered, What fool would dare to wander out in this rain?

He walked over to the door and opened it, and there she was.

It was a shock really, a terrible shock to see her standing there in the rain with a gash on her head and blood streaming down her face. The first thing he thought was, That's a nasty cut—it may need some stitches.

She was soaking wet, her clothes all soaked through. It was as if she were dressed in a kind of cling wrap the way her clothes clung to every inch of her body, every curve and contour. Daniel could see right through her sheer white top to her breast; her nipples were enormously round and erect. Daniel thought, She's exquisite.

"You deaf?" Nana interrupted his thoughts. "Who is it?" His grandmother appeared at his side, ducked under his arm that was holding on to the frame of the door, and spotted the wet and bleeding stranger.

"Girl, you done lost your mind! Get in here!" Nana yelled while pulling the nearly naked young woman in from the freezing rain.

There weren't many things that made Nana nervous, not after all her years in nursing and all the living she'd done. She'd seen distraught young women quietly trying to hold back their sobbing. She'd tended to women in torn clothes and even some who have been soaked to the bone in rain water. But this stranger who showed up on her doorstep in tears and ripped clothing and with bare feet cut up and bleeding in the rain storm shook her.

"Daniel, call 911, baby!"

Daniel knew his grandmother all too well. He could hear the fear in her voice despite her tough talk as he got through to the emergency operator.

Nana lead the girl to the sofa, reached for a cashmere throw, and wrapped her in it. "Daniel!" she shouted. "What's wrong with you? Get me some towels! You the medicine man. Why I got to tell you everything?" Medicine Man is Nana's nick name for him, which masks her pride of her grandson who recently began medical school.

"Girl, what has happened?" Nana spoke to the wet creature softly all along looking into her eyes.

The young lady began to speak but was interrupted when Daniel returned with the towels. Nana realized that she had better get the girl into some warm, dry clothes. "I'm gonna get you outta these wet things. That alright with you?"

The young lady, between shivers and chattering teeth, nodded yes.

"What's your name?" Nana wanted to know.

She managed to chatter out, "Jeannie."

"Well come on Jeannie, let's get you out of these soaking wet clothes. What kind of crazy you mixed up in? You done something wrong? Let me know now! The ambulance is on its way, but I'll call the cops on you too!" Nana searched her eyes for some signal as to how to proceed.

The young lady made a movement of her head and parted her lips as if to respond, but nothing came out.

"I don't know what that means," Nana let her know.

Daniel stood out of the way by the bedroom door while Nana sat the girl down. Nana could be rough, but he knew this girl was in good hands. The best actually.

Pondering this strange, wet, bruised creature that had shown up on their doorstep, he found himself mesmerized. Normally there was a calmness about him. Not much phased him. It worked both ways: he was not unsettled easily or easily moved.

He mused to himself, There's nothing in the medical books that addresses the shock that comes over first-year medical students when a gorgeous, bruised woman shows up at one's door.

Nana closed the door with him on the other side of it, interrupting his thoughts. She opened it quickly again as he was stepping away and whispered, "Keep an eye out for the EMTs."

Standing over Jeannie who was sitting on the bed, Nana lifted Jeannie's arms up in the air and pulled her wet silk T-shirt up and off. While Jeannie stood up she wrapped her arms around Nana's shoulders and stepped out of her pajama-like silk bottoms and then put on the cotton night shirt that Nana had given to her to cover up.

Jeannie was beginning to gain her composure a bit and said through her diminishing tears, "First, I was silly enough to lock myself out of my house. And . . . then when I tried to climb through the window I slipped and gashed my head. I cut my feet as well. How awful is it?"

"You can speak," Nana teased her as she sat next to her on the bed. She gently wiped Jeannie's face with a soft towel to dry her tears.

"You'll need to calm down now or your face is bound to swell up even more from so much crying. Maybe this here cream with aloe vera will keep the swelling down." Nana, keeping with the quiet that had taken over the room, spoke in a whisper as she gently rubbed the cream on Jeannie's face.

Daniel showed the paramedics the way to the bedroom when they arrived. He watched as the girl and Nana talked with them. One of the paramedics reached for the telephone and made a call while the other skillfully cleaned Jeannie's wounds even more thoroughly. Before packing up to leave, he placed a bandage over the cut on her head, which turned out to be bloodier than deep.

He certainly keeps his distance, Jeannie thought to herself as she looked up and saw Daniel standing in the corner. Her heart pounded incredibly quickly inside her chest. Seeing him this close up took her breath away.

"So she'll be alright?" Nana asked the paramedics.

"Yes, ma'am, she'll be fine. Just bruised and terribly sore I imagine. We've asked her to come in first thing in the morning just to run a few tests for precautionary measures, but she'll be alright." The paramedics confided in Nana on their way out.

"Daniel, can you walk Jeannie home? The paramedics called her house and spoke with her brother. He's at home now waiting for her. They moved into the Johanson's old house just down the street."

With great care, Daniel took Jeannie's hand and gently placed his arms around her waist. She even smells good, he thought.

He was grateful that the rain had stopped making it easier for her to walk outdoors with his help.

"Just a few doors down?" he confirmed with Jeannie in regards to her home.

"Yes," she whimpered in response.

"Oh you are our new neighbors?"

Before Jeannie could respond Daniel asked, "Is that him? Is that your brother at the door of your house?"

Jeannie nodded her head as she walked with her head on Daniel's shoulder as he supported her.

Standing in front of their house holding the door open, Jeannie's brother couldn't believe what he was seeing.

Gingerly, Daniel handed Jeannie over to her brother keeping an eye on her as she struggled to stand on her own. He asked her, "Is it alright if I come by tomorrow to see how you are or if I can help in any way?"

Jeannie nodded signaling a pitiful yes and then disappeared into her house with her brother closing the door behind them.

Overwhelmed with a mix of emotions, Daniel took his time getting back home. Shaken, he allowed himself to rest in knowing she'd be alright, and that he could see her tomorrow.

Inside Jeannie's house, her brother was furious with her. "Well, I hope you got what you wanted." He spits out.

"It worked didn't it? He's coming over tomorrow."

About the Author:

Tinka Harvard is a writer and theologian from Brooklyn, New York. A graduate of Union Theological Seminary at Columbia University in New York City with a Master's in Divinity, she seeks to write stories, essays and poetry that lend ideas toward inspired living. www.tinkaharvard.com

UNUSED MILES

Richard Bentley

This happened in San Francisco in the 1960s, but in the early sixties San Francisco wasn't quite as we picture it now. There didn't seem to be an unusual amount of freedom or rebellion in the air. Allen Ginsberg was a store clerk.

Back in Chicago, I had been captivated for many years by a girl named Mary Banz, beginning when she was fourteen and I was twenty-seven.

A few years later, she was studying art in a summer program at a Colorado college. I had just moved to San Francisco, not to wear flowers in my hair but because of a job promotion. How square. To demonstrate my newly acquired executive power, I invited Mary for a visit when her art school was over.

"Are you out of your mind? I know what you're up to, and do you think I'm going to do something stupid like come visit you? I'm not even drinking age in most states."

"We don't have to go to bars. We could drink at home."

I heard a faint giggle in the background, followed by silence.

"No," Mary said sharply, "I don't think so." Did she say it to me? Or did she say it to someone else?

There was a muffled conversation with hand held over the speaker. I thought of how far away she was and what an embarrassing blunder I was making. There was another muffled giggle, more silence.

After a while Mary said, "How about if I send you someone?"

"Someone."

"Her name's Patty. She's a sculptor. My age. She's from Johnstown, Pennsylvania. Says she wants to go to San Francisco, wear some flowers in her hair. Says she wants to walk around the Haight-Ashbury and smoke dope and fuck some really nice people. Preferably monks."

"Typical tourist."

There was more muffled conversation.

"A week from next Thursday," Mary said. "You can meet her at the airport. She'll be in a crate with holes punched in it. Go to baggage claim, ha ha."

Patty was smart and articulate in a foulmouthed sort of way, but what she said was always cheerful. She was funny and her beauty was unusual, with soft red hair fluffing outward as if a halo of static electricity circled her head. She liked to sit naked on the bed, practicing Handel's Recorder Sonata in F major. Over and over—da-da-da-da-da-dah-da...da-da-da-da-dah-da.

She practiced her recorder on the bed; in the car going up to Mount Tamalpais; on the Mad River Beach at Arcata; on the Skunk Train from Fort Bragg to Willits; in Golden Gate Park; in the Ukiah redwood forest; in a canoe on the Russian River; at a picnic table at the Souverain winery. A typical tourist.

She spoke as if she had a habit of authority.

"They haven't made any decent music since the fucking eighteenth century," she declared, slapping the recorder against her palm. "Stravinsky, the Beach Boys, it's all the same stuff." She was especially disrespectful of the Beatles:

"You say you want a revolution

"Oh no—oo…

"I don't wanna change the world

"What kind of insipid middle-class crap is that?"

On the other hand, she said there was no good sculpture until the twentieth century. I couldn't argue with her, even when I spoke of the ancient Greeks and all their Apollos and Aphrodites.

"Come over here," she said.

I moved closer to the bed and she reached out. "You see? A nice sculptural assemblage… ornamentally baroque and complex. You'd rather look at fig leaves?" She sighed. "One of these days I'm going to have to go back to school, back to sophomore year. But who knows when? This apartment's a real tourist trap."

"Just stay in San Francisco," I said. "You have plenty of unused miles."

About the Author:

Richard Bentley's fiction, poetry, and memoir have been published in over 250 journals, magazines and anthologies on three continents. His books, Post-Freudian Dreaming and A General Theory of Desire, are available on Amazon, Powell's Books, or at www.dickbentley.com. His new book, All Rise, contains recently published stories, poems, and graphic "wall poetry" that has been displayed in art galleries. Richard Bentley served on the board of the Modern Poetry Association (now known as the Poetry Foundation). He was a Pushcart Prize nominee and a prizewinner in the Paris Review/Paris Writers Workshop International Fiction Awards. In 2012 and 2013, he gave readings of his poetry at the famous Paris bistro, Au Chat Noir. Before teaching writing at the University of Massachusetts, he was Chief Planner for the Mayor's Office of Housing in Boston. Richard is a Yale graduate with an MFA from Vermont College.

O MITO DA FÉNIX
Vera Lúcia Gonçalves

Quando me debruço sobre a mitologia grega tendo a abrandar sempre no mito da Fénix. Há algo nela que me seduz, que parece ter sido urdido na malha de que se revestem os mundos por onde caminho quando mergulho na interioridade.

É como se a visse ao longe, numa pira sagrada sobre um altar, a incandescer em sintonia com a luminescência da canela, da salva e da mirra, salientando-se no fundo fúlvido de um sol poente. A noite consumindo a ardência até se extinguir no frio pardacento da cinza. O amanhecer dourando a formação poeirenta que o sopro de Zéfiro faz dançar no cântico sublimado da aurora. E essa formação poeirenta materializando-se pena a pena, tomando a forma cada vez mais evidente de uma ave.

O sentir da Fénix flutua entre as expectativas de uma pulsação idealizada ainda por ouvir e o reconhecimento das cinzas obscuras em que foram tecidas as suas penas mais refulgentes. A sua angústia, porém, será a consciência de que no momento em que estender toda a áurea magnitude das suas asas para se dirigir ao sol de um mundo novo, estará apenas a sentir a liberdade mais efêmera da vida antes de cair e de se tornar poeira outra vez.

A PLACE OF BUSINESS
Bill Schillaci

When I first entered its life, it was a stamp store, or seemed to be. It had no business sign, but there was a storefront window that was so grimy I had to walk up close and squint to see what was behind it. There, lined up on narrow, unfinished pine shelves were stamps, rubber stamps with names and addresses or PAID or DECLINED or MEAT IS MURDER or LOCAL 706 or giraffes or the Taj Mahal. Behind the stamps was darkness. I didn't need a rubber stamp. But the place called to me. So strange, so small, the size of a one-car garage, the single commercial establishment on the lip of a couple of acres of undeveloped scrubland, like a clapboard general store standing alone on a tiny prairie and otherwise surrounded by suburban homes.

With a slip of paper on which I had carefully signed my name, I took the single stone step and gripped the door handle, feeling like I was about to sneak into someone's living room. The latch clicked and I entered. An acrid chemical smell streaked up my nostrils. Inside, forming in the shadows there was...nothing. No counter, no desk, no person, just a wall of cracked brown paint with a doorless doorway that was marginally taller than what you would see in a kindergarten playhouse.

"Hello," I said.

There was a sound, like a chair sliding across the floor, and the doorway filled with a faint reddish light. The figure who came forward had to dip just a bit to pass through the miniature opening. The figure wore a hoodie, hood up, way up so that it covered three-quarters of the face inside.

An upward curve of the hood created a narrow aperture surrounding blackness, through which, I supposed, an eye observed me.

"Yes?" the figure said in a genderless whisper.

"I'd like to have a stamp made."

"Ahhh."

I advanced the slip of paper into the space between us. A narrow hand with long, bumpy fingers egressed from the sleeve of the hoodie, and I placed my signature on the upturned palm. As the figure examined the slip, my widening pupils noted that the hoodie wasn't a hoodie at all. It was a cowled cape or a cloak that fell to the figure's knees and was sealed in front with knots instead of buttons.

"Who is this?" the figure said.

"Me."

"And why does a young man like you need such a thing?"

"Excuse me."

"Your name signed. What is the purpose?"

"School art project."

There was movement inside the garment, a nod maybe.

"Fifteen dollars. In advance."

"All of it?"

The figure took a step toward the window and waved its creepy hand at the shelves.

"Do you see those?" said the figure. "Each of them never picked up and never paid for."

Apparent in the somewhat stronger daylight was a spiral design sewn with white thread into the fabric of the cowl.

"Is that Andromeda?" I asked.

"Indeed it is. Are you an astronomer?"

"I have a telescope. Nothing special."

I had a five and a lot of ones and pocket change, all of which I paid out on the figure's other upturned palm. It didn't add up to fifteen.

"Sufficient. Come back in a week."

The figure faded through the doorway and the red light went out.

That night I lugged my little National Geographic reflector telescope and tripod out behind the garage away from the house lights. I had the book of constellations that came with the scope and a flashlight, and I kept going from the book to the telescope, trying to locate Alpha Andromedae and the other stars in the cluster where the Greek Ptolemy discovered the naked princess chained to a rock waiting to be devoured by a sea serpent. The best I could do was find pieces, maybe a leg, part of an arm, but nothing complete. So I just scanned the sky, which I thought of as layered, the brightest objects the lowest layer, then the middle layer, then the faintest points on the unimaginable other side of the universe. This I did until my mother tracked me down and told me to put out the recycling barrel.

The idea came to me that the stamp person could join me behind the garage and help me find Andromeda. There were only four streets between us, one long one on the main road where the store was and then three short ones up a mild hill. We could wait until darkness and walk together under the clear sky, me and this mysterious being, like an androgynous time traveler from the Carolingian epoch. Crazy, of course, but that didn't stop the pictures in my mind, all unfolding from what I fantasized was the traveler's potent magic, undefined but something akin to ET levitating oranges.

As instructed, I waited until the seventh day after I dropped off my name. Again I looked hard through the window, this time finding that the shelves had been swept clean. On the inside of the glass panel of the front door hung a sign – For Rent and a phone number. It seemed the stamp person – if it was a person – had used me to procure revenge on all those customers who stiffed her or him or it. I tried the doorknob, it didn't turn. After peering for a time into the interior, trying to will the figure back into the store, I sat on the stone step. Beside me, one on top of the other, were two red bricks, and tucked behind them a small white bag folded shut. On the bag were two images – my signature in basic blue and above it in radiant emerald the Andromeda galaxy – and inside it were the two rubber stamps that made them.

She was two places ahead of me on the line at Starbucks, a line I had not intended to get on until, walking by, I spotted her. She ordered a grande straight and was still doctoring it at the condiment station when I caught up.

"Hey, Thalia."

Her hair was a helmet of tight orangey cornrows pulled back from her broad umber brown, tied at her neck and cascading down her back. Her sleepy eyes squinted a smile.

"Eddie," she said, stirring her drink. "Now you know my weakness."

"You and half the school."

"All of us teenage caffeine junkies."

"My mom's from Utah. Says she didn't have her first cup of coffee until she was twenty eight."

"Is she Latter Day Saints?"

"No, but everybody else was. So there was no peer pressure."

"I started at ten, my sisters earlier than that. In an enlightened society that would be child abuse."

She was, arguably, the smartest kid in the school. The bot her team built was a finalist in the FIRST Robotics Competition. Someone told me that her senior thesis had something to do with reading Dante's Inferno – in Italian. She was also the top pitcher on our otherwise pathetic softball team, and one muggy Saturday, after we had slipped into the county tournament because another school, ravaged by the flu, had forfeited, had thrown the entirety of two extra-inning games, nineteen innings all told. I'm tall but she was taller and today she smelled like a lilac bush in May. We joined the procession of lethargic classmates on the quarter-mile walk to the school.

"Do you ever drink tea?" I said.

"When I'm sick."

"I know a place with incredible tea."

"I never heard those two words side by side."

"I know. Do you want to try it?"

She glanced at me.

"Eddie, are you asking me for a date before the first bell?"

"No, no, I just like the tea and thought you might too."

"Sounds like a date to me."

Me? Asking Thalia Roberts out was above my pay grade, but it did seem that that's what I was doing .

"Alright, I'm asking, but only if you say yes."

"Hmm. I'd better accept. Who knows when I'll get asked out to tea again."

The next day after school Thalia rode the bus with me to my side of town. The weathered cedar siding of the shop had been painted a forest green, and the new asphalt shingles on the peaked roof had canted sides forming two sloping fields of linked trapezoids. Above the door, there was now a sign, an oval slab of timber printed with the words "Instant Gratification."

"Are you taking me to a massage parlor?" Thalia asked.

In the shop there was a single table with a green-veined white marble top the size of a manhole cover surrounded by three wrought iron lawn chairs. Grass paper the color of a subtle forest mist covered the walls, except in a corner of the ceiling where a leak before the roof was finished left a dark stain the shape of holly leaf with a single berry.

"So cute," said Thalia struggling to demurely fold her WBA legs in the cramped space under the table. She shifted her knees one way, I shifted mine the other, thereby eliminating the risk of contact. Her shoulders were glistening globes of power draped in a sleeveless Cleveland Cavaliers jersey. She surveyed the table.

"Is this the business?"

"They sell in bulk, mostly by mail," I said, pointing to the price list on a blackboard screwed to the wall. "This is kind of a tasting table."

"Thirty five bucks for a pound of sencha?" she said, studying the blackboard. "Is that a deal?"

"We don't have to buy anything. The owner knows me."

On cue, flashing through the doorway in his brilliant saffron robe, we were joined by Venerable Gyosei.

"Edward," he said, palm to his heart and bowing slightly. I returned both gestures. "And you must be Thalia."

"I am," she said, sitting up straighter. Her knees made contact with mine and there she left them.

Gyosei begged for our patience and withdrew. Thalia cast me a what-the-heck look.

"You told him my name?"

"I made a reservation."

"Smart. I mean, one table. How do you know, um...?"

"His name is Venerable Gyosei."

"How do you know Venerable Goysei?"

"It's more the store than him. I've sort of adopted it. Or it's adopted me."

"What?"

That story would need to come later since Venerable Gyosei reappeared with a tray. On the table he precisely placed a steaming blue clay pot inscribed with yellow Japanese characters, two matching cups, a bronze bowl, and a small wooden mallet. Goysei filled the cups with the pot's smoky contents and then struck the bowl with the mallet. A sound that was less a ringing than the hum of a musical instrument that vibrated the air for several moments. He then began a chant, a guttural recitation that barely escaped his throat. Thalia eyed me as if someone had emptied a tray of ice cubes down her back, but managed to dip her head until Gyosei concluded and once again disappeared.

"What was that?" she whispered, leaning across the table.

"I think it was this," I said, running my forefinger over the characters on the teapot. "It's a Buddhist sutra."

She nodded, and lifting her cup blew across the top of it. A vanilla aroma floated against my face. I would always think of it as the first time Thalia Roberts kissed me.

Smiling mercifully, Venerable Gyosei refused the ten dollar bill I offered. He gave us each two small bags containing samples of the tea we had sipped. On the walk back, Thalia stopped and opened her bag. Inside was a slip of paper with what I told her was the English version of the sutra on the tea pot, the one Gyosei had chanted. Still as a statue, she read it through. Then she slipped her arm through mine and we continued our thoughtful walk to her side of town.

"Fucking A, Eddie," she said softly. "Fucking A."

The walls inside the shower in my folks' bedroom bathroom didn't need to be replaced. Okay, there was mold, spotty infestations blackening the grout between the tiles. But with a stiff brush, some super-concentrated bleach and a little focused violence, the stains vanished. My father wasn't convinced. He said the tiles had been there for thirty years, maybe longer, since before we owned the house, and no amount of scrubbing would make them clean. With his toolbox he knelt inside the bathtub and went to work, first with a hammer and cold chisel, then, after a trip to Home Depot, a miniature circular saw that obliterated the grout and allowed him to squeeze the tip of a crowbar behind the tiles and rip them off the wall one shattered piece at a time. Of course some of the plywood to which to tiles were glued was coming off as well, but he seemed unconcerned.

"We can patch that," he said, and then he'd go to the next tile and claw it off with another chunk of plywood.

We both started off with dust masks, but the sweat inside his mask was getting to him and he let it drop around his neck and was now inhaling the white puffs of porcelain he was creating. His breaths came in gasps at shorter and shorter intervals. He'd been at it since breakfast and had destroyed maybe a square yard of perfectly good tiles, although bits that would also have to be scraped away were still stuck in place.

I stood behind him, sweeping the fallen debris into a contractor's trash bag. I kept pestering him to take a break and let me take over. When he finally agreed, I had to help him stand because his knees had locked. He was a dead weight, drained of energy, like a sack of dried beans in the shape of a man. He shuffled to the bedroom window and looked to the backyard where he had placed a lounge chair under our great elm tree. There in the speckled August sunlight, my mother reclined, folded up in a thermal blanket, a tartan cancer bandana encasing her hairless head. Her book lay on the grass beside her. My father never exactly voiced a belief that the mold in the bathroom had caused her illness or if he thought removing it would help her get well. But when he told her that was his plan, she smiled and said good idea. Even I, sitting in on this exchange simply out of inertia that rendered me incapable of walking out on another of their exhausting dialogs about what to do next, saw clearly that this had nothing to do with disease. It was just swabbing the deck on a sinking ship.

He hobbled down the stairs and out to the yard and sunk onto his back on the grass beside her. Wordlessly their hands connected as the leaves above them trembled and whispered in a hot breeze. There would be no more demo today. I cleaned up the rest of the mess, stashed his toolbox in a remote part of the basement and drove down to EnTILEment.

After Venerable Goysei turned in his robe, grew back a head of goldfinch-colored hair and exited the tea business, he converted the little shop into an outlet for wall and flooring tiles. Of course he hadn't the space for any inventory, and the shop was packed with black flannel display boards mounted with samples. I unlocked the front door and switched on the lights. Goysei had reverted to his birth name of Andy Laemmle, but he let me continue to call him Goysei, and had hired me to work twelve to five on Saturdays so he could drive down Washington Heights where her grew up and play pickup basketball with his cous-ins. It took him under an hour to teach me every-thing he knew about tiles, which wasn't much more than knowing which of the different types – porcelain, stone, glass, terra cotta – were water-proof and which just water resistant and some insights into the cost range, which, for a medium size bathroom went from under five hundred dol-lars for basic white porcelain to the cost of a small yacht for Italian marble. The prices were on the back of each tile so there wasn't much to do in that regard. Sometimes people brought in their square footage needs, and I had to work up an estimate on the calculator. When they wanted to negotiate, I told them to call Gyosei on Monday. If there were questions about installation, I pulled up a list of local contractors on the computer.

I stuck a rubber stop under the front door, put in my ear buds and sat under the awning out front to wait for customers. Hours later I was typing up a few notes for Gyosei when a very small Europe-an car pulled up in front and out stepped Jennifer Cartelli, my twelfth grade English teacher.

"Um, I'm closing," I mumbled, my eyes fixed to the computer screen and pretending not to rec-ognize her.

"Hello, Edward," she said. "I heard you were working here."

"Yeah, I'm closing. We close at five."

"I'm not here to buy anything."

I saved my notes, turned off the computer, put the pencils in a tin can and pocketed my phone. When I looked up she was still there.

"I heard about your mom," she said. I'm sorry."

That's something you say after a person dies, I wanted to tell her.

"Thanks, she's getting better," I lied. "I really have to close now."

She followed me to the door and stood very close. Ms. Cartelli was one of those teachers who had skipped the paragraph in the teacher's manu-al about respecting the personal space of stu-dents. In the classroom, trying to whip up our interest in Edith Wharton and Robert Penn War-ren, she was always on the move, up and down the aisles, bending over a desk and putting her face right up to yours so you could see the micro-freckles between her eyebrows.

"What does the Great Sleep tell us about Jack Burden?" she'd ask quietly as if she and the lucky student were the only people in the room.

Although I knew it was there and told myself not to look, my eyes went straight to the scar on her forehead, the one created after my mother's Jeep crashed into the driver's side of Ms. Cartelli's vin-tage Mustang when she was picking me up in the high school parking lot. My mother had been on her phone, which she witlessly was still holding when she rushed out. I followed, learning firsthand how much blood courses through the human head. Witnesses had seen my mother chatting on the phone when she backed up. There was a civil trial and Ms. Cartelli won a lot of money. The last I heard she had not returned to teaching.

She had packed on the makeup and there might have been some cosmetic repair, but the scar could not be hidden. It had the contours of Flori-da, I thought. She saw me looking and touched it.

"Ah," she said. "My Harry Potter symbol."

After she drove off I carried the two cartons of bathroom tiles to the trunk of the car. When I told Gyosei what my father was up to, he wanted to give them to us for nothing, but my father re-sisted and they settled on at-cost. The tiles were a muted salmon color although after I told Gyosei my mother was an Aquarian, he included a few of the water bearer, a draped maiden with luxuriant purple hair and a jug on her shoulder. The blank envelope Ms. Cartelli had given me was on the passenger seat. In the shop she told me that she had been talked into suing by a lawyer and now regretted it. She knew that what was in the enve-lope wouldn't change anything, and she expected that my mother would likely not accept it. Before she got in her car, she said I could open the enve-lope if I wanted. It was for all of us really, she said, because she knew it was all of us she had wounded. But when I pulled into our driveway, I still hadn't lifted the flap. There I sat, unable to move, until my father opened the front door and squinted at me.

It was my father's special look. Drooping jaw, heavy eyelids, exhausted inclination of his head, everything dipping south. The look signaled disapproval, all-purpose, suitable for any occasion or subject, the weather, the time, the stock market, the government, the Yankees, me. Here, it was the condo. He told the agent to give us a minute and gestured for me to follow him into one of the bedrooms. Through double windows the size of two placemats side-to-side there was a view of a brook that after a short run sunk out of sight into a culvert under the developmment's blacktop parking lot. A duck couple serenely paddling with the current disappeared under the parking lot as well.

"What?" I said.

"It's too small."

"Four rooms, a full bathroom, and a parking spot. What more do you need?"

"What about my tools?

"When was the last time you did anything with your tools?"

"That's not the point."

"What's the point?"

He slid aside the door to the clothes closet and the shallow space within received the look. It was the fifth Sunday running I'd taken the train up from New Brunswick because he wanted my input on living options. The condo was overpriced, probably more than he could get for the house, an observation I kept to myself. But money wasn't the obstacle. Following a month of bereavement leave, he was back in the village commercial district ably selling Dux beds on commission. Also, there was my mother's life insurance, and there was the mythical gesture from Ms. Cartelli. As she predicted, my mother wanted no part of it, but my father felt differently. Their disagreement proved to be the type of problem everyone should have, prompting several weeks of lively ethical discussion that distracted us from the clock ticking down the hours on my mother's life. The day before they powered off the ventilator, she whispered in my father's ear that he should do what he wanted. My father never voiced a reason for selling the house. After the funeral, he just said he that's what he was going to do. In the fog of loss it seemed perfectly reasonable, and there was no further discussion about it. But having made the decision, he promptly lapsed into

homeowner paralysis, not lifting a finger to make the house sale-ready or even do daily cleanup. Old food stains on the kitchen counters had so darkened they looked like tire skid marks; everything that fell on the floor stayed on the floor, including on the stairs a baseball cap and one slipper that were filigreed with spider webs; paint in tiny scallop formations peeled off the dining room walls; and only half the raw space in the second-floor bathroom had been filled in with Gyosei's tiles, the entire disastrous enterprise now covered with a plastic drop cloth held in place with duct tape. On each of my visits, the place looked more and more like a crack den. My father seemed oblivious to it all, drifting though the rooms like a ghost trying to remember what he was looking for.

This complex was new, not even complete. Construction of the road winding through the grounds was ongoing and landscaping had not been started, the fresh four-unit structures surrounded by hillocks of top soil and gravel. No unit in the building the agent showed us had been sold, so we had our pick. The two apartments on one side were mirror images of the two on the other side except for the different views through the windows. She walked us through each one, and right away, at the end of the tour, it was obvious the fourth had impressed my father no more than the first three.

"What's the point?" I persisted.

"The point is they're my tools."

The agent, a young, moderately aggressive woman with a shoulder bag stuffed with blank contract forms and brochures, cleared her throat at the door and said she had another appointment and had to lock up. She gave us her card and said we were free to explore the grounds. Outside my father virtually ran for the front gate that halved the patch of land, now the beginning of the main driveway, where the store had stood. Gyoshi had accepted the developer's offer to break his lease, bought a canoe and a camper and moved to the Adirondacks. It was left to me to watch from across the road as the CAT dozer flattened the store as if it was a paper cup. The scene was pure The Grapes of Wrath complete with a perfectly timed breeze blowing demolition dust into my face.

Following twenty feet behind my father, I called, "I'm not doing this with you anymore."

"Why not?"

"You don't want to move."

He glanced back at me, looking surprised, as if this thought had never occurred to him.

"Yes I do."

"You haven't even put the house on the market."

"It needs work."

"I can help with that instead of wasting time like this."

He had gotten so far ahead that he didn't hear my offer or pretended not to. The faster he walked the slower I went. Without looking back, he cut into our street and out of sight. I groaned and threw my hands heavenward. Above me the street's lone metal halide lamp on a wooden post was warming up in the November sunset, surrounding itself with an incipient pale halo. Eleven days to Thanksgiving, the first my father and I would have alone, and neither of had the balls to say a word about it or how we would get through it. The image that came to me was brutal – the two of us sitting down across from each other over microwaved stuffing and sweet potatoes in the mausoleum our home had become. Since Halloween, I'd been working on excuses for staying at school, all transparent, all feeble. Of course I would show up and my only hope was that the Lions would put up a fight so for three hours at least we wouldn't have to talk about condos or how my mother used to fill the house with her sister's blaring brood, who drove up from Dover for the entire four-day weekend.

When I reached the corner, I saw my father speaking with a person who was standing, oddly, in the middle the azalea bushes on our front lawn. As I approached my father turned toward me and so did the person. They spoke a little more and then my father walked up the path and into the house. The figure bent down between the bushes. Even in the fading light, I recognized her at once, but recognition was not accompanied by comprehension. My mother was not much of a gardener, but she had a fondness for the azaleas, which, she said, enhanced the house's curb appeal, and which she dutifully

pruned and fertilized. That's what Jennifer Cartelli seemed to be doing, on her knees, wearing a beat up pair of gardening gloves and clipping excess growth in early winter preparation for spring growth. She sat back on her heels when I reached her.

"I thought I would tidy up your yard a bit," she said to me.

I shrugged, which I realized was impolite, and quickly added an encouraging nod.

"I wanted to work on the inside," she said. "But your dad didn't think I should without you agreeing first."

"The inside?"

"Yes, inside your house, straighten up, a little vacuuming."

"Our house?"

"Yes, would that be alright with you?"

Making no effort to conceal himself, my father stood at a window, watching us. Ms. Cartelli followed my glance. She placed both hands to the ground and pushed herself to her feet.

"I don't get it," I said.

She took off the gloves – I wondered if they were hers or my mother's – and swiped at the front of her jeans.

"Well, here's what went down," she said. "Your father gave me a terrific deal on a mattress. Really hard for a girl to resist after that."

This has to be a joke, I thought. But I didn't get it. I didn't get any of it. In fact, I had the sense that Ms. Cartelli was observing my face melting from a phenomenal excess of stupidity.

She packed her gardening gear into a Whole Foods canvas bag, smiled, said goodbye, Edward and departed on foot. Down the road, her form coalesced with the thickening darkness. My father was still at the window. Watching her? Watching me? I couldn't tell. In the house we didn't speak, and the silence had yet to be broken as he drove me to the train station parking lot.

"See ya," I said, but just sat, unable to open the car door.

"Are you coming next week?" he said.

The train was already pulling into the elevated platform. I felt no urgency.

"Only if I don't have to look at condos."

"Deal," he said.

I sprinted up the stairs to the platform. The conductor had spotted me running and waited until I was on board before closing the doors.

About the Author:

Bill Schillaci was a busy writer of short stories in the 1980s. After a hiatus of 25 years, he resumed story writing in 2014. Since then his work has appeared in Printers Row, 34th Parallel Magazine, Palooka, East Bay Review, Poydras, and others. Bill was born in the Bronx and attended New York University. He was a technical writer for engineering firms in San Francisco and New York and is currently a freelance environmental writer. He enjoys building furniture and fixing up his old house in Ridgewood, New Jesey.

OPEN SECRET

Charlotte Freccia

Cheap white wine and good cocaine at Hen's house. Scrimp on one to score on the other, I guess. What's a sweetheart like you doing in a place like this, my dad used to say, when I was a kid waiting by the bike racks and he'd come pick me up from school. What's a sweetheart like you doing in a place like this, I want to say to myself, now.

I'm here with Pearl because I go everywhere with Pearl. Pearl is here because she knows Hen from high school. In high school, Hen was one year older than us and played doubles on the tennis team. She had some friends, but never a boyfriend, on account of her terrible cystic acne. Pearl and I know each other from growing up, when her mom drove her to my house every morning thirty minutes before school started so we could walk together, even though I lived farther from the school than she did. We tried out for the middle-school cheerleading team together, and we both got spots; we tried out for the high-school cheerleading team together, and we both got cut. We found other things to do. Pearl played the mother character in three different musicals—Hairspray, Footloose, and Bye Bye Birdie— and wrote the advice column for the student newspaper under the pseudonym of Cousin Cassie and got a lacrosse-player boyfriend one year younger than us who sold everyone mid-grade weed and was inexplicably called Blister, even though his name was Tom. I was on the debate team and played first chair in the cello section of the symphonic orchestra. I never got a boyfriend—was never all too interested in getting a boyfriend, really—but I fucked around with Blister's friend Dennis because he was always around

anyway, and because I liked hooking up with stoners: they smoked you out and kissed you slow, and you never had to be afraid that they would hurt you.

But now we're in college, and I sit outside the law library watching the pre-JD kids walk in and out in their Bean boots and Pirates caps and practice my cello in my dorm room at night. But now we're in college, and everyone loves Pearl because she sings a capella, and everyone loves Hen because she went on Accutane and now has smooth pink skin, the skin of a peach, plus a rickety duplex off-campus on Ten and Patterson where there is cheap white wine and good cocaine. Hen and Pearl both have 8 AMs, and they have breakfast together every morning. On one of those mornings, Hen invited Pearl to come over tonight, and told her to bring me along. When Hen told Pearl to invite me along I knew she must not know about what happened between me and her brother Jameson, or she wouldn't invite me at all, you know, because she'd feel too bad. What's a sweetheart like me doing in a place like this?

"P&P" by Kendrick Lamar starts playing and someone turns up the bass so the walls of the house shudder and shake like somebody with a fever. I'm going through something with life, but pussy and patron make you feel alright. Pearl materializes by my side.

Our song, Priscilla! she squeals into my shoulder. "P&P" is our song because we, too, are P&P, Pearl and Priscilla, Priscilla and Pearl. We have only recently become familiar with this song. It has only recently become ours.

I'm known to use big words when I'm drunk, and that's how I can tell I'm drunk. Is it possible to be blackout and metacognitive at the same time, I ask Pearl.

PUSSY AND PATRON THAT'S SOME GREAT ADVICE! she screams in my ear by way of a response.

Uh-huh, I say.

No one knows about me and Jameson except me —not even Jameson knows about me and Jameson. Hen doesn't know about Jameson. She doesn't know because he couldn't tell her. Pearl doesn't know about Jameson. She doesn't know because I didn't tell her. She knows him, though. Knew him. Jameson was friends with Blister for awhile, and he used to buy us alcohol from the drive-through in Ferguson the summer we were sixteen, even though when we were sixteen he was fifteen but looked twelve. The summer we were seventeen we asked him to get us a forty and a handle of the cheapest whiskey on Memorial Day weekend, the first weekend of summer, and he'd said he'd get it for us and he wouldn't even charge us, if I'd let him finger me. I didn't let him finger me, and Pearl and I took to lingering outside the convenience store on Old Boalsburg, stopping college students in the parking lot and asking them to buy us beer. In mid-June, Blister and Pearl and Dennis and me were looking for a place to smoke without getting caught and Blister texted Jameson and Jameson said that we could smoke in his yard if I blew him. I didn't blow him and for the rest of the summer we smoked under the slide at the playground at Kaywood Park, holding the smoke inside our mouths, almost choking, every time we heard a car roll by. After the Fourth of July, I was at the back of the CVS near the middle school looking at nail polish colors when I felt a hand flat and wet grab up a handful of my ass like wet sand. I knew it was his hand without turning to look, and I knew it was his voice that said that he got hard when he thought about me in my middle-school cheerleading uniform without turning to look. I didn't turn to look, just stayed still until he walked away. Two weeks later, he told everyone he ate me out in the grass under the ferris wheel at the carnival at Holy Trinity and that my pussy tasted like rotting fish. I didn't mind much. I was sure everyone knew that Jameson was full of shit, and I thought that this would be the end of it.

It wasn't the end of it. In mid-August, he stopped me behind the garage at a party. I had been throwing away some empty beer bottles in the alley and had dropped one and cut my hand on a jagged lip of broken glass when I tried to pick it up, and I was standing there with the blood suddenly blooming, wondering what to do, when he stopped me. He must have asked Pearl where I was, and she must have told him. Or he must have followed me, and waited. I like to think he must have followed me, and waited. I don't like to think that he asked Pearl where I was and she told him. That was when it happened. Behind the garage. My hand cut so there was blood on his forearm, and his shirt, and his face from the places where I tried to push him away. My tongue thick from the beers I'd drunk which I'd tried to throw away, which was why I was in the alley, to throw the beers away, and why I guess no one heard me, even though I thought I was yelling as loud as I could. My head sore and screaming against the whitewashed wood siding of the garage, which is where he ground it, one hand flat against my face, the fingers brushing my hairline, the palm flattening my nose, the heel slipping into my mouth; the other hand occupied elsewhere. I tried to bite. My teeth made tiny indentations in his flesh. I kneed him in the balls. He swore, and dropped to his knees. I pushed him onto his back in the alley. His head hit the ground where the broken glass was scattered. For a minute, both of us were motionless. I watched him close his eyes as he laid there on the pavement, and thought that he looked almost peaceful with his eyes closed and his mouth open just a little in the shape of the vowel in the middle of the swear that he swore at me when I kicked him. When I felt like I could move again I walked to the side of the garage, where tall weeds pricked my legs, and I pulled my underwear back up under my skirt. There was still the blood on my hand from the broken bottle, and blood on the inside of my thighs, now, too.

I stumbled back to the party with my hands in tight fists like there was something in my hand, which of course there was. I stumbled back into the kitchen and started asking everyone where they'd last seen Pearl in a voice like there was something at the back of my throat, which of course there was. I stumbled through the narrow hall to the laundry room once I found Dennis and he told me she was there, dragging my body against the wall like there was something inside my head, which of course there was. I stumbled against the laundry room door and stayed stuck in the doorway for a few moments, watching her make out with Blister, before I stumbled over to her like there was something between my legs, which of course there was.

Pearl, I said, in a voice which stumbled, too. We gotta go. We gotta go home. They hadn't heard me come in, but stopped making out when they heard my voice.

Blister turned his body so he was half facing me and half facing Pearl, who was sitting on top of the dryer. His face was scruffy and sullen from the moonlight which leaked in through the window over the washer.

Oh, Priscilla, she said. What happened? She knew that something had happened even though I hadn't told her, because that was the kind of friends we were.

No—nothing happened, I stuttered. I just want to go home.

I'm not ready to go home yet, she said. If you want to leave, you can, though—don't feel like you have to wait for me. Tom can drive me home. She knew I wanted to leave but didn't feel like she needed to leave with me, because that was the kind of friends we were.

I will, I said. I will leave. Before I had even finished saying it Blister had turned away from me and back to Pearl again, and their single body blocked the moonlight and the room was dark again, dark to me.

I navigated back through that narrow hallway, back through that crowded kitchen, back past Dennis who kept asking me what was wrong. I kept walking through the house until I was out of it and then I walked straight across the yard which was littered with red cups which glinted with the multicolored glow of the lights which were strung around the railings of the porch of the house. I left. And when I left I swore there was a car parked across the street from of the house and I swore that there was a light on in that car and I swear that by that light I could see that Hen was in that car, talking with another girl from the tennis team, but it couldn't have been

true because Hen didn't go to parties in those days, wasn't invited, and it couldn't have been true because Hen and Jameson couldn't have been in the same place on the same night, doing such different things. Or maybe it was true. It must have been, because when I saw her I stopped and looked at her, and before long she stopped talking to whomever she was talking to and looked at me, and it took too long after she started looking at me for her to lift her hand in a cautious sort of wave, and once she did it it took too long for me to lift and unfold my own fist into a hand which waved back at her and when it did the blood which had pooled in the fist rolled down my wrist the way a broken beer bottle rolls down an alley. When she saw the blood her mouth dropped open and her hand dropped back into her lap, and then I saw her make a move to open her car door and took off down the side-walk, hard as a head against a stretch of broken asphalt which glitters with broken glass. I didn't stop until I was home, and when I got there I cracked the door open and climbed the stairs to my room and got under the covers still in my clothes and slept hard and didn't think about Jameson until the next morning, when I woke up and smelled the rusty smell of zinc, the blood dried brown on my arms and legs.

Jameson didn't tell anyone where he was going that night when he disappeared from the party to find me in the alley, and because he didn't tell anyone where he was going no one looked for him and after I kicked him out of me and onto his knees and into the ground he hit his head so hard that he didn't wake up, at least not for awhile. When he did it was the next morning, right after the sun came up when the host of the party began to clean up the yard before her parents got home from taking her sister on a college visit and she found him, still lying there, and it took her six full minutes to get him to open his eyes. I heard that her parents found out about the party because she needed their help knowing what to do with him. I heard that two years later his hands still shake uncontrollably and that he's home-schooled now because he has trouble remembering. I have trouble remembering too, sometimes, but for different reasons.

Cheap white wine and good cocaine at Hen's house, and if you're going through something with life, Pussy and Patron will make you feel alright. Cheap white wine and good cocaine at Hen's house and somehow a sweetheart like me ended up in a place like this, with Pearl, who is here because of Hen, whose brother is Jameson who once did something to me in an alley behind a garage and Jameson can't know what he did because he can't remember, and because boys who do that sort of thing never know that they've done that sort of thing and Pearl can't know because then she might tell me that she was the one who told him where I was that night, and Hen can't know because if she knew she wouldn't have told Pearl to bring me along to her house where there is cheap white wine and good cocaine which by now I've had too much of so the party is moving fast in front of my eyes like it's being played back for me by some sort of machine and Pearl is telling me something and I'm saying something back but no one can hear me, you know, too loud. I wonder who I'm telling this story to, anyway—her or me?

About the Author:

Charlotte Freccia is a third-year student of English, Creative Writing, and Women's and Gender Studies at Kenyon College in Gambier, Ohio, where she also enjoys an associateship with the Kenyon Review. She is a 2016 winner of the Philip Wolcott Timberlake Writing Award, and has recently published poetry in Zaum Magazine, short fiction in Potluck Magazine, and creative nonfiction in Newfound. Her short story "Young Enough To Be Afraid" was published in Adelaide Literary Magazine in July 2017.

SLEEPWALKING IN THE FROST

Lily Wright

It was still dark when Ben drove the Gator out to the back paddocks to feed the fillies. The sun was slow to rise and a chill rose from the earth. Ben parked and cut the engine. It made hot tinks as it cooled. Margie was the first filly to the fence. She pinned her ears back at him and threw up her head in an exaggerated show of youth. The other fillies followed, the sounds of their skinny legs swishing through the recently bush-hogged grass. Unshod feet clopped against the cold ground. Next week was Ben's seventieth birthday. It made him think of his first small herd nearly thirty-eight years ago. He had learned a lot since then. His horses bore his own name and reputation. All flawless sport horses with intelligence and trainability, conformation and soundness.

Margie ran the other fillies off a few paces and waited by the gate which Ben opened as he'd done ten thousand times before, placing a hand against her shoulder and pushing past, hanging the bucket on the fence and moving a kicking distance down before placing the next bucket, and then the next, and so on. Eloise was the last to her bucket, the bottom of the pecking order. It was Ben's wife Ann-Margaret that named her.

"She'll be a little thing," said Ann-Margaret as she watched the foal take its first few steps, its gangly legs splayed out beneath it. Ann-Margaret had once been an avid rider herself before a bad fall left her in the hospital with brain swelling and a hip replacement. She wasn't even fifty and she'd been shook to her core and never wanted to sit on another one, even after so many years passed. Ben knew that she missed it.

Eloise was by the same sire as Margie, but had a completely different personality. Not one to argue, she would follow Ben around the paddock and stand quietly. She was the easiest to ground-break and would no doubt be the easiest to back. Ben thought she would make a nice kid's horse, but not much of a performance horse. She didn't have that drive, that extra glamour that Margie had.

Ben stood back and watched the fillies munching. Margie swished her tail and stuck her head up every now and then, picking up a back foot to warn off another filly. The colts in the adjacent field called to them mockingly, screaming like young teenagers in a crowded cafeteria. They watched for them eagerly, ears pricked forward, smelling the molasses in the sweet feed and waiting their turn.

Ben walked to the gate and unchained it, but felt a sudden pang in his arm that caught him off guard. He looked around the paddock, expecting to see Margie trotting off after having let a hoof fly in his direction. He felt dizzy and all at once, collapsed in a heap by the gate.

Ann-Margaret went to her husband's funeral, but couldn't help but feel the entire time that she was comforting others. She kept her composure, as all Midwestern girls are expected to do, and only cried in the privacy of her own home or in the barn. They had had a long, happy marriage, and Ben had gone out doing what he loved.

Ann-Margaret always expected to be the first one to go. Her health was far worse off than Ben's ever was. A series of riding injuries left her body sore and cumbersome, and the heart condition she developed finally caught up to her. She only ever envisioned Ben standing at her coffin on the day of her burial, never the other way around. Ben was always stoic about looking after her. He never complained.

The routine in which Ann-Margaret and Ben had lived their lives vanished once he was gone. That was perhaps the hardest thing for Ann-Margaret to cope with on a day-to-day basis. His muddy boots stopped waiting for him by the door, his six-thirty dinnertime was no longer mandatory. Ann-Margaret had to turn his alarm off after it woke her at 5:15 a.m.; the time Ben rose to go feed the horses. The inconsistency was frazzling and only added to her loneliness.

Perhaps what bothered Ann-Margaret most, however, was what began to happen in the weeks that followed Ben's death. Ann-Margaret caught herself sleep walking down to the barn in the middle of the night. She woke in the cold, her night-gown swaying in the breeze. She could see the barn cat Tilly's eyes glowing in the dark. Ann-Margaret rushed back to the house, trying not to overexert herself. It was a curious thing; she had never slept-walked before. She wrapped herself in blankets and climbed back into bed. She only fell back to sleep once the sun had come up again.

In the weeks that followed, Ann-Margaret continued to sleep walk down to the barn. She'd taken to dressing warmly before bed in anticipation for it. She thought of calling her sister to come look after her, but that display of weakness would only cause more discomfort within her family. She worried they might take her back with them, when all she wanted was to stay and watch the horses and go for brief walks down through the little garden.

Instead she called, Joel, Ben's farmhand. He'd worked for them since he was eighteen. At first he was confused when she tried to explain what was happening at night.

"Are you sure you aren't just dreaming that this is happening? Ann-Margaret, you've been under a lot of stress lately. You've just gone through a lot."

"No, no! I am absolutely certain, Joel. I'm not senile!"

Joel didn't respond right away. He had never encountered an angry and yelling Ann-Margaret.

Ann-Margaret collected herself. She was trying not to lose her composure, but this lack of control in addition to her other health issues scared her. She had never been so scared in her life.

"You could come stay with us," Joel said finally, "we've got a guest room. It might be good for you to get off the property for a while."

Ann-Margaret sighed.

"No, Joel. But thank you."

The sleep walking continued and Ann-Margaret began to catch herself imagining Ben's ghost. This of course was nonsense, but it made Ann-Margaret consider reaching out to her doctor. She thought of all the medications she was on, and wondered if they might be messing with her mind.

"No," the doctor had said, "you've just had a huge loss. Go stay with your family and take a little break. Let them help you."

This response irritated Ann-Margaret further. She nearly told the posh woman to "fuck off". She needed real help, not condescending advice.

The sleep walking occurred nearly every night. It was an unsettling routine. The only comfort she took was in watching the farm continue to function despite Ben's absence, this was all thanks to Joel. Ann-Margaret watched Joel catch horses and bring them into the barn. She watched him start to ride the young ones. She watched him feed and water them. All the care they needed, all the work that went into them; it exhausted her to watch. Dark circles had formed under her eyes from the lack of sleep. Joel's wife started to come by with home-cooked meals. They played cards and she once brought the young children over. It revived Ann-Margaret a bit, but she worried that her visible deterioration would force them to do something drastic, like contact her sister or make her move to assisted living or some such thing.

Ann-Margaret stopped taking her meds. Only the walks helped relieve her anxiety, but she couldn't stay out too long before she could feel her heart struggle and sputter like an over-heated engine. She began to go down to the barn more often in search of a sign. Clearly, there was something there drawing her to it at night. She inspected the stalls, the tack room, the feed room. She even climbed up into the hay loft. It all looked the same, nothing unusual.

One night, Ann-Margaret woke at the filly paddock. She looked down at her hands which held the rusting chain that wrapped around the gate and the fence post. She was undoing it in her sleep, something new she had never done before. The filly's watched her, Margie especially. Her ears flitted forward and back, she breathed heavily through her nose. The other fillies were riled up as well, looking at Ann-Margaret, but not wanting to get too close. Eloise had her front legs out slightly, ready to bolt at any slight, sudden movement.

Ann-Margaret looked down at the chain and then at the horses who stood watching her. Clearly they could sense something that only her unconscious was aware of, too. She let the chain slip through her fingers, and let the gate swing open. She backed away. One by one, the fillies trotted out in natural, floaty extension. Ann-Margaret watched them go, and they eyed her cautiously as they traveled. Ann-Margaret took a seat in the frosted grass. She was bundled up, as she had been doing before bed for some time now. She laid down in the grass and closed her eyes, and fell into a deep sleep.

About the Author:

Lillian C. Wright is a third year MFA Fiction candidate at George Mason University. She is originally from Massachusetts, but has been a long time resident of Virginia. She writes often of horses and rural life.

THE CAPPUCCINO

David Heath

Jackie Jacobs, helping sort and organize clothing items donated for the church rummage sale, came across a woman's tangerine linen jacket just like the one her friend Maggie had worn when they attended the symphony last month. As she held it to the light to check it over, she noticed something in one of the pockets. Reaching inside, she retrieved two used symphony tickets and a folded piece of paper.

Throwing the tickets in the trash she unfolded the paper. She couldn't believe her eyes. It was a suicide note written, dated and signed by her friend Maggie over a month ago...but Maggie was still alive. Jackie knew she had been going through a lot of depression with the divorce but lately she seemed to be happily adjusted. Being the inquisitive person she is, Jackie decided to give the note back to Maggie and perhaps see if she could prevent something terrible from happening.

She found Maggie at home enjoying a Danish and some coffee. "Hey there! Just thought I'd drop by and see how you're doing."

"What a surprise. You want some coffee and a Danish?" Maggie offered as she opened the door inviting her in. "Aren't you supposed to be getting things ready for the rummage sale this weekend?"

"Well yes and that's why I'm here," Jackie said following her to the kitchen table.

"Oh sweet Jesus honey, I already donated," Maggie said sitting her coffee and Danish down.

"I know, but I found something I think we should talk about because I'm your best friend," she continued as she handed the note to Maggie.

"Oh Lord! Where did you find this? I thought I had thrown it in the trash," she said clutching the imaginary pearls at her throat.

"In that linen jacket you donated, but what I want to know is why you wrote it?" Jackie said.

"I was dangerously depressed with that bastard husband of mine running off with his young secretary and filing for a divorce. But things have changed," she smiled.

"So...no suicide – Right?

"Why the hell would I to do that?" Maggie said wrinkling her brow.

"I don't know...you tell me." Jackie put her hands in the air.

"Can you keep a secret for a week?"

"Holy shit! You know I'm the worst gossip in the neighborhood, and you ask me to keep a secret?" Jackie smirked.

"You'll have to swear a blood oath."

"You're joking!" Jackie exclaimed.

"No. I'm dead serious – pardon the pun," said Maggie.

"Ok - for one week only...but please don't use that term...dead."

Pricking their fingers and pressing them together Jackie swore her oath.

A smile spread across Maggie's face as she looked around, "I won the lottery."

"You're joking," screamed Jackie.

"Lord! Will you stop repeating that phrase and listen to me? My divorce is final in three days. After that I can claim my winnings and the lawyer says Bozo can't touch a penny of it."

"How much did you win?" Jackie whispered.

"$324 million dollars." Jackie grabbed the table with both hands.

Maggie smiled. "It's the jack-pot power ball ticket...and next month we're going shopping."

"You're joking!" Jackie squealed. Maggie held up her finger to Jackie.

"Ooops...sorry about that. Shopping where?" she whispered.

"Paris, France honey - and while we're there we'll pop down to Italy for a cappuccino. I've always wanted to visit Rome."

About the Author:

At the age of 75, **David Heath** is currently enjoying life as a writer in the tropics of the Yucatan along with John, his life-partner of 48 years. Originally from Ft. Worth, Texas, David worked as a lifeguard, a Latin dance instructor, an interior designer, and a private secretary before moving to Los Angles, where he sold real estate, wrote music, did some fashion modeling and founded his own visual merchandising company. For twenty years, David & John owned and operated the Rancho de San Juan Country Inn and Restaurant northwest of Santa Fe, New Mexico, where they were honored with numerous awards in the hospitality industry. Having traveled most of Europe, the continental United States and Canada, David is busy writing, poetry, mysteries and a memoir titled Adventures in Life. His recent published works include: Tales from a Country Inn – The Rancho de San Juan Story. The D.G. Heath - Mystery Collection(Double Martini - Web of Intrigue & Codes and Confessions). David is currently writing - D.G. Heath - Mystery Collection – Book Two (Vortex – Casting Shadows & Blood Moon). Fiction, fantasy and mystery are his tools.

EPIPHANY AND THE ALABASTER ROSE
Adrian Encomienda

Daylight dimmed beyond Lazaro's bedroom window, leaving cold fluorescence. He sat at the edge of his bed with a cigarette sticking out of his mouth, in waist-deep memories. On his bed was a naked prostitute, Elvira, who he instead called Elva. She reached out to caress his rough skin, only to be met with a sigh of discomfort.

Two months prior, he was there on the balcony smoking and basking in the rays of the sun when he received a call that his mother, Rose, was hospitalized. Such news came not as a shock to him; she was in and out of hospitals for many months. After all, she was an Alzheimer patient with kidney failure. On the other line was his brother, Omar.

"She's in again, L. She ain't lookin' so good," Omar said, through what Lazaro assumed to be snivels.

"You know how far I am, hermanito," replied Lazaro, nonchalantly. While on the balcony of his apartment, he turned toward the window and saw that his girlfriend, Cora, was waving him inside.

"We're all down here, even some of our distant cousins."

Lazaro sighed and bowed his head. "They hate my every fuckin' inch. You think Tayo and them want me around? You think I want them around me after he called me a drunk, 'good-for-nothin' son?"

"Show up for ma," said Omar.

Then, Lazaro ended the call and put out his cigarette. He walked back inside and sat himself in the corner of the bedroom, on a cushioned seat.

"What is it?" Cora asked, fastening her robe.

"Same thing as usual."

"Your brother? Is he in jail again?" she asked, with her antique, Spanish accentuation.

"Na, its my mother. Shes in the hospital again," then replied Lazaro, removing his shirt and tossing it across the room.

"Well," Cora said, seemingly shocked, "will you fly out to the states to see her? Shes your mother."

"Ah, I've lived this moment many times. Each time I fly out to the states I am greeted like a family outcast. My own mother doesn't even recognize me. She sure as hell recognizes Omar, though."

Cora then approached him, sitting herself on his lap. She placed her sweet-scented palm to his cheek and said, "But, if she did recognize you, would that change anything? Perhaps you would find another excuse not to see her."

He then moved her hand away as an uncomfortable grimace came across his face. Then she stood and said to him, "I remember the photos you showed me of Rose when she was young. She is beautiful. That milky white face of hers -- those green, dark-rimmed eyes. I sometimes am reminded of her when looking into the mirror."

Lazaro then looked at her and stood from the chair. She did remind him of his mother, Rose. Their eyes were the same shade of green. Their skin colors were similar; milky white, except that Rose's was lighter. So, after looking at Cora and seeing Rose, he left the bedroom and went to the kitchen. He poured himself a glass of sangria and left the apartment for a drive around Valencia.

While driving, he began thinking of Rose and her faithfulness to Christ. Such faith, he thought, was fruitless. He then thought about Omar and how he went out of his way a few years back to tattoo, "Rose", across his chest. Growing up, Lazaro never knew his father well. The times he did remember with his father were brief and he was able to count them on one hand. At a red light, Lazaro leaned his head back and became lost in one of the several memories of Rose.

Rose stood outside beneath the large apple tree in the front lawn of the family's San Jose home. In a small, baby-blue basket were about five apples. The basket was there on the ground beside the playing siblings, Lazaro, Omar, and Euria. Lazaro took an apple and ran to the neighbor's lawn. The woman that lived there had a daughter, Jessica, and Lazaro fell in love with her the second he saw her in her bathing suit. Jessica was 12 and he was just a boy -- 7.

When he ran onto their lawn, he tugged the woman's shoulder and said to her, "Is Jessica home?" to which the red-haired woman smiled and told him to wait there. She then briefly went inside and after a moment -- maybe two, Jessica came out of the house and stood there before Lazaro. She had thick, brown hair and big blue eyes. Her eyebrows were the most perfect brows he had ever laid eyes on. When Lazaro looked back toward his mother, he saw her smiling and leaning against the large apple tree. He then gave Jessica the shiny red apple and ran, embarrassed, back to his mother. While Rose hugged him, Lazaro looked and saw Omar and Euria giggling.

Then Rose said to her son, "Mi hijo, when you become a grown man you will find a woman, but you will treat her well. You will treat her how you want daddy to treat me. You won't leave her. You will see that you will be strong, but she will be like a little, thin leaf; frail and prone to giving away. But, you will hold onto her, right? Because, son, a heart isn't easily mended."

To which Lazaro, with his small, round eyes replied, "Yes mama. She will be like you and I will love her for it."

Lazaro then heard the honking of cars behind him and saw that the red light had turned green, so he picked up speed in haste and continued his stroll around Valencia, Spain. He knew only few people there -- most were prostitutes and the others were just acquaintances. So, as he drove through the city, espying many beautiful sights, he continued to picture frail little mother lying in a bed of drab, white hospital linen. He continued to think of her even when he stopped to buy a new jug of sangria at a corner shop. His thoughts of Rose continued even upon his arrival at home.

The next week he came home from the woodshop where he worked and approached Cora with a long, sentimental kiss. Then he said to her, "I am leaving tonight. You were right -- she is my mother and I must be there. It is only right."

Cora then gave him a wide smile and nodded. "Before my mother died, I spent as much time as possible with her. I had no regrets when she passed because I knew I was there and I knew that she knew that. But," she said sitting Lazaro down on the sofa, "I don't want you losing yourself when Rose leaves."

"She won't remember me -- I already know that. Euria, Omar, and Hilda will be there with her and give me dirty looks. I have been through this so many times, babe."

"But, at any time it can end."

Lazaro then nodded. He knew she was correct in her thinking. So, that night, after making love to Cora, he packed a few bags and set them by the door. He waited on the sofa, in silence, for Cora to finish showering. The running water played like an endless loop to the dreadful 'what-ifs' he played in his head. 'At any moment', he thought to himself, 'at any given moment'. When he heard the water cease it's dancing, he hurried to the bathroom and entered without even a knock. He saw Cora standing like a naked, white pillar of daffodils. Her breasts looked as soft as beds of cotton and were, from experience, sweeter than honey.

"Goodbye," said Lazaro, reaching for her hand.

"Goodbye? Oh, Lazaro, what means this?"

Lazaro started to speak, but then abandoned it all at once. He then kissed her hand and hurried to the door. As soon as he entered his car, he shook his head and called Omar on his cell phone. After a few rings, Omar answered, saying, "Yo."

To which Lazaro enthusiastically replied, "Hermano! I am coming down there. I am on my way to the airport. How's ma?"

"She asked for you. Well, I assume its you shes speaking of. We showed her pictures, but she didn't remember a lot of shit. As soon as we showed her a picture of Papa, she began to tear up, saying 'Lavaro! Lavaro!'"

"You think she is meaning to call my name?"

"Well, no one else has a similar name to that which she is calling."

Then, Lazaro became silent. He remembered her voice -- it wasn't old. Her voice was not like an elderly person's voice; her voice was like that of a forty-year-old woman. Or, perhaps, Lazaro thought, her voice sounded that way in his head because the last time he heard her was when she was forty-years-old.

"She prayed again last night," Omar said, breaking the silence. "I saw how her eye lit up when she proclaimed that Jesus is Lord."

Lazaro then ended the call and tossed the phone into the passenger seat. Her faith angered him not because it was ridiculous or dubious, but because such faith he had never seen in a suffering person. So, the question often pained his heart, What has her faith begot her but misery? He thought about the question his entire drive to the airport. When he was on the plane, he continued thinking of Rose. He also had wandering thoughts of Cora.

When he arrived at the San Jose International Airport, after the flight, he walked through the familiar terminal, remembering the last time he was there. The last time he was there he had one black eye, a broken finger, and blurry vision. He had fought with the boyfriend of a girl whom he had sexual relations with in a parking lot. Such memories were both sweet and sour. As he stood bethinking himself of prior days, he was approached by his sister, Euria.

"Laz!" she cried, hugging him from behind.

Startled, he turned around and kissed her on the head. "Where did you come from? Did everyone come along?"

"It is just I alone," she replied, still smiling and examining him as if she hadn't seen him in a decade.

"Tell me -- how bad is she?"

Euria's smile died and she then softly said, "She is worse now than before. Laz, I don't even think she has a week."

After the brief exchange, the two left to Euria's car and began their drive to Santa Clara Valley Medical Center. On the road there, Lazaro saw many familiar places, such as his old high school which was now repainted and renovated. The entire drive, Euria was silent save for a yawn or cough here and there. She resembled Rose in the slightest; Euria's skin and eyes were both darker than Rose's. Hilda, who was the only sibling from a different father, looked more like her father than Rose. But, despite their blood-relation, Lazaro was never close to Hilda. She seemed more like a cousin to him than a sister.

"How is Hilda?" Lazaro then asked, still looking out the window.

Euria sighed and replied, "She is well. She had her baby boy two months ago. We had tried to call you -- to invite you to her baby shower a few months back, but you seemed to have been busy."

Lazaro then nodded. He wanted to argue and claim how unfair it was to conceal family matters from him, but he hadn't the energy.

The rest of the drive was silent. Even as they entered the hospital and walked to the elevator, they were silent. Euria pressed the round '10' button inside the elevator and they were taken to the floor where Rose's room was.

As soon as they began toward her room, Lazaro saw many familiar faces. He first saw Tayo, Rose's half-brother. When Tayo saw Lazaro, he nodded at him and gave a weak smile. Lazaro, in response, smiled and reached out to shake his hand. He heard a faint sob and turned to see Hilda standing with her baby boy cradled in her arms.

"Hilda, oh baby," Lazaro muttered and walked toward her. He embraced her, feeling her warm tears against the side of his face. Lazaro then looked at the baby boy and gave him a kiss on his tiny hand. "What is his name?" he then whispered.

"He has his father's name," she then replied, with what seemed like a forced smile.

After speaking very briefly to Tayo, Hilda, and some other distant family members, Lazaro entered Rose's room. It almost killed him; her pink gowned, tiny body was there in the bed looking cold and abandoned. She was still milky white and she still had emerald eyes. She was still bosomy. She still wore her dark hair down. Most of all, she was still Rose -- his mother.

Beside the bed, on a chair, was Omar. He still looked as he did before; a black tank-top, a baseball cap, and tattooed from the neck down. On the stand, beside the bed, was Rose's Bible. The Bible that was there beside her was the same one she had read from when Lazaro, Omar, and Euria were just children. It had a ruby on the top right corner of it's burgundy, leather cover. Lazaro knew that if he had turned to the Book of Matthew, he would find a family photo -- which was rare for it included the siblings' father. When he was a child, he remembered scribbling Jessica's name on the backside of the photograph in red pen. He was tempted to open the Bible, but instead knelt beside the bed and said to Rose, "I'm here mama. It is me, your son, Lazaro."

Lazaro then held onto his younger brother's hand, waiting for a response from his mother. She seemed indifferent; she looked at him, but said nothing. She acted as if he had been there kneeling the entire day.

"Ma, its Lavaro. Your oldest son is here!" Omar then said, pointing toward Lazaro.

"My son?"

"Yes, ma, it is me," Lazaro said, letting out a sole tear.

"But, you're my son," said Rose unto Omar. "Do I have more than one son?"

"Yes, ma!" exclaimed her eldest son. "I am Lazaro -- your first born son. Remember me?"

When she gawked confusedly, Omar reached for the photo of the siblings' father, Roses' widower, Lazaro. He showed Rose the photo, saying, "Ma, your first born son looks just like your husband.

Do you remember him -- the first child you ever had?"

Rose's eyes then widened as she reached out for her eldest son's hand. She caressed his hand as her smile grew. When she began smiling, she became the mother Lazaro remembered. Then, after a few stutters, she spoke, saying, "Oh, Lazaro. I thought you had died a long, long, time ago, love. You did not die?"

"No, ma. It is really I. I am really here."

"But, I remember I lived without you for a long time. I - I - I thought you had died."

He then heard a squeak and turned to see that Hilda and Euria had entered the room. Turning back to Rose, he kissed her hand and said, "I am very alive. I was away, but I am not dead."

"Oh, love, I remember how you were laid in that box -- that casket. I remember how I tried so hard to save you from being lowered into that grave. I cried for weeks; my eyes were red every day and every night. My sons, they tried keeping me happy -- it worked, well for a few years at least. But, love, that doesn't matter anymore, for you are here with me again."

After she had said this, Lazaro looked at Omar. He continued looking at him as if Omar's gaze would somehow aid him in speaking -- in thinking. Then Euria beckoned at Rose's right side and said to her, "Mama, don't you see your son there?"

To which she replied, "Yes, Euria, I see my son. That is him there beside your father!"

"Ma --"

"No! Let her continue," Lazaro said, cutting off Hilda.

Then, Rose looked about the room at her children. But, Lazaro knew she saw not four of her children, but three children and her husband. "My children, they kept me strong during your time away," said she, still caressing Lazaro's hand, "I was strong enough to find a new love -- my second love. Well, we had a new child. So, I had four children in total once she was born."

"You have four children? Tell me their names, Rose," said Lazaro, anticipating the answer.

"Omar is my son."

"Yes, but what about the other three?"

"I had two beautiful girls. There!" she said, pointing at Hilda. "She is there!"

"Yes, but what about the other girl? You said you had two beautiful girls."

"My other beautiful girl is named Euria. She has the fairest features," said Rose, looking around the room. Lazaro glanced at Euria and saw her in tears, in the corner of the room.

"Ma, look, there she is," he said, pointing at Euria. "There is your fair child!"

Rose then looked toward Euria. Right as her eyes were laid upon her daughter, her smile grew again. With her right hand, she reached out toward Euria, saying, "Oh, my sweet, beautiful little girl. How long have you been standing there?"

"Ma, you've seen me just yesterday," she said, through what Lazaro saw were heavy tears.

"Yesterday? Is that when my husband died and was lowered into the grave?"

But, before anyone could answer her precarious question, Lazaro stood up and said, "Rose, what about your other child? You have told me about Omar, Euria, and Hilda, the child from your second love. You said you had four children; tell me about this fourth child."

"Calmate, L," Omar said, just below a whisper.

Lazaro ignored his brother and said unto his mother, "Rose, my wife, talk to me about your other son. Please, tell me about your first-born son!"

After he said this, there was a moment of unbroken silence. The beeping of machines still continued beyond the great, loud silence. Beyond his mother's eyes, Lazaro saw her winding memory; it was like a roll of film that she was direly searching through. After a few moments, Rose began humming, "Pescador De Hombres", with her eyes set upon the ceiling. When Lazaro saw this, he figured Rose had abandoned whatever she'd been summoning up in her memories. He placed his hand on Omar's shoulder and saluted his sisters. With that, he was off toward the door. But, as he stepped out briefly, he heard Hilda frantically call out his name. He stood, with one foot in the room and one beyond the door, contemplating whether to continue with the trials and tribulations of forgetfulness, or to abandon the ordeal. As he stood, wavering this way and that way, Rose called out, in her maternal voice, "Lazaro!"

When he heard his name being carried by her voice, he hurried back to her side. He cupped her hand in his and said, "Yes?" like a curious child.

She looked at him with emerald eyes and cleared her throat of excess fluid build-up. She then spoke, "I did have another son. I remember his voice -- it was like the sound of cascading water! He was a great son; in his youth, he was always close to me. But, as time went on, he became distant. Before I had time to notice, he had moved away with a girl. Since then, he has not come to see me. I loved him. I remember the day I found out I was pregnant -- it was pure joy! Oh, my sweet baby boy. I pray each day that the Lord blesses me with just enough time to see his face again. But, I am nearing the end -- I feel it." She then gazed longingly into Lazaro's eyes.

"The Lord," Lazaro said with a sigh, "has answered your prayer."

"My obstinate son, I hope, is still faithful. When I leave, my children will inherit only the memory of me, along with the faith I have gifted them. I know that my son, wherever he may be, has inherited the greatest thing about me -- my light."

"And if he hasn't?"

"Well," she said, and Lazaro thought,for a fragment of a second, that she was going to come to her senses and realize that he was her son. "If he ever loved me, he'll learn to not loathe my faith, but loathe that which tried so hard to hinder my faith -- darkness."

And after Rose said this, she turned her head toward Euria, seemingly dismissing Lazaro. Lazaro kissed his mother's cupped hand and slowly began toward the door. He felt the pity his siblings felt for him -- it radiated, like a scent or a radio wave. As he walked through the door, he took a fleeting glance at his milky white mother who was laid out in a bed of linen and photographs. The door came to a halt behind him.

Within the next week, while at a local motel, he received what he had been expecting -- news of his mother's death. She had died at 3:08 PM in her sleep the day after he had last seen her. Upon receiving the news, he sat, forcing himself to cry.

A tear -- maybe two, fell onto his lap, but that was it. He spent the remainder of the night drinking wine and making love to a former high school sweetheart.

The next morning, Omar drove by to take him to the airport for his flight back to Valencia, Spain. While in the car smoking, the two laughed at jokes of the olden days. Lazaro attempted to re-kindle the spark of brotherhood that he and Omar once possessed, but the conversation was dry; it was devoid of any true emotion and interest.

The car then parked. Before Lazaro left, Omar took a hold of his wrist. "Hermano," he said, a somber reverb in his voice, "did she truly think it was Pa she was speaking to?"

Lazaro closed his eyes momentarily as he realized where the conversation was headed. "I believe she did."

"Well," Omar said, lowering the volume of the car radio, "here is what I think. I think that ma knew it was you. You heard the way she was speaking; she seemed all there in the head. She knew it was you -- or so I believe."

"She knew it was me? Well, hell, if that is true, then why did she speak to me that way?"

"L, she hasn't seen you in many years. She likely couldn't manage the shock of finally seeing you again. Perhaps she spoke about you in that way because she longed to say goodbye. Maybe she felt like a burden with all her health issues and whatnot. But, that night, after you had left, she said to me, 'Omar, you're like your brother -- stubborn, but full of love'. When she said, 'brother', she motioned her hand toward the area where you were kneeling."

"Na," Lazaro muttered , after a brief moment of silence, "she thought I was Pa." After he said this, he kissed his brother on the head and left for the terminal with his belongings.

A month or so after his arrival in Valencia, when he beckoned Cora in tears on the bathroom floor, he sat on the balcony, drinking a cup of red wine. He knew that Rose's funeral was weeks ago, but he refused to attend it. His reason for not attending wasn't spite, but fear and sadness. Had he attended, he'd be standing amidst other mourning loved ones in a cycle of 'remember, cry, smile,

remember, cry, smile…'. Seeing her alive and speaking was how he had envisioned her final day. But, what pained his heart was what Omar had told him. He could not help but question whether she truly saw him as his father, or if she knew it was really he all along. If she knew it was he, then he assumed it was her final wish for him to 'be faithful'. She wanted him to not loath her faith, but the illness. She spoke, many times, about her faith being the uplifting device in her constant falling. The loathing of such strength, he knew, was to be loathed itself. So, he finished the last drop of wine and nodded, as if to say, 'you were right, ma. You were right all along'. He left the glass on the marble balcony rail as he went inside.

With Cora away in Jerusalem for work, Lazaro confided in Elvira, the prettiest prostitute in Valencia. She was there on the bed wearing nothing but salmon-colored lip balm and golden earrings. With the last light of day behind some distant hills, Lazaro placed a cigarette in his mouth and sat at the edge of the bed, waist-deep in memories. Elva reached out to caress his rough skin only to be met with phlegmatic passiveness and a sigh.

About the Author:

Adrian Encomienda was born in Phoenix, Arizona. His writing is influenced by authors such as John Bunyan and John Milton. His latest short story, "Cicatrin", can be read in the Summer 2017 issue of Dark Gothic Resurrected. He is currently working on his first full-length novel.

THE FINAL WATCH

Jonathan Ferrini

Interstate 8 climbs west out of the Imperial Valley and twists through the rugged mountains upward into East San Diego County. My name is Tommy and I recently graduated from the Border Patrol Academy. I'm assigned to work the graveyard shift at the Campo checkpoint along Interstate 8 which is 65 miles west from the Mexican border crossing and fifty miles east from San Diego. The checkpoint is surrounded by rugged, isolated terrain accessible solely by four-wheel drive vehicles. Thousands of vehicles pass through our checkpoint daily but you wouldn't realize it working the graveyard shift as wild animals outnumber the vehicles.

My Senior Agent and mentor is Ben who reached mandatory retirement age. He loves his job and is a widower without children. He is kind, fatherly, and enjoys telling tales of his storied career more than training me. His rotund body is showing wear and tear. He has a limp and bouts of memory loss. Ben's faithful partner is a drug sniffing German shepherd named "Ruger" who can hold his own in a brawl. We spend most of our shift relaxing in recliner chairs and keep a cooler filled with soft drinks and water. Ben and Ruger nod off from time to time which I don't mind. Our office is a small trailer. It's a full moon tonight and the sky is full of stars. A breeze is kicking up the fragrance of the chaparral.

It's 0230 and Ruger barks. Ben wakes and grabs the binoculars looking east down the freeway which is dark. "It looks like CHP Officer Wally is on the beat", Ben remarks. Although I see nothing, I won't question a Senior Agent. Ruger is barking relentlessly and dragging Ben to the checkpoint.

Ben says, "Hand me a Coke for Wally, Tommy." I comply but remain dumfounded. The checkpoint is lit with floodlights but I see nothing. Ben and Ruger cross the two lane freeway to the checkpoint.

Ben crouches down and leans as if peering into a vehicle to speak to a driver. Ruger stands on both legs and Ben holds him close. I watch in disbelief as Ben holds a conversation with an apparition. Ruger barks and pulls Ben towards our chase car. Ben yells, "Wally just received a radio call to respond to an overturned tanker truck at mile marker 4. I'm going to assist. Man the fort!" Wally and Ruger race down Interstate 8 with lights and siren. I'm tense and confused. I radio Ben who doesn't answer. To my relief, I hear Ben request radio assistance from CAL FIRE Station 44, "Overturned fuel truck on fire. Driver trapped. Assisting CHP Officer Wally. Send fire engine and ambulance." Within minutes, CAL FIRE Engine 44 and an ambulance race by the checkpoint. I run to our four wheel drive truck and speed towards mile marker 4 to assist.

Mile marker 4 is several miles west from the checkpoint. I see Ben's chase car emergency lights flashing ahead and his chase car is positioned across the two lane freeway as a safety measure to prevent vehicles from approaching. A coyote darts from the brush, crosses my lane, and disappears into the wilderness. I swerve and narrowly miss the animal but at ninety miles per hour I struggle to gain control and keep from flipping. I maintain control of the truck and park but don't see Ben or Ruger. There is no overturned tanker truck. Engine 44 is parked alongside the freeway with its emergency lights off. The ambulance is leaving empty. A masculine, calming voice calls to me, "Up here on the bluff, kid." I climb up on to the bluff and meet Chief Johnny of Engine Company 44. He is tall, thin, and has a thick mane of silver hair and handlebar moustache. He is handsome and I suspect many are happy to be rescued by Johnnie. "Call it a night fellas", Johnnie commands his men who conclude their search for Ben and Ruger.

Johnnie asks, "What's your name Agent?" I reply, Tommy, Captain. Johnnie places his arm around my shoulder and raises his head towards the sky remarking, "You can practically count every star". I'm flustered and quivering. Johnnie holds me tight and looks me in the eye. In a hushed voice he says, "About thirty years ago, I responded to a tanker truck fire at this very place. Ben and CHP Officer Wally were attempting to extricate the driver. Just as we began spraying the tanker with foam retardant, it blew into flames. The driver was pulled to safety, Ben suffered singed eyebrows but CHP Officer Wally burned to death. There's no earthly explanation for what happened here tonight but I've seen it before. Agents like Ben never forget losing a fellow officer. When their time to die comes, they prefer it occurs doing the job they love and choose to vanish forever into the wilderness. The San Diego Commander of the Border Patrol and I go way back. I'll call him tonight and explain everything. He'll understand". Captain Johnnie and I walk down the bluff to our vehicles. Captain Johnnie waves as Engine 44 returns to the firehouse. I park Ben's chase car alongside the meridian and will retrieve it later.

I return to the checkpoint confused. I stare at the star filled sky and learned tonight life holds many secrets. I miss Ben and Ruger and will never forget them. I hope they are together in a better place. Across the freeway a lone coyote exits the brush, sits and stares directly at me. Our eyes meet for a moment and the coyote belts out a howl before returning to the wilderness.

About the Author:

Jonathan Ferrini is a published author who lives in San Diego. He received his MFA in Motion Picture and Television Production from UCLA.

SEARCHING FOR AMELIA ERHART

by Ben Orlando

The way I remember that day, Amelia and I are two women chattering along with the song birds around us. She stands next to me in her beige fatigues while I sit on a bench in our back yard high above the ocean, gutting the three-foot tuna my father caught that morning. Behind us the rain rat-a-tat-tats on the aluminum roof but there's no roof above us. In this heat the rain is a blessing, and the constant shower helps with the cleanup. While Amelia and I stare out into the ocean, the entrails at my feet slowly bleed down the soft slope of the yard, over the edge, and eventually into the Pacific. The way I remember it, while I clean the fish, we talk about boys and breadfruit and all the things you can't find on the island.

I don't know who she is, only that she's a woman who suddenly appeared. When I first notice her standing at the edge of the trees staring at me, I miss the fish and nearly plunge the knife into my leg. But my alarm subsides as she smiles and starts to walk towards me. And she's a white woman. At the time there aren't many on Samoa. Definitely more since the treaty ratification in 1929, but still not where we live. This white woman is either military or government. I guess military.

At some point she asks me "How far to town?" Her voice is soft, refined, a stylized way of speaking that reminds me now of Katharine Hepburn.

When I really remember that day, I realize this was all she ever said, and the rest I'd just said for the both of us. For the first fourteen years of my life I often talked out loud to myself, to the point that when I was with other people, I had a hard time remembering what they said and what I said

for them. But when Amelia Earhart stopped by, she spoke only those four words. For the length of time it took me to gut that fish she never made a sound. She simply walked up to me and smiled, and stared out at the ocean while I prepared our dinner.

After I answer her question, she tilts her head towards the sky, and walks off without saying goodbye.

"Hey!" I shout, but she keeps walking and soon disappears into the nearby copse of banyans.

Once she's gone, I think about her question. The dirt road near our cabin leads to the village of Masefau, and because we're so close to the shore, there is no other road, nowhere else to go, and she appeared from the side of the woods that faces the coastline.

Maybe a boat then, I decide.

My father retired from the U.S. Navy in 1923, nine months after the Teapot Dome Scandal, when supposedly I was conceived in a rowboat docked near Pago Pago. If my father had known about the scandal at the time, he never would have dropped his pants that day. The timing of my conception was certainly bad luck. But maybe if my father hadn't gone on about President Harding's corrupt behavior and the scandal marking a low point in American morality, my superstitious mother would not have died the instant I was born. And Amelia Earhart would not have come along.

On a tiny speck in the South Pacific, first Lieutenant Harry Levant made a critical decision not to return to the mainland with his new daughter. When I asked him why we never went back to the states, he only ever said that America was a land of depravity. I think the real reason was that he didn't want to be too far from my mother even though she was dead. Somehow he expected her to return.

Sometimes when I was being difficult, I asked him why he couldn't marry someone else and give me a new mother to love. Of all the things I ever said to hurt him, this question seemed to gut him the worst. Knowing this, I'd wait until my anger was at its peak before asking the question again.

After retiring as a reconnaissance pilot at the age of forty-five, my father continued to give lessons on the airbase three days a week, or he worked at a small shop in town, building and selling mechanical contraptions. We lived in Pago Pago until, when I was two, he decided to use his savings to build a rustic lamina-roofed cabin on the eastern, undeveloped side of the island, where we lived without many problems for the next twelve years.

He taught me to fish and to hunt, and we kept a small garden surrounded by mango and orange and jackfruit trees. Because of my father's skills and what he taught me, we rarely had to buy food supplies from the outside.

My father ordered books of every sort: math, science, history, literature, astronomy, war. At first he gave me lessons on each subject, but when I was old enough to read and learn for myself, he left me to choose what I wanted to learn and how. Mostly I wanted to learn about the United States.

I had a few friends in the nearby villages, and during the holidays I'd spend all day playing and listening to the gossip about the people I hardly ever saw. I learned the traditional siva, which is a dance performed by both men and women during the 'Ava ceremonies, and I also learned the maulu'ulu, which only the women are allowed to perform.

Every morning I walked with my father to his shop in Masefau, and then I'd chat with some friends and stop by Papa Pulau's on the way home. Papa Pulau was an old blind man who lived alone in a

shack more decrepit than ours. He used to spend his days just staring out into the jungle, or fiddling with a one-stringed guitar until my father fixed up an old transistor radio for him. After that, Papa Pulau spent all of his waking hours trying to tune his radio to a German waltz station he'd only ever heard once for three minutes. But the song was so beautiful, somehow so important, he said, that he'd happily spend what was left of his life trying to find it again.

Otherwise I spent my days around the house, fishing, hunting, reading, or writing stories about the United States. From my writing and from the books I read, I was trying to paint a picture of the country where my father was born. I was trying to understand why I would probably never see his home. I was not often bored, but near the end of my time on the island I spent many hours wondering if one could die from a lack of social interaction.

When I told my father about the woman who'd walked out of the woods, he stared at me for a while, waiting for the joke. When I didn't smile, he didn't smile. He walked out the door.

"No," I said, as if he didn't quite understand, except he understood every word. It was getting late but still he began to walk in the direction of town. I ran outside and shouted in irrefutable detail my encounter with the morose, friendly woman who'd asked me how far to town and then disappeared into the trees.

I kept shouting the details of the story but my father only heard it once. He walked off, back to Masefau, and that's when he heard about Amelia Earhart's missing plane, her last known transmission sent three days before she appeared in our backyard.

I know he heard about it because this was big news on the island and around the world. But he didn't tell me. I heard it from Papa Pulau the next day.

When I approached the small hut, I saw the eighty-three-year-old wrinkled Samoan smiling as if he'd just walked into a surprise party and all the people he'd ever loved were in the room.

He'd heard his song the day before, except this time the entire seven-minute waltz played through before the station was swallowed by static. He described every detail, slowly, thinking carefully before translating his experience into words. After that we ate lunch together in silence, and when I rose to leave he remembered what else had happened the day before. About Amelia Earhart and her missing plane.

"It was her," I told my father that night.

"That was fifteen hundred miles from here."

"Still," I reasoned, "we should tell someone."

He told no one, and told me to forget it, but I wouldn't stop talking about Amelia. Maybe she'd washed up onshore, I told him. She needed help and right now she was lost, wandering through the jungle. Hurt. Tired. Lonely. During our meals together I described everything I could remember about our encounter and pleaded with him to let someone know.

"I'm not going to eat with you if you don't be quiet," he said, but I didn't listen. I kept talking, and he continued to eat with me, never responding or moving his head to show that he was listening.

The next month we flew to Sydney. He told me it was a vacation, but in truth he'd enrolled me in an all-girls school, St. Christina the Astonishing. He stayed until he was sure I wasn't talking to any corpses, although the people at St. Christina talked to corpses all the time.

I spoke to many living people during our visit but after I learned what he had in mind I didn't say a word to my father.

He left and joined the largest search party in U.S. history and spent the next five years sweeping the limitless Pacific for a tiny plane and even tinier human remains. In his letters he told me there was a lot of money in the search, but I knew he was spending his savings on this preoccupation. I wondered how many times they asked him why he was doing it, why he'd dismantled his life and broken his family to spend so many hours and weeks and months and years searching for a woman he'd never known.

After graduating from St. Christina's, I went to a dull university in Brisbane and then moved with a friend to Seattle. I knew my father was born in a section of town called Georgetown, but I never went there or asked anyone about it. I experienced the America I'd read about for so many years, while my father spent his days at the bottom of a hole. In 1943 he and all the men on his ship had been captured by a Japanese patrol. He spent the next three years underground. To me he was already long-dead.

When he showed up at the office where I worked, I fell backwards into the wall. I didn't believe he was real until the man next to him asked if he could help, and even then I didn't believe it. He looked nothing like my father. The flesh was gone from his cheeks. The bump had disappeared from his nose, and where a full head of blonde hair had been, now there was only a dome of glazed sunburned skin and liver spots. His eyes had sunken so far back into his skull that when he stood in the shadows I couldn't see them at all.

My boss gave me the rest of the day off. We walked to a small café around the corner, empty at that time of day.

I asked him questions, and each time he parted his lips nothing came. After a while I wondered if he was actually trying to talk, or if the motion was simply a way to let air into his mouth.

The silence between us churned the bitterness from milk into sour cream. He did nothing to explain why he'd done what he'd done.

I did give him a chance, but when he didn't speak, I swallowed, and I began to talk about Amelia Earhart. I described the light tint to her curly hair, and I watched my father wince. I told him about the rips in her beige jacket, and the smudge of dirt on the right side of her face, and the near-perfect teeth when she smiled, and the way she talked, just like in the news clips. I kept on for the next twenty minutes until he walked out of the café.

The next year he knocked on my door while I was near orgasm with an older man I'd just met. I'd never experienced an orgasm although I'd slept with a number of men. While the stranger knocked on my door, my lover pleaded with me to ignore it, but I could never withstand for long the ringing of a telephone or knocking at the door.

When I stood up, my legs wobbled, and the muggy area between my thighs tingled. But when I opened the door, the site of my gaunt father standing there crooked, hat in hand, turned my vagina into a sapless pocket of skin.

I waited ten seconds and when he didn't speak I closed the door, but he managed to wedge his shoe into the remaining space. I pushed harder, knowing I was crushing his foot, but his face did not register any pain.

"When you were four," he said, "you called out to me. I was in the front yard sanding the legs for the kitchen table. You shouted to me. You said there was a woman, and she wanted to talk to me." He dropped his head. "You were persistent, you said she knew me, but I didn't listen. I didn't believe you."

He struggled to breathe deep but his tortured lungs would only grant him a shallow swig. "Afterwards," he continued, "you described her. You described every detail. And then you forgot."

I stood, my robe coming undone, as my father walked away. He disappeared into a clump of Japanese maples.

About the Author:

Ben Orlando is a professor of English at George Mason University. His novel, Lost Journals of Sundown, recently received the runner-up prize for the Bath Novel Award.

GIN BLOSSOM

Michael LeBlanc

To him it was magic. All of it: The projector cutting through darkness luring flies into the spotlight. The rows of chrome bumpers polished so bright he could watch the towering screen that presided over the lot in their reflections. The sound of the night's feature, Shane, played from car radios and it gave the movie an indistinct quality something like a whisper. It occurred to the man, as he turned back to face the screen, that the strangers listening in their cars were like old pals huddled together to listen a shared secret. It was a sad movie, but the thought had him smiling.

He didn't belong with the laughing families and kissing couples in their bright cars. He knew that, but for a short for a time he forgot he was out of place. He forgot that the rust in his wheel wells and the peeling red paint made his truck parked at the end of a row of handsome Cadillacs look like a punchline.

No, tonight his windows were rolled down and cool air flooded the truck's cabin, making him glad he'd snatched a blanket from its usual perch on the chair by the television. Out of habit he reached for the soft pack resting in his chest pocket. Struck by an impulse, he returned the loose cigarette to the pack and stuck his head out the window to enjoy the night air like a dog might. It was funny to him that a lifetime of smoking made cool air assault the lungs in the way smoke should, but he supressed a cough and continued to appreciate the night despite its distinct lack of nicotine. He was rewarded by the faint smell of the popcorn waiting for him at the concession stand.

The girl's eyes drifted back to the truck parked diagonally in the row ahead. The red paint peeling from the rusted body of truck, and the knotted mess of gray hair surrounding the driver's otherwise bald head stank of neglect, and struck the girl as somehow sinister. As the girl went to turn her attention back to the movie, the man stuck his head out the window to probe the air like a dog. She watched the man's nose, gin blossoms visible even in the low light, and imagined for a moment he was trying to catch the scent of her perfume on the air.

"Creepy." She'd said it without really meaning to, forgetting for a moment the man was well within earshot.

"What's that?"

She shook her head, horrified, hushing her date with a hurried pat on his shoulder. He turned back to the screen with a shrug.

Had the man heard her? He'd retreated into his truck as though burned by the cool night air, whacking his bald head against the door frame. Why would she say anything at all? With a twinge it occurred to the girl that her mother would attribute her rudeness to the "wild imagination" that had plagued her since grade school. She cursed under her breath.

It was apparent Shane was captivating her date by the way his jaw hung a little slack, but even more so by the fact that the effort he'd made to explore the boundaries of what was allowed on a fourth date had felt cursory. This would've annoyed the girl most nights, but tonight she was occupied, catching only snippets of a brawl or gunfight before her attention was drawn back to the bald man in the red truck.

The girl watched the man, hoping to see some sign she had invented the man's overhearing her. An hour into the movie and the man's window stayed firmly shut, opening only a crack when the man smoked two cigarettes in quick succession before rolling the window back up again. With that, the girl abandoned hope that the man with the gin blossomed nose hadn't heard her, and instead she set her over active imagination on the task of setting it right. After a short while staring at the screen without really seeing, she decided on cornering the man at the concession stand at intermission.

She waited, her eyes flicking to and from the bald man and Shane. When the intermission came, the girl hopped out of the Chevy with a word to her date about popcorn. She'd only just closed the door when the rusted red truck started with a rumble and a cough. The bald man pulled his truck out of the row of cars and drove off into the night.

The girl didn't watch much the second half of Shane either, not until the ending. Shane was wounded, shot in the gut. Little Joe stood at the corner of his cabin pleading with Shane to stay, but Shane rode on limp on his horse into the sunset. Little Joe's cries of "Shane, come back!" echoed feebly into the barren landscape and went unanswered.

"Can we go?"

The boy looked deflated at the girl's suggestion. Wondering if he should have paid her a little more attention, the boy started the car taking note of the tears in the girl's eyes.

It was four months before the girl spotted the truck again. It was parked outside B & G Hardware on Main Street, hiding is plain sight. She hadn't been looking for the truck. Not really, anyway, but she had turned whenever she spotted a red pickup out of the corner of her eye, and her heart had skipped a beat whenever she heard somebody start a particularly guttural engine. When she'd confided her interest in finding the truck and her reasons behind it to her date from that night (now her boyfriend), he had called it an "obsession". The word echoed in her head as she pulled the family dog by the leash to the entrance of B & G Hardware, but she took small comfort in the fact her boyfriend had also said persistence was part of her charm.

She braved the cold December air out on the sidewalk until her hands shook and had taken on a blue hue. She reconsidered the wisdom of keeping her dog out in the cold for so long, but when she decided to speed things along by going in to find the man, the bell above the entrance to B& G rang. There he was. The bald man with the gin blossomed nose, his gray hair matted as ever, with a load of lumber under his right arm, a paper bag in the other.

"Can I help you with that?"

The man looked over at the girl, but kept walking apparently convinced she must have spoken to somebody else, despite the fact the street was empty on account of the cold. The girl tried again.

"Need a little help?"

The man stopped. "No." His voice was deep and when he spoke it sounded like his mouth was packed full of cotton balls.

"I think I've seen you around."

The bald man looked around, as though sure he'd find the second party to this conversation standing behind him. Seeing there was no one, he nodded once before loading the lumber and bag into the back of his rusted truck. She looked down at her dog shivering at the other end of her leash.

"Do you like dogs?" Do you like dogs? The girl felt blood rushing to her face.

The man reached for his chest pocket and brought out a pack of cigarettes and a book of matches. The wind had started blowing and he struggled to light the match. The girl stepped closer and cupped her hands to block the wind. She caught a whiff of alcohol before the smell of the cigarette smoke drowned it out.

The man looked a little embarrassed himself as he

reached for the truck's door handle. He went to sit down, but paused. "What's her name?"

It was a moment before the girl realized he was talking about the dog.

"Ruby."

The man reached down and patted Ruby's head. Ruby went to lick his hand, but the man was back in his car before she had the chance.

"She's a good dog." With that the truck coughed, rumbled, and for a second time the girl watched the man's bald head as he pulled away.

It was not the satisfied ending she had hoped for. The girl's "wild imagination," as her mother called it, had constructed a scene in which the bald man joined her family around the dining room table for Christmas dinner. Over the years, maybe they would share a correspondence. She would tell the bald man all about college, her career, and family (when it came time for that). Again, the girl was forced to confront the fact that her imagination was in fact capable of taking enormous liberties. She wondered, as her and Ruby retraced their steps home, what else her mother might be right about.

The following July, and the girl and her boyfriend were back at the drive-in, the bald man long since forgotten along with much of last year's curriculum. They'd arrived early to claim a spot for Rear Window, after the boy had spent nine long months convincing the girl that it wasn't a horror film. It was a good thing they'd come early because even nine months after the movie's initial release, the lot was filling fast. The boy was admiring their view of the screen when the girl spoke.

"Should we move back?"

The boy looked at her, bewildered, until he followed her gaze and spotted a rusted red pickup truck in the back row. He shook his head, laughing, but started the car.

"Hi there."

The rusted red tuck's window was only open a crack and the man with gin blossomed nose sat inside staring straight ahead in silence. It was

hardly inviting, but the girl tried once again to speak with the man nonetheless.

"Remember me?"

The man seemed at a loss for what to do, but apparently saw no other option but to roll the window down. Still, the man didn't answer.

The girl looked over at her boyfriend, and his eyebrows were raised. The boy turned to the spot the couple had just vacated, which had already been filled, his meaning clear. The girl ignored him, turning back to the truck.

"Where's Ruby?"

The bald man's voice was so low the girl struggled to hear him. She laughed. "Jack would never let Ruby in his car."

At this Jack leaned forward in his seat and waved at the bald man. "She'd chew up the seats."

The man gave a small nod before pulling a cigarette from his chest pocket.

"Do you have a cigarette for me?" She wasn't sure why she'd asked, she'd never smoked a day in her life and had no plans to before this very moment. If the girl was confused by her new habit, it was nothing compared to Jack.

Without a word the bald man pulled a second cigarette from his pocket and held it out the window. She took it and it hung awkwardly from her mouth for a moment.

"Right," the bald man grunted and fished a book of matches from his pocket. The girl was careful not to inhale, but couldn't help but let out a small cough anyway. The man didn't seem to notice.

"Thank you," she said, reaching back out across the gap between the truck and car to hand him back his matches. "My name is Judith."

The man preoccupied himself carefully replacing the book of matches to his pocket. His gaze then dropped down to his feet. Judith had all but given up hope for a response when the man spoke. "Charles."

She smiled and the lit cigarette fell from her mouth. She returned it, her eyes squinting against the smoke and she made a wordless apology to Jack, patting his lap, before turning back to Charles.

"Hi, Charles," Judith said.

Charles' nodded, his eyes trained on his feet, as though afraid they might take off without him if he did. "Hello, Judith." Then he rolled his window back up, leaving only a crack for the smoke to escape into the summer night.

The sun dropped in the sky, and the shadows on the dirt lot grew longer and longer. Charles sat quietly in his rusted red truck watching the lot fill one bright car at a time.

Judith tried to catch his eye when the movie began, but by the time the ads were playing she could see through the window that Charles was enthralled.

In the end Judith loved Rear Window, though she could never admit it to Jack. Not after making the boy wait nine long months to see it. She watched, bringing her knees up on the seat when the suspense of it all got to be too much. When she saw Charles move in his truck out of the corner of her eye, she turned and found him holding another cigarette out the window for her. Judith's chest still hurt from the first, but she didn't hesitate in reaching out. She didn't want Jack to see her taking another in case he protested, however, so she whispered her thanks, and gave Charles a small wink. It would be their shared secret, like they were old pals.

When Rear Window played out its dramatic conclusion, Judith couldn't help looking over at Charles. The man with the gin blossomed nose was staring at the screen, but his face reflected none of the fear or apprehension Judith saw on the faces in all the bright cars. Instead, a grin had taken over the man's face. When Judith turned her attention back to the movie, she found that she, too, was smiling.

About the Author:

Michael LeBlanc is an emerging writer whose work has appeared in the Queen's University literary anthology, Lake Effect. He lives in Morristown, New Jersey where he work as an editorial assistant.

RUDE AWAKENING

Michael Washburn

Chris Sievert didn't know whether the disturbing visions he began to experience in his thirteenth year grew from a long-ignored brain injury, or whose fault the neglect of that injury might have been. The question that troubled him was whether the visions were pure fantasy, or harbingers of events soon to unfold.

The beginnings of the strange events were fairly low key. One blazing afternoon in August, the boy walked up to the front door of the farmhouse. He badly needed a drink of water, and people in rural Wisconsin are so friendly and kind. He thought he'd just knock on the door and ask the farm hand for relief from the sun, which was closer to the earth than he could remember it having been in his life. But no one answered, so he thought it might be time for a bit of derring-do, an act reminiscent of when he and his pal Mike had tucked bottles of Coke inside their jackets while Mr. Robbins was in the restroom of the ice cream shop. He opened the door and stepped inside.

The farmhouse was an oblong box pierced by beams of light at many points along its rotting sides. Bits of dust drifted, the only motion in a space full of disused tables and chests and with rakes, shovels, and spades encrusted with dirt and mud. Chris tried pulling a string dangling near the entrance, and the light came on. Well, someone's been payin' the bills. He yanked the string again, walked over to the sink halfway into the place, and twisted one of the rusty handles. This drew groans from within the building's infrastructure, but no water. Then he looked around and saw a ladder leading to a dark rectangle of space near the far wall. His footsteps echoed as mites of dust eddied in the light coming through on either side of this hushed place.

At the foot of the ladder, Chris paused, in doubt about the stability of the rungs leading up into the darkness. Then he grabbed a rung, and then the one above it, and lifted himself up into the unseen space. On this floor, light filtering through the opaque window at the far end of the building gave everything the kind of glow you saw in some of the paintings Mr. Pratt showed in art class. Here was even more dust, floating in the silence and mingling with the spider webs that had sprouted in the corners.

He peeked into the small room off the hallway running from the window to another room at the front of the building. Here was a bathroom, almost clean enough to suggest that someone used it regularly. This sink produced water, clean water as far the boy could tell, and he drank and drank before stepping back into the hall.

I have to know what's down there!

In trepidation, Chris took five steps. Then he stopped in his tracks, thinking he'd heard a clack! on the floor below, like the locking or unlocking of a door. He waited. Silence reigned again. He proceeded down the hall, straining to hear anything besides his feet on the aged boards. Then he was inside the room at the front of the farmhouse, where the weak light made the outlines of the chests and shelves just visible. There, lying against the wall, was a chest to compare with the one where Chris's father kept all the photos of the family on their treks to other regions of the state. It was a heavy wooden affair sealed by two black clasps and coated with dust and debris, including bits of plaster from the ceiling.

He had to know what was in the chest. Maybe it was money, or maybe someone had left a lifetime's collection of baseball cards or comics inside. Sometimes you heard about the discovery of such valuables in an abandoned or nearly disused place like this one.

To his amazement, the clasps did not resist. He pushed them up and flung the top of the box into the wall. Shooing dust from his eyes, he coughed hard for a full minute. Maybe it had been decades since someone opened this. He looked inside, and it was as if he were privy to something only adults are supposed to know about. Here was a yellowed stack of newspapers, all written in a language he didn't know. The pictures formed a panorama of tanks, phalanxes of marching soldiers, officers addressing troops, and parades through a city that wasn't Chicago. He studied one of these parades. It was on a different scale from the spectacles you around here saw on July 4. Filling much of the street was an enormous flag, above men in a truck who seemed to command awe on the part of the onlookers, awe of a kind you rarely saw even in church. In those instances where you could make out the spectators' faces, they appeared to be ordinary men and women who had found their saviors after years of wandering in a wasteland of the spirit.

Dust spilled off the top newspaper as he picked it up and unfolded it. At least the articles were in a format he recognized, and there were even cartoons, but not the kind with talking animals and other funny characters. Well, actually, one page featured several panels showing someone who looked like an animal—a pig, to be exact—and who wore a symbol Chris did not recognize. But he had seen it before—what was it called? The pig-man was holding up a sign with writing in the weird language.

Another cartoon taught you how to use a device that looked like a baseball bat with a huge snub nose. Four separate frames showed a man holding and manipulating the device, with arrows and instructions sharing one word throughout:

Panzerfaust. He flipped through the pages, surveying the pictures and images. The people on parade were

on some kind of holy mission against the pig-men. If pig-men came and knocked on your door, you could use the Panzerfaust on them. Again and again, creatures with that symbol—that star—had a hideous appearance. To the extent that he could follow the content of the newspapers, Chris did not like it. The unease it engendered overpowered the thrill of uncovering the secret and forbidden. He thought: This is weird. There are no Nazis in Wisconsin!

Climbing down the ladder, Chris thought he heard again the sound that had briefly paralyzed him. He stood at the base of the ladder and gazed into every corner of the farmhouse, and silence prevailed once more.

Outside, the sun had not relented a bit. In his chest, he had the heavy feeling that comes when you have done something bad, and the foundations of your world are not sound. He wanted to run, to take off over the expanses of green and violet, but he didn't want to start sweating. Chris started off down the hill, and got a hundred yards before something in the air made him stop and turn. A tall man gazed down at him from a spot on the plateau just to the right of the farmhouse. He couldn't make out any traits except that it was a man at least six feet in height, most of whose body was covered in spite of the heat. He had no idea how long the man had been gazing at him. Chris took off.

Chris was at a loss to explain why he disliked his social studies teacher, thirty-one-year-old Ms. Watkins, so intensely. But he thought it was partly her air of sanctimony, her contempt for views that didn't comport well with her own, and her tendency to use terms loaded with historical significance that he didn't fully grasp, as when she alluded to certain "fascists" holding seats in Congress. One day, she threatened him with detention for his rude reactions to her remarks in class.

On the following morning, Chris didn't see the stormtrooper until he'd raised the muzzle of his machine pistol, pointing it right at the school bus. The kids inside were laughing and carrying on and seemed oblivious to the man outside. Chris leaned back in his seat, resting his lunchbox on his knees, and rubbed his eyes with both hands. He couldn't believe there could be a Nazi here, raising the barrel of his gun against a bus full of children.

He looked out the window again. A policeman was waving a baton at the bus, which had stopped at a packed intersection on the outskirts of Medford. The bus got moving again, and Chris wondered what was happening to him.

Chris had seen his father's brutal side, had felt it deeply throughout his life, but never more so than when he had become friends with a big shaggy dog he met in the park. The boy was dribbling a basketball, and the thing just bounded up to him out of nowhere. The dog was so friendly, like a lovable stuffed animal come to life. It nuzzled you and licked you, it was nearly as long as you were tall, and it also seemed at times like a loving elder sibling. It taught you how to play games, rather than vice versa. They played for hours, Chris throwing balls and then going to the store and coming back with a packet of crackers. The dog could catch anything in its maw! They romped and played for half and hour before the carload of adults came and they jumped out and grabbed the dog and Chris's father wrenched the boy away, his thumb leaving a purple mark just inches above Chris's left elbow. "Goddamn it, Chris, what the fuck are you doing?" he bellowed at the confused boy, who nearly wet his pants. Then the father checked himself mentally, realizing he'd been a bit too rough. Instead of yelling at the boy, he explained why the dog couldn't be his friend. It was sick. That was part of the reason it was so friendly. They had to take the big fellow away, to where it couldn't make people sick.

He didn't know where the dog went, only that he would not see it again. It had seemed so happy and so well-adjusted to its own existence, and how they had made it yelp when they grabbed it! How little Chris or the dog had suspected that anything was wrong until that awful moment. Now he brooded over the fact that they were going to do to the dog what fascists did to people they didn't like. Perhaps in certain ways the world of today was not all that different from the bygone era he'd read about and heard about from Ms. Emery.

When the man in the white coat gave Chris a shot, an inoculation against what the dog carried, he felt none of the sharp pain he expected, only pressure, as if someone had punched him through a pillow. Then he felt dizzy and wobbly and had to sit down, but he was already on the floor and the doctor and nurse were pulling at his elbows and calling his name as he blacked out. Before losing consciousness, he wondered where his father was. He'd see that man, and his father's equally ill-tempered friends, soon enough, what with the parade coming up.

He woke up in his room back home. Someone was watching television in the other room, a sound that would come and go for days as Chris came and went.

He put one foot on the floor. Someone on the television was talking about the possibility of hurricanes this summer. The other foot touched down, as Chris touched his temples and wondered what the ringing meant. Maybe I'm dying. He was a kid! Why hadn't they stood over the bed, waiting to explain things and comfort him as soon as he woke? He staggered out of the room and down the stairs. When he had descended a few steps, the remaining stairs looked like a pattern on a rug, winding down and down in an intimation of infinity, and you could lose yourself in relation to the top or bottom, down and down and down—I'm falling!—he screamed, calling for the unseen occupant of the room down the hall from his room, and then he was passing through the empty air and then his skull crashed.

The sounds and the haze attacked his senses again, but now there was a form, a face, poised above him in the shroud, expecting something from him. "Chris," said his father, "you's a decent boy, you gonna be o.k. Don't try to do nothin' now, kid, you'll rue it. Rest." The face withdrew. For some reason, Chris thought that others had been in the room with his father. How desperately he needed help right now. Bad visions were coming, he could feel it, yes, Chris Sievert could sense the coming of mental dislocation as ominous and unavoidable as the most fearsome hurricane.

Grinding metal. The sound made the haze go away. The rattle of tracks turning over and over and the shouts of scores of people tore through the air. Chris sat bolt upright in his bed. He clutched the windowsill and peered outside.

The Tiger tanks were moving steadily along the road that served as the town's prime point of entry, past the gas station with the plastic green mushroom bearing its name, past the mighty tankers parked perpendicular to the road, then past the Kentucky Fried Chicken with its children's park full of hot red, orange, and yellow ladders and slides. The incongruity of the scene amused no one. Townspeople yelled and cried and ran. A man in overalls tore by, pointing to the routes leading out of town, and a fat woman in a pink t-shirt struggled to keep up, followed by three small kids. Another man came out of the KFC and just stood dumbfounded. More people were clambering into cars and dashing every which way through Medford's streets.

Amid the shouting, Chris made out an effort by the police to mobilize resistance. Two deputies standing behind a squad car parked near the center of town were yelling orders to a group of men running toward them with rifles and shot-guns. Behind another squad car, just yards from the courthouse, the sheriff and a third deputy watched in disbelief, training their pistols on the advancing column.

The dust had obscured the infantry moving in along with the tanks. But as they drew closer, Chris could make out the helmets of the Werhmacht troops crouching in the spaces be-tween the vehicles. A flash came from the MP-38 of one of these men, and the fellow standing out-side the KFC grabbed his abdomen and collapsed into a ball as blood spattered the door and the ground near the kids' park. Several more flashes followed, and suddenly one of the deputies near the center of town had no head. The glass of his car exploded into a million fragments, and the second deputy was lying on the ground with his face in his hands.

The sheriff and the deputy with him popped up from behind their car, fired, and ducked as rounds whizzed by and more glass sprayed the hot concrete. Then the sheriff, taking over from the dead and wounded deputies, waved at the group of men carrying arms and indicated the positions they were to take. A few

of them made it to those places while others fell and screamed with jets of red spurting from their arms, legs, bellies, and guts.

As if the soldiers had realized his im-portance, fire now focused on the sheriff's posi-tion. Rounds obliterated what remained of the windows of the squad car by the courthouse, and then the sheriff popped up and fired repeatedly until only a click! came from his pistol. One of the men of the Wehrmacht fell and clutched his neck, gasping. Then the sheriff was kneeling behind the car and yelling at the deputy. One of the men from town, a big fellow with a hunting cap, kneeled and fired his shotgun at the column, making several soldiers fall at once. Whether they were hit or just going for cover, Chris couldn't tell. Then an MP-38 opened up from another position, and parts of the man flew all over the street.

Chris stared in horror as the muzzle of one of the Tigers turned. The invaders were moving out from between the tanks and spilling into the streets, pausing to spray the wounded townspeo-ple with fire and to train their sights on the few resisters who hadn't perished or fled. The sheriff, who had reloaded, and his deputy fired stubborn-ly, and yet another soldier fell with his hand on his spurting neck. The muzzle of the Tiger belched smoke and fire, and then the squad car was spinning in the air and the two cops were nowhere to be seen. The invaders were spraying the street indiscriminately. A few Medford folk who had hid behind a car tried to flee, only to see parts of themselves spraying the ground in front of them before they fell. Another belch from the lead Tiger, and the courthouse imploded in a shroud of plaster and brick. A man with bloody stumps where his legs had been was trying vainly to pull to safety.

One of the deputies, whose partner had died at the start of the onslaught, was just barely alive. A bespectacled officer with a dignified, aris-tocratic Prussian bearing strode over, aimed care-fully, and shot him through the right temple. An-other officer was waving his Luger at a handful of terrified residents, who obediently moved into the corner formed by the post office and pharma-cy. That was when Chris walked out of his hiding place, stepping over bodies until he came to a dead farmer clutching a pitchfork. He picked it up and charged at the back of the murderous Prussian.

"It's all so hard to make sense of, all so overwhelming for a kid," said the voice in the gray blur of the hospital room, somewhere to the right of where the boy lay, with a gash running from his right nipple to his belly, as if raked by some ferocious carnivore. "Adults make assumptions about what a kid will understand. They don't know what might flower unexpectedly like weeds from depths of his imagination. They use words that you don't know, and your mind gropes and flounders and tries to figure out what's what."

Slowly, the shape that was talking grew distinct. An old man, maybe sixty, prone in the next bed, with his grizzled head turned toward the boy.

"But Chris, there's a lot more going on here. After you attacked a man on the street during the parade, a man you thought you recognized from a recent visit to a farmhouse, people thought you were plain crazy and should spend the rest of your existence in a padded room. They were most uncharitable to you, Chris. I knew your dad, I knew how he was with that drink in him. He went after you and called you all kinds of things that I won't repeat and one time he hit you in the head and chipped your skull and loosed the gray matter into other regions of your little brain. But I won't go too far into that, there's no point."

Chris tried to speak but couldn't. He went on listening to the voice from the next bed.

"So the question is whether you're wrong in the head, or have this smarts, this ability to extrapolate. Ain't that a fifty-dollar word? I think you have both the ability to extrapolate, and the knowledge to extrapolate from. Because you just might have gotten a hint of the history of this area. During the war, they interred a whole lot of Kraut POWs in a camp near here. No one knows for sure, but a few of them, or maybe just one of them, may have gotten out. You'd think you'd have to scour the earth, go looking in the east Texas bush or in Paraguay or some place, but as they said about Hitler's book, the obvious place to check out may be where no one thinks to search. Or maybe some among us knew, but no one cared. In any case, there is at least one very bitter

and determined National Socialist in our midst. You are not crazy, Chris. You are not crazy. You are curious, and prone to speculation, and so am I.

"What does this fugitive, this renegade, have planned? His kids, his nephews, his stepkids, his grandchildren—how do they figure into all of this, and how many other adherents to the sick cause are out there? Who on God's earth knows, Chris? Who knows?"

About the Author:

Michael Washburn is a Brooklyn-based writer. His fiction has appeared in Rosebud, The New Orphic Review, The Long Story, Valley Voices, The Tishman Review, and other publications.

VIXEN

D. A. Cairns

'A few rules to lay down, first, okay?'

Vixen ignored the man's melodramatic groan, and stepped away from him. She wasn't going to be deterred by his impatience. It was important to set the correct tone at the beginning, and to ensure that the customer understood what was expected of him if he was to avail himself of her services. I am in control, Vixen reminded herself, and I will maintain control. She had used this same spiel every time she had followed a man into this room. Despite the occasional temptation to abandon the procedure in the face of actual physical attraction, Vixen had consistently laid down the ground rules for these engagements.

'I don't like to be disrespected. If you swear at me or insult me, it's all over. Understand?'

The customer's impatience had evaporated as quickly as sun shower raindrops on hot concrete. He nodded whilst maintaining eye contact with Vixen. His eyes were dark, like his hair. Resigned obedience resonated in his tone when he spoke, 'Yes, mam.' If the smile that followed was intended to disarm her, it worked. Vixen returned the smile and temporarily forgot what she was doing. His charm was weakening her resolve, eroding her control. Quickly she summoned her reserve power, the override which was necessary to sustain professionalism.

'Secondly, I don't like rough play. I'm not into pain. If you hit me, push me, or even squeeze me too hard, I'll give you a warning. If you do it again...'

'It's all over,' he said, as he edged along the bed from where he was sitting toward where Vixen was standing. Although dressed for business in black lingerie, Vixen was unprepared for the intoxicating effect of his magnetism. She allowed her eyes to explore his body. It was the body of a late thirties, early forties guy who was making concerted efforts to fight the impact of time. His skin was a little loose in places: under his chin and over his pectorals. The onset of middle aged paunch was manifest but Vixen had seen a lot of worse bodies on a lot younger men. He was undoubtedly someone who cared about his appearance, and his legs and arms displayed toning which could only have come from hard work in the gym.

While Vixen conducted her examination, the customer continued speaking and she noticed for the first time a slight accent. 'I've never really understood that,' he said. 'I'm not an animal and neither are you, so I don't see why sex should be so animalistic.'

She realized that he had generously allowed her visual probing without showing the slightest sign of discomfort. Many of her clients were very awkward and uncomfortable during the introductions and explanations phase of their encounters.

'Some people seem to confuse passion with violence.'

'Or excuse violence as passion,' he added, gently correcting her.

'Finally,' said Vixen, wrestling control back again, though she was fighting herself now, her own burgeoning impatience. Arousal. Stupidly, she imagined herself falling in love with him, smitten, head over heels. She averted her eyes. Turned away from him, hoping her back would protect her. Shield her from the arrows. 'Finally, I'm clean but I don't know about you so, no condom, no...' A gasp stole her final words. He had come up behind her and gently entwined his arms around her. One across her breasts, the other across her stomach. His grip was beautifully tight. When he breathed into her ear, she almost fainted.

'I understand,' he whispered. Then he caressed Vixen into absolute submission.

Amy's first trip to England didn't go as planned. Not that she had a plan, but even her vague idea of what she wanted to do, and where she wanted to go, was insufficient nourishment for whatever hunger she was trying to suppress with this holiday. Was it wanderlust or pure discontent? Was it fear or boredom? What had driven her from security and familiarity into the clutches of chaotic uncertainty? Was it a vacation or an escape? Was she fleeing persistent vestiges of him? She didn't want to say his name, or even think it but she had not been able to shake the memory of him, his quiet and confident masculinity. She was drowning in a sea of nostalgia, floundering in a desert, arid and desolate. Amy had lost herself in his arms, and though he had long since departed, a significant part of her remained missing.

Heathrow Airport exacerbated her sense of lostness. On arrival, exhausted and disoriented by lack of sleep during the ridiculously lengthy journey, Amy was overwhelmed by the enormity of one of the world's largest airports. Both the size and scale of it, and of what lay before her was dizzying. Delays en route seemed to have been arranged conspiratorially. It began at Brisbane with a late departure due to inclement weather. Then, a mechanical problem with the Airbus 380 was investigated during an extended layover in Hong Kong, and resulted in a long wait for the passengers travelling on to London. Amy had passed the time with window shopping and cigarettes which she enjoyed in tiny glass cages labeled Smoking Lounges. Finally, somewhere in English airspace over London, the captain of the Airbus had politely informed them that due to unusual air traffic they would have to circle Heathrow until they were cleared to land. Amy

had regretted her decision to make this trip twenty nine times already.

'May I help you miss?'

As an interruption to her misery, the question was most welcome. Amy shook her head and then realized that she actually did require assistance. 'Sorry. Yes. I don't know where to go.'

The kind voice emanating from a face adorned with sympathy answered, 'If you follow this crowd, Miss, they'll lead you to baggage where you can collect your luggage. Do you have luggage to collect?'

Amy smiled and hurriedly rejoined the flock as it proceeded along the corridor. She desperately wanted a cigarette, and she wouldn't mind some sex either. Amy was not used to going more than a couple of hours without the former, or more than a day without the latter. First things first, Amy told herself. Get my bags and get out of here. Get to my hotel. Don't catch a taxi, too expensive. She used the shuffling time to try to recall all the words of advice she had received from friends and family back home in Coolangatta. All those experienced travelers who had showered her with the combined wisdom of years of living, working and travelling in foreign lands. She could have compiled a book based on what they had done and seen and learned. Such a book would have been handy right then, as she couldn't remember anything save the warning about the cost of London taxis. Between 50 and 80 pounds to Central London. Ouch. Better to shell out a mere five pounds to ride the Piccadilly line into town. That's what they said anyway, but Amy wasn't on a budget holiday. Stuff the cost! There was no need to scrimp. She'd worked hard for a couple of years without a break and had managed to save most of her earnings courtesy of her parent's magnanimity in allowing her to stay at home while she furthered her studies. Their reluctance to involve themselves in her personal affairs without a clear invitation had also worked in her favour. Loving her job and the money and freedom it afforded her meant that Amy would drag out her degree for as long as possible.

Terminal 3. Twenty nine hours after she left Brisbane. Amy stood at the luggage carousel watching bags and suitcases of all shapes and sizes cruising leisurely around the circuit until grabbed by their owners. She watched a few people struggle with massive trunks, while others liberated their bags as easily as scratching their noses. Airport staff were on hand to provide assistance as required. The proud resisted as is their bent, while the humble made gestures of gratitude, and Amy kept waiting. Where was her suitcase? One simple red medium sized suitcase: built by Antler, packed by Amy's mother.

The crowd at the baggage carousel thinned out like people at the beach as the sun went down and the chilly southerly wind began to kick sand in their faces. Amy loved Coolangatta Beach but preferred it without the masses of humanity spoiling the serenity with their noise and pungent presence. Early mornings were the only time to seize an adequate portion of sand and surf, but unfortunately she was usually asleep. Working nights had its down side, no question. During her reminiscing, travelers kept leaving the baggage claim area. The steady reduction in human density was disconcerting. Where the hell was her suitcase?

'I think we struck out,' said an American standing beside her. 'I don't see any more bags, and I haven't got mine yet.'

Amy ignored him and stared at the flap in the wall from where the seemingly endless procession of luggage had erupted and flowed, and then abated and now apparently ceased. She was in the process of regretting this trip for the thirtieth time, when the American suggested they head over to the help desk. Showing wonderful, even if slightly bombastic leadership, the man gathered the remnants of baggage seekers and mustered them together for an assault on customer service.

She glanced over to the help desk and saw a small queue formed at each of four counter niches. While the self appointed leader of the pack ordered the group to divide themselves up and choose a line to join, Amy studied the man serving at counter four. Although she'd only spent three hours with him, she instantly recognized him and quickly joined the queue for counter four, dismissing some mumbled protests as she did so. Her heart was pounding. Her mouth was dry. Impossible as it seemed, fate had brought them together again. She felt flushed and breathless as she brought to mind an image of that first

embrace, and the very unprofessional kiss that followed. Then she knew that it was him. He was the reason she had travelled to the other side of the world.

Fighting the impulse to fling all the people in front of her, out of the way, to get to him, Amy inched forward. She tried to catch his eye but he was engrossed. Would he remember her? A puff of arrogance answered the unspoken question. Of course he would. How could he have forgotten her? Still, so much time had passed and...

'How may I help you?'

Amy had reached the front of the line without noticing the passing of time or her progress. When he looked up at her, presumably wondering why she hadn't answered, their eyes met, and a spark of recognition electrocuted her doubts, and rekindled the smoldering embers of her desire.

'Hi', he breathed.

A light snow was falling as Charlie Tate left the cafe and made his way down Madison Street. He checked his watch and quickened his pace. The ground resisted his attempted acceleration with reduced traction, and he cursed as he lost his footing and fell: scrambling and scraping. Embarrassing.

'Are you okay there?' a friendly voice enquired.

'Sure,' said Charlie. 'I was just trying to go faster than my legs would carry me.'

'Take it easy then. The ground is slippery and there's no fire is there?'

Charlie smiled and thanked the man while inwardly deriding his irritating good humour and unsolicited advice. Truth be told, there was a fire. In his heart. Charlie groaned inwardly. He was thinking in clichés, and that could mean only one thing: he was in love. Amy's flight was due in at eleven fourteen, and he needed to get a wriggle on if he was going to make it. A friend of his had infamously arrived late to pick up his new wife from the airport. Married in Bangkok then forced to wait three months while her application for residency was processed, she had marched through the terminal and exited into the arrivals area, searching for her husband; the only face in the crowd she would know. The only face in the whole country she would know. He found her in tears. Not a great start to their married life.

Amy and Charlie weren't married. Not yet anyway. In the history of whirlwind romances, there had never been a more tempestuous and volcanically passionate love affair than theirs. Charlie still didn't understand how it had happened. He had been holidaying in Australia, on the Gold Coast with a couple of friends. One of them suggested they visit Coolangatta's most famous gentlemen's club, Le Penthouse Grand. Charlie had reckoned the idea of going there, questionable at best, and insane at worst but he had gone along anyway. Even the name was stupid. It had been his first time. Vixen had made sure it had not been his last. He had loved her when she first presented herself to him in the lounge at Le Grand Penthouse. There were other ladies available of course, but not for Charlie.

He had never expected to see her again when he returned to England. His pitiful pining was ridiculed by his mates who told him to enjoy the memories but get on with his life. The job at Heathrow had been comforting, pacifying in its monotony, and gradually she faded from his mental library. Then she was there, back in his life, standing in front of him at the customer service desk, and boom, bang, bing, three days later she was gone again. Moving on to more European adventures. He had wanted her to stay. Very nearly fell to his knees and pleaded with her not to go. His heart lacerated at the thought of losing her once more. But he held his tongue and she left, giving him nothing but a kiss and her mobile phone number. Amy had taken his number, as well as more of his heart than he could survive without.

Wanting to place as much distance as possible between himself and Amy, or even memories of her, Charlie sought a transfer. Although originally moving to Los Angeles airport, a position had subsequently opened up at Denver International, and he found the suggestion magically appealing. He was renting a small apartment in the city but had booked a room at the Hyatt Regency for three nights in the hope that Amy appreciated

opulence, and would find the ambience of both the city and his presence, relaxing and romantic. Denver offered plenty for tourists, more than three days worth but perhaps they wouldn't always be out and about. Maybe they wouldn't leave the hotel at all. Perhaps she would prefer to stay in. The spacious and luxurious room offered a king sized bed and spectacular views of the Rocky Mountains. Throw in a mini bar, TV, room service and double spa, and there were plenty of reasons for them to stay in. Whatever they did, or didn't do, Charlie wanted it to be special.

Charlie had barely unpacked his bags on arrival in Denver when Amy had called from her home on the Gold Coast to say that she had been thinking about him, and was considering a visit. As Charlie unlocked his car, climbed in and started the engine, he recalled the exact words of the conversation.

'Are you still in Los Angeles?'

'Denver.'

'I can't stand not being with you. Are you busy?'

'I'm just having breakfast.'

'Oh yeah, it's yesterday morning there. Would you like to meet me for lunch?'

'More than anything.'

'Are you hungry?'

'Ravenous.'

'The first available flight gets me there Sunday morning. Can you pick me up?'

'Easily. With one arm. Just let me know when and I'll be there.'

'I want to be there now. With you.

'I want to be with you all the time.'

Charlie might have been a fifteen year old in the throes of his first crush. All the gushing sentiment, the heart fluttering and palpitating, the dizziness. That conversation was so corny, he would have laughed at it had he heard it spoken by other people. Where did it come from? How had seven brief encounters led to an overwhelming feeling that he had to marry Amy and spend the rest of his life with her? It was madness. A prostitute? He'd never imagined paying for sex, let alone falling in love with a provider of adult services. Yet his feelings were undeniable, irresistible. Looking back, he had known this would happen when he first held her soft hand in his as she introduced herself as Vixen. The fuse had been lit during that initial introduction. Charlie had tried to stamp it out, to extinguish the subsequent blaze which burned in his heart but it was hopeless. He was in love.

What would these three days reveal about him, about her, about them? Charlie swallowed hard and wished he had a drink handy. There was so much against them: his friends and family, her past, the distance between them. Maybe Denver was going to be the place where the planets aligned, and if Amy fell victim to its charm, as he had done, who knew, maybe they could settle there. Could a woman of the night transform herself into a regular woman? A wife? A mother? The thought of settling down made him laugh, but God knew how he would have, at that point, sold his soul, to have this crazy dream. And she had promised him that her days of spreading her legs for strangers were over. Vixen was officially in retirement.

The short trip to the airport passed in an inebriated haze. He was drunk on the fantasy of happily ever after, and wondered whether his intoxication would register on a breath test if the police should pull him over. Could he walk in a straight line? Charlie was definitely having trouble thinking straight.

Sometimes when it's quiet, I can remember what my life was like before moving to Cedar Springs. It's not easy. It feels like someone else lived that life and I only saw it in a movie. The chasm between what is and what was, seems impossibly, implausibly wide. I'm not Amy Edwards anymore. I'm not Vixen. I'm Amy Tate. I've been her for three months now since our wedding in Denver which was so beautiful, I was almost constantly crying or fighting back tears of gratitude. I couldn't, and I still can't figure out what I ever did to deserve Charlie Tate. He is the man every girl dreams of. He's the man I dreamed of, when I dared dream such adolescent fantasy. Charlie's the one who makes all those women who don't

have him, sickly envious of the one who does. That's me. I'm lucky but I feel wrong. I feel like a faker, a fraud. I told Charlie I would quit my job at Le Penthouse Grand when fate reunited us at Heathrow airport. It defied credulity that I would travel to the other side of the world and accidentally bump into the only man who ever touched me. I mean, hundreds of men have touched me, pawed me, mauled me, used their hands, their fingers, their mouths, their erect penises to pleasure themselves whilst pretending to care about me. My body was a toy, a tool but none of them ever reached inside and touched me. Charlie somehow crashed through my walls of seductive indifference and simulated gratification, and touched me.

I'm bored too, as well as guilt ridden. I have no job, nor any qualifications, nor any desire to pursue either. I had a job, and I was good at it. I don't have money now, save what Charlie gives me and he's generous of course. I have everything. Our home is Vogue magazine perfect. I have everything, and I have Charlie who loves me with a frightening fervor. I love him. How could I not love such a man, but something is missing. I don't feel right. I've started drinking, and I spend part of each day playing stupid games, planning deceptions, imagining, fantasizing. Wishing I was still Vixen. Charlie is a wonderful lover: passionate and considerate but he's just one man. I'm lonely, but not because I'm an Australian living in the United States, or because there aren't any beautiful, caring people in my life. I've made friends, and I have been sincerely embraced as a member of the Cedar Springs community. In some ways, I have never felt so at home, but I still don't feel right. Something's definitely wrong with me.

Charlie wants to start a family. He's always in a rush. I mean we hadn't even spent four whole days together when he asked me to marry him. He knew what I did, if not yet exactly who I was, and it didn't matter to him. He didn't even ask me to quit. His grace, the way he accepted me and loved me, made me want to quit, so I did. I left my home voluntarily. He said he would live anywhere in the whole world if only he could live there with me. So I let him choose Cedar Springs in Michigan. I liked Denver but Cedar Springs is lovely too. Now he wants a baby. I don't think I want to be a mother. In fact, I think I would suck as a mother, but Charlie has always been so undemanding of me that I feel obliged to carry, deliver and nurture a child for him. He'll make a great dad. Considering all Charlie has done for me, and the beautiful man he is, I feel duty-bound to be imperturbably grateful and joyful. Why aren't I?

It's becoming clear to me now. I'm a glutton, my avarice is limitless so I'm going back to work. Only frequent sex with men I don't know and don't care about can fill the gaping hole that has been torn in me as a result of this foolish dalliance with normalcy. Vixen is going to have to make a comeback. I know this will require a seriously dangerous level of duplicity but I don't think I have a choice. I'm going to lose my mind. If I'm very careful, if I'm discreet and clever about it, it might be okay. And if I destroy the wonderful life Charlie has given me, then I'll merely be back to where I started, before he imprisoned me in his love. Anyway, Charlie will get over me. He deserves better. He deserves a better woman than me.

About the Author:

Heavy metal lover and cricket tragic, **D.A. Cairns** lives in Darwin in Australia's Northern Territory, where he works as an English language teacher and writes stories in his very limited spare time. He has had over 50 short stories published (but who's counting right?) He blogs at Square pegs http://dacairns.blogspot.com.au and has authored five novels, Devolution, Loathe Your Neighbor, Ashmore Grief, A Muddy Red River and Love Sick Love which will be available in November, from Rogue Phoenix Press.

EASTERLY

Ronald Kovach

Lately I have been studying the towering silver maple tree in my neighbor's yard two doors down, and the burden it poses for me in an already trying time. Facing me are two highly undesirable prospects, and the chance of a third. The immediate problem: those of us with the misfortune of living close by must ready ourselves for autumn's assault. Those leaves -- you can't imagine! They're everywhere, an annual aggravation to me and the other neighbors (though we only grouse among ourselves, never to the tree's owner). They fall by the thousands, brown and crispy, layered over lawns and flowerbeds, tracked into homes, snagged in shrubs and fences. For a couple hours you rake the stuff onto blue tarps, drag it to the street and empty. Repeat, endlessly. Nice to get out into the fall air, but not good for the back when you're my age and out of shape.

But that's not the end of it. Around mid-year the tree provides us our annual deluge of helicopter seedlings, each wishing to take root and flourish. Pull them out quickly by the roots or find yourself living in a forest of miniature maple trees, your life transformed into some odd children's tale. Finally, there is the abiding danger of our increasingly weird weather smacking the tree a good one during one of our easterly storms off Lake Michigan and a huge branch – or worse – toppling into a yard or smashing right through a roof. It happens, you know.

We have a little east-facing place that looks out toward Lake Michigan in the Bay View section of Milwaukee. Allison and I kid each other about the bravery it takes to endure the fierce easterlies that occasionally blow in off the lake, slamming the waves into the breakwall down by the yacht club with powerful thuds, throwing explosions of spray fifteen feet into the air. One winter, around 2011, when we still had the original cheapo front door on our home, an easterly suddenly rose up out of the lake and blew blinding snow directly at our home throughout the night, as Allison and I slept upstairs under our warm down. In the morning, we found a cake-size mound of snow inside our front door, the flakes having been driven like bullets through the tiny vertical crack along the door's edge.

This was when Justin, our now wayward son, was still living at home and immersed in his early attempts at drawing. That day, as the city brought in heavy equipment to remove three feet of snow clogging our street, Justin was up at his desk for hours with his watercolors, depicting the easterly as a giant silver-and-black-scaled reptile arising out of Lake Michigan and blowing enormous gusts of snow that topple buildings and bury the city. The creature had a Miller Lite firmly grasped in its claws. The drawing showed some talent, I thought, perhaps the promise of a lifelong hobby.

Justin is off at school now, UWM, living off-campus with three other juniors and turning into a goof-off. For a time he was on track toward a business degree. Now any semblance of a stable career in the making has gone down a rathole. His always natural ability at guitar – as I, an unmusical sort, perceived it -- has taken over his energies. He has reduced his class load, joined a band, and started bartendering twice weekly. (I hadn't realized his knowledge of alcohol extended beyond Budweiser.) He told me he's thinking of "taking a little break from school" for a while. He seems completely at sea, dog-paddling. To Allison: "Remind me again why we thought it was so neat to give him guitar lessons at age eight." I am beyond upset. "This is not how you build a life," I add. "This is called: floating around like a jellyfish." Allison: "Be patient." Easy to say.

To return to the burdens of my neighbor's silver maple, over the years I have managed to keep them mostly off my mind. Until now, I have always been so busy. Some small part of me even credited the giant tree for its shaded charm and golden fall colors. I should add that in our otherwise friendly neighborhood of closely tucked-together houses, I have never gotten to know the owner of this property, a retired fellow who drives an inordinately ugly, rust-splotched pine-green pickup, is reputed to be a grump, and is rarely seen. He is apparently clueless, or uncaring, about the labor his tree causes his neighbors. Here my wife sometimes interjects, "So Henry, do you expect him to spend thousands of dollars he doesn't have to take down an enormous tree, just because a few of his neighbors hate raking up its helicopters and leaves a couple times a year? It's part of urban living. Like barking dogs and closely packed houses. Deal with it." A school teacher, Allison is the voice of reason. I wish she had been on my team at work.

This year I have much more time to deal with the leaf problem. In fact, over a couple days I've already raked the mess in my yard, front and back, all the way into the rear alley running along the garages. Recall, I could have brought the leaves out to the front curb for pick-up. But I have a different plan. I form my leaves into a pile roughly eight feet long and four feet high and slowly, methodically, begin to move my bounty forward, on a direct line to the garage apron of the maple tree owner, Mr. Grumpy.

I have always tried to be helpful, and I fashion myself a man of generous spirit. I am a good neighbor. It is how I am put together. I join, I volunteer, I participate, I help, I try to make things work, or to make them work better. In the neighborhood you can find me running the snow blower up and down the street when blizzards come, collecting for charities, and hosting big neighborhood cookouts with my wife. At Our Savior Lutheran, I'm a longtime member of the vestry (just

as my father was), usher most every Sunday, and help coordinate the after-service socials featuring freshly baked white bread with strawberry preserves (which, unfortunately, have added five pounds to my already chubby waist). At work, as a veteran and fairly high-ranking employee, you could always find me on committees, collecting for United Way, charmingly (if I may say so) leading our occasional building tours for visiting groups, helping to plan the company's holiday parties, earnestly grilling the burgers and playing ring toss with our top execs at our annual "Welcome to Summer" tent lunch, even invariably leading a vigorous round of "Happy Birthday" at departmental lunches in my passable baritone. I had a great staff; it was the least I could do.

You may think, given these admittedly fluffy workplace activities, that I was a lightweight. Wrong. I was good at my job, which I attributed to three things: analytical savvy, a bucket load of experience, and an ability to focus for many hours with the persistence of a pit bull with a juicy bone (or, if you wish, given what happened in one of our Bay View parks recently, a finger). I had even managed to keep up with technology, not easy for my generation. A few months shy of age 60, I felt I had reached a new level of effectiveness. My written evaluations were, for the most part, glowing; I kept copies of them filed at home, where I could read them at any time. I won't bore you with them, but they're in my Ego File, for those dark, rainy days.

My superiors said they liked to put me on committees because of my experience, my rigor, and my "easy, folksy manner." I always appreciated hearing that, though there were times I felt my calm exterior fooled people. I was appointed one of the early leaders of Customer Focus: Building Efficiency in the Workplace, spearheading a new program aimed at getting our three hundred employees to think about their external and internal customer needs in an informed way. The program's good intentions appealed to me from the start. Granted, it required a never-ending round of mandatory monthly departmental meetings filled with official note-taking and long silences, but I kept my eye on the long-term benefits. I labored my group through the awkward pauses, even calling on people for discussion -- which, Justin reminded me, is just the thing you dreaded in school if you were shy or unprepared. "Dad, don't call on people," he said when I mentioned this at the dinner table one evening. "People hate that."

Everything got written down, circulated for review, and codified in enormous red Customer Focus notebooks. I don't think the Ten Commandments in stone ever looked this good. It was all sort of biblical, really. And then, in a couple of years, you started the whole process all over again, revisiting the same round of topics. I had never read Kafka, but I heard a couple of our more literary types at the company call the process "Kafkaesque" on a number of occasions. Fortunately, Customer Focus had the buy-in of our top people, who made it clear that snide remarks would be looked upon with corporate disfavor. The message was: Get on board. Then I started hearing quiet cracks about our "North Korean-style work environment" and, even harsher, "Like we have time for this silliness with the company headed into the crapper." I got on board.

Having completed the strategic relocation of my leaves, I start in on Joe and Doris' lot three doors down, again raking in the disciplined manner you would expect from me and moving their leaves to my existing pile in Grumpy's driveway. I try to stay in the moment; once I start looking back and remembering, in no time at all I feel lost and lonely. My present labor serves as a welcome distraction. I aim to thoroughly preoccupy myself for some time. This will take some doing.

At work, my Customer Focus leadership was well underway when I was asked to head up the first of a company-wide series of Thinking Smart workflow assessment sessions led by Job Walters, a consultant hired in from Houston who had a buzz cut and a persistent, inquisitive manner. I had long been pushing for this kind of outside review as a way to know our systems and procedures better. When I made the rounds of my colleagues in the company, I would fill them in on how Thinking Smart was going. "Very focused sessions, good discussions about where we're at, how we get our work done, where it's all going," I'd say.

One of my underlings, a capable but persnickety fellow in supply chain management named Mike Samuels, said he had had experience with a similar "work assessment" group at his previous employer in Kansas City and that what it really was was a cloak.

"Define what you mean by cloak," I challenged him. I had heard his naysaying before; I was not in the mood.

"You watch, Henry," he replied. "This is the prelude to a downsizing; this becomes their pretext for sizing up perceived redundancies and getting rid of people."

"Michael, with all due respect: no," I countered firmly. "That is not what is going on. You are not there; you are not seeing the whole picture. We've got the big pad out on the easel and Walters is keeping us all on point and jotting down all of the relevant points about who does what, when and how our workflow works, and the whole makeup of the department. How all the pieces fit. What is essential and what isn't." I was really rolling now. "It's refreshing to get a sense of just what a well-oiled machine we are, and how we might get even better. This is a real opportunity for departmental analysis, that's all."

"Well, the machine can limp along with a few more parts missing," Michael said. "Henry, do me a favor -- don't turn your back on Walter. And you need to ask yourself why the company comptroller is always in on those meetings. And why the bean-counters have scheduled these sessions just ahead of the Strategic Review."

By now I've achieved a pile in Grumpy's driveway roughly twelve feet long and six feet high. My project—at least as I initially conceived it--seems complete. I stretch out on my back on the grass to rest, my limbs diagonally extended, something I haven't done since childhood. What's next for me, snow angels come January? I look out at the choppy lake and see the Michigan-to-Milwaukee ferry approaching its dock at the end of a run. Grayish black clouds are slowly moving in. I feel a sense of unease. Justin texts to say he plans to pop over to pick up some paints and chalks from his old room. I text back: "Not a problem."

A couple months after my encounter with Michael, it was a beautiful day through the windows, about 11:30 in the morning, and Fred, my boss, had me walk down with him to Chad's office. Chad's a VP. I go back a long ways with both of them. Great relationships. We'd even socialized together outside work, with the wives and everything.

I figured we'd joke around a little, as per usual, then settle down to some workplace discussion. There was always some new initiative to work on, and I usually had good analytical insights to contribute. Fred hadn't told me what was on the agenda that day, which was unusual. Perhaps it was an unscheduled raise. I had gotten a few of those over the years. Terrific -- I'd take it. Put it toward the Mediterranean cruise two years off that Allison and I had been planning.

Chad's tone of voice didn't change at all – it was the same old Chad – when he immediately launched into the thing that must happen that very day due to "the long revenue slide" the company had been in.

And of course they were pulling my leg -- I understood that, I wasn't born yesterday. They were just toying with me. Guy humor. The joke was coming. There was a punchline in there somewhere. I waited for it.

Chad kept talking in a monotone. I was still half-smiling, waiting for the joke, when I felt the blood start to drain from my face. And then I was into an out-of-body experience, a parallel universe, and found myself unable to talk.

Later I would wish I had said, "Chad, once more – with feeling." And, "A thank you for all my great work would be appreciated too." But, of course, you never think of those things at the right time.

I could not form whole sentences. I was permitted to finish the day but then, it was somehow made clear, I must be out and gone – permanently disappeared, as it were. Like someone who had been fired for incompetence, or who had a horrible infectious disease.

But this I could not do; I could not finish the day and knew I must leave as quickly as possible. It was such a beautiful day out, sunshine filling the well-kept grounds. I noticed the usual stream of trucks pulling out from our adjacent warehouse. I passed a few colleagues in the hall as well as Jeb Walters. They nodded or said hello. They had no idea. Also, the carpet seemed so loud for our kind of company. Why would you go with red and blue plaid squares in a straitlaced place like this? I felt it shouting at me.

I simply could not speak. Hugs from my coworkers. Distraught looks all around. I was looking

down at myself from a distance. Who would pack up my things? Seventeen years' worth. It was not going to be me. All the money in the world would not make me step foot in this building again.

I stay sprawled on my neighbor's grass, remembering. My mind is swimming in my river of autumn leaves. Each of them has served nature's function and been discarded---jettisoned, if you will--to float aimlessly about.

From Joe and Doris' place I move on to LeRoy's, then John's. Good neighbors all. I bring out some stale chunks of bread for John's beloved birds. I sweep the leaves out of their backyards and garage aprons and the alley itself, merging their mess with mine. Talk about helpful. Too bad everyone's away at work; not a soul around to bear witness or thank me. It's OK. I do not require applause. My generosity keeps me going.

I knew that if I placed a phone call to Allison at the school where she taught and told her what had transpired, she could be distracted enough to get in an auto accident on the way home. I dissembled. I simply told her I was not feeling well and that it would be helpful if she could come home as soon as possible to provide some TLC. She bought it.

Two hours later, we were sipping a cup of tea and still analyzing. "Henry," she said, "did it ever occur to you that you may have been an instrument in your own demise?"

I chewed on that a bit. Alison could be quite articulate.

In the alley I grasp how I can easily expand my vision. I get out my leaf blower, spread about sixty, seventy feet of orange extension cord, and plug the beast in. I move much farther down the pathway now – two hundred feet or more – to add even more leaves to my monument. I blow everything toward Grumpy's garage.

At my stage of life I could not grow new stripes. It was too late for me to learn a new trade or to move. I was unable to miraculously increase the number of job opportunities in my field, or in my mid-size city. Nor could I look younger.

The job counselor heard so much bitterness in my voice about the sudden manner of my departure that he suggested I "journal" my feelings. Now there was a first for me. It felt weird. But after a few false starts I wrote, "The brutal abrupt-departure approach for valued longtime employees has the stench of paranoid lawyers and HR theorists who are robots at heart. All of my years of good work have gotten me this? To be suddenly treated like a leper and shoved out the door?" I kept going: "Makes me think of what Allison and I had the misfortune of witnessing when we were vacationing in Cape Cod last summer – the cute whiskery brown seal off Chatham Pier suddenly gone. Where did it go? Into the jaws of a shark – chomp -- right in front of a hundred vacationers, in their shorts and sandals with Starbucks in hand, gathered at dockside on a beautiful sunny day to take in the view and enjoy nature. Ha! The seal had done his time, and now it was time. Big spurt of blood gushing into the air. Nothing personal, seal. Just business."

There's simply no more room for leaves in Grumpy's driveway; the alley there is completely full right up to the top of the door of his garage and the one facing it. Unless I wish to get up on a ladder and keep adding to the height, there is no more possibly to be done.

I set up my ladder, a twelve-footer, tear open a fresh box of big black plastic bags, and begin stuffing them full of leaves. In all I slowly make about fifteen trips up the ladder, enjoying the novel view from on high. The clouds over the lake keep blackening. They're really something. Despite my growing fatigue, the day still feels fresh with possibility.

Sometimes in the early afternoons in my basement den, when I was bored, listless, and worn out from the incredibly boring search for a new job at my highly inconvenient age, and Allison was away at school, I would hold my head in my hands in despair. But I never let her see this.

When I stood in line to register for unemployment benefits, the people were a study in diversity, though I seemed the oldest. I acutely felt my years, my chubbiness, my baldness, even my outdated eyeglasses. Would handsomeness, hair, and slenderness have made a difference right then? No. No one knew me and no one cared in the least about my accomplishments or abilities. Repeat ten times, with feeling: No one cares who you are or what you've done.

As I was waiting in line, I would feel my body start

to disappear. I was there, but unseen. I felt completely invisible: All that I was. All that I had become in my life. Allison sometimes would use "invisible" to describe the feelings of middle-aged women caught in the undertow of youth. At last I got it.

Some nights as I was falling asleep or tossing about in the throes of sleeplessness, I found myself listening closely to the warning whistle of the trains coming through Bay View. I'd get a lonely vision of just a conductor or two in the front-most locomotive as the only human beings on board a winding, mile-long line of freight cars -- a moving, softly clanking mass of steel in the pitch black, destination unknown.

And on those mornings when the lake was badly fogged in as a freighter headed into the Port of Milwaukee, I would hear the ship's foghorn not in my usual romantic way, as an appealing manifestation of centuries of brave men at sea, earnestly moving the world's commerce, but rather as an alarm that the pilot was actually lost and afraid, and flailing about in confusion. It was as if his vessel has become a ghost ship, unseen and ignored. The series of breakwalls that could punch a big hole in his ship were coming up soon, perhaps any second, but precisely where, he wondered, were they in all this whitish-gray soup, and would his instruments show them in time? Or, was he just helplessly adrift?

I heard the early morning jets leaving Mitchell Airport nearby and I wanted so badly to be on a flight right then with Allison, headed to the Mediterranean (or really, anywhere), escaping to 30,000 feet to evade, or at least put off, my near future. But the Mediterranean trip had collapsed, along with a portion of our well-laid financial plans.

Inspired by the view from my new elevation, I am moved to expand my project into the rest of the alley. If only I can keep this up, I'll eventually have the entire length of the alley—ten houses' worth-- packed fifteen feet high. I wonder if the Guinness Book of World Records might take an interest.

I was not going to retire, at least not by choice. I had too much ability, I wanted to work, and we needed the money.

So many pleasant relationships I had at work -- coworkers all over the building. I knew that despite what had happened, they were all rooting for me and would be sure to stay in touch. The enjoyable web of relationships I had that extended beyond the strict topical limits of "work," would be maintained; I was just an email away, after all. I was gone so quick that last day that I'm sure they're still catching up to the news and are planning to contact me at some point soon.

I still took my long walks with Allison. We'd run into neighbors and chat. "I'm staying busy and staying in the hunt," I'd tell them with forced cheerfulness. I didn't tell them what it was really like feeling completely unmoored and getting nowhere in my job search. I'm not sure what was worse, the formal rejections of my job applications, or the certain feeling that they had gone into a corporate black hole never to be answered at all.

Justin dropped by for dinner soon after I lost my job, his way of showing concern. He gave me a hug, and on his back I felt a strange clump of hair that I eventually concluded was a ponytail. This took me a minute to process. Allison had made a great pork roast, with a fabulous underlayer of garlic. I smothered the meat and mashed potatoes in her sublime gravy. Good food and family as centers of gravity. You could do worse. Soon enough we got on the topic of Justin's future. The hybrid lifestyle he had cobbled together, he said, felt great right then, but was always subject to change. He was practicing guitar a lot, was getting pretty regular gigs with the band, and was now back to drawing and painting with discipline and purpose. He'd been spending a lot of time systematically visiting all of the local art galleries, often in the company of a girl he had met in one of his courses, and was planning to alter his line of business courses in favor of some art classes. He was also developing a rhythm and personality as a bartender that was generating a decent amount of tips, he says. "It's partly a show," he said. What next, I wonder.

Allison was more encouraging than I was. She felt he was simply a work in progress. Part of me felt too worn down to argue. Though I must admit, Justin seemed happier and less confused than you might expect.

If you actually saw how huge my leafy ark has become, would you believe your eyes? You would think you were hallucinating. I am willing to warrant that no one has seen anything quite like this. In fact, no one does see it. There's not a neighbor in sight, nor has a car passed in the last two hours. Strange. I keep at it.

While in my new life I was not the greatest company for her, Allison was amazed at my energy and organizational skills around the house. "Well, how do you think I got to where I was?" I blurted out. I felt multiple emotions crowding into that uncharacteristic outburst. So much was packed into it. She felt the heat in my words, and looked at me strangely.

I would perfect and control what I could. Inside, I cleaned and organized my workshop (long overdue), threw out old files, shredded twenty-year-old checking account statements. Outside, I slowly but persistently pulled out a couple seasons' worth of weeds. We budgeted $250 max for some long-needed improvements, figuring I might as well use my new-found free time to jump on them, in between the job-hunting. Over a week, I installed a smart-looking pink brick border across the front flower beds and planted a few shrubs at key spots. In the garage, I took all the tools and implements off the walls and dropped them in a large pile. I laid down tarps, put on plastic gloves and a foolish-looking shower hat, then hooked up the powered sprayer and applied a handsome creamy coat of pre-primed white all over the interior walls. I was sore for a couple days from all the bending, but there was more to come. After the walls dried and I felt better, everything went back up and the garage floor got three coats of heavy-duty concrete paint in medium gray. Walls and floor, it was a lot of work. When I finished, though, I had a garage I actually wanted to spend time in.

I get a lawn chair and sit out by the alley. Who sits looking at a three hundred foot leaf mountain when they have a lake view? Answer: He who built the mountain. What if my neighbors come home? What will they say? What will I say? Suppose Grumpy comes home in his pickup and sees me here, sitting with a rake and a leaf blower, in the shadow of his entombed property? Never mind. I am too filled with wonder to consider consequences at this moment. Unlike Rome, my Leaf Empire was built in a day. Amazing.

I'm not sitting long at all when a chill Canadian breeze starts coming up from the lake bluff and I head inside for a jacket and a hat. I also grab a beer and my copy of Originals: How Nonconformists Move the World; if I read one more book about job-searching I may scream. When I step out of the house, the wind is coming up much stronger. I see the surf slamming into the breakwall now, making its dull thuds and violently shooting spray. I zip up my jacket, and just after I do, an easterly arrives in force. This one is so violent that it tilts our birdfeeder in its base and snares a white plastic grocery bag littering our flower bed. The bag darts about in a frenzy, like a kite without a string.

Gusts tear into my giant project and start blowing and scattering all of it, this way and that, the scratchy sound of a million leaves on skittering little feet, my Leaf Mountain, my masterpiece, redistributed now all over the entire neighborhood, leaving no trace whatever of my ferocious labor, of my generosity, nor even the obstacle in Grumpy's path that was its genesis.

Soon enough, the alley is empty. So am I.

Just then, Justin arrives in his beater. "What have you been up to, anyway" he asks. I picture his incredulous look were I to tell him the truth. I debate my answer. "Oh, just kicking back," I say. There's a line he's never heard from me. His new dad.

And here comes Grumpy himself, returning in his pickup from some errand, ignoring me as he passes by. He taps his garage door opener and drives in. The door lowers and he trudges inside. Perhaps he'll spend the rest of his afternoon pulling the wings off flies.

"So what have you been up to today?" I ask Justin. The ponytail's gone and his long hair is parted in the middle. Still a trace of acne. None of his dad's tubbiness. A nice smile. "Busy weekend," he says. "A shift at the bar tonight, playing tomorrow at the Nomad. Trying to get into this small gallery show for 'emerging talent.' Studying."

"Well, do what you want," I say, without an edge but with a tired feeling about my own life. "More power to you."

He takes that in, then blurts out, "Whoa! Dad, we've got to move it indoors now, it's getting seriously nasty." A few fat raindrops plop down. A sudden gust tears off a lower branch of the silver maple and sends it flying toward my lawn. Any moment the sky will let loose entirely. As Justin hustles to fold the lawn chairs and close up the garage, I take one last look back. It's as if I hadn't done a spec of work in the alley.

The wind knocks over one of John's garbage cans. I'm expecting a big mess of trash all over the alley, which of course I will feel compelled to clean up. Instead, only a few green corn husks come spilling out, their golden strands fluttering wildly. The wind catches the husks and flings them about like they're nothing, formless and weightless. As I follow my son into the house, I find myself laboring to keep up with his stride. It's like he's off to the races.

About the Author:

Ronald Kovach is a writer, editor and musician in Milwaukee, Wisconsin. After working in newspaper journalism for 24 years, he held high-ranking editorial positions in three national magazines. "Easterly" is his first published fiction.

GRIEF'S CRADLE

Mark Gunther

When I was born, after penicillin but before the Internet, death and grief were shrouded in euphemism. Elisabeth Kübler-Ross changed that when she published "On Death and Dying" in 1969. She observed her terminal patients go through a five-step process: Denial, Anger, Bargaining, Depression, Acceptance. Yet in practice, patients were denied knowledge of their impending death. Heroic doctors doing the utmost bankrupted families and degraded the end-of-life quality for the patient. Kübler-Ross wanted people—doctors, patients, and families—to be comfortable with the inevitability of death and to talk to each other about it. Her paradigm became the language for this conversation, and has led to the whole world of advanced directives, hospice care, and dying with dignity. Yet now a "good death" has become as idealized as natural childbirth. The dying patient is granted the ability to pull the cables out of the switchboard one at a time until 24/7 connectivity is peacefully and joyously abandoned.

Though some deaths may be that well-ordered, many are not. Each death is completely specific. For a family, a death disorders the world. When my twelve-year-old daughter Eva died, there was none of this. She was alive, I was holding her hand, she stepped away, the car hit her, and she was dead. No stages there, so whatever you think about the stages, the concept does not apply to every death. Kübler-Ross clearly said that, not that this important caveat survived the denuancing maw of popular American journalism. Although "stages of dying" ideologues now allow the experience of dying to be emotionally variable, the paradigm still remains "stages."

Kübler-Ross' ideas became so influential that they were applied to bereavement too: "stages of grief." While this is quite popular and generally useful as a conceptual framework, an unfortunate subtextual byproduct of this construction makes grief a thing, rather than a state. Subject to analysis, this thing can be dissected, quantified, and then managed as if it's a project at work. Such a simple arithmetic forces grief into a Euclidian framework when it belongs in a quantum one. The mourner checks off the boxes until grief is gone. The message? Grief not only is something to be got over, but it in fact is get-overable.

Kübler-Ross appreciated grief's subtleties. She weighed in posthumously (and there is a delicious irony in that) with the co-authored publication of On Grief and Grieving in 2005. She says this in the opening paragraph of the book:

"The stages have evolved since their introduction, and they have been very misunderstood over the past three decades. They were never meant to help tuck messy emotions into neat packages. They are responses to loss that many people have, but there is not a typical response to loss, as there is no typical loss. Our grief is as individual as our lives. Not everyone goes through all of them or goes in a prescribed order."

There you have it. Society's focus on relieving the mourner of the symptoms of bereavement belies the truth that the palpable experience of grief is ever accessible. Grief invades the mourner's conscious awareness, and it is never, ever over. It is a sensual, full-body experience, entering like a virus and pulsing to every corner of every cell; it inhibits serotonin and rides the messenger RNA and subverts the ATP cycle and weighs on the transmission of every synaptic impulse or waft of neurotransmitter. I grieve often for Eva, for myself, for what my family has lost. I know because grief manifests in my body. The skin below my eyes contracts; my lips stretch across my teeth. My chest caves in just a bit, drawing my arms into my chest as a feeling of terrible despair and hopelessness forms within and moves upward past my heart and under my sternum to lodge in my throat. I may cry, in that moment, or I may curse or bang the table or the wall of the shower or replace the pots in their drawer with particularly emphatic force. Sometimes the moment simply passes; most often I can talk myself down. It often is useful to exhaust myself physically.

It is the rare first-person account of grief, whether memoir or fiction, that does not include physicalized symptoms: a deadened feeling, listlessness, searing pain in the heart, uncontrollable sobbing, blurring of vision, ringing in the ears, throwing things or pounding them, lack of appetite, slowness of gait, tripping often, inability to exert physical strength, disappearance of sexual desire or the physical ability to perform sex, dissociation, compulsion, self-mutilation, or other unconscious compensatory behaviors. I suspect the full list is much longer. For me there is a constant feeling of broken-heartedness, a big dead space in the middle of my chest. Memory resides in the body, and the physical experience of grief now is imprinted in me. Triggers abound in daily life, and have the power to reignite the grief state. Around my house we call that a PTSD moment.

Indeed, given all this authentic psychophysical imprinting, how is it possible for grief to do anything but linger? This experience, "Complicated Grief," has become a candidate for definition as a psychological disorder. Maybe so, in some cases, but really. Of course grief is complicated. Your loved one has been ripped away; that part of your soul is an open, visible wound. The role that relationship played in your unconscious is, by its absence, fully and irreconcilably conscious, its failures and forgotten chances as memorable as the good. The loss remembers and anticipates every other loss large and small: of crying inconsolably as a child, of the womb, the nipple, mother, childhood, father, career, and as we age even our basic physical and cognitive competence. Grief extracts fear of death from the subconscious and

hangs it like a glittery mobile right in the mind's lobby. It is an essential and honorable human experience.

As C.S. Lewis notes in A Grief Observed:

"For all pairs of lovers, without exception, bereavement is a universal and integral part of our experience of love. It follows marriage as normally as marriage follows courtship or as autumn follows summer. It is not a truncation of the process but one of its' phases; not the interruption of the dance, but its next figure. We are 'taken out of ourselves' by the loved one while she is here. Then comes the tragic figure of the dance in which we must learn to still be taken out of ourselves though the bodily presence is withdrawn, to love the very Her, and not fall back to loving our past, or our memory or our sorrow, or our relief from sorrow, or our own love (p. 59)."

Despite this knowing, every mourner is surprised by his grief. Isolated behind his loss, the mourner needs one who already knows, a loving companion who tolerates his pain, an anchored point of reference in a world that is suddenly, utterly, different. The day-to-day bustle of the rest of the world is unheard in the face of the mourner's clamorous loss. In intact communities, the bereaved are served by networks that allow their grief to flower. I had Judaism: friends, family and co-religionists buffered me against the Common World's oppressive normality. Lewis, a lifelong bachelor, married at fifty-four and lost his beloved to cancer four years later. He was a devout Catholic and perhaps he found his way out of himself through the Church. And to "once again love the very Her," the mourner must yield to the transformative power of his grief.

Joan Didion's The Year of Magical Thinking angered me the first time I read it. Honestly,

I don't think I read it very carefully. She published so quickly, I thought. Only a year? She couldn't possibly know a thing yet. But grief only lets you do what you can do. Now, I honor that. Didion is a writer, so she wrote. It's what she could do. I rode my bike a lot. I'm sorry, Joan; I should not have disrespected you. You moved between your disasters, making impossible decisions, getting through each day. She was dealing with her daughter's illness, as well, and, later, Quintana died; we are in the same club now.

Didion says the book is her "attempt to make sense of...months that cut loose any fixed idea I ever had about death...about grief, about the ways in which people do and do not deal with the fact that life ends, about the shallowness of sanity, about life itself." Didion found herself expecting her husband, John Gregory Dunne, to be there in all of the ways he always had been. By following the rituals of their life together, she would hold up her part of the bargain, without which there was no chance for him to once again fulfill his. Ultimately, she writes, "we must relinquish the dead, let them go, keep them dead." I had to keep Eva dead so I didn't try to parachute into the other world to find her. I checked daily. "Still dead," I would say to myself. "Still dead."

Death is not of this life, but grief is. When I was in shock, the first three or four months, I often dissociated. I experienced the universal human struggle inside of me, as if universe-size blocks of good and evil were thrusting against each other with the torque of gears the size of a galaxy. Because my daughter had died, I straddled the worlds of living and dead. I was graced with a special vision. Maybe I was supposed to be a prophet now, because I had experienced such a devastating enlightenment. I had existential conversations about it with my rabbi; what was my duty in light of this new inner knowledge?

Fortunately, Rabbi Lew convinced me to abandon the prophetic calling, but the next thing that happened was that I developed X-ray vision. I mean this explicitly. I saw the space in things rather than their substance; I looked between the electrons and the protons to see what was beyond. When I hugged my wife, her body was warm and soft and muscular—even though from across the room, I could look straight through her like she was a piece of tissue held up to the light. When she held up the newspaper, I could see the type floating freely in the air with her face clearly visible beyond. To my perception, these phenomena were exact and observable; therefore, true. Given this, I reasoned, the world of things must be arbitrary and exist due to some prehistoric and subconscious human agreement. This excited me, because if my X-ray vison was real, it broke the agreement. And if the agreement could be broken

for me, maybe I could blow up the whole thing and perhaps, in the ensuing chaos, find Eva again. Besides, I had lost track of her only for a few seconds. Maybe there could be a do-over.

It was not to be. The wall remained true, the floor solid, yet for a time my world included an additional dimension. The conflict was poignant. It went on for six months. It seemed absurd to be a body that breathed and ate and slept and did all kinds of other things that rooted me in the world. In my grief calculus, this was the core dialectic— the tension between the day-to-day requirements of real-world participation as mediated by the constant demands of my body, and my heartfelt emotional and spiritual desire to remain connected to Eva in world of the dead. Believing in these impossibilities inoculated me against the overwhelming despair, guilt, and sorrow that descended like a tidal wave in the second and third year of our bereavement. This is my analog of what Didion calls magical thinking: an authentic experience in a delusional context. Over the ensuing twenty years, through endless fits and starts, bouts of the deepest shame or vainglorious pride, I have had to learn how to live acceptably despite betraying my lost child every time I take a breath.

Both of these stories, mine and Joan's, are personal accounts of an incident of bereavement and a subsequent unique experience of grief. We each have moved on from the acute phase. Didion's grief seemingly finds a place; publishing a book certainly is an act of communal connection. My experience is more one of reconstruction, like after a hurricane—the things that got destroyed are still destroyed, even if something gets rebuilt on the site. There is no place in any world where I can "Accept" my child being dead.

This must be Complicated Grief. Here I am, two decades later, and I'm accompanied always by that unbearable moment—being unable to protect her when it counted. So even though my grief looks Ordinary because I work, exercise, play music, have a living daughter, maintain a marriage and friendships, my inner world is patrolled by a platoon of wounded archetypes, holding each other up, the unique experience of grieving their bond and the uncertain foundation of my daily life. There must be a purpose to grief more sublime than simply proving one's emotional capacitance. Why would our biology demand grief of us if it wasn't good for our survival?

What grief breaks is neither comprehensible nor repairable. Grief emerges from one's deepest soul and can only be incorporated, welcomed, allowed to establish a secure home in a conscious and generous part of the self. It weaves itself indelibly into the survivor's landscape, infecting everything with its richness and pathos, laying for each mourner a unique path that nonetheless has been walked by every single human being who ever loved anyone. I could not join Eva in the world of the dead. I could not return her to the living. I could not abandon her death to the past. I could not abolish my grief. Instead, it threaded itself onto my deepest soul, drawing the unbearable pain of my loss away from Eva's memory until I could love her once again.

About the Author:

Mark Gunther has been many things in his life—student, hippie, cook, husband, carpenter, father, administrator, entrepreneur, athlete—but always an activist, musician, and dancer. In 2015 he received an MFA in Creative Writing from the University of San Francisco. Since then, his work has appeared in Thin Air, Ducts, Noctua Journal, Still Standing and Nonprofit Quarterly. His novel, Living With Jenny, will be published in March of 2018.

DARES

John Bliss

March 2003, I received a flyer about a conference exploring the psychoanalytic collaboration of Masud Khan and Donald Winnicott. The two men were prominent members of the British Psychoanalytic Society. Their collaboration ran parallel to Khan's self-destruction. His intoxicated uncontrolled rants earned him a street reputation as an inebriated, abusive, anti-Semitic crank. Khan's infamy eclipsed the popularity he enjoyed as a brilliant psychoanalyst. He ruined his career, friendships and marriages. I admired Khan; the luminous outsider intrigued me. Khan was Winnicott's patient. The two men wrote and edited articles, socialized and had drinks together. I wondered if their relationship was like trying to be "friends" with someone you're madly in love with: pure torture.

It is difficult, sometimes devastating, to dare and push the boundaries that we invisibly impose. Winnicott died of heart failure in 1971. Khan's delinquency escalated after his mentor's ticker gave out. Heavy drinking expedited his demise. He died in 1989 at the age of 67. I thought tragedy like this could only be explained by the intense love the two men felt for one another. Love was a conundrum for me. I hadn't been able to love romantically without destructive heartache. I registered for the conference.

My ex-wife, Janet and I had started dating when I was fresh out of a two-year stay in a rehab for heroin addiction. I was working full time as a truck driver and going to college full time. While using heroin, I had contracted hepatitis C. At 25, I was already way behind schedule and my life expectancy predicted by a prominent gastrointestinal specialist was another 30 years. I felt lucky that someone loved me.

We had good times and two daughters, Jenna and Jillian. They were great company and collaborators. They also kept me close to home. I was growing too, became a psychoanalyst, opened up my own private substance abuse clinic, was teaching and felt successful. My progress threw my relationship with Janet out of balance. I wanted to go out more, make new friends and play music. The division between my wife and I became more pronounced after 9/11. The impermanence that we all confronted that day sparked me to assert myself in the world more.

I bought a tenor saxophone and started taking lessons. Jenna and Jillian developed strong senses of themselves and their independence gave me more time to pursue interests. Janet would loudly accuse me of loving the saxophone more than my family. Music had always made me want to love everyone more.

During my training to become a psychoanalyst I befriended an instructor, named Anastasia. We became close friends. Anastasia was happily married to James who I also became friends with. Janet was threatened by my friendship with Anastasia and James. Janet mobilized her family and convinced them I was committing transgressions that were ruining our marriage and destroying our family. Their narrative was basically that Anastasia and James were evil and brainwashed the idiot husband and father, me.

Janet specifically accused me of having an affair with Anastasia. I wasn't having an affair but I was finding understanding and closeness in my relationship with Anastasia that I craved. The rumor of an affair got Janet's sister and her husband very excited. They frequently appeared at our house. It always perplexed me what they thought they'd accomplish. The more I was pressured to stop seeing Anastasia, the more I dug in. I refused to be bullied and wouldn't stop seeing her just because they were uncomfortable with my relationship. Their interventions made it clear I had to stand my ground.

I was naïve as to the rigidity I was confronting from Janet, her sister and her husband. What I learned was that building new ways of relating entailed destroying old ones. I told myself love would prevail. Janet and I had been together almost twenty years. I incorrectly calculated the strength of our foundation.

We saw a therapist who predicted if we broke up, I would reproduce the same angst in another situation. I told him that was a pretty dismal critique of the effectiveness of therapy and protested.

"Angst, I just want to meet, make new friends and blow my horn. Just leave me alone. I won't compromise the integrity of our marriage. I need to see what else I can do in life. Your sister and her family are boring. I want to be around people who are interesting. It's got nothing to do with love."

The therapist and Janet challenged me, most likely the dare was unintentional. They kept the pressure on. In hindsight, maybe it was the hepatitis C volcano smoldering in my psyche. Mortality was daring me to see what I could do before the Banshee came calling for my soul. The saxophone and Anastasia represented survival and life. If I quit growing and pushing the boundaries, I was sealing my coffin before I was dead. Quitting any of it was death.

Hurting my children defied qualities that defined me. I wanted my daughters to depend on me without doubt. Fatherhood was the source of so much of my joy. How would a divorce affect my relationship with them? There was a battle raging inside of me. I was supposed to protect them not be the person hurting them. Could I live with myself if I inflicted this kind of nightmarish pain on them, my precious girls who for years were my closest associates?

After a few rounds of this, I packed my shame, my doubt and I left. Destruction wasn't so bad. Losing stuff was liberating; hanging on was torture. I

eventually became closer to my daughters yet still worry about how they were hurt by the divorce.

About six months after I left my home and a year before the conference about Winnicott and Khan, Anastasia her husband James and I planned to go out to dinner and met at their home. While they were getting ready, I browsed through a photo album. A single print drifted like a solitary autumn leaf out of the collection onto the glass coffee table. In the picture was a strikingly attractive woman. She reminded me of a young dark haired Jeanne Moreau.

"Who is she?" I asked Anastasia. "She is beautiful."

"Oh, that's my friend Leslie," Anastasia answered.

She told a story that during a trip to Italy, Leslie was able to return a blouse she had brought from a street vendor in Rome two days after the purchase. Leslie got her money back. The formidable grit it must have taken to return something for cash from those hawkers was impressive. I admired intensity and persistence. James added that Leslie was also a psychoanalyst and a graduate of Cooper Union.

At that time, I lacked the imagination that anything good could come of an introduction to this beautiful woman. It was difficult for me to shake an archaic conviction that I was bad. My mother had predicted that I would ruin Janet's life just like I ruined hers. Frances (my mom) claims she was addicted to morphine when she was pregnant with me. It was a difficult pregnancy, birth, adolescence and adulthood with her son John. Frances claimed she almost died carrying me. Whenever she mentioned this it always filled me with apologetic confusion. That shame followed me for years. I wouldn't doubt I was in trouble or even did wrong but would be perplexed as to what I had done exactly. Wrestling with the conviction that I was bad news was a consistent theme of mine. I was cautious and didn't want to hurt anyone else or get hurt.

After my divorce, the consideration of any romantic harmony was a blur. I was lonely but couldn't envision being in love without what I believed was the inherent destruction that went with it. After all I almost killed my mom before I could literally lift a finger. My focus was on my daughters, my therapy practice and playing music. It was as if I was cranky because I was hungry but wouldn't realize it until after I ate. My ambiguous famine could only be fed by the transformation that one experiences from being in love.

Slowly, the generosity and love from my daughters, friends and colleagues was convincing me that I might be safely lovable. Surprisingly, my mother was very supportive. I had more time to see her and take care of my dad who was very ill. Frances was grateful to have me around and I felt lucky to be there. The archaic belief of my own malevolence was being metabolized with everyone's kindness. My future was brighter.

My thoughts about Leslie were fractured by Anastasia's enthusiastic offer to make an introduction. I declined. If I was to meet Leslie and screw it up I would be lonely and hopeless. I also wanted to protect Anastasia. If I ruined Leslie's life then Anastasia was implicated in the destruction. I needed to take the risk, the dare had to come from me alone. That way I would be solely responsible. I was scared shitless.

I had a unique and intimate relationship with fear. My determination to confront the jitters was founded in the dares and double dares of my youth. These provocations assisted me in having the town record for stealing 31 pumpkins on Halloween when I was 12. On a double dare, John Monsees and I swam across the Kensico Reservoir one night and topped off the feat by jumping off the Rye Outlet Bridge where route 22 passes over the water in Armonk, N.Y.

These achievements gave me the fortitude to kiss Geraldine Moore with her encouragement, the way they did in France at a graduation party held at Katy Kork's house. I was thirteen; the quest for love was the behemoth double dare. Pursuing love became magical when you met someone who shared your appetite for the wonderful mutating lunacy it brings.

I failed to reach out to Geraldine after our kiss. That blunder became a vehement affliction that haunted me. No one dared me to call her. Geraldine unknowingly taught me that risking everything was the only way to wind up with something. I missed my chance with her. I kept pushing myself and was surprised by what I was able to

do. The dare and double dares became part of me. I learned from my mistakes, usually after repeating them several times.

The conference about Winnicott and Khan's collaboration was on April 17, 2004, at a psychoanalytic institute on the upper west side of Manhattan. Unbeknownst to me, Leslie was a member there. It was one year since I'd seen her photograph. I took a seat in the back of the institute's library where the presentation was to take place.

"Hi Leslie!" Someone called out.

I quivered at the sound of her name. Was she the glossy Leslie, who had been framed on four sides flat on Kodak paper, now walking among 84 people, and eight rows in front of me? (I counted). My excitement surprised me, it was as if I had been looking for Leslie for months but was so busy looking I didn't know who or what I was looking for. My vague budding belief in providence blossomed at that moment. I thought, of course she is here. It's destiny.

Her dark brown hair was different; she had let it grow, it was now outlining her sculpted chin. She wore a beige suit with a silk scarf loosely tied around her neck. She reminded me of Maureen O'Hare's Esmeralda from 'The Hunchback of Notre Dame" unaware that Quasimodo was about to swing down and save her from the gallows. Her stroll looked as if she might erupt into an arabesque or toss a bowling ball. Leslie's right hand dangled behind her thigh with her fingers poised to snap. At intermission, she stood and turned around with a beating heart I swore I could feel.

The possibility of her being as special as I thought and falling in love or not was terrifying. I thought of my archaic and grisly fascination with great white sharks.

Stan Waterman was an underwater cinematographer. Once while filming great white sharks off the Great Barrier Reef in Australia, he left the safety cage and used his camera to bang the first shark that came up to him squarely in the nose. By shocking the predator, Stan communicated he would not be its victim. He then swam comfortably with the school of sharks. This approach was a bit intense but I wanted to make a distinct first impression. At an intermission, minus camera, I walked directly to Leslie.

"Excuse me, my name is John Bliss, Are you Leslie Pendleton?"

"It's Hendelman, Leslie Hendelman."

"Are you sure?" I asked.

Leslie chuckled with a slightly furrowed eyebrow.

"Yes it's Hendelman. I am certain. Are you interested in one of the training programs?"

I briefly considered attending one of the programs as a way of getting to know her and promptly dismissed this strategy as inefficient. I had taught for several years and to become a student again to possibly get to know Leslie was silly. Plus my psychoanalytic training had taken eleven years. Doing another training would take way too long; much better to just ask her to go out sometime.

"No, I'm friends with Anastasia and James. I saw a picture of you at their home and was struck by how beautiful you are. I asked Anastasia who you were and I promised myself whenever I ran into you I would introduce myself."

I had the distinct sense she was suspiciously charmed by this encounter. She had faintly smiled; it reminded me of a salacious smirk Mae West might make. The intermission was over. I sat down and breathed, in, held it, out, three times. At the conclusion of the conference, I went to tell Leslie how happy I was to meet her. We exchanged business cards. I offered to call her.

"Well then call me sometime." Leslie answered with a distinctly different furrow of her brow. The telltale eyebrow crinkle and her tone had dare all over it. I was so grateful that I was a 49-year-old man and not the 13-year-old boy afraid to call Geraldine after our kiss.

Proudly demonstrating restraint, I waited until after 11AM the following day and called. I suggested we go listen to music and then have dinner somewhere. We made a date for the week after next on a Saturday. I was grateful to Stan, the shark man and Geraldine's kiss for their help with this dare.

When our first date finally arrived Leslie was late. She called.

"I'm a few blocks away, I'll be there in a few minutes."

"No worries, I got seats, I'll meet you upstairs. I know the drummer; he agreed to delay the show, he saw how excited I am."

This was an embellishment. I had met the drummer previously, he often plays with a good friend of mine and did say hello. My excitement was real. The club was on 27th street in the basement connected to a BBQ restaurant. We planned to eat after the show. BBQ wasn't food for a first date. I had made reservations at an Italian restaurant a couple of blocks away. The headliner was a guitarist I had known about but never heard live. Leslie arrived and I went to open the door to the cab. She looked like a dame from one of the 4 o'clock movies I watched as a child after school on rainy days. Leslie wore red silk blouse, black pants with an embroidered rose pattern, black leather hip length jacket, red ankle high boots and purple scarf. My calm was noticeable to me as I held my hand out to guide her out of the cab. Somehow, as she took my hand and gracefully got out of the cab her intimidating beauty and physical strength put me at ease. In retrospect, it felt safe. I wouldn't have to pull punches.

I never learned to appreciate free jazz and am wedded to melody. The music was a succession of bus stops in the middle of nowhere; the passenger gets off and is baffled about where they are and how they got there and could get home. Henry Mancini, the wonderful composer once said that jazz was the only art form he knew of that committed suicide. I thought of Henry during the set. I was uneasy and worried if Leslie was enjoying it. This show was not a good choice. Dares were often bound by dissonance and false starts. Fortunately, the set only lasted an hour.

The spring night air was refreshing and beckoned a new start. As we walked to dinner, I asked, "How did you like it?"

Leslie squinted and tilted her head. I assumed that she was cautiously disappointed and possibly didn't want to offend me. This was my cue.

"I was ready to pull the fire alarm! I was afraid it would turn into a version of "No Exit" and we'd be stuck there forever. I'd never get to talk to you, trapped in an abyss of incoherent choruses. Then there was that looming threat of an encore. I just wanted to shout 'Hey that's OK, we've had enough, we're tired and hungry and just want to get going.' The tunes were cleverly disguised as if the band was playing some self absorbed trivia game."

"Yes, like 'I Bet You Can't Name This Tune." Leslie said.

"Exactly, music should be a social interaction not some secret language, like twins develop." Leslie and I were getting in sync.

She didn't miss a beat and said, "Idioglossia!"

" Ah! Jesus! Great word! How do you spell it?" I said as I looked up and vigorously praised the evening sky.

As if in a spelling bee Leslie responded with flawless elocution, "I-D-I-O-G-L-O-S-S-I-A."

"Nice!" I said.

"He kept his back to the audience the entire time. Did he know this was a show? I did like your drummer friend." Leslie said.

This was very funny to us. I was grateful for the disappointment in the show. Laughter when shared burrows into your body. I always remembered who I had a good laugh with long after the punch line has waned. The admission of my foolish choice in the show led us to a verbal volley that was sweet collaboration.

I looked at Leslie, "I'm so happy to be out of there and be talking to you." The restaurant was in walking distance but far enough to give us time to talk.

The Italian restaurant was a much better choice, quiet, familiar food and attentive service. During dinner, Leslie talked about traveling, living in Spain, her career as an artist, a psychoanalyst and how she avoided marriage. She had this twinkle in her dark brown eyes that revealed an engaging sorrow. I dared to see her sadness as similar to mine. Her intelligence and a great sense of humor made this 5 feet 7 inches tall dark-haired beauty even more alluring than her photograph. She wasn't skinny and liked to eat. This was a great relief to me. Federico Fellini once said never trust a woman who doesn't like to eat.

I never found success or gratification when I adhered to a general policy as to when was a good time to let someone know something. Thanks to

Einstein I knew time was relative. Regardless of the form our relationship might take, I needed to know if we could become close which meant could we dare to reveal ourselves. I was definitely intrigued by Leslie. After dinner I drove her home. I glanced over and looked at the side of her face with her chiseled jaw line.

"I had a great time, I'd like to see you again."

We were at a red light; Leslie studied me for a moment and with a subtle smile answered, "That would be nice." Dares can create a volley, an exchange of challenges that makes the tension build.

I found out later the refreshing impact my decisiveness had on Leslie, I said, "How about next Saturday? We could drive up to the museum in Beacon?"

Just like that we began dating.

We did go up to DIA Beacon. Leslie was chilly. I ran back to the car to get her jacket and I started skipping at one point until I got a hold of myself. On our third date Leslie insisted on taking me out to dinner. We went to a new tapas restaurant in SoHo in Manhattan. Leslie's generosity and appreciation were new to me. It was weird and wonderful. After dinner we strolled up West Broadway. There was a pause in our conversation and we looked at each other. It felt as if a magnetic tow pulled me towards her, Leslie stayed buoyed to her spot. I leaned and caressed her cheek with my right hand; my left hand circled her shoulder blade. Our eyes met as I moved my head closer, our lips found each other then our tongues met.

After, Leslie smiled and exhaled, "Well!" I felt as if I plunged into a mountain stream after hiking in suffocating heat. The water was so cold that my body sizzled as the frigid liquid surrounded it. Leslie's heat and my archaic chill welded us together in that moment.

We realized the magic in our story by telling it. People asked, "So how did you two meet?" I was grateful to hear Leslie's side of our introduction and courtship. I swallowed her version like an antidote to my poisoned romantic past. As she told others about my daring approach, I felt special. I had made her happy and sure of herself. She made me feel certain. Her story about us meeting taught me so much. I was getting to know parts of myself through Leslie's experience of me.

Leslie appreciated my certainty. I was going with what I felt and always thought I lacked the polish and sophistication to play games in the romantic arena. Leslie experienced it as confidence and I was someone who knew what he wanted and would go after it. This was true. When I asked her out twice on Saturday nights, she knew that I wasn't coy or courting another relationship. The futility of that kind of juggling always perplexed me. Trying to handle multiple romances was an invitation to wasteful chaos. I devoted my time to improving as a person. Wilhelm Reich referred to it as becoming a "Citizen of the Earth."

Leslie felt my directness gave her space to consider what she may want in a relationship with me. She felt she could trust me. Up until hearing all this from her, I figured I was just simple.

Leslie was the same person who took off and traveled throughout Europe when she was twenty, settled in Spain for a year and pursued her photography career. It was invigorating to talk with her about how entrenched she was with art. On one of our early dates we went to the Whitney Biennial. She had studied and worked with some of the artists who were in the exhibition. Leslie told people her shyness was obliterated when she talked about her artwork with me. She found my curiosity encouraging and felt like an artist again.

Over coffee after the art show, Leslie talked about the struggle she had maintaining all the facets of her personality. She claimed I was unlike anyone she had been with. She saw my reinventing myself, trying to grow and improve as indications that I wouldn't constrain her and would able to surprise her and be surprised. She said I was a nut, a good kind of crazy. She saw me skipping back to my car up in Beacon when I volunteered to get her jacket. Leslie was touched that I observed she was chilly and that sparked me into action. She was not intimidated by my youthfulness. I was relieved when I found out that was okay with her.

She told me once that I must be a very good therapist because I was out of my mind; in order to understand what went on in other people's minds it helped to be out of your own. We laughed a lot.

We had both worked hard and at times gambled with conviction. Inevitably, we had paid dearly for some of the dares and double dares we exposed ourselves to. We had both ended relationships with the hope that there was greater love awaiting us in our future. Taking a chance of finding this ambiguous greatness were dares of humungous intensity. Leslie and I had performed the trapeze of life without any safety net.

We both embraced the dreaded loneliness when we couldn't live with the vacuum that only two people can create. We had been in serious relationships and felt the harrowing distance that is created when you feel misunderstood or unappreciated. When we embraced that heartache we used the solitude to improve ourselves and got ready for the possibility of finding love again.

Unbeknownst to me at the time, Leslie wasn't going to just let the two of us fall in love. She had formulated a plan, a dare, probably a double dare. One Saturday afternoon, she called me at my office while walking her friend Donatella home from having a few drinks at a birthday party. I answered on the second ring.

"I am in the neighborhood and wondered if you would like some company?"

"I'll meet you downstairs, the door is locked."

Years later after seeming to laugh for no reason, Leslie told me after she called that day she saw me waving from a block and a half away, oblivious to the confusion I was creating. (Everyone on the block thought I was fluttering at them).

Once upstairs, Leslie sat on my black leather couch I sat in my shrink's chair. Her hair was tied back as it was on our first date. She looked serious and I was concerned. She took a deep breath and said "I want to talk to you about something and you may want me to just get out of here or have me leave after I tell you."

I felt a visceral tightness that froze my body. I focused on Leslie like a man who cuts diamonds for a living. She continued.

"I decided that the next man I sleep with would have to be someone I could spend the rest of my life with."

I was the shark that had just gotten banged in the

nose. Did Leslie know Stan Waterman? Leslie was a heavy weight and had just challenged me. Bernard Hopkins was a world champion boxer at age 49. Here I was at 49, being given a shot at the title.

"Leslie, are you telling me I'm a contender?"

She smiled, a tear welled up in the corner of her left eye as she answered, "Yes, John you are indeed a contender."

I took her hand and she let me take her in my arms, we were laughing, crying, we hugged each other and we kissed.

"Leslie you are one of a kind, I'm in love with you."

"I know John."

We announced in unison, "I'm hungry."

I couldn't have predicted what was at stake when I dared to introduce myself to Leslie. In the most literal and physical sense, I would have died without our dares to one another. We got married on July 24, 2005. Five years later she dared me to try a new treatment for Hepatitis C. This was the fourth time I was to be treated. The three previous treatments failed and I was certain that this would fail also. I only did it to humor my wonderful wife. The new drug killed the Hep C, but an MRI towards the end of the treatment detected liver cancer. The medical community referred to liver cancer as the silent killer. Usually, when you found out you had the cancer it was too late to treat it. My cancer was found early and Myron Schwartz, a wonderful surgeon at Mt. Sinai, was able to cut it out.

I have grown accustomed to living happily growing as a couple, a father and a step-mom; free of hepatitis C and cancer for over four years now.

I looked at Winnicott and Khan differently after all of this. The two men dared to stretch the boundaries of the therapeutic process. Dares depended on the courage of the players. The risk and the bravery were subject to the gravity of chance and time. I had taken many chances that hadn't worked out.

It seemed to me the baseball player who stole the most bases also got tagged out the most. The great Mickey Mantle's nickname was the 'strike out king'. Muhammad Ali without losing wouldn't

have had the distinction of being the only boxer who won the World Heavyweight Title three times.

Winnicott and Khan wrote such wonderful books and helped so many people and helped many therapists to help many more. Wasn't that the real celebration of their relationship? None of it would have happened if they cowered from one another.

In the spring of 2016, Leslie and I went to hear the wonderful psychoanalyst and writer Adam Phillips, who had been analyzed by Masud Khan. During a Q & A, Mr. Phillips was asked about his treatment with Khan. Adam told us that when he first called Masud to make an appointment, he quoted a fee that was nonnegotiable; Adam countered with what he could afford. Masud responded to Adam's dare with a day and a time to meet. Adam said, "I loved him."

Dares and double dares start out as challenging invitations. The arrangement can lead to collaboration that brings you to a place you wanted to go to but never knew existed. Daring took Leslie and I beyond what we thought we were capable of on our own and luckily it took us to love. I liked to think it took Winnicott and Khan there as well.

About the Author:

John Bliss lives with his wife Leslie in New York City. He is a psychoanalyst and clinical social worker that co-founded an outpatient licensed substance abuse clinic thirty years ago where he continues to work. He has focused on writing about personal experiences at the encouragement of his wife, daughters Jenna, and Jillian, and musician friends and now his writing buddies. Map Literary is publishing his story 'Keep The Change' in the fall of 2017. The process of developing narratives in his therapy practice, playing saxophone, and writing is exhilarating to him. Writing has a special appeal, he can do it anytime and it doesn't wake up the neighbors the way the horn does.

CLIO

Alicia Marie Devers

"You have no idea what you're doing, do you?" he asked.

I stood on the edge of a high cliff where the water far below me hit the rocky enclosure. I knew that was the understatement of the century, but Kyle would never hear me say it.

"Of course I do," I said, "You just have to jump."

"If you say so," he said, crossing his arms. He had a smug look on his face. I wanted him to eat his words.

I could jump off this cliff. People did it all the time on TV. It was just water on the other end. It would be a safe landing, unless I whacked my head on the way down. But dying in a watery grave with bragging rights at my funeral seemed more reasonable than the humiliation I'd face if I didn't jump.

"What? Scared?"

"No!"

"Well, hurry up, it's gonna start storming."

"Quit rushing me."

He was right. The sky in the distance was inky black, the feel of electricity in the air made my hair stand up on my arms. The waves were gray and harsh from the wind that made its way across Lake Superior. Kyle moved back as I tiptoed closer to the edge, willing myself to jump and hoping someone would call us in and we'd have to ditch this idea until tomorrow, where something new and more intimidating would catch Kyle's eye.

I took a deep breath, let it out. How far could this cliff really be? 20 feet? 30?

Most things on TV tell you that you'll hang there, time will slow down to an unnatural pace and you'll be able to count the raindrops as they fall in arcs in the sky. That's not how that works. You plummet and you hit the water hard. Water shouldn't be that hard, but it is. It knocks the breath out of your lungs and everything you told yourself you'd do once you're down there goes completely out the window.

As my body fell through the water, the current washed over me. My feet and head changed places. I lost track of where the top of the water was, the bubbles and foggy water making it impossible to see. I started trying to swim up toward the blurry distorted picture of the sun but my arms and legs couldn't seem to move fast enough. Eventually my body evened out. I swam up until my head broke the surface, my lungs reaching out for air.

I didn't get a breath before a wave crashed over my head, sending me back under. It was cold against my skin. I came back up again, gasping, rain pelting me hard in the shoulders. I managed to swim toward shore, walking once it was shallow enough.

Kyle was gone, the rain had sent him running inside. I could just make out the color of his swim trunks hopping up the steps to his house. I shivered and went over to grab my glasses, put them on, my towel drenched in icy water.

My house backed up to the beach with a set of stairs leading from my patio down into the water. There were beach weeds tall enough to block my fence along with some well placed bushes. But what really kept my house secluded from the beach were the tall pine trees that sat up and down the street and the path leading up to the cliff.

I wrapped my arms around myself and jogged to my house which was only an arm's reach to Kyle's. The bathroom window in my house was close enough to his that if we had stretched out our hands we could've touched. I slid open the door wall and stepped into the kitchen.

"Mom?"

"In here," she said.

Her voice came from the living room. I walked in to see her on her knees scrubbing the bookshelf, her books scattered on the floor. She had finally hung up the pictures that had been stacked in a cardboard box in the corner. There were mostly just pictures of me and a few of the two of us but all the pictures that had had my dad in them were only obvious by their absence.

"What are you doing?"

"Just some spring cleaning," she said. She stood up, wiped her hands on her pants.

"It's the middle of July," I said.

"It's never too early to do spring cleaning," she said, "Your lips are a little blue. What have you been doing?"

"Swimming, with Kyle."

Her lips thinned, but she didn't say anything. Ever since we had moved in after the divorce and I had started hanging out with him, she would get this sour look on her face like she sucked on a lemon. She spent time with his mom but mostly to get dirt on everyone's children. She walked toward the kitchen leaving me in the middle of a puddle on the hallway floor.

"Make sure you wipe up that water."

I dropped my towel on top of the puddle before going upstairs and into the bathroom. I locked the door behind me. I leaned against the sink, my fingers white as they held on like at any moment the world would stop and I'd need something to hold onto. My breath was caught behind my teeth as soon as I was alone. I splashed water on my face. Everything was fine. I was fine. I turned the shower on until steam was fogging the mirror, making it impossible for me to see my reflection.

The hot water fell onto my skin, thawing me until I was red. My throat was tight, but no one was looking now. Not even me.

"Clio," my mom's voice came from under the door. "Dinner's ready."

I turned the knob off, the water dripping to a halt. I put on the pair of pajama bottoms I had left on the floor that morning. I wrapped the towel around my head before going downstairs to the smell of lasagna.

My mom set our plates down, "We need to talk about Kyle." She unfolded her napkin, put it on her lap and then faced me. "I don't think you should hang around him."

"Why not?"

"He's a bad influence."

"Well, he's my friend," I said. I supposed that was true. He was about as much my friend as anyone here could be.

"Not a very good one," she said. "I've talked to his mother and he's been in trouble since he started high school. He's bad for you."

"Who else am I supposed to hang out with? I don't know anyone!"

She swallowed a bite of lasagna. "There's plenty of people to be friends with here. You just have to try."

My mom was that person that never went to the same school for more than a semester. So, naturally she thought this was normal.

"I don't want to try. I want to go home. Kyle's all I have. Do you want me to be alone all summer?"

"Stop being dramatic."

She was right. Kyle was a bad friend, but no one wanted to be my friend, not when they could be friends with the same people they had been friends with before they left the womb.

Their grandparents probably hung out together and played bingo. Kyle was the only person I had. My mom just didn't understand.

After my parents had gotten divorced we had moved to this desolate little town far away where my father couldn't just drop in. Not that he would try. The only downfall was I was out of district and had to change schools. My old school was in the suburbs right outside of Detroit. My new school was here, in Marquette, 455 miles from where I wished I was.

"Whatever," I said.

We sat in silence, the only noise our forks scraping against the plates. They were same blue plates my grandmother had packed away for us so my mom didn't have to run into my dad at the house. We still had boxes along the floor my grandmother had taped closed, her block writing labeling them as kitchen, living room, bathroom.

I was finishing my dinner when the doorbell rang. Mom's chair scraped along the floor as she got up to answer it. I looked down the hallway to the door and could see Kyle's face was hidden behind a large black umbrella. It was raining now, the wind picking up as the storm closed over us.

"She can't talk right now," my mom said.

"Yes, I can. I'm right here."

My mom looked between the two of us before sighing. "Five minutes." She left us standing by the door.

"What do you want?"

"That was so sick! I didn't think you had the guts to do it."

He turned around and sat on the porch swing. There was an awning above us so he stashed his umbrella under our feet, we faced the storm and the water at this angle, not enough to see the cliff. The rainwater slid down the awning, a small waterfall of sorts in front of us making a mud puddle in the grass in front of us. The wrought iron fence around the porch was rusting where the water landed, flecks of red swimming in the muddy water.

"Yeah, whatever."

"Well, I'm sure I can think of something for you to chicken out over," he said.

"Like what?"

"I'll let you know tomorrow."

I heard his screen door slam shut before going back inside.

My mom was on her phone, her voice low like she didn't want me to hear, but she couldn't hide the anger. She was leaning against the fireplace, her back to me. I could see her face in the window and she had her eyes closed as she listened to whoever it was on the other end.

"You're not speaking to her," she said as I passed her on my way upstairs. I took my foot off the bottom step to try and listen to what she was saying but she snapped her phone onto the mantel piece and was silent.

When she opened her eyes she saw me standing in the doorway. "Everything okay?" she asked.

"Yeah, why?"

"You just seem down," she said.

"I'm fine. Everything okay with you," I said nodding toward the phone.

"What? Oh, yeah, it'll be okay," she said.

I knew my mom felt guilty about the divorce, it was in every line of her face. But I also knew I didn't blame her for it. He was the dad sleeping on the couch, a bottle of something on the table, a ring of water under it from where it had been placed over and over again. I had learned pretty young not to wake him up when I came home, or I had the chance of being yelled at, hit or both. My mom would be standing at the doorway leading into the kitchen and immediately usher me in, watched me do homework as he slept. It was quiet there. It didn't surprise me when she decided one day while he was at work to leave to my grandmother's house and not come back.

I walked up stairs to my room, closed the door behind me and put my face in the pillows.

That night the storm settled into a light mist in the early hours of the morning but the wind still circled our house. The tree next to my window scrapped the glass, my eyes open because of the noise. The wind was howling as it raced through the cliff face and into my yard, swirling in angry zig zags lifting sand and pelting the side of the house. I was just about to grab my blanket and sleep on the couch hoping the tv might drown out the noise when I heard a little tap.

It was Kyle. I had no screen in my window so when I opened it, we were face to face.

"What are you doing? It's like midnight," I said.

"Actually it's almost one."

"Doesn't change anything. Why are you here?"

He pushed me aside and pulled himself into my room. The moonlight behind him casting his face into shadow. My front yard was deserted without him, the gravel road now just mud and puddles.

"Listen, I know you don't have a fun bone in your body, but there's a party. On the beach. We should go."

"A party. In a storm?"

"It's not storming. It's a little mist."

"Sure."

"It's not that big of a deal," he said.

He sat down on my bed in front of the mirror. He smoothed his hand over his face and then laced his fingers in his lap. His blue eyes looked even bluer as the street light outside hit half his face. His dark hair drying in ringlets across of his forehead reminded me of the mud swirling in the grass earlier. "What time does your mom go to work in the morning?"

"Like 6."

"Okay, so be back by 5:30."

I was positive this was probably the worst decision of my life, but he was sitting there so smug. I only had a month tops to make my reputation a good one and so far, with Kyle's help, I was failing miserably. If it really was a party, maybe I could make some different friends.

"Fine, let me get dressed."

"Knew you had it in you."

"Yeah, whatever."

I put the clothes I wore the day before back on, then watched as Kyle went out my window, his feet leaving footprints on my windowsill.

"Are you sure this is a good idea," I asked.

"Yes, come on."

I slipped out into my front yard behind Kyle hoping to whoever was in the sky my mom wouldn't wake up as soon as I was out and come and check on me. I hoped the tv she kept on at night would drown out any noise I was likely to make.

Kyle walked like he had no fear but I tried to at least stay somewhat out of the only street light on this side of the street, my shadow dancing between the bushes along the side of the house. We rounded my house and went down the stairs onto the beach. In the distance, closer to the pier, I could see they had lit a fire.

We passed Kyle's house and then came up to the party. There was probably only 30 people at this point. I wondered why exactly they lit a fire, seeing as there was still mist hanging in the air around our shoulders but it was smoldering, the other light coming from a few burning embers. A few guys were crouched in front of it trying to make it bigger.

"Don't embarrass me, okay," Kyle said. He set his shoulders back before knocking his way through people.

I rolled my eyes and followed him into the crowd congregated under the pier. It was people I had seen around town but had never spoken to. They were sitting on driftwood, glass bottles in their hands. The fire was in the center of the crowd, a few people drenching the wood in lighter fluid. There was the occasional shriek from some girl as her group of friends arrived. The girls were closer to the fire, their faces clouded in shadows flickering from the tiny flames that flashed before dying out again, the boys were the outer circle, like they had shepherded us between them.

Kyle slapped backs with some boy who managed to fit a bottle in each of his back pockets, plus one in each hand. He had tan skin, blue eyes and his hair was pushed in directions like he had just gotten out of bed.

"I got the beer like you said," he said to Kyle.

"Cool, did my old man notice anything," Kyle asked.

"No, passed out from what I could see." He turned towards me, "Do you want one? I'm sure I could spare it."

"No, thanks," I said but Kyle cut me off.

"She'll take one."

The boy handed me one from his back pocket. I wasn't so sure this was a good idea but I took a sip anyway.

"Ew, what is that?"

"Beer. I stole it out of the garage. Kyle's dad had a whole case in there," the boy said.

"Uh, here. You can finish it."

I handed it back to the boy who took a gulp before going over to a group of girls who had just arrived. Kyle pulled me over.

"What are you doing?"

"I'm not drinking beer."

"Listen, if you want to make a good impression, you might want to act like it," he said.

He left me alone next to the beams of the pier. Someone had turned on some music, so people were beginning to dance, if you could call grinding against each other dancing. The guys looked at the girls like they were sheep about to be hunted, their eyebrows heavy over their eyes in the firelight.

I was about ready to leave the party and go home when someone else slid up to me. He was pimply and lanky, and he was dressed more plainly, like he wasn't supposed to be here but had somehow snagged an invitation.

"Hey, why are you all alone?"

"I'm not. I came with Kyle. He went to get drinks."

"Well, until he gets back…"

The boy took a seat next to me on the thin piece of driftwood. His dingy plaid jacket smelled like smoke and pineapples. He took his vape pen out and took a drag, letting the thick, heavy smoke cloud his face. It smelled like pineapple.

I think I'm just going to go home. I shouldn't be here anyway," I said.

"Don't leave. You can hang out with me," he said. "I'm Todd."

"Clio."

He got closer to me. "Cute name."

I put more distance between us. "Yeah. Sure is."

Todd handed me his drink. I took a sip. It was still the bitter nasty taste of beer but this time I didn't almost gag. I took another sip before handing it to him.

"That's nasty," I said.

"It was the only thing we could get. Kyle's dad drinks for a living so he doesn't notice."

"Oh."

We stood in silence, the air around us heavy with awkward. I had not heard much about Kyle's father and anytime it got brought up he'd change the subject. A few more people had arrived but just as many had left, a few couples sneaking into the seclusion offered by the trees.

"So, how long have you lived here?"

"I just moved this summer," I said pushing his arm off.

"Why? This town is in the middle of nowhere."

"I don't know. My mom picked it. I think because it's far away," I lied.

Todd thought about this for a second, the side of his body coming closer to mine. "Why did she want to get away?"

When I finally faced him face on, he seemed a little older than most of the people here. He seemed a little older than someone who was in high school and I wondered how many grades he had failed.

"My parents got divorced."

"I know how that is. My dad left when I was seven."

He almost seemed sincere when he said it but his face was getting closer to mine and I backed away. That wasn't happening, in any lifetime.

"Well, look at that. Time for me to go."

I walked toward Kyle, through the crowd that was stuck together from hips to mouth. Bottles were clicking together, the voices way too loud for the beach at this hour. If they weren't careful someone would end up calling the police.

Todd grabbed my wrist from behind and spun me around. His eyes were a lot glassier now he was bathed in the light from the pier.

"Where you going?"

"Away from you."

He laughed and pulled me over to Kyle, his arm like steel around my shoulders.

I pushed him off again. He was just about to say something when Kyle interrupted. "Todd. Aaron and I want to go get snacks. Aaron said he'd drive."

"Wanna come, Clio?" Todd had a grin on his face and my gut was telling me not to go, just go back to bed. But if Kyle was going, I was sure I'd be back in time to sneak into my house without my mom knowing.

"Sure, why not?"

The four of us, Aaron, Kyle, Todd and I, walked up the sand into the lot near the beach. We piled into his four door car. I was wedged in the back next to Todd and some garbage Aaron didn't seem to want to part with.

We had the windows down, the music up, as we pulled out of the beach parking lot. It was a long twisting road lined with oak trees, their branches lazily stretching over the road, wet leaves sticking to the cement. When we got to the main road there were more street lights but everything was closed up for the night. The small family restaurant had a few cars in it but someone was out back taking out the trash. The gas station on this side of town was open but I could see the guy behind the counter had his eyes closed as we stopped at the stop sign.

We turned again, taking a back way, houses flashing past our car. Old houses that had two stories and wrap around porches, most with an American flag by the door. The trees in the front yard waved to us as we sloshed past through rain puddles.

Todd's hands were on my thigh and at first it was a nice weight on my skin. It seemed to anchor me there along with the music pulsing through the frame of the car and my chest. But then his hands ever so slowly were coming closer and closer to the inside of my thigh. I grabbed his hand between mine and just held it there, crossing my legs so hopefully he got the idea.

I didn't make eye contact with him as I moved his hand back to his own leg, the Walmart coming into view as we passed a McDonalds and a gas station. I wasn't actually positive where we were, my summer confined by the sandy beaches near the house. The four of us got out of the car and walked over to the door. We were loud, but the workers didn't look at us as we yelled down the aisles.

It was ghostly silent. The lights were dimmed overhead, the few workers we did see where leaning against their counters reading magazines. They glanced up when we came in but they looked back down again when we went over to the food section of the store. We went to the snack aisle in the back of the grocery section, the only camera two aisles over and looking in the wrong direction. The boys started pulling things off the shelf, stuffing things into their jackets.

"Here, Clio, put this in your pocket," said Kyle. He was handing me candy bars.

"No way. You're crazy."

"God, come on. It's just a few candy bars."

"It's illegal."

"Listen, we do it all the time. You won't get caught," said Kyle.

"And even if you do, Kyle's dad is a police officer. We'll be fine," said Todd.

"No, way," I said. "My mom would skin me alive."

I tossed the candy bars back to Kyle and turned around to leave. Jumping off cliffs, sneaking out and now he wanted me to steal.

I was walking toward the door and out of the store when Todd caught up to me. I only knew he was behind me because of his smell invading my space.

"What are you gonna do? Walk home?"

"Maybe," I said.

"Let's just go sit by the car," he said.

I went down the aisle that we had parked down and found Aaron's gross beat up green car that looked like it was between baby vomit and something less pleasant. One of the windows was broken so a plastic garbage bag was covering the hole.

I sat on the hood of the car, Todd taking the spot next to me.

"They should just be a minute," said Todd.

"Why do you do that," I asked.

"It's fun," he said shrugging his shoulders.

We were parked so that we could see into the large windows on the front of the building. Todd took out his pen again and sent the water cycle into overdrive leaving my glasses fogged up. I took my glasses off and was wiping them on my shirt when--

"Oh, shit," he said.

"What?" I jammed them back on to see that Kyle and Aaron had been stopped just inside the door to the store by a guy dressed in a grey security uniform. I stood up to go into the store.

"No, way," said Todd. "Are you crazy?"

"Do you have a phone?"

"Yes, why?"

"I'm calling my mom," I said.

"You can't call your mom."

"Got any better ideas," I asked.

"Yeah, we get out of here."

"Wow, what a great friend, you are," I said.

"I won't be much help if I get busted too," he said showing me the stuff he had in his pockets.

"You guys are not the brightest, are you," I asked, "Give me your phone."

"I swear man, Kyle and Aaron will be real pissed if you call your mom," he said.

"Yeah and I'm sure Kyle's drunk cop father will be so pleased to see him at the station," I said.

It seemed to have dawned on Todd what that would mean if Aaron got sent to his dad and he slowly handed me his phone and I was glad my mom insisted I memorize her phone number instead of just putting it in my phone.

When my mom finally got there to pick me up from the Walmart, she strolled in like it was nothing and talked to the police officer. Kyle and Aaron were slouched together, at least from what it looked like from the parking lot. My mom went over to them and they stood up and followed her out of the store. She walked the two of them to her car and pulled me along with them.

"Get in," she said and the four of us got in.

"Where do you two live," she said to Aaron and Todd.

"Just on the other side of town," said Aaron, "On Westchester."

So we drove in silence. Eventually she turned onto their street. Aaron didn't bother saying thank you but got out and started laughing with Todd. Todd looked over his shoulder and waved goodbye to me. I didn't wave back.

"Now, I don't know what you two were thinking--"

"Mrs. Chase," said Kyle, "Are you--going to tell my dad?"

"Yes, I am," she said. She faltered a little when she saw the look on his face.

He seemed, almost, afraid. My mom pursed her lips, in the middle of thought.

"You know what, Kyle. I'll give you this one," she said, "But if it ever happens again..."

"Thank you, Mrs. Chase."

The rest of the way was silent and we pulled into our driveway a little while later, Kyle going one way and us going the other.

"Are you okay," she asked.

"I don't know."

"I'm sorry, Clio," she said.

"For what?"

"Judging Kyle," she said.

"What do you mean," I asked.

She took the keys out of her purse and opened the door. I squeezed into the hallway behind her.

"You might not need him, but I think he needs you," she said. "His dad--"

"I've never seen Kyle look like that," I said.

"Yes, well, keep him close, I think he needs it."

"Yeah, maybe."

About the Author:

Alicia Marie Devers grew up in Roseville, Michigan, where she lives with her mom, Kim and dad, Bryan. She is currently a senior at Siena Heights University where she is studying Creative Writing.

THE DELUGE

Gracjan Kraszewski

"We'd like to extend a special welcome to any viewers joining us following that wild conclusion to the Atlanta-Carolina game. What a finish, huh, Bob?"

"That's right, Schenectady. Wild, more like hogwild if you ask me."

Schenectady Tourismmadeeasy nods and laughs. "A hogwild finish indeed, Bob. Remember, folks, when you need that one of a kind glossy sheen for your outdoor deck, Hogwildfinish.com is the place for you. Hogwildfinish.com, the official deck stain depot of the NFL."

"Looks like we got a good one brewin' here, too" Bob says.

"No doubt about it. And when you find yourself in need of a good brew don't forget to check out Sudsy Gordos, the official beverage retailer of the NFL. Sudsy Gordos, brought to you by the Anheuser-Busch Coors Miller Pabst Yuengling Imitation Chimay Cooperative. So," Schenectady says before pausing to catch his breath and exhale, "fourth quarter and it's a close one. The visiting Kraft Packers of Green Bay lead the Winnie the Pooh Remade Cartoon Classic Bears of Chicago 17-13. The WPs have the ball on the Kraft twenty-six yard line; two timeouts left and just about to come out of the two-minute warning. Speaking of warnings, folks, don't wait until Black Friday to get all of your holiday shopping done. Get the Yuletide Automatic Pocket Siren today. Set your timer and forget about it; the YAPS will activate exactly thirty-six hours before Black Friday giving you that friendly reminder that it's time to beat the holiday rush. 'Let the

YAPS zap you when it's time for shopping, you focus on couch-plopping;' The Yuletide Automatic Pocket Siren, official sponsor of the two-minute warning."

"Here we go," Bob says, giddily rubbing his hands together as the teams retake the field. "This is shaping up to be one heck'of'a hogwild finish if you ask me."

"Absolutely," Schenectady says. "Winnie the Pooh U.S. Department of the Treasury Quarterback Milt Peralta hasn't been his usual self. The two time NFL MVP, brought to you by AVP 'your local Scranton portal to the great beyond,' has completed less than half of his passes today and thrown two interceptions. But, if there's one thing we've learned about Peralta it's that he responds well to adversity and preforms best under pressure. Just like the new and improved gold plated Duplex DoubleYummy Pressure Cooker, the off-...and Johnson is tackled at the Kraft nineteen yard line."

"Peralta made a really good decision there," Bob says. "He recognized that Kraft was playing Tampa 2—brought to you by the Tampa 2 Buccaneers of Tampa Bay—and made the proper check-down to Johnson. Now it's second and three and they've got the whole playbook to work with."

"With that last completion the Winnie the Poohs are into the redzone for just the second time today. The redzone, brought to you by Redzone Canine Pacification Services. 'When your pooch goes into the redzone, it's time to punt; bark us at 1-800-pscyhosaliva.' Peralta's pass falls incomplete. He was looking for Willard on a fade to the back of the end zone. Looks like the Extra Crispy Bacon Company football just got away from him there."

"That's exactly it," Bob says. "Peralta has an absolutely fantastic Arm & Hammer arm but sometimes he forgets about touch. Plus, the conditions here at G.I. Joe field have been typically difficult with the occasional driving gust of wind making throwing and kicking a complete crapshoot."

Schenectady looks at his partner. He is silent. He just keeps staring at Bob. After a brief pause, Bob remembers; he throws his head back and nods. "The wind, brought to you by Febreze Air Effects, official meteorological sponsor of the National Football League and the half of the CFL."

While Bob is speaking the WPs pick up eleven yards on a halfback draw. First and goal at the Kraft eight yard line. Chicago takes its second timeout.

"You know," Schenectady says. "Peralta's Arm & Hammer arm is fantastic, like you said, but I'd like to see him utilize his legs a bit more; especially down here so close to the goal line."

"Which leg?"

"Both." Schenectady says. "His left leg, sponsored by Kick in the Pants Homeschooling Services for Delinquient Children, and that right leg, too, brought to you by Right as Rain Hydraulic Rental Cisterns. If he ever finds a way to combine the talents of those two legs, well, the league better watch out."

"I'm just thinking that this game is really looking like it's going to come down to a hogwild finish," Bob says.

"Shotgun snap, Perlata rolls to his right, he looks, he keeps rolling, throws it out of the back of the end zone. Second down....Bob, I have breaking news. I just received a notice from my agent that the city of Schenectady has sold my naming rights to Jonathan Porto Portable Waste Disposal Management Services. Partner," he says with a chuckle, "you can call me Johnny Porto! Effective immediately."

Bob laughs. "You know, come ta'think of it, I think that name suits you best. Well, I'll be. Not since you were that Adam's apple abrasions cream

spokesman, Redneck Cackalacka, have I heard a name that suits you so well. Congratulations."

Two yard gain up the middle by the WP running back. Third and goal at the six.

"Well, thanks, Bob," Johnny says. "In other exciting news, folks, it just so happens to be a third and goal with less than two minutes left in the game. You know what that means!"

The game stops and the TV cameras cut from the field. Everyone focuses on the booth; even the players look up. Bob, his hands tied behind his back, sticks his face into a large, canary yellow washing bin filled to the brim with root beer. He is hunting three Red Delicious specimens that have been plopped in, causing some soda to lap out over the sides and pool in a foamy puddle around the base of his microphone.

There is a special scoreboard in every NFL stadium for this moment. A timer counts down from one minute. If the man formerly known as Derek Smith can retrieve all three apples from the liquid every fan physically in attendance at an NFL game that week receives a packet of coupons to the Great Oregon-Yakima Apple Company. The GOYAC is America's number one distributor of produce—not simply pommes but also pommes de terre, and much more—and pays Smith, a two-time All-American linebacker in college before becoming a five time Pro Bowler in the league and now America's favorite color commentator, more than $20m/annum for his name change and involvement in the "Fourth Quarter Apple Hunt" which GOYAC claims has led to a 23% increase in overall sales since the game-within-the-game's inception four years ago.

Bob Babobbingham pulls out apple #3 with 0:04 left on the clock. The crowd roars. They rise to their feet. Johnny unties Bob's hands. Bob stands and waves to the cheering crowd.

The game resumes shortly thereafter. On third down the WPs run a trick play, a halfback toss right that is really a halfback pass. The running back sells it well but no one is open. He pump fakes, stumbles, then tucks and runs down the sideline before getting blown up by the free safety at the five yard line. He careems trough the air and crashes hard into a camera man who pays the price for inching ever closer to the field for that photo-of-the-year potential shot. The WPs take their final timeout in advance of the fourth down try.

"Now that's a good hit," Bob says. "You know, Schen-, Johnny, I just keep watching this game and I've got to say. Brother, we're in for a hogwild finish."

"It's really come down to the wire, folks," Johnny says. "Fourth down, four point Kraft lead. The Winnie the Poohs have got to try to get all the Queen Bee Golden Organic Honey here. Field goal won't help. Need help with your homework, kids? Check out Onlineteacherbuddy.com, official educational sponsor of the NFL. Eleven seconds left in the game. Let's see what they're going to do. And when you really want to see what anyone's going to do run on over to Clear Vision Warehouse, the official eye care sponsor of the NFL. They break the huddle. Peralta is in the shotgun, sponsored by the Beretta Firearms Catalog, flanked by two running backs. Willard is split out wide left. Speaking of left, too much turkey leftover? Why don't you-...Peralta changing the play; puts Dennison in motion and out into the slot, the NFL slot brought to you by Vegas Slots for Tots. Ten seconds on the playclock. Speaking of clocks, how about an antique mod-...Peralta changing the play again. Five, four, here we go... Peralta looks left, he shuffles to his left, here comes Smith on the cornerback blitz! Peralta gets away! Smith just whiffed on the sack! Perlata still moving to his left, he looks, he looks..."

The game clock reads 0:00. As such, hundreds of fireworks—brought to you by Sixty-yard Heave into the End Zone Fireworks, "when it's time to chuck, light it up and duck," official pyrotechnic of the NFL—are going off above the stadium as the usually green AstroPlay undergoes metamorphosis into flashing hot pink while the stadium speakers blare DJ Frankie Scot-Kizzle's chart topping remix of the Star Spangled Banner, all as Peralta finally sets his feet and lightly flicks the bacon ball over a leaping defender's outstretched hands as another crashes hard into his thighs, knocking him down.

The pass is intended for Willard, who is blanketed by two defenders, all three of them heading for the back pylon, tracking the floating pass—neither a tight spiral nor a duck—against a resplendent although bothersome fireworks show

above an equally distracting spastic pink field at their feet. The three leap simultaneously as now the ball appears within reach. Out of the corner of his eye, Willard sees something else. Just for a split-second, but that is enough. The WPs are on the cutting edge of postgame entertainment; for two seasons now, after every home game, they flood G.I. Joe field and recreate famous naval battles from history. The Battle of Naxos is scheduled for today. But after the game! It's supposed to be after the game!!

Willard takes his eye off the bacon for that crucial moment, his eye drawn across the field to the far endzone, far across the field, where someone (or is it perhaps just a malfunction?) has jumped the gun. The fireworks keep popping, the music keeps thumping and the azure water crashes out from the tunnel with terrifying speed. The football falls softly to the ground, untouched.

About the Author:

Gracjan Kraszewski's fiction has appeared in Eclectica Magazine, Wilderness House Literary Review, The Dead Mule School of Southern Literature, PILGRIM, The Southern Distinctive, Five on the Fifth, and on The Short Humour Site. Author of an absurdist-existentialist novel, Job Search, set in a American future 100 years from now, treating questions of free will, cultural value, and the pursuit of happiness (currently in circulation). Holder of a PhD in history. Played baseball in college, professionally in Europe, and for the Polish National Team.

ECHO

Andy Tu

The first time I met Elana, during freshmen orientation at college, I thought she was a loser. There wasn't much to warrant this judgement, just a feeling of aversion when she asked to walk back to the dorms together from campus. I agreed, of course. After all, this was the precursor to the next four years of my life. I didn't want to get into a habit of being anti-social, even if it was with someone I never thought I'd see again.

"It was Pamela, right?"

"Yup," I said.

"So where you from?" she asked.

"South Haven."

"Oh."

"You know it?"

"Yeah," she said. "I'm from Livonia."

"Wow, we're actually not that far from each other."

She nodded.

"Cool," I offered.

We walked side by side in silence. I felt the typical awkward aura of strangers being in each other's presence to avoid being alone. It was bright out, and humid. My tank-top stuck to my back like tape. In the distance to our left, crowds of freshmen roamed past the bookstore, cafes, and movie theater.

"You wanna check out Main Street?" she asked.

I knew it was an effort to socialize, to possibly even form a bond, however unlikely to last. I was going to be social, active, and popular in college, unlike my nerdy self in high school. But still, I said, "No, I'm okay. I just want to get back and out of the heat." Which was true, anyways.

She shrugged. "I'll see you later then."

She headed toward the activity, waving goodbye. I really didn't think she would end up becoming my best friend.

I didn't realize that I'd subconsciously rejected until years later. Getting home from orientation, like every other incoming freshmen in the world, I went on Facebook and friended those I'd met. No one in our group had particularly interested me. In fact, I'd found them to be kind of strange. A guy and a girl, even though they hadn't known each other before, ended up spending every moment together like they'd been best friends their entire lives. One girl wore all purple and pink and spoke too cheerfully during our scavenger hunt and "bonding activities", a few internationals spoke only Korean to each other, and my temporary roommate had brought her laptop, headgear, gaming mouse, and customized keyboard to play World of Warcraft. I didn't even know girls did that.

It turned out that Elana had been assigned to the same dorm and floor as mine. She messaged me, saying, "hey, guess I'll be seeing you soon."

I didn't think anything of it.

That first year, though, I ended up eating most of my meals with her in the dining hall. We were in the same introductory math class first semester, an 8am that was too early for our tendencies to stay up late into the night screwing around in random chatrooms. It was a hobby I was both ashamed of and addicted to during high school, and the reason why I'd spent so many Saturday nights alone as my friends tried to make a social life for themselves by hanging out at late-night diners sipping on sodas and munching fries, a social life that I didn't really believe was real. I'd been determined to transform into a new person; misleading strangers in chatrooms was not going to help. Yet I spent most of my nights with Elana catfishing both girls and guys, cackling each time a guy tried to sell us a line about his dark and mysterious self or a girl we'd hooked messaged us asking why we'd suddenly stopped talking to her. We had such guilty fun. We created our own world and laughingly outcasted ourselves from our floor mates, who we'd mock in private. One time we even mixed our urine into Elana's roommate's mouthwash. We were terrible, and we enjoyed every moment of it. But times like those aren't meant to last.

After college, I taught English in Japan for a year. Elana, prone to slack off in her studies, extended a fifth year.

"Wait, I thought you were done," I said a few days after I'd come back and we met up.

"Yeah," she said. "There was an incident…"

"What do you mean?"

It was Saturday and we were in the kitchen at my home in South Haven, my parents out.

Elana sat down onto a stool along the counter. "I mean… well, there was this girl in one of my classes, and I got into a dispute with her… and so… yeah…"

"What? What do you mean?"

She laughed, sighing. "It was stupid, really. She said something during discussion against me, and we got into an argument. And then…" She laughed again. "I made a fake account on Facebook, and I started messing with her."

I smiled. "Oh man…"

By then it'd been years since we'd engaged in that nonsense together, since our second year when we'd shared a room. Our third and fourth years, I'd lived in an apartment with a friend from my hometown, and Elana had commuted. I'd gradually stopped screwing around in those chatrooms, realizing it was for cheap laughs and unfulfilling. And after my trip to Japan, I felt wholly different. Transformed and becoming someone I was, for the first time in my life, proud of. But it seemed Elana was still living in the past.

"Yeah," she said. "Anyways, long story short, she somehow found out it was me. It was stupid, because I accidentally used an old email account that was linked to me. But yeah, she reported me to the Dean's office, and they suspended me."

"Shit…" I said.

"Yeah, whatever though." She shrugged. "So what's the plan for the evening? You still drink?"

"Not really…"

She was looking out the window into the hill of grass that climbed toward the sunset, light sliding through the shutters in stripes across her face.

"Only on special occasions, though," I said.

The special occasion rule I'd self-imposed was a result of my inability to control my worsening drinking habit. Sometime during our second year, Elana and I, despite neither of us having ever tasted a sip of alcohol our entire lives, decided to steal a bottle of Tequila from a fraternity party, one of the few we ever attended.

In our dorm room we took swig after swig, wincing as that noxious liquid staggered down our throats.

"You feel anything?" I asked her.

"Not really…"

I took out a couple of cups and filled them up like I was pouring coffee. We tapped them and said cheers, then gulped down as much as we could before nearly choking and spitting some out in laughter.

"Oh… fuck," I said.

"Oh my God," she said. "I'm… I'm like… about to hit the wall."

She tried to stand from her bed but immediately fell to the floor, knocking over the lamp on her desk. We cracked up so hard I thought I was going to die from lack of breathing.

I don't remember a single thing that actually happened that night, just our laughter.

I started drinking alone in secret during my third and fourth years of college. It'd started with a single cup at night when I was bored, to getting wasted alone when my roommates went home for the weekend. I felt more connected to my real self when intoxicated. I'd giggle hysterically, shouting at the television and cussing people out in chatrooms, the joy of mischief rushing back along with the spin of the walls and ceiling. It was on a night alone when I couldn't stop myself from walking to the supermarket to select a bottle that I realized I had a problem.

Just a week before my reunion with Elana, though, when I was still in Japan, getting drunk by myself at a sushi bar, I formed that 'special occasion' rule, and told myself that I'd wait at least two months before taking another sip.

Which is why I was already beginning to feel regret as Elana and I clinked our shot glasses together at the bar.

"Bottom's up," she said cheerfully.

We tossed them down.

Once I got started, I was in for it. A drink led to another, then another, and another. I was an all-or-nothing kind of girl, and by the time evening settled in, people chatting it up and an upbeat song jazzing around, I was drunk. And loving it.

"You're fucking crazy," I said, giggling. "That's not going to work."

"Just watch—just watch," Elana said, raising her arms into the air. "Hey, Bartender!"

The guy, who was filling a mug on the other end, glanced over.

"Get your sexy ass over here!" Elana yelled.

"Oh God…" I ducked my head and covered my face with my hands.

The bartender smiled, but looked away quickly.

"Hey! I'm fucking talking to you! Don't make a girl wait!"

He kept his focus on the other customers.

"He doesn't look interested," I said, slumping forward into my stool. As usual, I'd drank too much in too little time. My stomach felt like it was trying to shimmy its way out of my body.

"Oh, trust me," she said. "When a guy's into me, I know."

I laughed. "This isn't Random Chat. Guys can see straight through you here."

"Just watch," she said.

She continued shouting and waving her arms. The music volume seemed to have increased, my eardrums rattling with the heavy bass of a now hip-hop music. A guy tapped my shoulder and asked if I was okay. I nodded.

The bartender didn't come until he had to cross where we were sitting, right in the center.

"Hey!" Elana said, splashing some of her pink Margarita Sunrise onto the counter. The guy looked down at the mess she was making. "Girls like me don't come around all the time, you know."

The guy took a deep breath. "I'm sure they don't," he said. He let out a near-silent, pitiful laugh. I smiled apologetically at him. He smiled back.

"You're really cute," he said to me. "Maybe I can call you sometime."

This shook me out of my haze. "Uh…" I couldn't bear to look at Elana. I didn't know if this guy was messing around, or what, but…

"People are waiting for you," I said, flicking my head toward the other end of the bar.

He shrugged, and left.

"What a douche," said Elana, looking down at the pink liquid in her glass. She took a long sip.

Elana and I were alike in so many deranged ways, from the way we'd dance stupidly when walking behind an unaware floormate in the hallway, legs wobbling and arms clucking like a chicken, to the moments we couldn't stop cracking up in class because a girl in our discussion group looked like she'd just applied a fresh layer of lipstick, which we assumed was because she had 'the hots' for our TA. Yet I did feel distinctly different than her in one way—I felt more attractive.

Of course, I never thought this consciously; it was similar to the unspoken feeling I had when I'd met her during orientation: a type of superiority, creeping silently along the back of our friendship as we stuffed our sweater pockets with muffins from the dining halls and snuck under the tarp of a fundraising tent in the middle of the night to scavenge through their goodies. Guys would sometimes show interest in me, striking up conversations while waiting in line at the dorm's cafe. Elana had been there sometimes to see it happen, and I always felt somewhat guilty that she seemed to receive less attention. In fact, not once did I see a guy approach her during those four years.

"That guy was a total asshole," she said in the car. We'd just left the diner we'd walked to after the bar, where we'd gotten coffee and scrambled eggs to sober up. I felt okay. Still a little buzzed, but I'd driven in worse conditions. During those couple of hours as we'd lounged in the booth, we'd stayed mostly silent. I'd been too focused on getting myself back together to even think about that bartender.

"Yeah," I said, making a careful left turn.

"I mean, he even asked you out just to like, be a dick to me. I can't believe I thought he was cute."

I nodded. "Yeah, I don't know... maybe he just wasn't into you, you know?"

"What do you mean?"

"I don't know. Never mind. That guy was a douche."

We were about twenty minutes from her place. I was taking all local streets, and starting to feel like maybe I should just pull over to sober up a while longer. But I kept going.

"Yeah, it's just me and you, you know?" She put her hand on mine, which was resting on the center console. I pulled it away.

I laughed awkwardly, but she didn't respond. As the silence in the car stretched, I began to feel, pressing between us, something unspoken.

Elana and I always had an on-going lesbian joke between us. We'd check each other out when one of us came in from the shower wrapped in towels and say something crude like, "Mmmm" or "Yeah, baby". Sometimes we'd blow kisses from across the classroom when other students were discussing topics with the TA. It was all just playful fun, much like the way we'd mimic the friendly girls on our floor who'd knock on our door and come in, saying an enthusiastic, 'heeeeyyy'.

Except that at one point when I'd been in Japan, Elana had told me, offhandedly through Facebook chat, that she thought one of her classmates was bi-sexual, and that Elana was 'curious'.

Curious, about what?

I don't know, just curious. Be yourself, right?

Nothing else had been said on this, but since then, I'd wondered if perhaps she'd been opening up to me. And I wondered this again as I drove us toward her house, the car quiet, the faint light of lampposts blinking slowly in and out through our windows along the dashboard. I'd turned on the radio after her strange gesture. Even though we'd joked about lesbianism in the past, neither of us had ever touched the other with any sort of affection. And I could feel it between us—something was off.

"Do you think you're like, better than me or something?" she said after some time.

We were stopped at a red light.

"What? What are you talking about?" Despite having sobered up to a large degree, I could feel the onset of a hangover already, rocking somewhere in my skull. A film of unbalance lingered before me.

"You always act like you're better than me," she said.

The light turned green.

"I don't know what you're getting at," I said, driving through the intersection. "Or where this is coming from."

"You know exactly what I'm talking about." Her voice was bitter.

The conversation didn't feel real. We'd always gotten along. I couldn't remember the last time—or if we'd ever—fought. She sounded serious, though. More serious than she'd ever spoken to me. I kept wondering—did she really have feelings for me? Or was this about something else... about that bartender, about all those guys over the years that passed their glance over her to look at me?

"You need to relax," I said.

She scoffed. "I'm not an idiot."

I shook my head again, wincing. "These are your words, not mine."

"Whatever," she said.

We drove for a short while. Then, glancing in the rearview mirror, I noticed that a police car had turned onto our street, following behind. I stiffened in my seat and gripped my fingers hard on the wheel, wondering if my breath still wreaked of alcohol.

"I know a shortcut," Elana said. "Turn left at this light."

The map on the navigation was telling me to continue straight, but I figured it'd be better to get away from this cop.

"Okay..." My hands were trembling, but just barely, a shiver running through my wrists. I'd just gotten hired as a school counselor; the last thing I needed was a DUI.

I was about to turn left but the light turned red, so I stopped. The police car crept up behind me. And then I saw the sign on the corner: One Way Street.

"What the hell?" I said. "This is a—"

"Oh sorry," she said. "I got it mixed up with another street."

"Right..." I said.

I followed the navigation the rest of the way home. We didn't say another word to each other. When we got to her place, I pulled up along her curb, and she got out and went into her house without a goodbye. And that was the last time I ever saw her.

A month later, she texted me, asking if I wanted to go to a bar. There was no mention of that night, as if nothing had even happened. I didn't know if I could trust her anymore. Was her telling me to turn into that one-way street an attempt to sabotage me? Or an honest mistake? Either way, it seemed that she'd always been hiding something from me—whether it was genuine feelings or resentment. Maybe, like all those profiles we'd created in the past, she, too, had been hiding behind a screen all these years, presenting to me who she thought I wanted her to be and never revealing her true self.

I replied saying that I was trying to quit drinking, which I was anyways. Thinking about our friendship then, I realized that all our bonding was based on guilty pleasures and self-destructive habits. We'd needed each other in college because we'd had no one else, because we'd had no responsibilities and no concern of the future. But I'd changed so much. Had she?

Four years have passed, but not a single word has exchanged between us since. Every once in a while I think about her, about all those times, those hours in our dorm room cracking up as we mercilessly sweet-talked strangers, raking them in like house money. I think about all the inside jokes, the shots we banged down, just the two of us. And remembering all the good times makes me wish there could be a future just like it, even though I know it's impossible. Best friends, gone in a whisper. Sometimes, though, I'll visit her social media pages and see what she's up to. There's hardly ever anything up, just a profile picture change every half year or so, her standing below a tree in a park or lying across the sand. And there, even though years have passed and I still haven't gotten myself to reach out again, to put some trust back into our old friendship, I send my best wishes to her in the silence.

About the Author:

Andy Tu is pursuing his first novel.

WHO YOU'RE DEALING WITH?

by Raymond Arcangel

Nothing ever looked like it did in the movies. No cozy warm lounge, a half-dozen chairs of leather and wood with their backs against the cream-colored walls, low mahogany table with magazines spread in a fan. No blithesome old secretary, her desk right there among you all, the interminable clacking of her typing slowing as she asked you if it was still as hot as an oven outside. This place was more reminiscent of a North Philly county assistance office: tile floor and drop ceiling with buzzing fluorescent rods, rows of hard plastic chairs facing a wall of bilious green. Twice in six weeks Ernie had sat staring at that wall—and the backs of the heads of the others, each silently seething—and it still made his stomach churn. To their right was a long counter, behind which the tops of three crimped, saffron hairdos were visible, chatting and answering unseen phones.

Before Olive had laid down the law—no more nookie until he stopped acting like a baby and made an appointment—it had been, what, well over a decade since his last time in a doctor's office? Perhaps there had been a time when they'd looked like the movie office; it was hard to say.

HMO's, a self-sustaining system. A maddening hour on the website and you needed a doctor, and a psychologist, and a dentist from the teeth-grinding. Olive had sat with him on the couch, calming him, navigating the site and reading reviews.

"This guy sounds good, baby," she'd said, clearly hoping against yet another veto. "He's right in Mayfair. You could just go into work a little late one day."

This was where she shined, situations where she got to be the adult, narrowing, effacing, the twenty-year difference in their ages. She had taught him how to file his taxes online, how to order a pizza on his cell without ever having to speak to an employee, and she would see to it that he saw to his health.

"I don't like his face."

"Oh, come on, Ernie. He's got four stars."

"He looks like a pervy assistant scoutmaster I used to know. Guy was always trying to show you wrestling moves and making weird jokes and breathing all over you. He tried to talk me into sharing his sleeping bag one night. Put me off camping for good."

"You're a man in his forties, not a sixth grader in danger of getting molested."

"You never know with these guys," he'd said, rubbing her pale knees, moving toward her denim cutoffs. "They get your pants off, get you hopping up on that table, wrapped in thin paper like a damn Christmas gift to themselves..."

"Ernie," she'd said, laughing, relenting, letting him take the laptop and set it on the coffee table. "This is important."

He guided her backwards, placing a throw pillow behind her head. She closed her eyes, exhaling audibly when his knuckles pushed against her warmth.

"I know, baby. So is this. This is the most important thing—"

"Mr. Bayag," one of the hairdos called in the general direction of the side of his face. He stood, finding none of the three revealed faces to be looking at him. After a long moment, the one in the middle—her flat gaze never moving from her desktop monitor—said, "You can go in back with Kim, honey, and she'll get you weighed and take your blood pressure."

The details of the first time were a bit hazy. You'd have to ask his mother. He wasn't sure if he'd ever had the story straight, hadn't thought about it much or put it into context until decades later. Their first apartment, that little two-bedroom on Knorr Street. He was a year old, his mother bathing him in the kitchen sink as she used to do. She reached over to flip on the light, her other hand in the water with him.

Was it that he too had felt the shock and cried out, but somehow it hadn't harmed him? Or was it that the shock had somehow not touched him at all? Whichever it was, in every retelling his mother had called it a miracle. She'd been knocked to the ground, the lights dimming, the hum that had run through her still ringing in her ears. She'd held him to her breast after, crying and rocking him and saying she was sorry again and again.

He sat on the leather examination table. He'd been weighed, had his vitals taken. His work boots were in the corner, his blue canvas jacket on a hook above them, but he'd been otherwise allowed to remain dressed. On the fourth floor of a six-floor, kidney-shaped medical center, he could hear the weekday sounds of the city below. Kim, the lovely Latina nurse, her red scrubs tight upon her ass like the skin of a cherry, she had given a slight tsk while reading his blood pressure.

"What, is it still high?"

"Actually it's a little better than last time. You been taking the meds?"

"Sure thing."

He had taken them for a week, stopping the instant they'd begun to turn his manhood into taffy. He'd rather have the high blood pressure.

His cell phone buzzed from somewhere within his jacket. It reminded him of a summer morning when he was a kid, the bedroom he shared with his older brother. A fat alien-looking wasp had gotten in and trapped itself between the two panes of glass above their old rickety air conditioner, droning and warbling and banging against the glass. Freeing it would've involved unscrewing the AC unit and holding it precariously above the concrete of their back alley two floors below while the other boy lifted the window. As his brother had said, one of them would've probably gotten a stinger in the hand for his trouble.

Hey there, Poppa Bear, the text read. Everything is gonna be fine, I know it. I just hope you ACTUALLY WENT. Love you.

Yes, Little Red Riding Hood. Where else would I be? Love you.

Who could say how many other times there had been, really? Routes driven home instead of other routes, blocks not walked down nights coming home from a bar, corners not turned. If you pulled back far enough, how many Mr. Magoo near-misses had there been? Even the incident that had led to this whole doctor thing could probably be listed among the almosts. About to gear up for a job, he'd just started up the warehouse staircase when everything went black. According to Matt, he'd suddenly collapsed, his upper back landing against the metal railing from shoulder to shoulder. He slid down, as perfectly as if it had been choreographed, his body crumpling at the bottom step and rolling to the floor. He'd gotten a bit bruised up, and he was embarrassed as hell, the guys standing around him, Lou splashing a Dixie cup of water in his face, but, hell—if he'd been higher up when it happened, he could have broken his goddamn neck.

But he hadn't been higher up. That's what his brother would've said. Would've told him that he looked too hard into things. He tried to find meaning in dumbass rock lyrics and he stared at things until patterns emerged. Some people turned down one street and met disaster and some people turned down another and did not. Some bugs forced themselves into a narrow crevice and got trapped and some flew right by, on to better things. It didn't mean shit. That's what his brother would've said.

There was no way of knowing how many windows he'd flown by, how many times he'd missed fate by a hair. But the second time, the second instance that had clearly been a thing, he was in his early thirties, working for a cardboard manufacturer way up in Huntington Valley.

He was one of the floor guys, the grunts, entire shifts spent taking the huge sleeves off the machine, binding them to pallets and wheeling them out to the dock. As was often the case over the course of his many jobs, he'd been friendlier with the folks up in the office, the reps and secretaries, the faces of the company.

The newly hired accounts manager was fresh out of college, a wife's cousin or something to one of the big bosses. Ernie found him a bit soft, but the kid had taken a liking to him after finding out he was a Vonnegut fan. There was something more than a little condescending in the wonderment he'd expressed—really? A commoner like him read Vonnegut?—but Ernie chose to not be insulted. Soon the kid was coming down and hanging around on the floor during lunch hour, or buzzing on the intercom for Ernie to come have a cigarette with him mid-shift. He was infatuated with Ernie's Philadelphia accent and working-class upbringing, adjusting his own speech patterns when they talked, laying on the curses and the comments about female bodies. For his part, Ernie mostly just laughed at the kid's jokes and nodded his head.

One night they got around to their long-planned drinks after work, in the back of a strip-mall spaghetti place between Somerton and Huntington Valley. The kid told him about every piece of ass he'd had, and which girls at the office he wanted to stick it to. Six Honey Browns sloshing around his gut, Ernie hit I-95 in his old Celebrity just after nine pm, regretting almost instantly not having visited the john before beginning the sixteen-mile drive.

By the Cottman exit he knew he was going to piss himself. Almost home, just a couple off-ramps to go, but holding it was like holding his breath, and the moment was coming when his body would do what it wanted and let go. Just beyond the Bridge/Harbison exit, the shoulder had been widened considerably, the result of some construction project that had been going on for as long as he could remember. He pulled over among the cones and barrels, throwing it into park with one hand and opening the door with the other, tearing at his jeans as he trotted to the concrete divider. It was one of those glorious, orgasmic pisses, clear as water. He looked to the autumn night sky, moaning, light traffic at his back.

He'd been back on the road for only a couple hundred yards when, after coming around a bend, he saw lights heading his way. They were higher up than his, clearly a truck of some make, and his first thought was that the vehicle had something to do with the construction. What the hell were these idiots doing, not even blocking off traffic before driving the wrong way down the highway? It was an old Ford pickup, slowing to thirty miles an hour as it passed him. Ernie tried to see into it, but the figure behind the wheel was cloaked in darkness.

"Real brilliant, jackass," he said to no one.

A quarter-mile down the road, he spotted a police cruiser pulled over to the shoulder, also facing the wrong way, and it began to dawn on him what he'd witnessed.

"Hey, I was worried about you," the woman he lived with in those years said, lifting her sleepy head from the couch, a Nick at Nite rerun on the television.

"Put on 3, 6 or 10. There's gotta be something about it. Some nut was going the wrong friggin' way on 95!"

"What?"

"He went right by me, as close as I am to you."

As soon as she clicked the remote, he saw the highway, shot from a helicopter.

"Jesus," his girlfriend said, lighting a Marlboro. "He must've been stoned."

The story, when all was said and done—an evening's worth of intense coverage followed by two or three nights of exponentially declining airtime; a few articles in the paper—would remain largely a mystery.

Gary Tomlin, twenty-eight, of Bridesburg, and his seventeen-year-old girlfriend, Amy Skurski, a senior at Little Flower High, were parked at a gas station on Richmond Ave when, for unknown reasons, Tomlin grabbed something out of an idling police car and fled. The officer, who'd been inside getting coffee, heard Tomlin peeling out, saw his own car door hanging open, and gave chase. He radioed for back-up as he tailed the pickup up and down the streets of Bridesburg and Port Richmond, Tomlin eventually barreling up the Richmond off-ramp.

The official police statement was that the officer had not followed once the truck had entered onto the highway.

Immediately after he'd passed Ernie's car, Tomlin had accelerated, witnesses stating he'd been going at least sixty miles per hour when taking the bend. His young girlfriend beside him, he plowed head-on into the car of Keisha Warner, a twenty-four-year-old mother of two. The women died on the scene, Tomlin succumbing a short while later. What he had taken from the cruiser was never stated, at least not in any of the stories Ernie read.

He was staring out the office window, listening to the traffic below. He almost dropped his phone when it buzzed again.

That's the wrong fairy tale, silly boy. Love you.

He could take anything but this damn waiting. Twenty minutes since Kim had said the doctor would be right in. Just bring it, doc. Grin that noncommittal, thin-lipped grin, exchange a few pleasantries about how he'd been feeling, how work was, blah blah, and then say it—what Ernie already knew he was going to say. Just goddamn bring it.

This was how his brother had gone, how he'd gotten word he was going. And their old man, too. Some office like this, both of them having been urged by women to go to the doctor, go to the doctor. Tests were run, follow-up appointments made. Time spent in the waiting room, and more time spent waiting in the examination room. But, eventually, the doctor came in, the grin got grinned, and what got said got said. And both of them, father and son, they decayed with alacrity, rushing to make the words real once they'd been spoken.

The door opened.

"Ernesto," Kim said, leaning in, her rear sneaker held slightly raised, ready to bolt once she'd delivered the message. "Doctor Murphy will be right with you, okay, hon?"

"Okay," he answered, moving away from the window, obeying the instruction given by her eyes and the tilt of her head that he retake his seat on the examination table.

"Just a few more minutes. You need anything, hon?"

"Nah. You want to wait with me maybe?"

She laughed and sucked her teeth. "You."

The third time he'd almost died was just a few years back, not long after he'd taken his current job with the industrial pest-control company.

Olive was one of the small group of telephone salespeople, cold-calling restauranteurs and other business owners, offering them a free inspection with one of their highly trained techs. Short punkish blonde hair, cruelly short skirts and tight blouses painted onto her thick-in-all-the-right-places frame, the word among Ernie's fellow techs—most of them at least a decade his juniors—was that she was unapproachable. Chuck, the phone room supervisor, would fax the next day's schedule over to the warehouse every afternoon, but Ernie began making a point of coming across the lot on his own. When word got around that he and Olive were becoming friendly—smoke breaks together behind the office building, grabbing lunch at the deli up the street—the guys were amazed.

"Ernie, no offense," Ronnie, a skinny twenty-something, said, his buddies chuckling and shaking their heads, "but you? Seriously?" Buzz-cut and sparse goatee, ugly green tattoos on his forearms and neck. Your typical Northeast Philadelphia white boy who both hated and emulated blacks. "Girly must have daddy issues."

"Shit, boy" answered Matt, the sole member of the crew older than Ernie and the guy who'd gotten him the job. "This is Ernie Bayag. You don't know who you're dealing with. You should've seen what this little bastard pulled in the old days."

They'd yet to go beyond talking, Olive and he. Mostly, she talked and he listened, offering advice or a joke when it felt right. Ronnie had been correct though: girly definitely had daddy issues. She had issues with her whole family, in fact, her father having abused her trust only slightly more than the others. But she was sweet and pretty and kind, bringing Ernie a batch of homemade escarole and meatball soup the day after he'd had to have his dog put down.

The company was two two-story buildings on a dead-end street of businesses off Keystone. There was a trucking company, a tool and die maker, a mammoth auto junkyard, and, at the end of the block, the pest-control company. Like the others, their lot was surrounded by a tall chain-link fence, the top garnished with rolling loops of razor wire like the spiky skeleton of a prehistoric eel. As protected against theft as they were at night, during business hours the gate, and the doors of both buildings, were left unlocked.

It was late afternoon when, having just returned from a job in South Jersey, Ernie parked his van and walked across the lot, Olive's Tupperware container in his hand, washed and ready to be returned. The ground floor of the office building held the cafeteria, bathrooms, a small conference room, and the office of the rarely seen owner of the company. Atop a wide staircase of lacquered wood was the phone room, which Ernie found empty. He'd later learn that the telesales crew had a great morning, filling up the schedule early. Olive had earned herself a twenty-dollar bonus for the most appointments and, along with the rest of the crew, the afternoon off.

He put the container on her desk and sat in her chair. Framed snapshots of her nieces, a prayer card from a favorite uncle's funeral, her Ron Burgundy coffee mug.

Something was happening outside, between the two buildings. Yelling, not of anger, but confusion and—fear. A voice—Matt's, Ernie was fairly certain—screamed for someone to call the cops. He went to the window at the rear of the room. His eyes fell first on Lou, the head tech, in the midst of an almost comic double-take, work boots skidding on the gravel, his big belly bouncing beneath his blue canvas shirt. Whatever humor the image held evaporated with the shot. It was like the splitting of a crisp piece of wood amplified by a cheap, tinny stereo speaker. Matt,

who in desperation had flattened himself against the wall of the office building, fell into Ernie's view. Another crack, and a cloud emerged from the stucco wall of the warehouse, a few feet above Lou's shoulder.

"April, no, no. I didn't have anything—"

He ran toward the narrow metal door, tripping as another cloud of white exploded above his head. The door opened and two canvas arms pulled him inside.

April walked slowly to the door and knocked, as calmly as a woman selling cosmetics. Early thirties, sickly thin, dressed in her usual of track pants and baggy t-shirt, her stringy bleached hair falling over her Martha Washington glasses. She'd been one of the telemarketers until earlier in the week when, after calling out yet again, Chuck let her go.

She'd not taken it well, calling back later that afternoon and begging Betty, the office apple polisher and Chuck's unofficial assistant, to please let her speak with him. Chuck wouldn't come to the phone, Betty informed her with polite glee. Ernie had gotten the whole story from Olive on one of their smoke breaks.

April turned from the metal door and started slowly toward the office building, putting another round into Matt's lifeless body as she passed.

911 had just answered when he heard April calling, almost sweetly, from the ground floor. Hello?

"911. What's your emergency?"

Her mane appeared on the horizon, ascending the wide steps. Ernie quietly put the receiver into the cradle and walked toward her, smiling, his hand extended in a friendly wave.

"Oh, my god—April. I heard they fired you. What the hell? Those idiots. You were, like, one of their best salespeople."

"Where's Chuck?"

"I don't know where that asshole is. I think he sent everybody home. You should sue. They can't just fire you like that."

She seemed to be struggling to match his warmth, like a shy kid not sure if she was being made fun of or not. The shiny revolver hung at her hip.

"Thanks. Betty's not here either?"

She moved to the older woman's desk, running the barrel of the gun along the grandmotherly cardigan slung over the chair.

"This isn't a damn coat room," she said to herself, lips contorting as she struggled against tears. "I like how she's always telling everybody, clean up after yourselves, clean the coffee machine."

"I know, right? Such a total bitch."

The phone on the rear desk went off in a loud, electronic trill, like a robotic bird that had been programmed to feel pain. April gave a low moan in commiseration.

"Who's that, you think?" She brought both hands to her head, the gun lying against her skull as she grabbed at her hair. "That about—what I did?"

She was unraveling. Her eyes locked onto his face. He could read the debate behind them like a news feed. What was the difference now? Take it all the way.

"We better get out of here, April."

"Oh, god. Oh, god." Her pale fingers turned purple as she gripped the gun harder, pointing it at his chest. "I'm sorry, Ernie. I messed up. Oh, god—Matt. I'm sorry."

He moved towards the stairs. Foot on the landing, he turned and waited for her.

"Come on, girl. Let's get the hell out of here."

When they reached the first level, she bolted, throwing open the glass door, running into the lot and through the gate. Hearing the sirens, she stopped, teetering on the road just before the perimeter of the company. As a cruiser pulled up to her, the roar of others on its heels, she put the gun to her heart and pulled the trigger.

Kim's instruction, dressed in good humor though it had been, was strong enough to keep him rooted to the examination table. He craned his neck toward the window, ears canine alert. Traffic,

yells and laughter, a group of teen girls singing a hip-hop song. He closed his eyes and saw Olive, walking ahead of him and looking over her shoulder. The backs of her legs, the small of her back. Her smile. Come on, mister...Oh, baby, wait up, wait up.

Fuck Kim's eyes. His teeth tearing at his bottom lip—slowly, perniciously, a friendly assault, we're all friends here, us body parts that attack each other—he went to the window. Blue sky, a hotel and a little mall across the street. Cars. The kids, still singing from somewhere below, would remain unseen.

The doctor they'd settled on, Olive and he, hip to hip like picking out floral arrangements or booking a room down the shore, was an older guy. Doctor Murphy. Big reddish nose, cherub cheeks, white hair, a beardless, somewhat less rotund Santa Claus. A guy who'd been around before the HMOs, before the six-floor medical centers shaped like a kidney. A guy who'd maybe once had a practice right off the street, up a few brownstone stairs, an office like the movie office. Olive read aloud his stellar reviews, which spoke of his years of experience, his personable nature.

Later that night Ernie had torn himself from the warmth of her body and gone back out to the parlor. On her laptop, he'd done some reading of his own. He knew the verdict, knew its name, before he'd ever set foot in the medical center. Doctor Murphy knew, or suspected, right away, too. The tests he'd ordered on Ernie's first visit were exactly the tests the website said would be run. It had all been right there on the web page, laid out like a recipe for gumbo. The headaches, the fainting spells—two more since the first, both of which he'd managed to keep from Olive—and, of course, the all-important family history. Thanks, Dad. Thanks for that. The headache yesterday, it had hit on the way back from a job in West Philly, so bad he'd pulled over and curled up in the back of the van, crying and begging.

You come in screaming and you go out screaming. That's what his brother had said, after they'd watched the old man wither like a time-elapsed film of rotting vegetables. No movie dignity. The old man had gone out bitching to the last, cursing, blaming God and everyone around him. Until the morphine took that last bit of fire.

Then he didn't even know their names, or his own name, or the name of any god to curse.

His brother had gone out better. His bravery may have been spite more than anything else, but he'd been brave.

"I can't even stand the occasional cold," Ernie said to himself, the windowpane against his forehead. "I'm going out the worst of bitches."

The door opened and there was the new and improved Kris Kringle's reflection in the glass, the naughty/nice list on a clipboard in his hands.

"Ernesto, hello," he said, grinning the tight-lipped noncommittal grin.

"Hey, doc."

"Have a seat."

All things must be said while you're on the leather table. You know that. We can't go further 'til you're on that table. Then don't get on that goddamn table, he imagined his brother saying with a cackle. Believe this: if I could do it over, I'd have never sat down.

"How have you been? How's work?"

Ernie sat, moved around, got comfortable, answered politely.

"Good. Now, we've got the results of your tests."

"Yeah, that was lucky, huh, that they were able to fit me in downstairs last time I was here? The woman said they can't usually see anyone on such short notice."

Bonham was playing "Moby Dick" inside his chest. The doctor smiled, gently. He adjusted the top sheet of the printout, a purely symbolic action, for the paper was held flat, trapped beneath the heavy snapping metal bar of the clipboard.

"Ernesto—"

"Please, doc—Ernie."

A banshee's bending cry tore the air. Damn good thing the windows were narrow and only opened inward, or the folks in the top floor psychiatric office would be hopping from the building like cliff divers. Ernie could barely endure it himself, painting on a smile so he didn't scream.

Kim came into the room, her eyes a tacit question about procedure.

"I'm sure it's just a false alarm," the doc said loudly, his hand on Ernie's shoulder, ushering him toward the door. "Keep everybody calm, Kim, and lead them to the stairs. I'm sure it's just a false alarm."

The enclosed staircase—cinder block walls the color of coffee ice cream, with drippings on the stairs, like the job had been done by a claustrophobic whose main concern was getting the hell out of there—was abuzz: people young and old, some obviously patients, others in lab coats or scrubs, and others still in the business casual of the medical administrative branch. The alarm wailed the entire way down, each rise and fall another call to panic, but the marchers, Ernie among them, maintained composure, looking at the backs of the person in front of them, more joining the stream at each turned corner.

The door let out at the rear of the building. Just before the curve, there was a similar door, with a similar stream of people exiting from it.

Ernie ran his eyes over as much of the building as he could see, looking for smoke or flames. A fire engine pulled silently onto the lot, rolling with the slow, desultory air of a giant awoken for no good reason. Waiting for word that it was safe to go back in, people were chatting, smiling, an exciting little break in their day. Doctor Murphy and his nurses stood off to Ernie's right. Santa and his lady elves.

He took a step back, watching them recede just a little. Another step, the doctor now all but obscured by a heavy-set man in a janitor's uniform. A third step, nearly tripping over a concrete parking bumper. He turned on the balls of his feet, toward the curve of the building and the avenue beyond it.

Olive was on a call, chair toward the window, the chord from her headset tethering her to the desk. Bare legs crossed one over the other, pen tapping against her chin, like she'd been set there from above for his viewing pleasure.

"Next Tuesday? Yes, sir. Our tech can be out at...two-thirty. Is that good? Okay, great. And keep in mind, sir, we're currently offering one-third off for anyone who signs up for monthly checkups on the first visit."

He returned Betty's plastic smile and sat on the edge of Olive's desk, making faces at her and grabbing her hands as she slapped at him. When the call was completed, she sighed and searched his eyes.

"Well, how did it go?"

"Fine."

"Fine. What did they say, Ernie?"

"Nothing to worry about, ma'am. Doc said I might be working a bit too hard. Take it easy, get some more sleep. You know."

"Yeah, baby?"

"Yeah, momma. We're good."

About the Author:

Raymond Arcangel writes and works crap jobs in the Fairmount section of Philadelphia, between the Art Museum and the Eastern State Penitentiary, which seems oddly appropriate. His short fiction has appeared in the Concho River Review and an anthology of the Silver Pen awards.

REVELATIONS OF TEN-YEAR-OLD

by Saul Hernandez

Every Sunday I walk with Him. I knock door to door with Brothers and Sisters from the Jehovah's Witness Congregation. It usually goes like this: we arrive around eight in the morning to the assigned streets, we then divide ourself into groups and go two by two, just like the animals that stepped into Noah's Ark, to spread the word of Jehovah and his promised kingdom. Brother Aguirre says that we are doing good by bringing the word of God right to people's front door. But they don't always answer. Other times they open the door and see us and bam, they slam it on us; I wondered what it must be like to be able to close the door on something you don't believe in.

Sometimes I day dream at church, I break the silence in the room with my laughter. I offend Brother and Sisters of the congregation who are giving a speech or the ones listening. My father looks at me and with his eyes whipping me again and again.

As if I'm not punished enough, at school I can't even participate in fun things. I've had the same teacher since I was in the third grade and she has moved with my class all the way to fifth grade so she knows what I can and cannot do. My parents remind her at the beginning of each year that I cannot participate in birthdays, holidays, say the pledge of allegiance or anything that would be praising something that isn't God.

Mrs. Balderrama sends me to the reading corner when these activities take place My parents don't know I read about magic, time traveling, people choosing their own destiny, or about worlds that exists outside of this realm, like the "promise kingdom."

I read all the The Magic Tree House series in the reading corner, but when I finished all 24 books that my teacher had bought I was sad that I couldn't figure out what came next, so I made up my own ending where Jack and Annie, alongside Morgana, destroy the time machine and stop traveling across places and time, and they live a normal life creating and choosing their own paths; yeah, that would be nice, choosing your own destiny.

I found the Harry Potter series in that reading corner too. It was while my class recited the pledge of allegiance. This dictionary type book caught my eye. I took it home with me because I needed to find out about Harry's destiny. Except his destiny was destroyed when my mother caught me reading it under the covers. My parents burned the book. They said I could not get sucked into the life of magic, people with powers, and wizards, Jehovah would not approve of this. I yelled and said, "The Bible is full of magic!" When has someone heard of a burning tree talking to you or a man with the power to split a sea or even walk on water. My parents didn't care. They were only following what the church had taught them: to fear the unknown.

The next day at school I was embarrassed to tell Mrs. Balderrama about the book. I waited until the end of the school day to tell her about Harry's tragedy. I cried and told her I could pay her for the book by cleaning her desk or cleaning the classroom. I apologized to her with every sentence I said. At first her eyes were firm and full of fire, her eyes had a different look from the one that my father gives me, but then she cried with me. This was the first time I had ever seen an adult cry.

In church we learn to love all people no matter what. I think this is a lie too. When a person didn't want to hear Brother Aleman preach at their door the Brother Aleman got red like a kettle and you could almost see the steam coming out of his ears and nose. It happened to brother Ibarra too. Except he stomped off of the persons lawn and stepped on the side flowers by the gate. I felt bad for the flower, it had nothing to do with the owner only the Brother's anger. It was just there being a flower, is this how God looks at us, as only flowers in a garden waiting to be stepped on?

They also tell us at church that God is always watching us. I think of myself as an observer too. I wonder if he's been keeping a close eye on me. I think he's on to me.

About the Author:

Saul Hernandez is currently a student in the Bilingual MFA in Creative Writing at UTEP. His work has been featured in The Rio Grande Review, labloga.blogspot.com, xicanation.com, and in The Brillantina Project. He's also the current Director for Barrio Writers at Borderlands in which, alongside other volunteers, teach a one-week free writing workshop for the youth in the community, so that at the end they may submit their work and get published in a yearly anthology through Stephen F. Austin State University Press.

THE LADY OF THE HOUSE

Dennis J. Dymek

No one quite remembered anymore when Bob and Emily Taylor had moved into their remote cottage on the outskirts of town. Everyone knew, however, they must have once been deeply in love. Why else would Bob have taken care of his slightly invalid wife by himself for so many years? It wasn't as though she had any kind of debilitating illness that required constant medical attention or one, that kept her from joining any of the town's social circles. To hear Bob tell it Emily had a withered leg from a prolonged childhood bout with polio and had always been self-conscious about appearing in public. Even as a young woman Emily was a reclusive sort. That suited Bob just fine as he himself was rather shy and rarely showed himself except when doing errands like picking up the mail at his post office box in town or doing the shopping at the local grocery store. Occasionally, he went to the town festivals.

They lived in Roaring Brook Cottage, (that's the name they had given their house) and had for the last twenty years. An entire generation of the town's kids had grown up and there were only a few of the older folks remaining who remembered when he first announced that he had taken a bride after visiting some relatives who lived way up "down east" along the Maine coast.

Bob had recently started to exhibit the first signs of dementia. His wife having died two years ago, he sometimes forgot that she was no longer among the living. It was small things at first: like when he went shopping. He might find that he had almost forgotten something that Emily would have especially wanted, like a certain type of soap or a particular type of cheese that she liked. He would suddenly remember that he had forgotten to get the particular item she would have wanted. He would think to himself, I'm glad I remembered that. Emily would be upset. She's so good I hate it when she's disappointed at something I forgot to get.

Sometimes, he wouldn't remember until he was in his car and about to leave. He would turn off the engine and go back into the store to pick up the forgotten item. At the check-out counter, he would say, "I'm glad I remembered this. Emily would wonder how I could have forgotten and take it personally. Oh, she won't say anything, but I've been with her long enough to know that I let her down."

Sally the check-out lady would look at Bob a little strangely. She would think, 'He's gotten a lot older since Emily passed away. I bet he's really lonely now. But where's the harm? He's just gotten so used to Emily's ways they have just become a habit, like a cow that comes in from the fields knows which stall is hers. Well, it's no wonder and besides, it's none of my business'

One day Bob was seen down at the hardware store. Phillip Grant was in the back of the store and in the process of restocking some of the shelves when he heard the small bell tinkle announcing the arrival of a customer.

"Hey Bob. How are you doing? Haven't seen you in a dog's age. What can I do for you?"

"That old vacuum cleaner we've had forever finally gave out. Emily sent me down to pick up a new one. Said it couldn't wait and I better go right away. I guess most women are like that. Can't stand a house that's untidy and isn't just to their liking."

"Ya. Funny how women are like that. God bless 'em, though. We'd probably turn our homes into pig-sties without them."

Phillip then remembered that Emily had died about two years back, but he thought, 'Heck, if I'm talking like she's still alive, well it's not that surprising that he's gotten into the habit of knowing that Emily would have sent him down right away'.

Bob automatically gave the standard reply

"Ya, it's funny how you get so used to them. Say, by any chance do you have a good one that's not too expensive but that's well made and is going to last? A fixed income can only go so far every month."

"You're in luck, Bob. I just got a consignment of a couple of new G.E. models and they offered a discount for a floor model. Don't have much room for a floor model, though. Let's see; I could pass on the discount to you. How would that do?"

Phillip showed him the price and Bob gave out a little whistle.

"Prices sure have gone up over the years. I must have paid half that amount for my old one."

"I bet. It's that darn inflation. Seems like the government can't ever do anything to keep it under control."

"I wish they wouldn't keep my pension check under control. Small chance of that happenin', I suppose."

"Not likely."

"How's the quality? Emily can't get around like she used to and doesn't take kindly to vacuuming the same spot twice."

Phillip thought, 'He's beginning to go downhill. I guess I'll have to tell everyone to keep an eye on him. If he gets much worse, I suppose we'll have to call Doc Wilson to see what's to be done with him.'

"It's a G.E. and made right here in the U.S. not like some of those foreign imports. You can be sure the quality is good and it's goin' to last."

"Hmm. If you say it's good quality then I'm sure that will please Emily."

"Speaking of Emily, how's she doin'? Never see her around." Phillip wanted to see just how far his faculties had deteriorated.

"Like I said. She's getting on like the rest of us. Her bum leg sure as heck ain't goin' to get any better. She's a real trooper, though. Never complains; just goes on with her business. Other than the leg she as healthy as can be expected. Won't see a Doctor. Says she doesn't believe in 'em and that they generally do more harm than good anyways."

"She's probably right. Once they've got you in their clutches, it's tests and more tests. Let me get the box with the vacuum cleaner. It's still in the back."

The transaction completed, they wished each other and their families well.

The noise from the new vacuum cleaner was noticeably less than the old one. "What do you think Emily? Looks like it's doing a fine job cleaning."

Emily just smiled with that slight smile she always showed when she agreed with her husband.

"How about I take a turn just to see how well it works and after that, maybe we can have some lunch together. How does that sound?"

Emily, once again, just looked at Bob and smiled.

He had grown to love that smile. One day he had taken her to a professional photographer to have her portrait taken for their 10th anniversary. Her smile was at once beautiful and yet, mysterious. It was simple and straightforward and yet it seemed to hold many deep and unexpressed thoughts.

He had two different pictures taken. One was downstairs on the table where the telephone was at the bottom of the stairs. He liked to look at her picture when he was talking on the phone. The other was placed on the bedside table that lay between the two beds upstairs. Ever since Emily had died, he had grown used to looking at them more and more until sometimes he would talk to the pictures and ask how Emily thought about his doing this or that.

Towards the evening after supper, he would take out his pipe and sit on the rocking chair opposite Emily's picture. When Emily was still alive, they would sit and talk about things that old married couples talk about. Mostly, though, they would just sit quietly and listen to the sounds of the house.

The house as its name implied was situated next to Roaring Brook. An old refurbished farmhouse, it was close enough so that they could hear the bubbling noise of the dark shadowy water flowing over the half hidden rocks. It was a very soothing sound and it complemented the slow regular ticking of the grandfather clock. It was a quiet house, like Bob and Emily were. The two sounds were so restful and continuous it seemed to Bob that they would go on forever. It gave the pair a comforting notion that God was looking down upon them and was giving them His blessing here on earth.

Every night when Bob was getting ready to go to bed he would look over at Emily's picture and softly tell her that he still loved her like the first day they met. He then said a little prayer thanking God for all the good things and the good life he bestowed upon them.

The next day Bob made breakfast, cleaned the pans and dishes and had a smoke. Everything that needed to be done, Bob already finished. On occasion Emily liked Bob to go to the library and pick out a book for her. She wouldn't give him a specific title. She knew that Bob knew her tastes well enough that she was confident enough to let him surprise her.

 What Emily never knew was that he relied entirely upon the Librarian, June, to pick out a book that she knew Emily would enjoy. He looked at the clock It was only eleven and the library didn't open until twelve. For some reason he became impatient as he waited and smoked. He thought. "I know that Emily is no longer here in person and so how could she be so impatient to read a book?"

It was a ten minute drive to town and the library. Bob couldn't wait any longer and left at twenty minutes to twelve and parked in front of the library, waiting for it to open.

June Barstow was right on time as usual She noticed Bob parked along the sidewalk and waved to him. She gave Bob a welcoming smile, then took the keys out from her purse and wiggled them at Bob to indicate that he could come in now.

The Marshal Field Memorial Library is a rather odd structure for a library. It was endowed by Marshall Field who inherited a fortune first meant for his brother who died too early to inherit it and so it was passed on to Marshal who grew up in Conway and attended the Pumpkin Hollow Elementary School.

It's an odd structure because it looks like a cross between a State Legislature building with two wings and a bank. It even has a dome atop it. However, it is far too small to be either. It looks like a miniature model of them. This characterized Conway itself, It's small, a bit quirky and yet quaint.

The interior, though, was warm, and like June, welcoming. The mid-day light splayed a dusty yellow glow of light onto the bookshelves and the marble floor.

Bob went up to the desk that June was just then sitting down behind. She began looking for some papers she was planning to work on that day. She looked up, saw Bob in front of the desk and smiled,

"Good Afternoon Bob. I haven't seen much of you since Emily passed away. What can I do for you?"

"You have always been so kind in picking out the books that Emily liked. I was wondering in you could pick out another book. I'm not going to read it myself. I'll just put next to where she sat and read downstairs. I guess one might call it a tradition."

There was no one else in the library and as she went to the particular bookshelf where she always went to get Emily's books, June felt free to talk.

"Hmm. Let me see . Ah! Here's one she might have liked." She handed it to Bob but continued.

"Bob, How are you doing these days? I mean you must get a little lonely once in a while."

"I guess so. I've known Emily for such a very long time, I often forget that she isn't still with us.. Don't tell anyone as I don't want everyone to thing that I'm losing my marbles, but I find myself talking to her or to her pictures once in a while."

"I wont. I find myself talking to Jim once in a while myself and he passed away almost five years ago."

Bob looked around to see that no one had come into the library.

"When you come to think about it, it's not really all that crazy. People talk to God don't they? And Philosophers, I suppose, talk to the ancients like Plate or Sophicles and ask them what they thought about certain problems they've been thinking about. I've asked for Emily's opinion on so many things over the years about how to go about doing this or that, that it's become a deeply ingrained habit."

June replied, "You know Bob, that's the best explanation I've heard so far. I'd like to hear more what you think about. It might sound a little silly, but I've been wanting to ask you over to dinner for sometime. It's been ages since I cooked for a man and I hate to say it but I actually miss it. I think I miss the conversation during and after the meal the most. What do you say? Would you like a nice home cooked meal?"

"Thanks for the kind offer June. Give me a little time to think about it and let men see how Emily might feel about it. Why don't you write down your home number and I'll call you tomorrow and let you know?. How's that?'"

"That would do just fine. I'll be available this Saturday if you don't have anything planned."

"OK. I'll call tomorrow. I guess that's all I need right now."

When Bob got home, he immediately filled his pipe and rather than sitting down started pacing back and forth. It wasn't like he didn't admire June's looks and down to earth type of thinking.

He did. He had known her all his life and knew her about as well as anyone in town.

They engaged in a playful type of banter at times during the various town festivals when he would run into her. The festivals were small affairs and one pretty much met all the people in town at them. Emily rarely attended them.

Bob always felt slightly guilty when he enjoyed his meeting up with June and having such a good time. He felt like he was somehow "cheating" on Emily. It was no wonder then that he now paced back and forth, undecided what to do.

"i wonder what Emily would think about my accepting a dinner date with another woman, especially June." The few times Emily went to the library with Bob, she could plainly see there was a kind of bond between them. She had become a little jealous of her.

Bob thought to himself, "Normally I'd know just what she was thinking as though she were talking to me. But now, now matter how hard I try to know what she would think, all I get is silence."

Bob went out for a walk. He thought that might clear his mind and give him some type of signal as to what to tell June. Still there was nothing forthcoming. He returned home and removed his hat and coat and listened to the clocks tick, tock, tick tock.

He sat down again and finally decided, "Well if Emily won't give me any advice, then she must be saying, 'It up to you what you want to do. You're free to choose what you want."

Bob surprised himself when he decided that Emily's non-response was in fact Emily's apparent blessing. Nevertheless, he wasn't the sort who just rushed into such possibly momentous changes in his life. He made supper, cleaned up and only then finally called June.

"Hello June? I thought about your offer and I've decided to accept, if you're still willing."

"How would seven on Saturday do? Just wear the clothes you always wear. We've known each other long enough, we don't have to be formal."

"Seven sounds fine. I'll see you then."

June was ten years younger than Bob. She only recently turned fifty six. Remarkably, she still retained her good looks. She was never a beauty, but she always had a ready smile and friendly disposition towards everyone. It made her appear to look prettier than she really was.

June looked out the kitchen window when she heard a car stop in front. When Bob got out and knocked on the door, June called out, "The door's unlocked. Come on in and make yourself comfortable. I'll be right out. I'm just finishing with the gravy."

When Bob came into the house he was greeted by a nicely decorated two-floor farm house. She lived in it ever since she married Jim and raised her two children there. The wooden floors and the warmth that came from the wood stove gave the house a simple cozy presence.

The table in the dining room had a new tablecloth over it. The plates and utensils were set out. There was a candle in the middle of the table along with a small flower arrangement.

"Wow!" Jim thought. "June's really gone out of her way." He felt a slight tingly feeling spread through him and now that he had Emily's blessing, he was nonetheless surprised not to feel any guilt, just the expectation of an unusual and pleasurable evening with a desirable woman.

June came out of the kitchen with a bowl of salad. Bob thought she looked perfect in her thin white sweater and black cotton dress that loosely fell to her knees. She had done up her hair a little and put on some basic simple makeup.

She laid the bowl on the table and greeted Bob, "Hi Bob. I'm so happy you could come. Would you like to start dinner right away? I know it's probably already a little late for most folks."

"Sure let's just start in. I'm pretty hungry and made only a light lunch so I wouldn't spoil my appetite."

They talked mostly about the funny incidents that occurred in the town over the years. Bob was in High School when June was just a child.

"How are your kids doing June?"

"Oh, the two finished College some time ago and moved to the big city. Jim Jr. is in New York now,

still single and Cathy is married with a little girl. She's living with her husband just outside Boston, so it's not too far for them to visit or on the other hand for me to visit them, not that it happens as much as I'd like. They have their own lives to live and I'm just an intrusion."

"I doubt that you could be an intrusion on anyone, let alone on your children and your grandchild."

"I try to keep a low profile when I do visit. That brings up the subject; did you ever want any children of your own?"

"I guess we did, but once Emily had that surgery, I was just happy she survived. After the surgery, the Doctors said it would be too dangerous for her to have a child. We thought of adopting a couple of times, but for some reason, we never got around to it. By then we had just got used to each other's company so much a child would have changed things too much. We finally accepted the idea of just being together ."

"Well enough of that for the moment. Let me bring out supper."

June brought out a typical homemade New England supper. It consisted of a roast beef with gravy, fresh steamed green beans and mashed potatoes.

"Would you like to carve the roast Bob?'"

"Sure. I always like doing that."

After dinner, June put the dishes away and brought out a freshly made Apple pie. It was Bob's favorite.

"June, I have to hand to you. That's the best dinner I've have in some time."

"I'm glad you liked it. Would you like to sit by the stove. I don't mind if you smoke your pipe."

"That sounds real inviting."

June put on a tape of old favorite songs, sung by Frank Sinatra and Bing Crosby and Andy Williams. They sat next to one another on the couch facing the wood stove. They were still reminiscing when June turned toward Bob and said.

'You know Bob, I haven't cooked or slept with a man since Jim died." She paused waiting for Bob.

"I haven't dated or slept with a woman since Emily died. Are you by chance asking that I share your bed tonight?"

"I suppose I am, but I was hoping for a little more than just sharing my bed."

"You know, I think I'd like that, -a lot."

"Do you think you could wait while I get ready? I'll call down to you when I am."

"O.K."

June was more than just ready when she called Bob to her bed. She pleasured Bob like he had never been before. It was more than he ever could have imagined and he fell asleep exhausted but with a grin on his face. He felt like a teenager who had just had sex for the first and second time.

They rose in the morning. June looked over at Bob. "Do you think you're up for seconds?"

Bob laughed a little.. "If this morning is anything like last night, I'm sure you'll be able to get me in the mood."

Bob left after breakfast. He felt a changed man. Everything tasted better. He enjoyed the cold air as he left and went to his car. The town looked different-

When Bob got home he walked upstairs and gave the picture of Emily a little kiss. He thanked her for her understanding and blessing. He unconsciously returned to his old ways of talking to Emily, however. In Bob's mind she was still there as real as ever since she had died.

He was a little unstable walking at times. He was going over the events last night at June's as he was descending the staircase. He tripped and fell and either broke or sprained his ankle. He also hit his head against the banister as well. The phone was on the table at the bottom of the stairs and because he didn't want to alarm Emily, he steadied himself on the table that held the second picture of Emily. He was able to call the Fire Department, but his words were slightly slurred

"Hi. This is Bob Taylor. I just fell down the stairs and I think I may have broken my ankle. My wife never did learn how to drive. Do you think you could send someone up and take me to the hospital?"

It took about fifteen minutes for the ambulance to arrive and when they knocked on the door they heard Bob shout out to them to come in; the door was unlocked.

The EMT's had been alerted to Bob's growing dementia and they had started a small file on him. They felt this was the perfect time for a psychologist to evaluate him while he was in the hospital. They opened the door and wheeled in a gurney, then gently lifted him up and secured Bob to it.

"Say Bob, where's your wife? While we're here, maybe we should see how's she's doin'. It's been a long time since any of us have seen her. Come to think of it, I don't remember ever having seen her."

"Oh. If you look out the back you'll see the cross on her grave that I made. There's a picture of her on the table. Doesn't she have a beautiful smile? She's still the lady of the house, you know.

Epilogue

Bob had to undergo surgery. No one knew if it was the stress of the surgery or the drugs they gave him for the pain or whether it was the knock on the head when he fell, but Bob's dementia quickly increased. He often wandered off into the past and would frequently ask when Emily was going to come and see him.

June came to visit him. She could hardly believe this was the same man she had over for dinner jut a couple of days ago. He was now experiencing short term memory loss and her couldn't remember having had dinner with her. It was almost as though she had lost another husband, though she knew that was crazy. Still she felt a remorse at what might have been. On the other hand, she also thought, maybe it was for the best.

Bob never returned home. He was eventually sent to a nursing hospital, where he spent the rest of his days.

HARD COAL

Terry Sanville

Two sisters climb the mine road that disappears into the hills above Cumbola, Pennsylvania. Their breaths smoke in the early light as they struggle through waist-deep snowdrifts. The wind tears at their coiled hair, causing tears to stream down flat cheeks from wide-spaced eyes.

"Why do I always have ta carry the bucket?" Gert complains

"Quit yer gripin'," Julia replies. "Mama put me in charge, and besides, I'll be carryin' it home when it's fulla coal."

Halfway up the slope they stop to brush snow from their mittens. Below them, the bells of Saint Anthony's announce the end of sunrise mass. They hurry onward. In a short while they too are expected to kneel in their Sunday best for communion.

At the top of the ridge, the road drops into a stream-cut valley. In places, the maples and oaks have been cleared, exposing abandoned mineshafts and water-filled stripping pits to the leaden sky.

"What about around that strippin'?" Gert points.

"Nah, we picked 'er clean weeks ago – and the last time ya fell in and almost drowned."

"I hardly got wet. You worry too much… just like Mama."

Julia glares at her younger sister and pushes past the black pool, partly covered with dirty ice. "There be nobody about at the Number 8. We'll try there."

"But the watchman?"

"He'll be too drunk to catch us. Come on."

At a massive black oak, still clutching its dead leaves, the sisters take off through the woods and creep to the edge of the colliery. The camp is deserted. But smoke pours from the chimney pipe of the watchman's shack next to the washhouse.

"He's in there," Gert whispers, "will see us for sure."

Julia frowns and thinks about their brother, just a year older than she and fighting the Boche somewhere in France. Chester would have come with them to help. Before the war, Papa and he dug hard coal from the seam in back of their house and didn't need to scavenge from the culm banks. Then the black lung and a Black Maria took Papa away.

"Come on, and be quick about it," Julia orders.

"You go first. I'll wait here till you're inside."

Julia's face splits wide with a grin, showing strong teeth. "You're such a sissy."

"Just be quiet. I'm the one that watchman will come after." Gert turns up her nose and looks away.

Julia sighs, knowing her sister is right. At sixteen, Gert's trim waist and well-proportioned figure far outshines Julia, who is built like a tough little teapot, short and stout. She dashes from the trees, skirts an iced-over strippin', and runs full tilt into the black mine entrance. Turning, she peers across the clearing at the watchman's shack. Something moves behind one of its windows, at least she thinks it does. She waits in the shadows, her heart thumping. A cardinal calls loudly from the trees, a spot of brilliance in the winter gloom.

Smoke drifts upward from the shack. The cold settles into Julia's shoulders. She steps to the opening and waves Gert on. Her sister moves forward with a hip-swinging gait that cuts a trough through the powdery snow.

"Ya walk like some Philadelphia harlot," Julia says when Gert reaches her.

"How would you know? You've never been beyond these hills."

"Chester has...told me stories."

"Let's just fill this darn bucket and get home. I can hardly feel ma feet."

Julia pulls a candle from her coat and lights it. The sisters follow the tracks into the mountain, stopping to retrieve rocks fallen from the coal cars on their way to the breaker. As a little girl, Julia used to take her father his lunch in a tin pail. She knew the other Polack miners, remembers their exhausted faces and dark staring eyes, the hopelessness of their coal-cracker families. She dreams of escaping to New York City, to work as a cook, to buy a train ticket west, far from these freezing winters, coal, and the company store.

"Whatcha moonin' about?" Gert asks.

"Oh, nothin'. Did ya ever think about leavin' this place?

"No. Mama needs us now more than ever."

"I mean, after Chester comes home."

"I figure, there's plenty of good men in these parts to marry. Why should I leave?"

"Well, I don' want no man of mine gettin' kilt working for the companies."

"Man of yours? Hah." Gert chuckles and dumps a fist-sized lump into the almost-full bucket. Julia staggers under its weight but keeps moving. They work fast, the effort warming their bodies.

Stopping to catch her breath, Julia notices that the light from the mine entrance momentarily dims. "Hush, now. Someone's there," she whispers.

"It's the clouds blockin' the sun."

"No, it ain't. I just..."

Footsteps advance toward them. Julia blows out the candle and they slip into a black side room. Crunching steps move nearer.

"I know you's in here," a man's voice calls.

Gert grabs Julia's arm and squeezes hard. Julia puts a hand over her sister's mouth and whispers in her ear, "Quiet."

The footsteps stop. The watchman strikes a match, lights a lantern, and sets it on the ground. He's no more than a dozen paces away, a grizzled figure hunched in heavy wool. Julia sees his narrow eyes focus, then widen. "Hey you two, come over here."

"Run!" Julia hollers and dashes past the man with her sister following.

The watchman whirls and grabs onto Gert's arm. "Not so fast, darlin'," he says, snickering.

"Let her go," Julia cries.

"Not before I teach her a lesson." He bends and mashes his greasy face into Gert's. She screams.

"Leave her alone," Julia mutters. "Ya can have me."

The watchman stares at her and laughs. "What would I do with a stumpy little girl like you?"

Without speaking, Julia slowly raises her skirt to expose white winter bloomers. The man releases Gert and advances.

"Run Gert, get outta here," Julia snaps.

Her sister whimpers and dashes for the mine entrance.

Julia smells him, his breath strong with hooch, his body stinking of coal dust mixed with old sweat. He reaches for her. Julia swings her left arm and smacks him alongside the head with a chunk of anthracite. The watchman yelps. She sprints down the tracks toward the light, her high-laced boots slamming against the crossties. Outside in the blinding snow, she heads for the trees. He catches her at the edge of the strippin'.

"You're a feisty little thief, aren't ya," he says, laughing. He surrounds her with his arms and pulls her body to his.

"Leave me alone, you…"

From behind him, Julia sees Gert's slender hands grasp a huge lump of coal and bring it down on the watchman's head. He grunts, his arms go slack and he staggers backward. Without hesitation, Julia shoves him over the edge. He falls headfirst into the strippin', breaking through its thin ice. He surfaces once, hands clawing at air, at ice shards, at the last vestiges of his life. Then he's gone and the pond's surface quiets once again. In her mind, Julia sees his body settle into the muck where the bluegill and catfish will feed on this unexpected meal. She shudders and covers her face with her hands.

"Come on," Gert pleads, sniffling loudly. "Let's get home."

"Yes, yes… but the bucket." Julia races back into the mine and returns with their costly prize. The sisters stagger up the road, clutching the handle between them. They don't pause until reaching the ridge top. Below, windswept Cumbola is quiet in its Sunday reverie.

"You gonna tell Mama?" Gert asks finally, her voice small in the cold air.

"Only if they come for us. We best hurry to church. I need to confess before communion."

"What we done weren't no sin," Gert says through tight lips.

"Maybe not. But I can chance it with the law, not with God."

"They'll find him tomorrow." Gert sighs and pulls her coat tight.

"No they won't. That pond 'll freeze over tonight and by spring he'll be…"

The sisters go silent and slowly hobble downhill, the coal bucket cutting a furrow between them in the soft white snow.

About the Author:

Terry Sanville lives in San Luis Obispo, California with his artist-poet wife (his in-house editor) and one skittery cat (his in-house critic). He writes full time, producing short stories, essays, poems, and novels. Since 2005, his short stories have been accepted by more than 230 literary and commercial journals, magazines, and anthologies including The Potomac Review, The Bitter Oleander, Shenandoah, and Conclave: A Journal of Character. He was nominated twice for a Pushcart Prize for his stories "The Sweeper," and "The Garage." Terry is a retired urban planner and an accomplished jazz and blues guitarist – who once played with a symphony orchestra backing up jazz legend George Shearing.

HOOK MAN

Michael Warren

"That's bull-shit! There's no such thing as a Hook Man." Inky was quite certain on this point. "That's just a story."

There were five of them: Martin, Teeter, Paz, Inky and Tom. The boys met on the old suspension bridge over the river, then moved to the swing tower in the city park. There were six swings hanging on chains from a tripod made of welded irrigation pipe. The swings were made for younger children, not for soon-to-be high school freshmen. The boys stood on the seats, pumping until they were upside down at the peak of their arc, then twisted and released in a chaotic top-spinning furry.

Few used the park, especially after dark. It was a good place to hang out on a summer evening, lit only by a few weak yellow argon lights. Some concerned parents wanted to close the park at night and chain off the entrance. The Mayor argued that a chain would not keep people out and would complicate the jobs of the city employees. It would also eliminate a favorite early morning rest stop for the lone night cop.

The town was small. This was rare free space where young boys could hang out un-observed. Everywhere else everyone saw everything. Here the boys could smoke their dad's stolen cigarettes and talk constantly. Ideas sprouted like weeds. They straddled that boarder between children and young adults, still entitled to be ridiculous while exploring thoughts and ideas not wholly adult, on the edge of adolescence. This was a dangerous age.

"My brother showed me a scratch on the car door from the Hook Man's hook. He said you have to lock your doors when you go out to Hook Bend to park. You have to leave quick when you hear him so he doesn't break the windows. He always tries to get the girls first." Paz was fully invested in the Hook Man legend.

"That's bull-shit. Besides, who's gonna go park with your brother. He don't have a girlfriend, how would he know"

"No, its not! I heard it! One of the seniors said he found a hay bail hook hanging from his bumper!"

"I heard they think the Hook Man is actually the old Holdeman Twins, that there are two of them." Tom had now entered the debate. "They do it because they were both in love with the same girl, and she got shunned and killed herself, and now they want to kill anyone who has a girlfriend because they never can. It makes sense."

The Holdemans were a religious sect similar to the Amish, locked in a time past, disdaining ornamentation and education beyond the required age of sixteen. Mostly farmers, they stood apart form modern life. Their church was located several miles from the distractions of town, among the fields beyond which they saw no need to venture.

The Twins gave the appearance of being sect members. Their long beards were neatly trimmed. They were tall and thin, wore the same denim overalls, the same caps and the same shoes. Even their smiles, which they shyly displayed easily, were interchangeable. They were identical in every respect, mirror images of each other. They never drove, but walked everywhere together, never alone.

"That's bull-shit! Those guys must be ninety years old. Besides, I don't think they're real Holdemans anyway."

By now the boys had moved on to the grassy space next to the old stone bathrooms where the they lay flat, looking at the cloudless moon-lit night sky. Martin remained quiet. This was an unusual night of freedom for him. His father had remained in Madison for business, and his mother was visiting her sister in Nebraska. Tom's mother had agreed to serve him dinner. Afterwards, he and Tom had ridden their bicycles to the park. They were walking their bikes across the "swinging" bridge when they met Teeter, Paz and Inky.

"They just don't act like real Holdemans. Don't you think they're creepy??" Tom's inflexion was not confident. He seemed to be expressing not a firm opinion, but to be asking for support for a position that he knew was shaky and blurted out on impulse.

Martin continued his silence. He had encountered the Twins while working at Sarge's, the local lunch counter with an old fashioned soda fountain. His job there was to clean the floors, wash dishes and make the occasional cherry Coke from syrup and soda water. Sydney, his father, thought a job on weekends and after school would prepare him to work in the appliance store when he was older.

Martin liked the Twins. He was uncomfortable wrapping them in a conspiracy. In his empathy he could feel the embarrassment they would feel if they heard these words. They were gentle, always courteous, always with a ready smile. He could not imagine them as the notorious Hook Man, or as anything other than kindly old Holdeman brothers living quietly in town.

"Ya know, dope-head may be right," said Teeter. "They could be faking it, You never see them with any other Holdemans." The idea appealed to Teeter, whose instinct to challenge was as strong as his inclination to scoff. "They dress like farmers but they don't farm, they don't work. And where does their money come from? I think they

might not be real Holdemans. I'll bet they're Hook Man."

The boys continued to field ideas on the subject as they left the park and walked up a darkened street, pushing their bicycles next to them. The town was silent. They walked in the middle of the street, safe from traffic since there was no traffic. In Newtown, traffic ended by seven in the evening, even in the summer. It would not start up again until early the next morning when work resumed. The only car likely to be on the street after seven was the night cop, and he would only be patrolling Main Street, past the grain elevator and the high school.

"Lets go to their house and look in the windows. See what we can see." Teeter was often the instigator of questionable adventures. He was not yet the bully he was to become, but he already had a way of shaming others into following his lead.

Martin cringed at the idea of doing something he knew would get him in trouble. This was the kind of hair-brained stunt his brother would do. If caught at something, he could not face his father.

"I don't know. It's getting late. I need to get home," he offered as a feeble excuse.

"Oh, come on! Lets go check them out."

They continued talking as they walked down the street. It did not require a noticeable deviation to wander towards the Holdeman Twin's house nearby. Every house in Newtown was nearby.

The house was dark. It was an old house, like most of the houses in town. There were a few that were newer, owned by people who drove to Madison every day for some kind of work. But most of the town's houses were old and plain, wooden structures with an occasional porch, a detached garage in the back facing the alley. The boys stopped at the curb in front of the house.

"I don't think they're home." Paz was looking for a way out, mistakenly thinking that if the twin's were not there, the boys could not intrude. "Maybe they're still down at Sarge's. They eat there almost every night. Might still be at Sarge's."

"Could be. Sarge is open 'till ten or so. Maybe they're still there."

"I'll bet that's it. We probably got fifteen, twenty minutes." Teeter sounded decisive.

"Fifteen twenty minutes for what?"

"To go have a look."

"What the hell you mean, go have a look?" Paz gave Teeter a look of astonishment.

"I mean, we go in the house and have a look. See if it's a real Holdeman house or a fake. Martin and me'll slip in, the rest of you keep an eye out for the Twins."

Martin stood speechless.

"Shit, what if Jazzy catches us?" Now Martin was alarmed. Jazzy was the night cop. "He'll throw us in jail."

"Newtown don't got no jail. Besides, Jazzy's probably up at Sarges too, having a cup of coffee. He won't be around here."

"That's stupid." Tom registered his opposition.

"Hey, its no more stupid than breaking into the high school and doing all that shit. Remember that? Nobody got in trouble for that." Teeter was referring to a never-resolved episode that occurred over the preceding winter.

"That was different. That wasn't someone's house."

"Bullshit. Martin, lets go."

Teeter started to walk around the house towards the back door. Martin continued to stand frozen and silent.

"Come on, dip shit," Teeter hissed. "Get your ass moving. You two keep a lookout."

Martin's feet were heavy. He slowly fell in behind Teeter.

The back door faced a garden and what looked like an old out-house. As with most doors in Newtown, it was unlocked. There was not much need for locks in Newtown, just as there was not much need for a night cop. Few things ever turned up missing.

It was a religious town, a mélange of protestants that included Methodists, Mennonites, the Holdemans, Baptists, plus a few isolated Catholics and Jews. Everyone knew everyone else. It was

inconceivable to enter someone's space uninvited. Once in a while some one might report a petty item that was lost or misplaced, but never stolen. Teeter was a collector of these lost items, but he did not have the courage to take anything of importance. Only the Madison people locked their doors.

The wooden screen door was stuck at the bottom corner. It gave a groan as Teeter pulled it open. The wooden back door opened without resistance onto an enclosed porch. There was another door from the porch into the kitchen. This door was also unlocked.

Martin walked on his toes, afraid of making the slightest sound. The anticipation of what they might find, of who might find them, hung on Martin like a heavy wet coat.

Inside the only light came from the half moon shining through curtain-less windows. Even in this dim light he could see a simple kitchen, with a few open cabinets, no doors, over a large and worn porcelain sink. A cast iron skillet rested on one burner of an old gas stove.

"Not much of a kitchen, huh!" whispered Teeter. The whisper was barely audible but Martin shrank back towards the door at the amplified hissing sound of Teeter's voice.

"Oh don't be such a pussy, no one's here." Teeter continued to whisper in spite of his confident assertion. He was not interested in the kitchen and quickly moved through the doorway into a dining room with a plain wooden table at its center. Everything was simple, and painfully ordered. The walls were barren except for a calendar and a picture of Jesus. A floor lamp with a faded cloth shade stood in a corner. There were no light switches.

The two boys slowly walked through the dining room, into a living room containing only four wooden chairs and an old cloth couch with a wooden frame . "I'll bet they don't even have a bathroom," hissed Teeter as he passed into a hallway leading from the living room.

Martin's breathing stopped! A clock somewhere in the living room began to chime the hour. It chimed in pairs of two with a single chime at the end. He was frozen and could not breathe. The chimes seemed loud enough to be heard on the street, to be heard in his father's house a few blocks away, to be heard by Jazzy in his patrol car. He counted nine chimes in the space of time necessary for ninety. After the last chime's reverberation, the silence of the room was dense.

Teeter had not returned from the hallway. Martin whispered after him, "Teeter, lets go. This is stupid. Lets go."

Teeter did not answer. Martin cautiously leaned into the hallway and saw Teeter standing in an open doorway. He was staring intently into a room, his mouth open. Martin made an almost inaudible "psst, Teeter" as he stepped next to Teeter and followed his gaze into the room. The same half moon light was shining like a beacon through another un-curtained window. There were two narrow beds, one either side of the window. For the second time in minutes Martin stopped breathing.

In the bed on the right was a body, covered by a thin sheet. Its hands were folded over its chest in a pose of supplication. The sheet was tightly tucked under its chin, a long white beard lying atop the sheet. Its eyes were closed. The sheet was perfectly smooth except for the large mound at its feet and a smaller mound where the groin would be.

In the other bed was the same body, only it was sitting upright and staring at Teeter and Martin with the gaunt face of a death camp survivor.

Seconds passed like minutes. Then wordlessly, Teeter turned into the hallway and ran. The noise of his feet hitting the bare wooden floor was deafening. He ran back through the house, out the door onto the porch, then through the stuck wooden screen door with a loud bang.

Martin stood transfixed by the stare of the twin. There was no expression on the twin's face. His eyes were wide and impassive, no fear, no anger, no surprise, no expectation. Only a willingness to face the truth of whatever Martin might do next.

Without taking his eyes from the face of the twin, Martin took a deep breath and said, "I'm sorry." He then turned back down the hall and walked out the front door of the house, closing it carefully behind him. He stepped into the street and walked through a tunnel of light towards the rest of the boys gathered at the end of the block.

About the Author:

Michael Warren is a retired executive and sailor living in Newport, RI. Raised in a Mennonite community in central Kansas, Michael has since traveled the world as a business manager and writer as well as a sailor. HOOK MAN is part of an as-yet unpublished novel INVENTED PEARLS.

THE OPPONENT

Mark Hannon

He sat on a folding chair, dripping sweat, his heart rate slowing down, the fight over for several minutes. Feeling the water run down his nose, he concentrated on timing when it would fall off the tip and drop to the towel he held in his lap. The towel was clean and smelled of alcohol and soap from a hospital laundry. There was an ice bag in the towel, and Ty was moving the muscles in his face carefully, trying to judge where the ice bag would have the best effect. He was slowly rolling his shoulders, expanding his chest and flexing and unflexing his fists to see if there was any damage in those parts of him that might be slow in showing pain as the adrenalin wore off.

The dressing room was a banquet room in a hotel, divided in half by a curtain so that the opposing fighters were separated. A middleweight named Billy, usually the coolest before a fight, was waiting to be called to the ring, tapping his left foot like he couldn't stop it. He looked from Ty's swelling face to his manager, to the ground. His manager, a retired fighter with a shaved head, placed himself between Billy and Ty and kept repeating their fight strategy. "Keep on the outside, use your jab. Don't try to slug with him. He comes at you, throw one, two, three jabs, step to the side. When he misses, step in, let your combinations go and step to the side, first one side, then the other. Get him from all angles, not straight on. And remember, if your head's not moving, your feet gotta be."

Feeling the swelling coming over his left eye, right where the doctor said it would, Ty applied the ice bag that his manager Jack had left him and looked at James the Preacher's entourage getting

their boy whipped up. The choir was dressed in red and white satin seconds' jackets, shouting, "The Lord is all I need!" with increasing volume while James bounced on two feet and rotated his neck.

In a far corner, a goateed father tapped his son on the knee with a punch mitt. "C'mon, boy, let's get you warmed up." The son got up, and the two of them came over by Ty to get some room to warm up with the punch mitts. As they approached, they got a closer look at Ty's bruised face, looked away and went to the business at hand. "Ok," the father said, "let's see the jab," holding up the right mitt. The son's eyes went from Ty to concentrate on the mitt. Pop. Pop, pop went the jab, the punch traveling a straight line from his shoulder to the mitt and springing back, ready to fire again.

A white haired chocolate colored man in a gray suit wearing a Commissioner's badge wandered into the dressing room and was stopped by a fighter's second. "Do they have latex gloves for seconds at ringside or do we have to have our own?"

"Yes, you have to wear the latex gloves at ringside."

"Yeah, but do they provide them at ringside or do we have to bring our own?"

The elderly man smiled, pointed to his badge and replied, "I'm a Commissioner, I know you have to wear the gloves." He then turned from his questioner, took a step towards Ty and said, "My. Have you seen the doctor yet?"

"Uh huh," Ty replied, "he says it'll be ok and I can start sparring again in a week," hoping everyone in the room heard him.

"Ok, ok," the old man said as he shuffled out of the room.

"Hey, Rock," Ty said, addressing the back of the shaved manager's wrinkled bulldog neck, "Jack outside?"

Turning his bullet head, he replied, "Yeah, said he and Mike were going to check out Angus' fight. Cut man had to work that one too."

"Hey, can I use your scissors, get the bandages off?"

"Sure, here you go," pulling a pair of trauma shears out of a side pocket and turning back to his conference with Billy. Leaning against the wall to hold the ice bag in place, Ty labored with the scissors to cut the tightly wrapped padding off his hands.

The show's promoter walked into the dressing room and stopped in the center, making sure his arrival was noticed by all. Hair freshly cut, blue suit sharp, he scanned the room, momentarily making eye contact with everyone and getting their attention. The choir quieted with heads bowed and the promoter stepped to James' manager and gave him a two handed shake. He turned to James, sized up the main event fighter's conditioning as good and wished him good luck, tapping his gloves with his fists. He spun to the rest and waved, wishing all the fighters luck. Stepping towards Ty, he said, "Tough fight you gave him, Ty. Tough fight," looking over the damage to Ty's face.

"Jack here?"

"He's outside, watching Angus' fight. Hey, how many rounds did you think I won?"

The promoter was already gone, back into the arena looking for another welterweight for next month's card.

Across the curtain divide, Ty could hear his defeat described by his opponent "He couldn't get out of the hook's way. Saw it comin', but didn't move fast enough. Then, when he did move, there was the right hand waitin' for him. Jab, hook off the jab, right hand. All night long. Takes a punch, though, he in shape."

He's right, Ty thought, it was the hook that he kept landing. Gotta work on more head movement, get away from that. I was getting to the body some in the first two rounds, but didn't slow him down enough. Pitty pat punk. I get him again, gonna duck that hook, step to it, bust his body up. Slow him down, crush him inside. Take Monday off, then do the bob and weave in the gym this week till I got it down pat.

"I knew I had him, second round. He come at me straight, I pivot, let him have it. Move. He couldn't keep up with my hands or my feet. Next? Bobby says he get me Force Recon from down in Virginia next month's show."

The next day was Sunday and Ty slept most of it. He didn't answer the phone all day. He left the newspaper outside the apartment door, stayed inside, ate and listened to music. On Monday, Ty woke up in the morning and had no pain in his ribs when he breathed deeply. No bruises on his arms, no pain in his hands when he opened and closed his fists. The weather was warm but he put on a hooded sweatshirt to run and kept the hood down. Jack says that burns up more calories. He took a deep breath, glanced at his amateur trophies on the shelf, and went out to run his five mile course, just like the one he read Shane Mosely did. Back in the apartment, he decided he didn't have time to shave before work and went in the back way.

Ty hung his coat up, glanced in the hall where the timecards were and seeing no one, punched in and went out onto the commercial laundry's garage. He had loaded up several of the bags of clean laundry when Tommy came by pushing a cart. He looked at Ty, and Ty just knew he was staring at the swelling.

"Mornin' Ty. You got the number six route today?"

"If it's Monday, gotta be the Allentown Road route. What else?"

He shrugged, "Nothin', just Monday," and went on pushing the cart by him.

That guy never had a fight in his life, Ty thought, but he'll talk about it, I'll bet. Never say a word to my face, but probably laugh it up in the lunch room about what they read in the paper.

At his first stop, he unloaded the clean laundry and was tossing the dirty laundry bags with all his might from the back door to the front of the truck when the manager came by with the manifest papers all signed. Ty turned to take them when he saw him looking at him.

"Jeese, Ty, fight last night?"

"Saturday night. One of Bobby M's pro shows at the arena..."

"Oh, well, take it easy. We'll see you Thursday before eight, right?"

"Yeah, I always get here early Thursday."

At lunchtime he went to Wendy's because they had the grilled chicken salad. Tossing away the dressings they gave him, Ty looked at both Sunday's and Monday's papers to see what they said about the fights Saturday. Sometimes they didn't get the results in on time to make Sunday's paper.

Nothing. Nothing about the fights, nothing about boxing at all. A bunch of bullshit about a wrestling show this Friday. Phony stuff about who might kill who. Fake W.W.F. wrestling bullshit.

He looked at himself in the mirror in the locker room after he got back to the garage when he was done with the route and decided to go to the gym. He was the first one there when Mike opened the door at five.

"Hey, kid, you feel good enough to work out today?" he inquired, looking at the swelling around the eye which was yellow, blue and green by this time.

"Yeah, fine. Just gotta lay off the sparring for a week the doctor says. Guy couldn't hit. I got him figured out for next time."

While he worked out, Ty noticed the looks and overheard the comments like "got clobbered," and "lucky to stay on his feet," but they could be talking about anyone. When he was getting changed, Jack came in and they all went into Mike's office, Mike behind the desk, Jack sitting on the desk and Ty leaning in the doorway, looking at pictures of the three of them behind Mike's desk.

Mike looked at Jack, and pointing to Ty said, "Kid worked out today, came here straight after work."

"Did four rounds shadow boxing under the strings, working on head movement. Hit the heavy bag four too, two of 'em on the uppercut bag. Next time I'll get'm, workin' the body and duckin' his hook."

"Ty," Jack started, "Bobby says he hasn't got room for you on the next card..."

Ty saw Mike looking him right in the eyes. He looked over Mike's shoulder and saw the picture of himself, hand raised in victory from the Golden Gloves two years ago. I fought that guy three times, Ty thought, lost the first two times, but when the Gloves Title was on the line, I beat him. Right hand to the body slowed him down in the second, he was all mine after that.

"...so I made some phone calls. Rick Benson out in Ohio has got a card in Toledo at the end of next month."

Jack was looking at him now, too. Behind him was a picture of Ty standing on the ropes, both arms in the air, Jack looking up at him and smiling after he'd knocked out Toby Green in his first pro fight.

"Says he can match you with Tom Peterson from out there. The guy's four and six, has trouble making weight. I said if we're gonna travel, he's gotta make weight or forfeit the whole purse to us."

It was a whole new world, the pros. Small gloves, no headgear. He touched his face, checking to see if it still hurt as much.

"Must not be training much if he can't make weight. He doesn't make weight, we ride to Ohio, just pick up the money. He does, he's outta shape, you beat 'em."

There weren't any more pictures of his other pro fights, though. He remembered an article from the paper mentioned him as a prospect that had lost a controversial decision to another local fighter. Great things still expected. Beat him in a rematch, too.

"The question is, Ty, how do you feel?" Mike asked, "Saturday night was your third loss in a row. You gonna want to fight in a month?"

The two handlers were waiting for an answer, looking right at him, just like the refs do when he's taken a knockdown.

"Yeah, I'm fine, I'll be ready. I'm already in shape, no problem with the weight, and I'll be back sparrin' next week, you'll see. I'll go to Ohio, take their money, beat their boy. Start getting back on the winning side."

Jack slapped him on the arm and said, "Atta boy. I'll call Benson later and tell him we'll take the fight. We'll get back on track in Ohio, take their money and beat their boy, just like you say."

With the fighting spirit restored, Ty went out of the office and said good night to everyone in the gym, once again a prospect.

Watching Ty leave, Mike said, "He peaked in the amateurs, Jack. He stays in shape but doesn't get any better. He's gotta know takin' him outta town like this puts him down as a guy listed as an 'opponent'."

"I give him about five years. He can still make a few bucks at it, Mike. He's young, he'll do it while he can, beat a few guys here and there. He'll quit when he gets tired of working out and the money ain't there."

"What made him an amateur champ is still in him and it'll keep him hanging on a lot longer than that, especially if the regular fans remember him. A guy like him, every time he gets beat, it just gets a little easier to lose."

About the Author:

Mark Hannon is a retired firefighter who boxed as an amateur, and trained amateur and professional fighters. He is the author of the novel "Every Man for Himself," published by Apprentice House Press. Other work has been published in Peninsula, Scribble, The Baltimore Sun, the Maryland Historical Society Magazine and The Carriage Horse Journal.

MARIA

Emily Peña Murphey

On that last day before the big storm, I first noticed something was funny when our family went to the mercado in Las Altas. We arrived very early, just as sunshine was coming over the tops of the mountains. Around the dusty little plaza the shops were opening, and vendores were setting up their stalls like always. But the grown-up people seemed worried and nervous. I could hear them whispering to each other as, if a secret, a certain word: "huracán."

What could it mean? I was sure I'd heard it before, as a word for an ocean storm, but just the same I asked my big brother Eduardo about it. He paused and looked up for a minute from where he and some friends were tossing stones into the fountain.

"Oh, huracanes are those storms we have at the end of the summer every year," he said. "But you're too little to remember any of the really big ones—like one that hit us when I was small. The strongest huracanes sweep right in from the ocean with days of heavy rain, and wind strong enough to knock over a tree. That's why the big coco near our house has always been growing kind of on its side." Then I guess he thought he'd explained enough, because he turned around went back to his game.

Mami came and took my hand and said we needed to shop for some extra food, and that she was lucky to have a good hijita like me to help her. We took our bags and baskets all around the square and bought as much food as we could carry up the steep trail to our house— nearly at the top of the mountain. Rice, gandules, cooking oil, and a few onions. When Mami had spent almost

all the coins from her apron pocket my little sister Arielis began to fuss, so Mami sat down on one of the old iron benches and swung her shawl around to the front to give her the breast.

I began to laugh when I looked at the big sacks of rice and beans we'd been carrying and said, "Mami, vamos a tener una gran fiesta, no? Aren't we going to have a big party?" But instead of smiling at my joke, Mami frowned and said, "Niña, callate! Lo que viene va a ser nada de fiesta!—Hush, little girl; what's coming will be no fiesta!" The way she said it sort of scared me and left me with a feeling I'd better keep my questions to myself.

Then Mami reached into her blusa and took out a bank note. It was decorated with fancy green designs and the picture of an important-looking man.

"Take this to the ferretería—the hardware shop—and ask for a flashlight and a package of batteries. Then with whatever's left over get us some more of the big candles and a box of wooden matches. I'll wait here with the baby and our bags of food." She folded the bill and pressed it into my hand. Feeling important, I took the money and hurried off.

In the hardware store people were in a hurry to buy up all sorts of things. There was a long line all the way from the door to the counter. A kindly old abuelo noticed me and said, "Let the little girl go first!" The others stood back and let me move to the front of the line while they all watched. This made me feel so embarrassed that I forgot the names of the things Mami had asked for! I knew one of them had something to do with flashing light, but all I could think of was the word "quiebraplata,"—which in Inglés means "firefly!"

When I said that word in my shy little voice, the people standing around began to laugh. But Señor Ramos, the shopkeeper, said, "Tienes buena suerte, my daughter—you're lucky—because you're getting the last "firefly" I've got left in the store!" A few of the men behind me grumbled, but someone pointed out that no family would need the light more than ours, since we lived so high up the mountain and so far from town! Several men I that I knew were my Papi's compadres nodded in agreement, and the viejito who had helped me in the line made the sign of the cross over me and muttered a prayer for God's protection .

Señor Ramos knew about the batteries I'd need, and took down from a shelf a packet of the right kind. When I asked for velas, he handed me several big, waxy white ones, and also added the matches I'd nearly forgotten! These things went into a plastic sack, and I paid for them with Mami's paper money. The ferretero gave me a few coins back and slipped a couple of bright-colored lollipops into the bag as a treat for Eduardo and me.

I thanked him and turned around to leave. Then I noticed that in just a few minutes the little store had become packed with people jostling each other to grab nearly anything that was left on the shelves. They seemed frightened, and I felt that way too as I made my way toward the door passing among many scuffed rancheros' boots, tattered long skirts, and brown legs in worn-out work pants.

What a relief it was when I got outside and saw Papi—all my fear went away, and I felt safe as if by magic! He was standing beside our little burro, el Chaparrito, tying some big pieces of wood onto the pack saddle on the shaggy one's back. Papi didn't notice me at first, so I ran up behind to surprise him by jumping onto his back with a big hug. When he reached around and saw it was me he took me in his arms and happily cried out, "Mi reina!" He tossed me high in the air still clutching my bolsa, and caught me and gave me a kiss on my way down.

"Looks like you've been helping your Mamá with shopping," he said, inspecting the contents of my bag. "Such a smart girl to be helping us get ready!"

Hoping I'd finally found someone who could explain all the ansiedad, I pleaded, "But Papi, what is it we're getting ready for?"

"Ay, mi hija," he replied, "Every so many years a really big huracán comes up from el Mar Carribe and vents its wrath on poor Borinquén! The people who have radios and wireless telephones are saying that a really strong one is coming soon to Puerto Rico, so everyone on the island is getting ready to keep safe in their homes until the storm is over!"

"But why is the sea so angry at us?"

"Well," said Papi, "That's how some people think about, it. But to me it's just something caused by our Mother Nature. She has her moods like any woman—sometimes she sends us sunshine and soft breezes, and sometimes she stirs up the waves and makes a great storm. It's according to God's will, and we must take shelter and be patient until it passes!"

"Are you going to build something with the boards?" I asked hopefully, remembering a picture I once saw in a magazine from Miami—a little pink house with some girls playing in it.

"Well, not really build anything new, Lupita, but try to make our house stronger by nailing these across our shutters and windows. Now let's go find the others and get ready to head up the hill." He took Chaparrito by his rope halter and turned his head toward the center of the square.

We found Mami, the baby, and Eduardo back near the fountain where I'd left them. Mami was still busy with Ariely, who after nursing had needed a change. Edi was impressed to see the large boards and other hardware we'd gotten, and offered to carry some of the heavier packages of food. We bundled all we could onto the burrito's back and made our way toward the trail that led up the mountainside to our casita. My rubber sandals skidded on the gravel as I walked up the path.

When we got home Papi started right away to latch all of the house's shutters and nail the big boards across them. Eduardo wanted a turn with the hammer, so Papi gave it to him and let him bang in some of the nails.

While Edi was hammering, Papi sat down on a stone to rest. He became thoughtful and said he felt sorry that when he built our house—back before I was born—there wasn't money to buy cement for all four walls. He kept promising himself he'd fix the last one, but somehow he was always too busy. So the fourth side of our house was made out of trees stripped of their branches and thatched with palm fans. We called it the bohío wall, because that's the name for the open wooden houses the country people used to make for themselves down in the valleys. It did sometimes let in wind and rain, but we covered it with a big plastic curtain and never thought much about it.

Mami went straight to the cooking area and built a big fire in the horno. She sent me with a jug to fetch water from the cistern under the house, and began to cook up a big pot of rice while the pigeon peas were soaking. When the rice was done she scraped it out into another pot and boiled the peas with some chiles, onions, and garlic. She sent Edi and me out to our little garden to pick all the vegetables that we could, even the ones that weren't quite ripe, since we needed to collect as much food as we could before the rain started. We also collected as much wild fruit as we could harvest from the nearby trees: plátanos, mangos, and guayabas. As I carried my heavy basket into the house I looked behind me at all the plants that now looked so empty and bare!

While Mami prepared the cena, I amused Arielita by bouncing her on my lap and singing to her. Like all little ones, she loved the song about the coquí, the tiny frog that sings all night long in the trees. I held her little hands and clapped them in time with the chorus, which made her laugh. "Coquí, coquí , coqui-quí-quí-quí!" While I sang, Mami looked over from the hearth and smiled at us.

We had a hearty dinner of the gandules and rice, and the ripest of the frutas. We put the leftovers in a big iron pot with a lid, which Papi carried down to the cisterna to set it on the stone shelf where the water would keep it cool for tomorrow.

From what my parents heard in the village we were expecting the rain to start falling that night, so while it was still daylight Edi and Papi searched the woods on our hillside for dead branches. Papi chopped them up with his axe and machete to lay in a store of extra firewood. Edi brought the wood into the house and stacked it next to the cooking fire where it would keep dry. Papi took his shovel and dug a trench around three sides of the house so that any heavy rainwater would flow away from us and run downhill. Then he and Edi penned up the goats and el Chaparrito, and shooed the rooster and chickens into their coop.

That night when we said our prayers and bedded down to sleep, we could hear the coquí frogs singing like they always did in the trees around our house. When Mami was done nursing Arielis, it seemed that she and Papi shared an extra-long hug and kiss before they blew out the candle in the lantern.

I'd been sleeping soundly, but in the middle of the night I woke up suddenly to loud sounds of rattling, whooshing, and bumping. Soon I realized I was hearing heavy rain drumming on our metal roof, and very strong winds flapping the banana trees growing around our little casita.

"Mami, I'm scared!" I cried out in the noisy darkness.

"Come here and get in bed with us, mi amor!"She said, and as soon as I climbed in with my parents I felt very warm and safe.

I dropped off for a while. When I woke up again the sky was starting to lighten up a little, though we all knew there would be no real dawn that morning. The rain and wind sounded stronger than ever, and I could tell that now even my parents were getting nervous. That made me nervous too, and I noticed that during the night even the brave Eduardo had crept over to join the rest of us in our parents' big matrimonio. We'd spent most of the night with all five of us huddled together, glad to be warm and dry.

But of course we were also worried. Papi finally quit his snoring and woke up to listen to the huracán. "I'm so glad that we moved our ancianos down to Ponce last year," he said to Mami, who nodded in agreement. She said, "Of course they still miss all of us and the mountains, but they're safer there in a special home in a lowland city where people take care of them. Though I still wish I could be there at their bedsides! At least my sister and cousins are nearby…"

Right after she said that, the sound of the wind grew so loud that it sounded like a roaring lion, and I hoped that the storm wasn't so fierce down in the city where my grandparents were now living. We were all wide awake now, and could see that one corner of our roof was being lifted up and then dropped down again by gusts of wind. After what had seemed like a very short morning, the sky had become very dark. A trickle of rain began leaking in from under the bohío wall. Papi put a battery into the flashlight and went over to the door. He opened it a crack and peered outside, shining the light around.

"We must move this bed closer to the fireplace and chimney—that's the strongest part of the house, "Papi said as he closed the door and latched it. So we got up and worked together to move the heavy piece of furniture. I didn't want to say anything but I was beginning to feel still more scared, since Papi seemed concerned for our safety. I remembered the American story of "The Three Little Pigs" that the teacher had read to us in English on the first day of school. I could imagine there was a huge wolf outside trying to blow our little house down!

"Papi, you built this house very strong, didn't you?" I asked at last.

"Yes, as strong as I could, mi hija!" But I could hear a worried tone in his voice and wondered what he had seen when he opened the door. We children had now been forbidden to look outside.

Mami got up and lit the fire and started to boil some water for coffee for the grown-ups. Once the coffee and hot water had been poured off into the pot to brew, she made some corn meal mush for the rest of us. While that was thickening she put on the heavy skillet. Then she sliced up some plantains and fried them in the tiniest bit of oil I ever saw her use. "I think I'll cook some extra plátanos in case we want them later!" she said, and soon had cut up and fried almost all of them. This seemed odd to me, but then I noticed that drops of rain were beginning to splash down the chimney and make a hissing noise as they fell in the fire. I wondered if my mother was worried that the cooking fire might go out. But I didn't say anything.

So that was how it was, and it was like that for days! Sometimes I felt like we were the family of

Noah in the Ark, and wondered when the rain would stop. Then maybe we could send out a dove to bring us back hopeful news. And I wondered fearfully what had become of our animals; our goats and chickens, and our dear, patient burrito who was almost a family pet. Surely by now their pens had been damaged by the wind and they were scattered far and wide across the hills and barrancas. I hoped they had not gotten hurt and didn't feel scared. And of course I was also worried about the other mountain families, whose daughters had become my playmates at the village school.

For soon it became clear that there was a great deal of water streaming down the mountainside, and each hour a little more of it came into our house! It was now our job just to do our best to keep warm and dry and keep our spirits up. Mami had set aside the lollipops that Edi and I got from the herradura, but she decided to give them to us now. Sucking on them cheered us up and helped us feel a little less hungry. Most of our food was gone and the tiny meals we were having were not very filling.

We tried to while away the time with songs and riddles and telling stories. We passed the hours curled up in the bed or crouched by the chimney, trying to chase away boredom by making every chore and activity last as long as possible.

When she wasn't busy cooking, Mami took out her sewing basket and by the light of the lantern made a new dress for my rag doll, Pepita. Then she took out her special needle and made a pretty band of lace to sew on Ari's little cap. The third morning Mami took a long time brushing my hair, and then braided ribbons into it like she'd done last winter for la Navidad. She held up her little mirror to show how pretty I looked, and we both laughed. During those days I learned that laughing is important—it works to break up and drive off that feeling of terror that can lodge in the belly when someone feels completely helpless.

From somewhere Papi took out a jackknife that we'd never known he had, and taught Eduardo how to open it up, sharpen the blade, and use it. Taking turns, they carved little fish and funny people from some sticks of firewood. "You must always take good care of the sharp edge of any sort of knife, mi hijo," Papi said, "and treat it with respect. Otherwise the orisha Ogún, who rules all blades of iron, might cause it to act against you." Edi nodded gravely, but looked confused about the name Ogún and the meaning of the word orisha.

Right after Papi had said these things, Mami glared at him, and he seemed embarrassed. "You know, mi amor," she chided, "That's not the Christian way of thinking that we want to teach our children!" "You're right, of course," our father admitted. "But when I was a boy how I loved to hear my bisabuelo tell the old stories of Santería!"

"What stories? Tell us, tell us!" Edi and I cried out, bouncing up and down. Papi looked at Mami and she shrugged her shoulders and gave him a look that said, "Well, alright!" So we spent a long afternoon feeding our sputtering fire and listening to Papi tell the ancient tales of our isla and the gods and goddesses of the Mar Carribe. These were the things the Taino Indians and African slaves of Borinquén once believed, before the Spanish priests came and baptized everyone into the Church of one God.

As Papi talked, we learned of the orishas: gods and goddesses of war; of dancing and drumming; of love, thunder, sunshine, and the ocean waves; tales of great storms, battles, and romances. It all seemed so delightful that somehow I couldn't imagine that our loving Jesús Cristo would disapprove. Especially if it helped a poor jíbaro family in danger to hold on to their hope and faith!

I think it was on the third night or perhaps the fourth when the earth floor of our little casa was finally streaming with water and the fire had completely gone out. Papá had made many trips to the cistern for water, but it had become too muddy to drink or cook with. So finally we gave up and just put our biggest kettle outside the door to fill with rain. Everything was soggy now and it was only by holding onto one another in the big bed that we could feel at all warm. We had eaten most of the food that we'd been able to gather and prepare.

Suddenly we heard the sound of the wind become ten times louder than we'd ever heard it, and with every bump the loose corner of the metal roof began to flap up higher and higher into the darkness. We were all on the bed together,

trembling under the soaking blankets, crying out "Ay! Ay!" and praying out loud to la Virgen de Divina Providencia to save us! Then, in a dreadful instant, there was a terrifying ripping noise, and we watched as our roof was torn completely away to sail off like a huge kite with a great, whistling roar. We could hear the big sheet of metal rattling and banging its way across rocks and treetops as it flew through the storm and away from our house forever.

Then we had nothing above us but the black and terrible sky with its ever more powerful winds and pelting water! We heard a creaking and cracking, and all at once we could see that the bohío wall too was breaking down and at any minute would be splintered to pieces. Papi leaped up and grabbed the wooden table, now starting to rock on its legs as heavy as it was. He lifted it up and lowered it over us on the flooded frame of the bed. "Children, keep under this for protection!" he shouted, as the wind whipped him and blew all sorts of things against his body.

Quickly, Mami handed me the baby and reached out to grab a corner of the plastic curtain just before it too flew away. She and Papi used it to make a kind of tent to cover the table and bed, and then crawled under it. There was barely room beneath this shelter for all of us.

To our horror we then heard fragments of what had once been our house's fourth wall as they rattled and scraped by just inches from our heads before disappearing into the howling darkness. The wind seemed stronger than ever now, with one less barrier to hold it back. Edi and I clutched our parents and moaned loudly, and little Ari added her baby's wailing to our cries.

What a long and miserable night it was, and how unprotected we were from the terrible huracán! I tied my braids together behind my head to stop them from lashing my face in the wind. The plastic tent that kept off some of the rain flapped wildly, and my parents held tightly to its corners. Papi gripped the table's legs with all of his strength to keep our last bit of protection from blowing off!

What was even worse was seeing the place where we'd once lived so happily destroyed before our eyes. We watched in horror as one by one each of the furnishings of our little home was snatched away by the wind and carried to someplace un-known. Even the big boards that Papi and Edi had nailed so firmly over the windows came loose and began to swing to and fro. We saw great branches and even whole trees go flying by overhead, along with boards and fences and all sorts of things that could only have come from other people's hous-es!

Finally, wanting to protect us from seeing any more, Mami made Edi and me close our eyes and put our heads down on her lap to try to sleep. In our bravest voices we all recited a bedtime pray-er, and Mami rocked us and sang to us softly. As I finally dropped off, it seemed as if the storm might be calming down just the tiniest bit.

We had gotten so used to pounding wind that when we finally heard silence, it seemed like thunder! It was truly a miracle, for when I woke up in the morning the storm had passed over. For the first time in days I saw faint sunlight. Beside me under the table, Mami was nursing little Ari as Eduardo dozed with his head in her lap. Papi was standing over us peeling back the dripping plastic, clearing away trash, and looking around at what was left of our world. He saw me open my eyes, and lifted me out from under the table. Then, taking my hand, he guided me toward the front door. We walked across a mud- and rubbish-filled space contained by what was left of our house's walls.

"Hija, ven conmigo y miremos juntos!" Papi said. "Daughter, come with me and let's look togeth-er!"

We walked through the frame of the door and into the midst of a shocking vista—the tops of the trees that had once been so green and shady had been stripped off so that only trunks and bare sticks remained. The spiky stalks on the far hillsides reminded me of bristles along the back of a wild boar. New streams that had never been there before now flowed into broadened gullies that led to the valley. The water gurgled softly.

I gasped and began to cry. My Papacito picked me up and hugged me so tightly against his chest that I could feel his heart-beat. I could tell from his breathing that he was weeping too.

Then Papi hoisted me up onto his shoulders so I could see far, far, down the side of the naked mountain. Though it had always been hidden by the forest, I could see the dome and cross of our lowland village church, la Iglesia de la Virgen de Divina Providencia—named for the Mother who watches over our island. The sunlight grew stronger until the cross gleamed in its rays.

"Figúrate, hiija," Papi said to me softly, "Sobrevivimos! Just think of it—we survived!" He lifted me over his head and set me down on the muddy ground.

"Sí, Papi!" I said, looking up at him. "Mother Na-ture is so very strong—now she'll make the trees grow back, and we'll raise food from the earth!"

My father gazed at his three cement walls. Within them, the others were beginning to stir and crawl out from under their shelter.

"A house can always be rebuilt," my Papi mur-mured, "but never a family!"

About the Author:

Emily Peña Murphey is a granddaughter of Mexi-can immigrants, with family roots in the Texas Rio Grande Valley and the Smoky Mountains of North Carolina. She worked for many years as a psycho-therapist, listening to people's life stories and accounts of their family histories. She has under-gone graduate training in psychology, social work, and Jungian psychoanalysis. Peña Murphey's current work on a trilogy of novels recreates the cultural and political milieu of Mexico and la Fron-tera of her ancestors in the decades spanning the Mexican Revolution, with special interest in the struggles of women. She uses writing to explore her cultural identity as a mixed race Mexican-American at the vanguard of the Latino diaspo-ra. She has published poetry and memoir pieces in the e-journals Jung in Vermont and the Smoky Blue Literary and Arts Magazine. Peña Murphey blogs at https://lafronterista.blogspot.com. In addition to being a writer, Emily is an avid garden-er, cook, folk artist, musician, and singer. She lives in Philadelphia.

NORMAL

Gina Miller-Meinema

"I know this guy. Glenn? Glenn, can you hear me?"

"He can't hear you." I say to the fireman, even though I knew it was pointless. They always kept yelling my dad's name no matter how many times I told them that he can't hear. I couldn't help myself. It was habit, really. Usually it irritated me to no end; why didn't they just listen? Even the ones who knew him did it; why did they insist on talking to him when he was like that?

As a nurse, years later, I got it. I was taught, as all emergency medical personnel are, to always assume that the patient can hear every word you say because hearing is the last sense to go. I was also taught never to use the word "normal" to describe a patient's condition. What is normal to one person may be completely out of the ordinary for another. As a twelve year old in 1983, I knew my family life was unusual, but to me it was still normal. So when the firemen paramedics didn't listen to what I was telling them, because I was the one in charge and I did know what was going on with my dad, I didn't get it.

That day in 1983 was slightly different. From the rushing rapids of my life, I was plucked up and deposited onto a soft, promising life raft. Clinging to that raft, the ineffable relief and gratitude I felt was so vast, I was sure I would drown in it anyway.

My dad, Glenn, was a brittle diabetic, prone to obscenely low blood sugar levels and grand mal seizures on a daily basis. His condition was so out-of-the-ordinary that doctors never believed it to be possible.

Then one day, during a routine visit, one lucky M. D. witnessed it for himself and saw how impassively my mom, Sue, handled Dad as he convulsed all over the doctor's office— banging into coat racks, kicking the contents of waste baskets to the floor, grunting and snorting like a wild boar. It happened so quickly and was accompanied by such violence, that the doctor actually accused my dad, who in that state was oblivious to the world around him, of faking it. A simple finger prick (which turned out to be not so simple while Dad rolled around on the floor and jerked his entire body at the most inopportune moments) quickly revealed to the doctor, the error in his thinking.

Fast food and convenience store employees in our area had called the paramedics for my dad on multiple occasions. If I was there, I tried to stop them. In the absence of my mom, I was the first to notice that Dad wasn't acting right, but because I needed to get some sugar into his body, I was forced to ask the employees if I could borrow a Pepsi (being a child, I was not in the habit of having money on hand) and then I implored them not to call the ambulance, "I'll get him out of it and he'll be fine. Really. This happens every day."

Unfailingly, the convenience store clerks and fast food employees dialed emergency medical services. What did a kid know?

Although Mom always told my siblings and me that we could call the ambulance (a regular number, along with other emergency numbers, posted near our phone) anytime we were alone with our Dad when he was "getting sick" (Mom's euphemism for Dad's grand mal seizures), I did everything I could not to call. My younger sister Cheri, on the other hand, dialed with gusto.

Or so I thought.

Whereas I was steadfast and practical about caring for our daddy (we didn't actually call him "Dad" until we were teens), Cheri was emotional and fearful, seeming unsure of what to do with our flailing father in the absence of Mom or me. Whereas I was embarrassed by the noise and commotion of the sirens and paramedics, Cheri seemed to relish it. Whereas I preferred to take care of Dad myself, Cheri preferred to let others do it for her.

Wherever I was, I would hear the sirens, run home, and yell at Cheri, "Why did you call?"

What a cruel and thoughtless sister I could be sometimes.

As a mom years later, even as an older teenager, I finally knew why Cheri always called. Our dad looked intimidating to most adults when he was having a grand mal seizure. The scariest part: his eyes. They remained wide open and staring, yet completely vacant of any trace of our real daddy. As a kindergartener, I was sure his bulging eyeballs belonged to the zombie who took over his body when he was like that; they were the hardest part for me to overcome, too. On some level, I think I always understood why Cheri called in the professionals.

(And what a smart little kid she was for keeping a level head! But to me, as a child only three years older, I thought she was something along the lines of hysterical for summoning the ambulance so often. Thankfully the years have made me wiser and more compassionate. She was right for calling when she felt like she could not or did not want to handle it on her own. Cheri helped me to be a better nurse. We all react differently to situations and no one reaction is wrong, only different.)

But as a shy kid wanting some measure of privacy, I had an aversion to the ambulance and fire trucks full of emergency workers who showed up on our street and crammed themselves into our tiny townhouse where Dad lay on the floor, upstairs, downstairs, or in the basement,

depending on the day. I resented the mobs of gawkers that shamelessly collected on our front lawn waiting to get a glimpse of our dad.

And the questions: "Gina, is your dad going to be okay?" "What's wrong with your dad anyway?" "Are they going to take him to the hospital this time?" And my favorite: "Don't you ever get tired of the ambulance and all these people coming to your house?"

As the oldest, I learned how to handle Dad alone by the time I was five years old. Mom was a teacher in Clinton Township, so she would leave to drop Cheri at our grandma's house long before my Tweety Bird alarm clock went off at 7:30 a.m. It was my job as a first grader to get myself up and ready for school, and to make sure Dad got up for work before I left.

Sometimes, while he slept, I could tell Dad's blood sugar was already too low. I knew by the way he began to purse his lips and roll around on the bed that I had to take care of him before I went to school.

I learned back then that even though my dad's eyes were open, he could not really see. I became an expert at feeding him the sugared juice in the baby bottle with the specially-cut nipple Mom had made, at just the right moment so he didn't snort it back into his lungs and aspirate; or, during one of his moments of puffing his cheeks up with air and pushing it out with puckered lips, he didn't spray it all over both of us. I learned to stand clear of his thrashing arms and legs that could, at any moment, suddenly spasm into a forceful blow at anything in the vicinity. Dad was known to break lamps and chairs with the explosive movements of his body.

It's strange what becomes normal in a life. Twenty some years later, about a month after Dad died in 2004, I was driving on a road near my house when I heard the familiar wail of sirens. I immediately grabbed my cell phone to call Mom. It took a few seconds and then it was a hard jolt to my heart. For the first time in my life I knew the sirens were not for my dad. I wondered at how I had not heard the sound of sirens for a full month. We lived just a mile from a hospital; they were ubiquitous. My parents live about three miles away, so inevitably I would wonder about Dad because quite often, it was for him. I can only guess that I needed that time of silence to be truly struck when I finally heard the sirens again.

It was the first time I thought: Maybe my family life was not as normal as I'd always thought.

The shock of it stayed with me for months, years, even.

Late or middle of the night phone calls were another normal phenomenon in my life. From hospitals: "Is this the residence of Glenn… Loooh…DAHV-ski?" There is no "k" or "ahh" in our last name, but they always seemed to add them in there to make Dad Polish, or maybe Russian. The mispronunciation was all I needed to hear: "Mo—omm," I would call out, "Dad's in the hospital again."

From Mom, when I was an adult: "Dad's at the hospital. Can you come stay with Tony and Katie so I can go get him?" Tony and Katie were the youngest of our family, ten and twelve years my junior. Tony was the result of Mom and Dad's successful attempt at trying for a boy one last time, and Katie was their happy "Ooops" who came two years later. Mom got her tubes tied immediately following Katie's birth.

From Mom again, slightly out of breath, but always matter-of-fact, when Tony and Katie were older, but out with friends: "Your Dad is convulsing on the bathroom floor. Will you come help me get him out of there so he'll stop banging his head between the toilet and the wall?"

And from a tearful teenaged Katie getting ready for school in the morning when Mom was out of town for a conference: "Gina? Will you come help me with Dad? He's lying outside on the front lawn! He's really cold, and he won't wake up!"

"Is he breathing?"

"I don't know!"

"Cover him with blankets and put pillows under his feet. I'll be right over."

When I arrived, the still figure of my unconscious father on the front lawn was a more disturbing sight than any I could remember. He

looked so little; so vulnerable under the towering pines. I stared, momentarily suspended by the thought that he could be dead. Then, my whole body released a sigh I had not realized I was holding, as I discerned the faint cloud of breath intermittently hovering over his face on the cold fall air.

Katie and I were unable to lift our dad's barely five feet two inch frame of completely inanimate weight, so I called my husband, who had not yet left for work, and still, we had difficulties. Thankfully, our dad was not the size of a normal man.

As we struggled at the doorway, I noticed a sack of Dad's favorite mini burgers on the side of the porch, unopened and completely cold. With Mom gone, I knew he had decided to sneak the extra car out. My dad was a night owl. At two or three in the morning, he probably figured there wouldn't be anybody on the roads. His driver's license had been revoked long ago for getting into one too many accidents due to his seizures. Though he had taken to riding an old red and white bike, the kind with the extra wide seat and a basket on the handle bars (the kids of the neighborhood called him "Pee-Wee"), he still loved to drive, and obstinacy was a trait that stayed with Dad until the day he died on his living room floor three and a half years later. Ironically, he did not die from complications caused by a seizure or his diabetes, but from the blood thinner he was taking for his new heart valve. It happened just minutes after midnight, the day after Easter, when an hour earlier, he had said to the spirit of death, and again to the spirits of his brother, his mother, and his father, and later again to the spirits of his mother-in-law, his brother-in-law, and his best friend, Bill, "Just give me another hour. One more hour."

Mom was unaware of the family reunion in their living room, but she sensed something amiss. It came out of her mouth disguised as irritation with her husband, "Glenn! Glenn? Who do you keep talking to?"

He was trying to stay alive long enough to prevent his living family from having to memorialize his death with every Easter celebration thereafter. But on that early fall morning, before Katie discovered him unconscious on the front lawn, his stubborn determination to get safely home before the seizure completely took hold of him only got our dad as far as the front porch, with his sack of steaming square burgers that smelled deliciously of greasy, cooked onions. It was then that he lost all control of his mind and his body and fell off of the porch onto the concrete walkway. He convulsed his way over to where Katie had found him on the lawn, hours later, fifty feet from where he started, between a metal rake left lying pointy side up, and the cement bricks surrounding the pine, that had been laid at sharp angles to resemble a circle of little red rooftops. There was blood on the side of Dad's head and also on the walkway. I easily deduced, from reading Nancy Drew mysteries throughout all of fifth and sixth grade, and sometimes seventh, that he had tumbled off the porch and smacked his noggin, as he so often did over the years.

Although he was unresponsive and in a diabetic coma, by that year, injection shots of glucagon were available by prescription for diabetic emergencies. It still took him a very long time to come out of it, but within three or four hours, Dad was basically okay. I always believed our dad led a life charmed by the providence of guardian spirits who watched over him.

Long after Dad died, a middle of the night phone call would still catch me off guard. The first one came more than a year after he'd been gone. Although I no longer slept with the phone near my bed, and although it was only a wrong number, I reflexively popped up and ran to the den to answer it with Dad as the star of my thoughts, and then: Wait. No. It can't be about Dad. He's not here anymore.

"Glenn? We're going to get you out of this car, okay?" It was the fireman who knew our dad. I didn't bother to tell him again that he had no idea what he or anyone else was saying and that they could do whatever they wanted when he was in that state. I was just overwhelmingly relieved to have the burden of keeping us all safe off of my shoulders.

Minutes earlier, I had been hanging over the front seat trying to keep the car from veering into oncoming traffic, while two year old Tony wailed from his front car seat, "Daaadddyyy! Daaadddyyy!"

My friend Mimi and nine year old Cheri were screaming and pounding on the windows of the car, "Help! Somebody help us! Why won't they stop and help us?"

I had been trying to wrestle the steering wheel from our dad's convulsive grip for the last ten minutes of the ride. His foot was pressed to the floor as we sped down the road. My twelve year old, gangly girl arms fought to keep us mostly in the turning lane until, without warning, a spasm of Dad's entire body caused him to let go of the steering wheel and lift his foot from the gas pedal. I inadvertently turned the car almost perpendicular to traffic in the middle of the turn lane. I did not know how a car worked; I only knew that the other pedal must be the brake, and that I had to get Dad's foot to press on it.

Since we were rolling slowly enough, I yelled for Mimi to jump out and run for help. Cheri continued to cry hopelessly and Tony was hysterical. Cars were zooming by, with horns blaring, swerving at the last minute to miss hitting us. I tried to climb to the front seat so that I could press on the brake pedal with my hand, but Dad was jerking too violently by that time; I realized that I still had better leverage by reaching over the front seat.

"Cheri! Stop crying! Roll the window down and wave your arms so someone can see that we're kids!"

I never found out his name, but a normal looking, twenty-something man finally stopped and came running over to ask if we needed help. He opened the car door and muscled Dad over toward the middle of the bench seat of the station wagon so he could straighten the car out and put it into park. I was finally able to lift my baby brother out of his car seat so that I could comfort and soothe him and even soothe myself. The man stayed with us, asking me questions about the goopy green gel I began forcing into Dad's mouth after handing Tony over to Cheri. He listened as three little girls rehashed the harrowing story of their adventure, until the fire trucks and ambulance that Mimi had summoned, arrived at last.

On that not-so-normal day, I had never been so happy to hear the sirens and see all of the trucks pulling up close to our car, forming a protective barrier around us. For once, I welcomed the attention of others into my normal life.

About the Author:

Gina Miller-Meinema is a nurse-turned-writer, living in Corona de Tucson, Arizona since August of 2013. To help make ends meet while she writes, Gina works part-time at the local desert mountain Corona Ace Hardware, where she enjoys the camaraderie of her bosses and coworkers, and the easy companionship of the regulars, with strong vintage names like Earl, Virgil, and beautiful Louise. "Normal" is Gina's first published story.

A WILD CHILD

Pamela Carter

I grew up in the 1950s in a small log cabin located in an inter-mountain valley west of Denver. Our lives were primitive; all our water had to be hauled in five-gallon cans from the community well three miles away, and we bathed once a week in an aluminum tub filled with water warmed atop the wood-burning stove that took up most of our kitchen. We had no central heating, even though temperatures frequently dropped below zero in the winter, so the house was drafty and cold much of the year. Still, it was heaven to me. Ranches and open spaces surrounded our cabin, and the natural beauty and abundant wildlife fired my already active imagination.

In the summer I often rose in the dusky dawn light and climbed out my bedroom window before anyone else in the household was awake. I would catch my horse, Tammy, grab a hank of her mane, and swing myself onto her bare back. Tammy had been abused as a filly, and it left her more feral than tame—one of the reasons I loved her so much. But she had come to trust me and, unencumbered by saddle or bridle, was responsive and well-behaved. I could guide her by pressing my knees against her sides, and together we would make our way in the hazy morning light, the air filled with birdsong, to a saddle of land on the Falcon Wing Ranch and, from this rise of land, watch the sun rise over the sleeping city below. The memory of the piercingly fresh air remains clear even now, almost sixty years later.

When the air warmed up some, I'd ride Tammy to a small pond on the ranch, strip off my clothes, and urge her into the still-cold water, then hang onto her mane as she pulled me to the other side. Later I'd climb out into the high grass growing at the edge of the pond and let the morning sun dry my naked body. I loved the sense of freedom I felt lying naked in the grass. I liked being naked, period, and wore clothes as little as possible. Other days I'd ride Tammy to an outcropping of rocks on the Holland Ranch and lie shirtless (free as a boy) as I made nooses of grass to try to catch the blue-tailed skinks that slithered across the rocks. I never caught any but I loved the feel of the sun-warmed roughness of the sandstone against my chest and belly. Maybe my father's worry over my "wildness" was a reasonable thing after all.

The best days were those when I led Tammy around the edge of the cattle guard on the Tall Timbers Ranch, where a herd of Black Angus grazed in the woodland meadows. There was an old "soddie"—a house built of sun-dried mud bricks—where I kept my Big Chief tablet and No. 2 pencils from my mother's prying eyes. She disapproved of my writing and would tear up any of my stories she found, so I wrote in secret here on the ranch. I loved these days when I didn't see or speak to another person.

I was born in 1948, half a century before Dmitri and Janice Papolos published their seminal work on childhood-onset bipolar disorder, The Bipolar Child, so I was seen as an exceptionally bright but difficult child rather than one with a treatable mental illness. In our small community I was known for my oppositional, defiant behavior, explosive temper, and love of risky adventures. Many mothers felt I'd be a bad influence on their daughters, and I received few invitations to birthday parties or sleepovers. Luckily my mother's best friend, Nigel, took me as I was, and she had four sons whom I counted as friends.

The year I was twelve, Nigel took me, her sons, and my two younger brothers on a four-day camping trip that gave rise to the most memorable escapade of my childhood. The last night of the trip, Guy, Nigel's eldest, who was my age and a good friend, and I were fishing in the river that ran through the Black Canyon of the Gunnison when we saw an enormous bird float through the air and disappear into a crack in the cliff on the opposite side of the canyon.

"That's a great horned owl, and I bet she's got some owlets up there," Guy said. "You don't see many of them."

I knew immediately I had to have one of the owlets to rear; they were uncommon and would grow to be so huge. It took me a while to talk Guy into capturing one of the young birds but I finally persuaded him. The next morning we crawled out of our sleeping bags just after dawn and set off for the place we'd seen the mother owl disappear into the cliff. Guy handed me a large stick. "The mother's going to attack if we take one of her babies, so you beat her off me before she can tear me to pieces." Guy had a rope slung over one shoulder to use to capture the young owl. We started climbing. It was hard going, having only one hand to grasp the rock and pull ourselves upward. We finally reached the aerie one hundred feet above the river. Inside were three fledgling owlets, but we didn't see the mother. It smelled musty inside and the owlets backed away from the opening when we stuck our heads inside. The young owls were much bigger than I expected, maybe two feet tall. They clicked their beaks at us but made no other sound. Guy was a ranch kid with excellent roping skills. He unwound the rope and snaked it out over the branches and bones that filled the aerie, snagged the owlet nearest us around its legs, and dragged it to us. The owlet continued to click its beak as we started back down the cliff. I watched out for the mother, but she floated up silently behind us and grabbed Guy by the small of his back with her talons before I had any idea she was close. I tried

to hit her but almost knocked Guy off the cliff instead. Going down was much harder than climbing up. I kept swinging my stick at the mother without much success, and within minutes Guy's shirt was blood-soaked and in tatters. I began to wonder what I'd gotten us into. Finally the mother flew back into the aerie, and we were free to climb down to the river, holding the owlet upside down and trying to avoid his clicking beak. I began to worry about what Nigel would say when she saw Guy's back and shirt; she'd know the idea to climb the cliff had been mine.

But all she said when we came into camp was, "I don't want to hear one word about how you got that owl." And she never did. We named the owl Al and fed him ground beef and mashed bananas, a diet that seemed to agree with him. Of course my mother wouldn't let me keep him, so Al went back to Nigel's ranch when they left near the end of summer. He never became fully wild. Guy told me, in one of his rare letters, that every night Al flew to Guy's bedroom window and sat on the sill, clicking his beak.

I didn't begin treatment for bipolar until the age of thirty, and as I approach seventy, I realize I have never become fully "tame."

I'm not sure I regret it.

About the Author:

Pamela S. Carter studied with Joelle Fraser, and her work has appeared in Midway and Pamplemousse. She graduated with honors from the University of Denver's Sturm College of Law and practiced law briefly after graduation. Pamela now considers herself a full-time writer.

EMAIL TO A DEAD FRIEND

Doug Weaver

Hey Michael – guess what. You died this morning at about 4 a.m. So weird, huh? Apparently you had a heart attack or something. Anyway, I just wanted to tell you because – well, who knows why I need to tell you the details of my life all the time. I just do. Like it or not (and I know sometimes very not) you are and always have been the repository of my details, all the stuff I read and watch and experience. For forty years I get excited at the thought of sharing something with you, with Michael, my Michael.

Anyway, I bet death is weird. You'll have to tell me about it sometime. I have to tell you, though, that literally more people than I knew existed are really really upset this morning. I'm sorry, Michael. That's not fair. It's just that one day I'm going along all normal and stuff and the universe makes some kind of sense because I know you're in it, and I'm reading books with precise sentences and walking the dog and eating watermelon and being pleasant to other people, and the very next day life changes to something else. Really, something like the surface of the moon: everything else is still here, but there's no Michael. It's just fucked up.

Wait a minute. This isn't a joke, is it? You'd never surprise me with something like this. You're too decent to jump out at four in the morning and say Boo! I'm dead! Because I know you loved me and that kind of thing would be totally uncool. It's something I might have done to you, but I know you would never have done it to me. Right? I hope not. Is it cool to use the past tense, you know, because you're dead, like in the past? Is that too morbid? I don't want to offend you so I'm just checking.

If you were here with me, I would tell you your death is actually really really hard for me. Wait, but since you're dead – no. Let me ask it this way: Do the dead have some special knowledge of stuff or have special powers, like Santa or God? I've seen movies that say so. If that's even a remote possibility, I will literally do anything if you just move a hair on my arm, become an annoying little itch somewhere, just to be even a little bit tangible, just for a minute or two. I know deep down that probably won't happen though. Come to think about it – if you really do have some special power – please don't do anything. That would be nice for about one second, and then I'd have to sort all this out again! So wherever you are, just chill.

I'm wondering if the dead have any need for memories. I wonder if I do. Part of me wants to suppress the recollection of all those years we were in love and did all that stuff. Because this is uncomfortable. By the way, I hope you're comfortable. I bet if you did remember stuff, you'd remember that trip to Mexico. I only learned years later that you didn't really care for Mexican food that much – which sort of makes sense because you're French and everything. But those enchiladas we got at that family café – I forgot which state we were in – but all these little towns kind of just popped up out of nowhere among all the church steeples. Remember? We talked about it, like which came first, the church or the town? We could see the café from the street, but there was no sidewalk or anything so we had to kind of jump down a dirt embankment to get to that squat little white building in the middle of this dirt yard that had all these dusty trees in it, with bicycle tires that were swings for the kids. There we were in all that heavy late afternoon heat and the dust and flies with all the dogs and the paper plates and really sweet drinks and the juke box that was all songs in Spanish, but sounded so cool, and the connection we had with the family who tried to speak English and we were trying to speak Español. It was so messy and sticky with laughing and grit and sweat...and god, was it fun. I remember it seemed like we were brave explorers discovering an unknown civilization, but mostly we were just in love. God I loved you then. Remember we were concerned that, being in Mexico, we'd get flack for being two men renting a room with one king-sized bed? But nobody said anything – or if they did, it was between themselves: I had to make the bed for those two sinners in room 214. And that Ford Tempo where you just popped the hood before we left Guadalajara and unhooked the speedometer? That poor Ford Tempo! What a fucking trip that was. Or all those other trips to Europe to see your family? The best life ever.

I know you hate academic stuff, but listen: it's a binary: Michael/No Michael. I think if one of those theorists showed up and reminded me that the point of binaries is to change them from either/or to both/and in an attempt to make me feel better about No Michael, I'd punch him in the face. Michael is better. Both/and Michael just seems like a load of shit right now because you're not here to touch me; to console me; to talk to me. And No Michael feels just like all those sad songs and poems that you always believe are for somebody else. Guess the joke's on me: I'm it this time. It's just really raw and searing and doesn't get smaller, just a big old lonely maw that looks like it would be ravenous, but just fucking sits there all by itself, right in the middle of my chest mocking me, right where – right where my heart is. Damn, Michael, that's it then, huh. I didn't know the heart was that much.

People tell me in their consolations that with time this hole will become a little cooler; flatten out into acceptability, but I don't want it to. No Michael is not acceptable, cannot be acceptable. So for now, I will hold you as close as I can because I can't bear to have No Michael, especially since just the other day I had Michael, the guy who

cried for the cars he sold; who un-self-consciously hugged trees in the Muir Woods. You were such a beautiful dork.

God, I've been thinking crazy thoughts since you died. Some of those thoughts weren't all that charitable either. Like I even felt for a minute that I just wanted to wash my hands of the whole thing, once and for all – just forget about you and live my life as if you'd never existed at all. Once and for all a free man where I could finally be effective, like you might have been responsible for my shortcomings that caused me to live such a fearful life. How fucked up is that? I mean think about when we met. I was so thrilled that I'd met a sexy good looking guy who acted like he wanted to see me again. And you were French! Over the moon! It was so easy like we were both on a steel track chugging away into the sunset. I right away confided to you that I was in AA, that's why I didn't get high or drink booze, which you thought added to my good character. You didn't know – you couldn't have known what I was like prior to getting to AA. But you found out. You were so shocked when I started using drugs again. You made valiant efforts to help, talking to various people who you thought might have insight or leverage. You had no idea that once I started using again that I would be transformed into a liberated Kamikaze Kraken literally existing to destroy everything, including myself. I'm so sorry for all that trouble, Michael. If I had it to do over again – no, that's bullshit. One thing that's become very clear since you died is that there are certain unchangeable "things" in the world: giant impregnable slabs of granite just planted right there in the middle of reality: The Way Things Are and The Way Things Were. For whatever reason there was no way we would have been able to live out our lives together like normal guys. I chose meth and heroin and cocaine over you, Michael, and it couldn't have been any other way. It's a bitter lesson for me, but, as I think about it, also sweet. Because I never found someone else after we separated. I knew I could never replace you, so I consigned myself to live alone, just me and Duffy, the greatest dog on the 7th floor. I've become the Miss Havisham of the East Village, but with a mustache, and always with hope that things would be resolved someday; that all that was needed was one more month, one more week, one more day, and finally, finally this dissonance would resolve, just like a renegade tri-tone screaming through space so it can get home, its existence defined by instability, but with the terrible knowledge that "home" would always be just around the next bend. That's the thing about tri-tones: they're made up of two parts a tri-tone away from each other and they exist only in their quest for resolution. Is that it, Michael? Were you and I destined to fail as a unit? It's a terrible realization to suspect that at least one of us was blind to the duties of maintaining stability. A fatal flaw. Did you finally figure this out? Is that what killed you? I know you knew about my loneliness, how I missed you about one trillion times more than I let on. I know you knew when I phoned you in Montana that I felt like I was intruding, so I kept our contact to a minimum. I know you knew how thrilled I'd be if you called, especially out of the blue; or even sent an unsolicited email to me. You knew that I knew that you could never, even if you'd wanted to, abandon your current partner Dan because that's who you were: a decent man. You were constitutionally incapable of going back on a promise. That's just the way things are.

I know you're gone and I need to treasure you now. I see your face. Your gentle face and your broad smile. I'm grieving. There's no doubt. I guess soon I will have to finally say good-bye and move on with my life. But if it's okay with you, I'll just hang out here by the door for a while, just sit here with my stuff for a minute before I hit the road.

About the Author:

Doug Weaver has earned degrees in piano performance and journalism, and has a graduate degree in creative writing from California State University. Earlier in his career, he also graduated from the Los Angeles Men's Central Jail, having conducted extensive research in the use and commodification of cocaine, methamphetamine and heroin. He teaches at a small liberal arts college in Los Angeles, and currently lives in Long Beach with a cairn terrier.

RESILIENT CHAINS

David Boyle

How many times have we looked within ourselves for an answer to the question What is happiness? More than any of us can imagine, I suppose. I first asked myself that question a number of years ago, well before I reached my thirties, when I began, without realizing it, to take an inventory of my life. And now that I'm fortunate to have reached my late forties, and being of relatively sound mind and body, my answer hasn't changed. I am happy, dear readers, happier than most people who have exceedingly more than I. No matter. I'm a reader, a writer, a film enthusiast, an advocate of the arts. I've numerous interests, hearty thoughts and ideas. I draw immense pleasure from spending the majority of my time experiencing, creating, sharing, and promoting creative ventures. I would find it an extraordinary privilege if one day, sooner rather than later, I could earn a living as a creative individual, never having to waste my precious time, passion, energy, and enthusiasm on trifling occupations. Other than that minor detail, I couldn't be more pleased by what I've done for myself, and with so little.

Life has shown me that each and every one of us has a different idea of happiness, of comfort, of success, of entitlement. I, for one, think that some of us expect too much out of life, or are taught—indoctrinated to believe, in fact—that we should never stop reaching for more and more and more, mindless of the abundance so many have already garnered. I think that rationality bogus. Like the millionaire who's never happy making millions upon millions a year, even middle-upper-class individuals find themselves working exhaustively to secure the so-called American Dream, whatever that may be. For the majority,

I'm sure, that dream translates to staggering wealth and high-living. However, somewhere along the way, while entertaining that fantasy, they glance back and realize they've forgotten where they started, where they were headed, where to pivot next. Then, unable to come to terms with their misconception of the dream, they start living beyond their means, to the point where the dream itself becomes irretrievably misplaced, bringing about further hardship and agitation. Depression, among other afflictions, sets in, dismantling one's life. Perhaps since I've never made a whopping salary (much less than the median income for my demographic), I've taught myself to be fiscally responsible, careful and resourceful with every dollar that comes in. I've got enough food to eat, a roof over my head, and ample outlets to keep my mind and imagination fully engaged and productive. That's quite a lot, in my view. Of course I'd like to sustain myself by focusing exclusively on my craft, but, all particulars considered, I have no legitimate reason to feel cheated, deprived, wronged, or to claim that my personal dream has somehow been ignored or blown to smithereens. After all, when I contemplate the grueling lives of the mentally and physically ill, as well as the degree of suffering around the world and the countless hard-working poor who struggle to avoid impoverishment, I can't help reminding myself that my life has turned out all right, that my petty desires are of little consequence in the grand design of the universe. Nevertheless, I try every day to be a decent person, to improve my standard of life and to maximize my potential, to find simple ways to savor what I hope will be a long, prosperous life, one with minimal physical, financial, and creative difficulty. Ultimately, I want to wake up in the morning for as many days as I may have, to do what inspires me, and maybe earn enough to do that full-time for as long as I am capable. I yearn not for millions, nor for fancy cars or boats or motorcycles, nor for fine foods or wines or clothes, nor for a mansion, nor for various other extravagances. No pampering necessary, folks, I'm not a hedonist. Hedonism, taken to extremes, tends to be a mindless, mirthless, fruitless existence, not to mention costly. Besides, I have my own goals, visions, aspirations, and I'm endeavoring to make them take form, while at the same time I constantly move forward, thinking practically and logically about how I can be the man I wish to be. I can envision him, hunger to be him, but I must keep working toward embodying him.

Insofar as I can tell, attitudes in recent years (in the last decade or so) have changed. When I look around—not far, mind you—I see, here and there, miserable, competitive, unsatisfied people. I know a number of them, and have talked with them; others I don't know personally but I have heard them utter complaints of one sort or another. Everywhere you go these days people, though seemingly well off, have no qualms about voicing their chagrin, even if it comes off as unwarranted, misdirected, or ill-conceived. In the opinion of these impossible-to-please individuals, the best is never sufficient. Some have achieved impressive stature and have accumulated substantial wealth, life-changing wealth. However, when you probe just beneath the surface and uncover more of their story, you often learn of discontent and disharmony; jealousy, envy of another's status. "I should be making more," they say. "I deserve better. Why settle for less? Why be dissatisfied?" Several times I've heard: "I have a college degree. My income, my lifestyle, should be commensurate." Well, ladies and gentlemen, what are these people telling me, telling the world? Are they the only ones worthy of being well circumstanced? I think not. How about the rest of us who haven't been through the channels of academia, who haven't been groomed for excellence and overachievement and stature, who haven't procured that prized piece of paper which seems to guarantee opportunities aplenty for its possessors?

Full disclosure: I don't have a college degree, and I'm not ashamed of that, not embarrassed at all. Though I don't have such a document framed and hanging on my wall or above my desk, to stare at and to be proud of, I've worked hard all my life, as hard as any man or woman, trying to maintain a comfortable existence. Not a man of excess, as I've already conveyed, but someone that can get by without feeling undue strain, undue loss of self-worth, without having to sell himself out and become cut-throat, arrogant, smug. In almost every aspect, I'm doing okay. I live a quiet, respectable life—a life difficult to classify by today's standards. Lest you wonder, I'm not being self-deprecating, I'm being completely honest, and judging by what the data suggests. Overall, though, my life is adequate, and it fills me with gratification to say that I've accomplished everything on my own, through consistency, determination, and honest work, even when the reward has been paltry, as it often has been. I have never taken handouts. No free rides. I've never asked for money without having something to offer in return. No blaming others for troubles that crop up, as is the norm with those who feel underpaid, overworked, as if their lives are stagnating, directionless. Sheer willingness to possibly fail and fail again has gotten me here, without derailing my original mindset, my original commitment to do something that incorporates the best of me. Through the years, having faced my share of triumph and adversity, I've stayed positive, thanks in no small part to a strong mind, an exemplary work ethic, supportive family and friends, and a blossoming interest in the arts. Yes, you heard correctly, the arts have helped me more than you might think. When I'm being creative or when I'm immersed in someone else's creativity—whether it be a good book, a movie, a piece of music, etc.—I'm content beyond measure. At such times I not infrequently ponder the only missing link in the chain that is my life: I hope to soon complete the chain, and live the reasonable, unproblematic life that this ordinary soul has asked for: To live on my own simple terms, using creativity as a means to financial freedom, personal stability, fulfillment in all areas, and to embracing my truest self. I live day to day, just like those of you who are reading this essay, experimenting with the moments as they pass, working toward formulating the answer to an everyday question:

What is happiness? I know what it is, though for me alone, and I must continue searching for the all-important link. Even without it, even if that link should fail to connect to and fill the gap in my chain, I fully comprehend the meaning of happiness. And it hasn't cost me a great deal, and for that I'm grateful.

About the Author:

A versatile writer, **David Boyle** has written two short story collections, published by independent presses. Five of his stories have been adapted to film. In 2014 four stories from his second book, Abandoned in the Dark, were made into a full-length anthology film of the same name. Though he earned his readership by writing reality-based dark fiction, Boyle has gained a reputation for literary stories, essays, articles, aphorisms, reviews, interviews, analyses, travel writing, and poems, a good number of which have appeared in both print and online magazines as well as in anthologies. Discover David Boyle: www.facebook.com/authordavidboyle.

NO TIME FOR TEARS

David Heath

I notice the caller ID number before I answered the phone. Mom and dad kept in touch with me almost every week since I moved to California. I should have called them this week, but between work and my so called busy social life, I simply forgot. My partner, John and I were living on the peninsula in Belmont Shores, California with the Pacific Ocean to the front of the house and the Bay of Naples on the backside. I lifted the receiver as I took a seat on the sofa, "Hi there! Sorry I haven't called. What are you guys up to?"

I was surprised to hear my dad's voice instead of my mom's. "Well son, I didn't want to bother you but I thought you'd want to know." I sensed from the sadness in his tone this was not good news. "I had to put your mother in the hospital yesterday. She's been having trouble breathing again even with the oxygen machine. It doesn't look good but they're doing all they can for her. I'm leaving now to check on her before my cancer treatments at the radiation center. She said not to bother you but you never know what can happen." Dad was never short for words.

How quickly a late spring day can change. Mom had been suffering from bronchitis and emphysema for several years but she wouldn't give up smoking. When they visited us for Thanksgiving at our house in the Tehachapi Mountains, I noticed how the altitude affected her, even though she tried not to show it. But it was dad's last sentence that worried me.

"I have some vacation time saved up and we aren't that busy at the store until the big sale in June. Maybe I can fly back for a visit. I'll check with my manager and see if he can spare me for a few days. I'll call you back tonight and let you know."

"Thanks son. I know she'd be happy to see you if you can get away. I have to go now or I'll be late. We can talk tonight and maybe I'll know more by then. I love you."

"Me too."

Business in the men's clothing department at Saks Fifth Avenue had dropped to a snail's pace since the "after Christmas" returns and the January Sale were over. Our next major events were Father's Day and the Men's Clothing Sale in June. With three other sales people working in the department, I didn't think I would be missed for a few days. I checked with the other salesmen first to see if they would mind

Billy and Michael understood but Marc wanted to know who was going to do my stock work and inventory while I was gone. I told him that would be up to Leith, our department manager and not his worry. Marc had been the top sales person in the department before I came on the scene. He had a cocky attitude and thought he ran the department. Leith said to take as much time as I needed – my job would be there when I returned.

John drove me to the airport the next morning. Sunday flights are always full and I would lose two hours going east to Texas, so I had booked the first direct flight to Dallas-Fort Worth airport, with a return on the following Friday evening. It had been five years since I'd been home. But changing jobs five times in fifteen years, getting settled in my new life on the west coast, meeting my life-time partner and moving six times in that same period could be the reason. Vacations were not spent visiting relatives. However, the urgency in my dad's voice and his concern for mom convinced me I needed to be there. He said he would pick me up at the airport and we could go straight to the hospital – no need to rent a car.

Having worked most of his life for the railroad as a brakeman and conductor on freight trains, my dad retired at the early age of 62. Diagnosed with mesothelioma cancer two years later, he and mom had named me as executor of their wills. Glenda, my older sister, didn't like the idea and Carol, my younger sister, couldn't have cared less.

Our grandfather told me my parents thought I had a better head on my shoulders than either of my sisters. Glenda, my older sister, had been married five times and Carol, who was a year younger than me, had been through three husbands. Neither of them had to work for a living unless they wanted to. I guess that made me the more stable sibling.

The heat and humidity hit me like a sauna as I stepped out the door of the plane and tread down the stairs to the tarmac. Dad was waiting in the lounge - I almost didn't recognize him. It's strange how people can age so much when you are not around them daily. On our way to the hospital, I noticed him shaking as he drove. I could tell that the radiation treatments and chemo therapy had taken their toll.

When last I saw him I recalled a vibrant man of sixty, his grey hair, cut in a flat-top and his square jaw always clean shaven, but sitting beside me was someone I didn't know. The deep wrinkles, sunken cheeks and dark circles under his eyes made his once handsome face like a skeleton. His strong muscular arms were now just sagging skin stretched over bones. Even when he tried to smile I could tell he was hiding the pain.

He said mom was out of intensive care and appeared to be doing better. He asked about John, our jobs and the house in the mountains which had so impressed him. He couldn't believe we had built it ourselves. In general he needed to talk. His actions told me he wanted to tell me

something but didn't know how to say it. I would learn later what he couldn't say.

Mom, sitting in up in bed eating some Jell-O when we arrived, smiled as I gave her a kiss on the cheek. "Wow! This is a surprised. When did you get here?"

"Just arrived today. A little bird told me you were in the hospital so I thought I'd come and rescue you."

"Well, more likely it was probably some old crow." She winked at dad. "But I'm so happy to see you sweetheart. Is John with you?"

"Not this time. He couldn't get off work – some big project or other. You must be feeling better, you look great. Why are they keeping you here? We should take you home."

"Oh boy! I would love that, but the nasty old doctor needs to run some more test tomorrow so I'll have to stay here over night." She grabbed my hand and whispered, "Can you bring me a Lotaburger and some fries? The food here sucks – even this Jell-O."

To tell the truth, mom was craving a cigarette, I could see it in her eyes. She was ready to get out of that place and light-up. I had tried to convince her and my sisters to stop smoking, but I couldn't be there to make it happen. Dad had already quit because of his lung cancer. Not that it made much difference after years of breathing asbestos from the brake-shoes on the trains. The doctors said he had from six months to three years left at best, even with the treatments. We visited for a while until mom began to tire. I gave her a hug and said we would see her at noon the next day. "Trust me," I said, "I'll have your burger and fries with me."

My grandfather, known to everyone as Gran, lived with my parents. Mom was an only child and Gran was her father. He cooked dinner at home that evening for the three of us. At the age of 84, he suffered sciatic nerve issues but still drove to work every weekday morning. An accountant for forty-three years with Mobil Oil, he now worked in a small, CPA office a short distance from the house.

Dad, looking exhausted, said he needed some rest. I gave his frail body a hug as he hung on to me. I told him I too was tired and said good night. I slept on the sofa in the living room even though it was a three bedroom house. Gran had his bedroom and my old room was being used for storage.

I awoke to the smell of coffee coming from the kitchen and checked my watch. It was still dark outside and the illuminated dial showed 5:30 am. Gran was an early riser. We had coffee together as we discussed mom's health. He wanted to go to the hospital with us at noon, so I said we would come by and pick him up at work. My sisters were coming over around ten o'clock to go with us.

The house was still and quiet as I roamed from living room to dining room and kitchen out to the den and dad's ham-radio workshop remembering the wonderful times we shared as a family. I peeked in my old room but didn't go in - boxes were stacked everywhere. My sister's shared room was now Gran's room and still had their twin beds, a dresser and a vanity with a beveled mirror.

I made myself some breakfast wondering what time dad would be up. I didn't want to disturbed his much needed rest. Glenda, with her wavy auburn hair, arrived at ten sharp. After we greeted each other, she began bustling around the kitchen. "Where's dad?" she asked.

"Not up yet. He was tired last night so I didn't want to wake him too early."

"Well you need to go wake him now. He'll want breakfast and we can't wait all morning. We should be at the hospital before the lunch hour or they'll shoo us out. They have strict visiting hours you know." Glenda sounded like an army sergeant barking orders.

I knock on his bedroom door but there was no sound. Perhaps he was in the shower. I open the door to a dark room and could barely make out a figure lying in bed. I went to the window on dad's side of the bed and opened the blinds. "Time to get up - Glenda's making breakfast." I turned to see his body still lying in bed. I touched his shoulder to wake him – it was stone cold. A shock went through me. He was dead. The soft morning light from the window behind me fell on his face ravaged in silent pain. I pulled the bed sheet up over his head, shut the blind and closed the door

behind as I entered the hallway. He had not uttered a sound during the night. Perhaps I was so tired I didn't hear him.

In the kitchen, Glenda had started fixing his breakfast. "You don't need to do that." I spoke with a lump in my throat. "Daddy's dead - he died in his sleep last night."

She quickly became hysterical - sobbing uncontrollably. "No – no, he can't be. This isn't happening."

I turned the stove off - grabbed her shoulders and shook her. "Glenda, he's dead, you have to get a hold of yourself. We have calls to make and things to take care of." I stopped her as she headed for the bedroom. "I don't think you should see him right now – it's not a pretty site and I don't want you to remember him that way." I hugged her tight and let her cry for a few more minutes. Carol arrived about that time and she and Glenda consoled each other while I made the necessary calls.

I phoned the funeral home first. Dad had made all the arrangements ahead when he learned of his cancer. He'd arranged everything for mom at the same time, even to their obituaries for the newspapers. Their headstones were carved and ready except for the date of death. The hearse arrived and they remove his body in less than an hour. They said his body would be ready for viewing the following day in the Garden of Gethsemane room at Forest Lawn Cemetery. The funeral would be held in three days. I notified their doctor so he could sign the death certificate at the funeral home.

I arranged a meeting with their lawyer for the next morning. Now it was time to break the news to our mom – a task I tried in my mind to prepare for. We stopped to get our grandfather and I told him the sad news while he sat at his desk. I knew when he got to the car he would wonder why dad wasn't there.

Standing in the hospital hallway, a nurse informed us visiting hours were over until after lunch had been served to the patients. I explained what had happened and why we were there. I asked her to have someone standing by in case mom needed a sedative when I told her about our father. I wasn't waiting for visiting hours. On hearing my sad message, she called another nurse over, told her to be prepared and allowed us to enter mom's room.

She had just started eating her lunch and was surprised to see all of us there. "Where's my Lotaburger and fries? Is your dad bringing them?"

I sat on the side of her bed and took both her hands in mine. "Daddy won't be here today." I whispered. "He's now with the angles." At first, she wasn't sure she heard me.

"He's where?" she said – and then it registered.

"Oh no! No – no…not my baby."

I wrapped my arms around her and told her he had died peacefully in his sleep at home. She shook with deep sobs and continued to cry on my shoulder. The nurse looked in and I nodded my head as mom leaned back in the bed - one hand in mine and the other covering her mouth, the tears rolling down her pale cheeks. The rosy color had drained from her face. The girls gather closer to comfort her while i chatted with the doctor by the nurse's station.

We stayed as long as we could until the sedative began to make her drowsy. The doctor said he would let us know if there were any changes. He phoned later that evening and recommended she stay in the hospital a few more days. She'd experienced a relapse with the news and her breathing had become irregular. He wouldn't sign her release until she improved.

I called the airlines to cancel my return trip and find out what they would need to reschedule a flight when I knew a date. They were understanding and most helpful. I then contacted the personnel office at Sax and arranged to take the additional time off until mom could return home.

Our dad had more friends than I realized and I was surprised to see such a large turnout for the funeral with standing room only at the back of the large chapel. A male vocalist sang I Come to the Garden Alone, and Clifford Williams our Presbyterian minister preached the eulogy. I took care of the floral arrangements with our family florist and made sure dad was buried with his Masonic ring and apron. Eight men from his lodge served as pallbearers. I had served as a DeMolay Grand Master in the same lodge.

As I stood by the open grave, and placed a single white carnation on the casket, I finally understood what he had wanted to tell me when I arrived. He knew he was dying and wanted me to be there when it happened. I would be the man of the family now and he trusted me to know what to do. How did I miss that?

Meanwhile, back at the house, neighbors had arrived with tons of food. It's traditional in Texas to gather at the home of the deceased and provide the family members with food and beverages as many people come to offer their condolences. No time to be alone and reflect on the happenings of the day. All will be well.

My sisters and I decided to redecorate mom's bedroom before we brought her home. We painted the yellowed, cigarette stained walls a bright cream color, purchased a new mattress that didn't sag, hung new floral drapes with a matching bed comforter and moved dad's clothes to the closet in my old bedroom until she decided what to give to Goodwill.

After collecting mom from the hospital, we drove out to the gravesite. She couldn't attend the funeral since she was still in the hospital. Sitting in her wheelchair beside the grave, she asked to be alone for a few minutes as we stepped away.

She had saved a white carnation from one of her many floral arrangements at the hospital and placed it on his grave.

Back at the house, the girls made her comfortable in her recliner chair, while I went to Lotaburger and returned with lunch. She smiled as I opened the bags and placed the cheeseburger, fries and a large coke on her TV tray. "Now that's what I call a lunch." She said.

So much had changed in so little time, but a Lotaburger will never change. Everyone dug into the bags for their burgers and fries as I filled her in on what we had done. Several neighbors dropped in to say hello. A few days later, when things calmed down, I returned to LA leaving mom in the care of my sisters.

John met me at the airport and I filed him in on all the details. He'd wanted to come to Texas for the funeral, but I told him there was nothing he could do and he shouldn't miss work. We ate dinner out that evening. Exhausted, I crawled into bed and passed out. John left for work early the next morning.

I fixed my breakfast and sat at the dining room table alone staring through the floor-to-ceiling windows at our lush patio garden and began to cry. I hadn't been able to shed a tear for the past three weeks and I couldn't stop. I hadn't told the store when I would return so I stayed home and talked to my dad the rest of the day. There hadn't been time for tears but I knew he would understand.

About the Author:

At the age of 75, **David Heath** is currently enjoying life as a writer in the tropics of the Yucatan along with John, his life-partner of 48 years. Originally from Ft. Worth, Texas, David worked as a lifeguard, a Latin dance instructor, an interior designer, and a private secretary before moving to Los Angles, where he sold real estate, wrote music, did some fashion modeling and founded his own visual merchandising company. For twenty years, David & John owned and operated the Rancho de San Juan Country Inn and Restaurant northwest of Santa Fe, New Mexico, where they were honored with numerous awards in the hospitality industry. Having traveled most of Europe, the continental United States and Canada, David is busy writing, poetry, mysteries and a memoir titled Adventures in Life. His recent published works include: Tales from a Country Inn – The Rancho de San Juan Story. The D.G. Heath - Mystery Collection(Double Martini - Web of Intrigue & Codes and Confessions). David is currently writing - D.G. Heath - Mystery Collection – Book Two (Vortex – Casting Shadows & Blood Moon). Fiction, fantasy and mystery are his tools.

MIMI

Pam Munter

Her most indelible appearance comes during the last segment of a silent and faded 8mm color film reel running just about three minutes, probably around 1949. The family is stiffly gathered on the lawn in the front of her spacious, rented two-story white, wooden Arts and Crafts house on Arroyo Verde Road in South Pasadena. My father, ever the family photographer, slowly and awkwardly pans the ensemble. There is the Cleveland family contingent of five here for a vacation escaping the Midwest humidity. At the end of the row is my wonderful Nana, my father's mother. There's someone standing very close to her. I can see it's me. I'm probably six, looking quizzically toward the camera. A short distance away, there are my parents and my baby brother, Johnny. No one seems to know how to behave in front of the Bell and Howell windup camera, standing as if they were impatiently posing for a still photograph, their faces frozen in uncomfortable smiles.

Then, suddenly from the left side of the frame, there is a blur of motion. The camera irresistibly pans over to capture a slim woman with burnt umber hair piled on top of her head, wearing a long, silky dark green dress and dancing as if the whole Copacabana orchestra is behind her. She is smiling and twirling her billowing skirt like a ballroom champion, making big circles around the yard. It is a moment of pure joy. Her exuberance is startling in contrast to the early part of the three-minute reel. The grainy film doesn't even seem to be in color until Mimi flounces into the picture. The film suddenly turns white and stops. Thinking about it immediately brings a huge smile to my face. No one ever expressed intemperate exhilaration like that in our tightly wrapped, conservative family.

Like her flamboyant persona, Mimi's history was fascinating and glamorous. I would later find out that sometime around 1919 or 1920, Mimi was the first of her eight siblings to emigrate from England to the United States, settling in Philadelphia. Her history is sketchy, so typical of black sheep, but it would seem she joined an opera company and met a tall handsome tenor named Frederick Etheridge. While in the troupe – one that also featured future MGM star Nelson Eddy - they fell in love, married and had a son, Fred. The marriage didn't work out, so like her own mother, she moved on - without her husband and without bothering to divorce him. Mimi and little Fred moved to Cleveland, Ohio and helped the rest of the family settle there as well, just as soon as they could get past the noisy, frightening scrutiny of Ellis Island.

After my father and mother moved to Santa Monica, California, they sent frequent letters touting the superior weather and job opportunities during the heavy hopelessness of the Depression. Mimi picked up her son and moved to nearby South Pasadena. Soon, her only sister, Rene, would join her in California, opening up a small health food manufacturing plant with her husband.

During my early childhood, I had seen Mimi only on special family occasions. Holidays were big extended family eating events with 20-30 people each Thanksgiving and Christmas, seated around a ping pong table set with bright holiday colors. Mimi would motor over from South Pasadena in her ancient, sputtering Dodge, arriving in a frazzled state and immediately demanding a bourbon and Seven Up. It wasn't until my parents wanted to park me somewhere that I began to spend more time with her. My younger brother Johnny would be dropped off with my mother's parents in nearby Ocean Park then they'd make the one-hour drive to South Pasadena on the brand new Pasadena Freeway.

I loved staying with Mimi. Unlike the other Osbornes, she seemed to have broken free of many constraints. She talked to me like a person, seemed to think about what might please me and introduced me to a world different from the one I saw at home. While she was never demonstrative, I got the feeling she wanted to spend time with me, enjoyed having me in her world.

Somehow I knew that Mimi was a family outcast. I thought it odd that my father and her own mother always called her by her proper name, Muriel, and there seemed to be some unspoken tension between all of them. Mimi's single marital status worked against her for sure, in our insecure, tradition-bound lower middle class community. Leaving one's husband? Just not done. She drank every day, which was far from my parents' occasional social tippling, so they considered her an alcoholic. She was overtly anxious, too, which likely made my parents uncomfortable with their own rigorously submerged emotions.

Mimi's younger sister, Rene, had died the week I was born - from a surprise cardiovascular accident, one of the many Osbornes who were to die at a relatively young age of that disease. Her widower didn't have the heart to carry on the business they had started together, so Mimi took it over. The small health food manufacturing company wasn't a big moneymaker but enough to keep her and Nana afloat in that big white, wooden house. Mimi's son, who fought for the RAF in World War II, had been a POW for several years, an event never discussed by anyone in the family. When he came back, he moved out and went to college on the GI Bill to become an aeronautical engineer, the family's first college graduate. I would become the second.

An hour or so after dinner, my parents said their goodbyes to return home. That meant my bedtime was coming up soon. Mimi would say, "Time to march up the little wooden hill, Ducky." It was an apt description of the winding staircase

leading to the second floor. It was dark on the stairs and upstairs, too, and I hesitated to go up there alone. I slept in the big double bed with Nana, both of us reading ourselves to sleep.

Sometime in the middle of the night the Santa Fe train would make its intrusive, almost deafening presence known, awakening me with fear and dread. It was so much scarier at night than the daytime runs, to which I often ran outside so I could wave at the engineer. The train tracks were only an empty lot and a narrow street away from the house and, in the calm of the night, it felt as if the engine would blast right through the bedroom wall.

In the early years there, I had nightmares about the bad things that could happen when all that noise could cover them up – a gruesome murder, for example. My twitchy fantasies had been informed by radio mysteries, movies and the reading of Mimi's Mickey Spillane paperbacks. Because the house was constructed of wood, I feared a fire breaking out. The house was so old it had the original gas fixtures, though they were no longer used. I saw potential peril everywhere. And yet, the two larger second floor bedrooms – Mimi's and Nana's - each had its own outdoor balcony.

In her efforts to protect me, Mimi inadvertently blocked my means of escape. "You must never go out there, Love. You'd fall right through to the ground and die." But I knew the forbidden rooftop balcony could provide an escape if only I could get to it before being burned to death.

During the days, I played cards with Nana or explored the neighborhood on foot. Sometimes, Nana would move to the ancient upright piano against the back wall and play. I always requested "The Blue Danube Waltz" because it was so melodic and made me feel warm and buoyant. Nana's tightly coiffed hair would gently sway to the rhythm of the ¾ time. She must have had other songs in her repertoire but that was the one I loved and would always associate with her.

When she would tire of entertaining me, Nana would give me a nickel for an orange Nehi and send me off to the gas station on the corner. Looking back, I realize I spent a lot of time alone in South Pasadena just as I had during much of my childhood at home.

Being such an anxious kid tended to constrict my world in many ways. But if much of my childhood seemed to be in black and white, it turned to glorious Technicolor when Mimi would come home from work.

Almost the first words out of her mouth were, "Be a good girl and fix me a drink, Popsie."

I had been instructed on the proper way to mix her Seagram's and Seven. If I mixed the magic concoction according to the acceptable formula, she might let me light her unfiltered Camel all by myself. I handed it to her and she'd take a long drag, then turn on the radio to listen to the news, Walter Winchell or to popular music. After she and Nana discussed the day's events, she would head to the kitchen to open something for dinner.

Her favorite seemed to be canned salmon, always accompanied by some vegetable like lima beans or green beans – all out of a metal container and all a khaki color. The less-than-luxe cuisine was in contrast to the formality of the sparkling white tablecloth and polished silver candlesticks on the dining room table where we ate all our meals. On special occasions she lit the candles, then proceeded to demonstrate for me the correct way to use the candle snuffer to end their lives at the end of the meal. After a few lessons, she gave me that task for the rest of our candlelit meals together. I relished that grave responsibility, always making sure she saw I was executing it correctly, flipping the silver snuffer over quickly so wax would never spill on the tablecloth.

"Good job, Ducks."

Mimi's voice sounded like she was forcing it out, due to its thin tone and her ambient level of tension. She tended to clip off her words at the end, a lingering artifact of a once thicker British accent. If I were to do anything wrong, she would caution me with a slight edge to her voice. "Don't be a gutter snipe, Dear." I didn't know what that was, but it sounded pretty awful, so I fell into line.

All the oversized and overstuffed furniture in the house looked old and beat up to my young eyes but many were probably antiques. The house had a unique smell, as if it had been hermetically preserved from an earlier century. The small dining room was consumed by an expandable wooden table and a big, matching credenza. On one wall

next to the doorway to the kitchen was an unexpected and almost grotesque caricature of Louis Armstrong that I examined every time I sat down to eat. Asking too many questions was rude, so I never knew why this particular picture was chosen or if she had a personal connection with it or to him in some way. I was almost hypnotized by that picture but now I can't remember if it was in black and white or in color. Its unique lines caught my eye every time, having never seen anything like it. Like many in that post World War II era, African Americans were seen as less than human and I'm pretty sure most of my family members agreed with that. Certainly in my house, there were no pictures of black people, even cartoonish ones. Later, I came to see it as one of Mimi's many admirable departures from family canon.

After dinner, we'd settle in the living room. Mimi had her second or third Seagrams, another Camel and listened to the radio. One of her favorite tunes was the 1951 hit, "I Get Ideas" a seductive tango sung by baritone Tony Martin. At eight years old, I didn't know what kind of ideas he might get, but Mimi certainly did. Her mask-like face would lose its tension and she would become radiant, listening to the lyrics and even sometimes singing along.

When we are dancing and you're dangerously near me

I Get Ideas, I Get Ideas

I want to hold you so much closer than I dare do,

I want to scold you 'cause I care more than I care to

And when you touch me and there's fire in every finger

I Get Ideas, I Get Ideas

And after we have kissed good night and still you linger

I kinda think you get ideas, too.

I could tell she was transported by the music and I loved watching her move her lithe body to its rhythm. Much later, of course, I would realize that Mimi was still a very sexual creature – something that would never be acknowledged in my family.

She was in her early 50s by now and was actively dating. Much of the time, she took me with her – at least, for the first part of the evening. I felt very grown up and fondly remember the atmosphere at the cozy Old Virginia restaurant, one of her favorites. There was live music from an accordion, red-checkered tablecloths and candles on the tables, all right out of a movie. As with most public places, the air was clogged with cigarette smoke, which was considered normal. They'd order me a Shirley Temple while they had their cocktails and let me have whatever I wanted for dinner. Then she'd take me back to the house and I was supposed to go to bed. I was often still awake when she'd come home late. I knew what was likely coming. Nearly every night before bed, she sat at her dressing table in her bedroom while she cleaned off her makeup and colored her hair with henna. I was fascinated by the whole process – from the idea of even having a dressing table to putting icky, gooey stuff on one's hair. I had never seen anything like that at home.

While I enjoyed my many adventures with Mimi, my favorite time was New Year's Eve. Surprisingly now, looking back, she never accepted a date for that night. It became our special night. Before I came into the family, Mimi spent many nights at the end of each year helping to decorate the floats for the Pasadena Rose Parade, pasting on the fresh flowers and seeds to create a colorful spectacle. That was history when I began spending more time with her in the big white house after Christmas.

On December 31, she'd bring in a big two-pound box of See's candies and stock my favorite Nehi orange soda, along with other cookies and treats. Nana inevitably complained.

"She's going to get sick from all that sugar, Muriel."

Mimi defended her largesse. "It's just for one night."

I struggled to stay awake until midnight because I knew it would be worth it. Around 10 p.m., Nana went upstairs to bed. Mimi turned on the newly purchased RCA console TV and there was Guy Lombardo and his orchestra. We watched the black and white images and waited. Then the countdown. Ten, nine, eight, seven, six, five, four,

three, two, one. Happy New Year!!! Mimi and I would holler that incantation over and over. Then after a conspiratorial grin, we'd run up the dark stairs to the Chinese gong that sat on the table at the top of the stairs. We both bonged it athletically, without any regard for poor Nana trying to sleep in an adjacent room, which always made us laugh hysterically. Once the gong had been rung, we went back downstairs. Mimi opened the front door, picked up the doormat and launched it into the yard.

"Why did you do that, Meem?" I asked.

"It's out with the old, in the with the new. It'll bring good luck." I didn't know why that would be true but went along with it, part of the tradition. I loved the exuberance with which she heaved that dirty old mat.

Serendipitously and without much fanfare, Mimi introduced me to what would become my lifelong fascination with the theater. On one of those New Year's stays, she took me to see a comedy at the historic Pasadena Playhouse. I can imagine my nine-year-old eyes gleaming, my mouth agape, sitting in the front row watching these people create bright and spellbinding entertainment just a few feet away. The name of the play has lost its way somewhere in my brain, but I remember it starred the comedienne Vera Vague. And I easily bring back the enchantment and sense of awe, much like a religious experience. Even now, I have those identical feelings when I walk into an historically rich theater, eager to be transported outside my own world.

One evening during a subsequent visit, Mimi called me over to the couch.

"Sit down, Popsie. I want to tell you something. Pretty soon, your cousin Nancy is coming here to live with us."

I had never met Nancy. At ten years of age, she was nearly a year older than I was and lived with her parents in Ohio. I knew that her father, Mimi's younger brother, had died suddenly years earlier, and that her mother had been ill and had died. I didn't then know that the mother had been schizophrenic. I was crestfallen.

"But don't you worry, Ducks. You and Nancy will get along fine." She paused and looked directly into my eyes while she reached for my hand. "Don't ever forget, Popsie, you'll always be my Queen Bee."

I nodded and hoped that were true. "OK."

I took some comfort in that reassurance, but I sensed something important was ending. There might not be so many spontaneous trips to Chinatown after dinner or to Fosselman's ice cream shop after Saturday errands. And I probably couldn't hang out with her in her business any more, either. Not with another kid there.

Nancy was there by the time I made my next visit. We got along well enough, played together every day. We went to the movies and walked to the Community Plunge to swim in the summers. We read movie magazines and comic books. But all we had in common were Mimi and Nana. I was curious about what had happened in Ohio, but it was completely against family rules to ask about something so personal.

To my relief, the New Year's Eve tradition stayed true. Now there was even more noisemaking at midnight, making it more fun.

But when I was 12, life as I had known it stopped cold. Nana died. She had a series of strokes and the family had made many urgent drives to the nursing home in Pasadena. I always brought her a little gift I had made or bought with my allowance. After she died and Mimi laid all her things on her bed, the same bed we shared when I'd visit. I saw she had kept all of them – my drawings, my little toys – everything I had ever given her. At the funeral, I was the only one crying. Later, I wondered if she was the one adult who loved me most of all.

Nana's dying felt bigger than the loss itself, though that was the hardest thing I had yet experienced in my young life. Looking back, I can see that Nana's death was the beginning of a bent toward melancholia that has never left me.

Mimi and Nancy moved to Long Beach where Mimi bought a small health food store. I visited now and again but it wasn't anywhere close to being the same. The pallor of Nana's death hung over me for years. And, true to the family ethic, no one discussed it. Nancy wasn't much interested in academics, reading or sports and seemed to spend much of her time at home, knitting and

taking care of Mimi. Now it was Nancy who poured the drinks every night and lit up her Camels. Like the emerging tides slowly eroding a treasured sand castle, my connection with both of them seem to dissipate over time.

Mimi died of the family curse, a massive CVA in 1964, at the age of 64. It was my senior year at Berkeley and, if there was a funeral, I wasn't told about it until after it was over. Nancy married soon thereafter, had two daughters, and moved to Oklahoma where she, too, had a series of strokes.

A couple of years ago, I was in the South Pasadena area and decided to drive by the house that had been the scene for so many abiding memories and recurrent dreams. Though everything had changed along with the increased traffic congestion, I knew exactly which turnoff to take off the Pasadena freeway, Avenue 64. I could feel my heart racing as I turned right past the green Arroyo Seco parkway then right on Arroyo Verde Road. I slowed down and looked to my left for the stately white house. To my shock and dismay, in its place was a parking lot for a small industrial complex. I circled the block several times, trying in vain to find that center of my childhood. Did I choose the wrong turnoff? Had I remembered the wrong address? I felt tears quickly well up and roll down my cheeks – it was all gone. Had it burned to the ground, as my little girl self had feared? It was the last vestige of important formative experiences and relationships. As if a symbol of the change, Arroyo Verde had become a busy thoroughfare and I couldn't so much as slow down amid all the traffic to consider the jolt.

It was really gone, every piece of it.

But now unfailingly each New Year's Eve, those South Pasadena scenes are replayed like home movies in my mind. Not just the fun and funny celebrations with the gong, but all the warmth and affirmation I got from Mimi and from Nana. Mimi seemed to know how to make the most of her life and, even considering whatever demons she might have fought, she knew how to make me feel special and loved.

It's hard to realize that Mimi, Nana and I shared those precious moments for only three short years, then three more once Nancy came to live there. Perhaps the intermittent flashes of passion and the possibility of a Technicolor life made it seem longer. In some ways, she was my very own Auntie Mame. She couldn't have been any more memorable.

About the Author:

Pam Munter has authored several books and a couple dozen articles, mostly about dead movie stars. She's a retired clinical psychologist and former performer. Pam is working on a deconstructed memoir and short stories based on old Hollywood. Her essays have appeared in Manifest-Station, The Coachella Review, Lady Literary Review, NoiseMedium, The Creative Truth and Angels Flight—Literary West. Her play, "Life Without," opened the staged reading season at Script2Stage2Screen in Rancho Mirage, California and was a semi-finalist in the Ebell of Los Angeles Playwriting Competition. Pam will finish her MFA in Creative Writing and Writing for the Performing Arts this June at the University of California at Riverside/Palm Desert.

Website: http://www.pammunter.com

TWENTY -SEVEN

Holley Hyler

The morning of my birthday, I opened the card my mother sent me. It was meant to be innocuous, but it opened the floodgates with only two sentences: "When I turned twenty-seven, your sister was three months old. Your life and mine are not at all alike, are they?"

The back of my armchair felt like his chest, so I pressed my face against it and wept.

The blood between my thighs agreed with my mother's statement, a birthday gift that my body had held on to for over two months. It heard him when he told me that he did not love me, a thought that made me tearful in the doctor's office days earlier. I shook my head when the nurse asked if anyone had hurt me, assuming she meant intentionally. I shook my head again when she asked if I could be pregnant, the "You Are Safe Here" sign on the wall mocking me.

People have a way of writing it off as insanity or low self-worth when you love so much. They classify it as "low libido" or "fear of intimacy" when there is only one person on the Earth that you dream of allowing inside you. Those who believe in that fear cannot see the paradox in it, thinking it normal to stand naked before partner after partner in a fruitless quest, the skin flushed before the soul is even warm.

The doctor walked in and pretended not to see as I wiped my eyes. I pretended to read the documents posted around the sign. He told me that my blood test results were normal, and then he left.

The evening of my birthday, the rusty Ferris wheel at the state fair loomed, encouraged by the night to show its true colors. The attendant at its gate pointed to a "No Single Riders" sign when I approached. He watched as I bent to walk underneath the chains and out of the line, people's gazes pressing the weight of shame on my back.

I wandered, taking in the sights and sounds, the feeling of mockery returning whenever I saw the Ferris wheel blinking in the distance.

"Join a sideshow," it seemed to say. "You could be the World's Loneliest Girl."

"You are as fake as the sign in my doctor's office," I thought. "After this is over, they will tear you down and put you in a truck. You have no home, no anchor."

It glowed fuchsia, then blue. "You wound me."

During my drive home, I wondered how many tears had sunk into the depths of my chair.

The day after my birthday, my tears mingled with my morning coffee until all I tasted was salt. I craved an anchor, other than the one inside me. People were sometimes fake, could not be anchors, could not be static like furniture. I leaned my head against the chair.

"You are safe here," I whispered.

About the Author:

Holley Hyler is from southern Virginia and currently lives in Rochester, New York. She graduated in 2013 from University of Mary Washington with a Bachelor of Arts in Creative Writing. Her first publication, a personal essay entitled "Meditation Session," was in Buck Off Magazine in May of 2016. She works as a consultant and plays the guitar in her down time.

THE PAINS AND PRIZE OF REMEMBERING TIME

by Angela Yurchenko

"Culture is love plus memory," a poet tells his students. I catch the reverberating echo of his voice refracting through decades. Having prepared myself, a few seconds back, for yet another thesis on the undefinable, overused word, in large the curse word of modern society, I jumped at the eye widening, brief, and anything but banal definition – better, equation - one that you'd never hear from academics, professors, or even men of art. Yet here it was, spoken by Nobel-Prize winning poet Joseph Brodsky. Poets are very precise in their choice of words and much of what is spoken by the great ones bears a sort of Old Testament prophet power. Love – memory - culture? Right away, his words carried me off on a train of accumulating thought.

I hasten to add - my first thoughts were not on love, but on memory. In fact, memory and everything having to do with Chronos is one of my favorite concepts in Art. Talking of memory, we also stumble upon remembrance, its more popular sibling. Though a part of memory, it is only a single and flatter side of it. Were we to forget, let's keep in mind that to "remember" means to recollect a certain event, thought, piece of information, etc. But "memory" is the accumulated baggage of these fragments which form into a single thick layer inside us. The former is momentary, dependent on the external, possible to be taken apart; the latter is a constant presence, be it conscious, or subconscious. Less casual, when it comes to art, Memory is more tangible.

As I saw it then, the greater Memory incarnated before my eyes as a sort of string - long, visible to few, stretching across centuries, connecting centuries, people, and thoughts. A fragile string that carried tremendous power, energy, force, like a thin wire loaded with a thousand-volt current. One where no part was torn, one which spun its way through great minds, through tragedies, through bliss, and finally reached us - living, doubting, laughing–today. And this string the poet called culture. How far have we come from academic definitions? Perhaps not that far.

Briefly: the first roots of the word go back to the Latin colere. As many words, it held a very practical and down-to-earth meaning: to cultivate, till the earth. In fact, only in 19th century English was the word started to be used figuratively, as "to cultivate the mind and senses." The efforts of tilling the earth were very well reflected in the effort of "tilling" [i.e. –obtaining by effort (old Germanic)] one self. This effort part is completely gone in most of the definitions we associate with the word nowadays – words like "popular" and "group culture." In the nineteenth century, the word held a distinctive personal definition – it was the very opposite of the mass- produced. Perhaps it's in this combination of the personal and the Chronos-conscious, that we might at last find truth. Most definitions we use as of this day will be shattered. Be that as it may.

Somewhere, in the far, far distance, goes on hushed conversation, pretty serious. But again, this is the far past, moreover, a realm of memory.

And love? What can one say about this even more oft-repeated, humiliated word?

"We must love one another or die."

But allow me then- aren't we dying this very day, this very moment? And in fact, aren't we already dead?!

A buzz, like the scratching of an old vinyl, accumulates in the tense air and suddenly switches off. The voice disappears. No one is to be seen.

Who cares for social neatness? If W.H Auden's commandment has become a stumbling stone – the price of the question really too high for too many – we should know that stumbling is the outcome of blindness, and not the poet's fault. Even more so, when in context - for the context was World War II. And yet, this was only a commandment of a commandment. Strange, that it would cause such debate.

Memory, love....I get the feeling that together, these two ancient words mean a lot more than their single, ambitious equivalent, reminiscent of sweaty tilling. Free of the many prejudices that still bind us, keeping the wire connecting us through centuries throbbing, transforming it into a vein which flows from the very source, perhaps we can survive only thus. By survive, I mean live up to our purpose down here, in each separate case. The power of keeping great art in our active, living memory is that as a living substance, it multiplies and births worlds beyond what we may have imagined at first glance. Its children are more multiple than the sand. Like the cosmos, the word has no end. The driving force, however, remains - as it was in the beginning - Love. If universal love still remains a matter of question, then from another viewpoint everything falls into place:

When we hate each other, we die.

The same holds true for memory. The same holds true for the sum of the equation, however we want to define it.

About the Author:

Angela Yurchenko is a classical pianist, translator and copywriter. She was raised in NYC where she studied at the Juilliard School of Music and started her performing arts career. Currently, Angela lives in Saint Petersburg, Russia where she works for an international company as a translator and copywriter, and continues her concert career. She loves writing about arts and culture.

GRADUATE

Robert Cardullo

"Fifty Years After: Some Thoughts on The Graduate and the New American Cinema"

When Mike Nichols' second film, The Graduate, was released on December 21, 1967 (fifty years ago, which is hard to believe), it proved that he was a genuine director—one to be admired as well as to be concerned about. It also marked the screen début, in a title role, of Dustin Hoffman, a young actor already known in the theater as an exceptional talent, who here increased his reputation. Also, after many months of prattle at the time about the New American Cinema,1 The Graduate gave some substance to the contention that American films were coming of age—of our age.

To wit, during the two years prior to the release of The Graduate, there had been a considerable shift in the filmmaking climate. American movies usually reflected the truth of American lives without intending to, because movies manufactured as commercial entertainments were nonetheless inescapably the products of contemporary psyches. But in the mid-1960s many American films started, quite consciously if not always successfully, to come to grips with various social phenomena and certain psychic states. (I'm speaking of a change in well-budgeted theatrical films. Underground films had always tried to treat those matters; one of their reasons for existence was to compensate for the lack of such honest encounter in aboveground films.) This is not to say that psychical substructure had disappeared from these new films, but much that used to be implied or that only seeped into movies because it couldn't be kept out, was now there by explicit design.

Obviously some "personal" films had been made in the United States before this time, but there was now a strong new direction of which Mike Nichols' The Graduate was the first visible marker. Let's define a "personal" film (yet again) as one made primarily because the maker wants to make it, not as a contract job: analogous—as far as the conditions of the medium permit—with a poet's writing a poem or a sculptor's making a sculpture. In most of these films from the mid-to-late sixties and early 1970s, the subject is some aspect of American society or some experience of the filmmaker's that he wants to investigate and correlate with the world. In more of these films than is usual, the director wrote or collaborated on the script.

Here are some of those pictures from the years 1967 to 1969, the period immediately surrounding The Graduate: Greetings, Last Summer, Easy Rider, The Wild Bunch, Putney Swope, Medium Cool, The Learning Tree, The Rain People, Who's That Knocking at My Door, Midnight Cowboy, Alice's Restaurant, and Goodbye, Columbus. All these films were (and are) of widely varying quality and proved yet again that to make a film "personally" is no guarantee of artistic success. A straight, contemporaneous commercial film like Hot Millions (1968) or Funny Girl (1968) is still a lot more rewarding than the trite and sentimental Learning Tree (notable only because it is an autobiographical film by a black man about his boyhood). And, in the cases of Midnight Cowboy, Easy Rider, and Medium Cool, the free souls were shown to have their own falsities and self-indulgences to beware of. Still, the promise in this new artistic situation could not be denied.

The reason for such a change in the filmic mainstream was, I believe, the ⊡presence in the audience of the millions⊡who had been pouring out of colleges since World War II and, perhaps ⊡more especially, the millions who were in colleges at the time: their growing interest⊡in the cinema, their reliance on it as they ⊡relied on no other art; their rejection of⊡the ludicrousness of the commercial formulas or at least their refusal to accept them as the totality of film (as they were then the totality of television); their concern with the society in which they were living and with themselves in that society; their shame at the difference between what was happening in the best postwar European film and what had been happening in the United States. The fulcrum on which the production change turned, the essential component, was of course the mind of the financier. He had seen where the money was; at least he had seen that the money was not unfailingly where it dependably used to be; and in his bewildered thrashings-about, he now sometimes thrashed toward the personal film—and a needed avenue was thus opened.

There were at least two possible results of this change. First, critical standards began to be applied to American film that were cognate (not identical) with those for any other art; as a result, there was less need for a lopsided critical theory like auteurism, imported from France and deliberately built askew so that it could slide past commercial distortions to judge whatever of merit was left inside. Second, as I point out above, American cinema started to engage, as consciously and explicitly as any other art, with social and psychical matters. Much, of course, remained mysterious and uncontrollable, perceptible only after the event, like so much in all art and in life. But the equation had shifted. More aesthetic matters now moved into the area of design and control; and what was left down there in the uncontrollable depths consequently resounded even deeper.

Now let's talk about the place of The Graduate itself in this seismic cinematic shift. The film's screenplay, based on a 1963 novel of the same name by Charles Webb,2 was written by Calder Willingham and Buck Henry. The latter man, like Nichols, was an experienced satiric performer. (Henry appears in this picture as a hotel clerk.) The dialogue is sharp, hip without rupturing itself in the effort, often moving, and frequently funny except for a few obtrusive gag lines. The story is about a young cop-out (in the jargon of the period) who—for well-dramatized reasons—cops at least partially in again.

Benjamin Braddock is a bright college graduate who returns from the east coast to his wealthy parents' home in Pasadena and flops—on his bed, on the rubber raft in the family pool. Politely and dispassionately, he declines the options thrust at him by bourgeois, barbecue-pit society: a scholarship to graduate school and a position in the plastics industry, among others. His mother and father, however, are keen for their son to get on with his life and are only interested in talking up his academic success, athletic prowess (as a track star at school), and possible future. Mrs. Robinson, the bored wife of his father's law partner, then proceeds to seduce Benjamin, though he is increasingly uncomfortable in the continuing affair—for moral reasons of an unpuritanical kind. The woman's daughter, Elaine, comes home from college and, against the mother's wishes but in obedience to his parents' insistence, Benjamin takes her out. Indeed, he falls in love with the girl, which is predictable but entirely credible. Eventually he is blackmailed into telling Elaine about his affair with her mother and, in revulsion, she flees—back to her university in Berkeley, in northern California, for the fall term. Benjamin follows, hangs about the campus, almost gets her to marry him, loses her (through her father's interference), pursues her, and finally gets her.

To dispose at once of the tedious subject of frankness, I note that some of the language and bedroom details pushed that frontier (in American films, at least) considerably ahead, but it is all so appropriate that it never has the slightest smack of daring, let alone opportunism. What is truly daring, and consequently refreshing, is The Graduate's moral stance. Its acceptance of the fact that a young man might have an adulterous affair with an older woman and still marry her daughter (a situation not exactly unheard of in America in the 1960s although not previously seen in the American cinema) is part of the film's fundamental insistence: that life, at any time in our world, is not worth living unless one can test it day by day, by values that ring true to the day.

Moral attitudes at the time, far from relaxing, were getting stricter and stricter among a certain segment of the population, with the result that many of the shoddy moralistic acceptances that dictated mindless actions for decades were being fiercely questioned, especially by the young. Benjamin himself is neither a laggard nor a lecher; he is, in the healthiest sense, a moralist: someone who wants to know the value of what he is doing. He does not rush into the affair with Mrs. Robinson out of any social rote of "scoring" any more than he avoids Elaine Robinson—because he has slept with her mother—out of any social rote of taboo. In fact, although he is male and eventually succumbs, he sees the older woman's advances as part of the syndrome of a suspect society. The result is that the sexual dynamics of the story propels Benjamin past the sexual sphere; it forces him to assess and locate himself in every aspect of his society.

Sheerly in terms of moral revolution, all of this would have seemed pretty commonplace in the late sixties to readers of contemporary American fiction. But we are dealing here with an art form that, because of its inescapable broad-based appeal, follows well behind the front lines of moral exploration. In the United States the cinema follows less closely than in some other countries, not because American audiences are necessarily less sophisticated than others but because the great expense of American production encourages a producer to cast the widest net possible. None of this is an apology for the film medium; it is a fact of film's existence. One might as sensibly apologize for painting because it cannot be seen simultaneously by millions the way a movie can.

Hence the arrival of The Graduate in 1967 can be viewed two ways. First, it was an index of moral change in a substantial segment of the American public, at least of an awakening of some doubts about past moral acceptances. Second, it is irrelevant that these changes were arriving in the cinema a decade or two decades or a half-century after the other arts, because their statement on film makes them intrinsically new and unique. If arts have textural differences and are not simply different envelopes for the same contents, then the way in which The Graduate affects us makes it quite a different work from the original novel and from dozens of novels of moral disruption or exploration around the time it was made. Nonetheless, some literary critics in the sixties deplored the adulation by young people of "serious" films, saying that the "messages" they got from Bergman, Antonioni, and Godard—and subsequently Nichols—had been stated by the novel and even the drama thirty or forty years earlier.[3] But this is not really true: for if art as art has any validity at all, then the cinema's peculiar sensory avenues were giving those "old" insights a presence—in sight and sound, time and space, intimacy and scope—they could not otherwise have.

Let me concentrate for the moment on the very novel from which the film of The Graduate was adapted. Besides the fact that a great deal of Webb's good dialogue (which comprises most of the book) is used in the screenplay,[4] the structure of the first two-thirds of the book—until Benjamin goes to Berkeley—is more or less the structure of the movie. The longest scene in the picture—the bedroom one in which Benjamin comically tries to get his mistress to talk to him—is taken almost intact from the novel. But Mike Nichols and his screenwriters rightly sensed that the last third of the book bogged down in a series of discussions, that the novel's device for Benjamin's finding the place of Elaine's wedding was not only mechanical but also visually sterile, and that in general this last third had to be both compressed and heightened.

Doesn't the film split in half as a result? This has been a recurrent question about The Graduate over the years, and it requires comment. Benjamin does not change, in my view, from the hero of a serious comedy about a frustrated youth to the hero of a glossy romance; he changes as Benjamin. It is the difference between the women in his life that changes him. Being the person he is, he could not have been dignified and assured with Mrs. Robinson any more than he could have been ridiculous and uncommanding with Elaine. We can actually see the change happen—during the scene with Elaine at the hamburger joint where Benjamin puts up the top of his sports car, closes the windows, and talks. Talks—for the first time in the film at any length. Those who insist that Mrs. Robinson's Benjamin should be the same as Elaine's Benjamin are denying the effect of love—particularly its effect on Ben, to whom it is not only joy but escape from the nullity of his affair with her mother and the impending nullity of himself. There is even a cinematic hint early in the picture of the change that is to come: our first glimpse of the nude Mrs. Robinson is a reflection in the glass covering her daughter's portrait on a wall.

In character and in moral focus, then, the film does not split, but there is a fundamental weakness in the novel that the movie tries, not entirely successfully, to escape. The pivot of the action shifts, after the story shifts to Berkeley, from Benjamin to Elaine. From then on, he knows what he wants; it is she who has to work through an internal crisis. It was Nichols' job to dramatize this crisis without abandoning his protagonist, to show the girl adjusting to the shocking fact of Benjamin's affair with her mother, and he had to show it with, so to speak, only a series of visits by the girl to the picture. To make matters worse, the environment—of the conventional campus romantic comedy—works against the seriousness of the material, the revisionary nature of this particular romantic comedy. The library, the quad, the rooming house, the classroom corridor have to be overcome, in a sense. Nichols never lets up his pressure on what he feels the film is about, but the obliqueness of the action at this point and the associative drawbacks of the locale never quite cease to be difficulties.

Charles Webb himself objected to the film of The Graduate on the ground that, unlike his novel, the movie does not take a moral stance.5 He based his objection on the fact that, in the book, Benjamin arrives at the church in time to prevent Elaine's marriage to another man, and in the film he arrives after the ceremony. I myself don't understand how the author of this book could equate morality with marriage licenses. In any event, not only does Nichols' solution avoid the destructive cliché of having Benjamin get there Just in Time, but it is also completely in character for Benjamin: he has impertinently had an affair with the married Mrs. Robinson, and now—at least for the time being—he will impertinently be having an affair with the married Elaine.

There is one point in Webb's novel, however, that I wish had been made explicit in the film. The author makes sure we know that Benjamin is not a virgin when he goes to the hotel room for the first time with Mrs. Robinson.6 I had always assumed that Benjamin was not "intact" simply because of his age, his kind, and the time period (again, the late sixties), but there is no evidence in the film one way or the other. Moreover, I know from anecdotal evidence that there are still many people who assume he is a virgin, and this makes a great difference in their view of the first hotel encounter. If that is a scene about a novice, it is a conventional skit about sexual initiation; if Benjamin is not a novice, then the scene is about the distress of a young man torn between shock—after all, this woman probably wheeled him around in his baby carriage!—and his sexual urges. Such a conflict, between rigid social conventions and surrogate Oedipal drives (Mr. Robinson says at one point that he regards Ben as a son), is the source of a deeper, darker comedy.

This brings us to the central artist of the entire enterprise, Mike Nichols. In his first picture, Who's Afraid of Virginia Woolf? (1966), he was shackled by Edward Albee's famous 1962 play and by the two powerhouse stars, Elizabeth Taylor and Richard Burton; but considering these handicaps, he did a creditable job, particularly with his actors. In The Graduate, uninhibited by the need to reproduce a Broadway hit and with freedom to select his cast, Nichols moved fully into film. Here he is perceptive, imaginative, witty; he has a shrewd eye, both for beautiful imagery and for visual comment; he knows how to compose as well as to juxtapose; and he has an innate sense of the manifold ways in which film can be better than he is and therefore how good he can be through it—particularly through its powers of expansion and ellipsis.

From the very first moment, Nichols sets the key. We see Benjamin's face large and absolutely alone. The camera then pulls back, we see that he is in an airliner, and the captain's voice tells us that it is approaching Los Angeles; but Benjamin has already been set for us as alone. We follow him through the terminal—aptly, on the airport treadmill, or moving walkway, but at the far right of the frame, not in the center where we would expect to see the protagonist (and with his image soon to be replaced by that of his suitcase on the conveyor belt). Benjamin seems just as completely isolated in the crowd here as he does later, in a scuba-diving suit at the bottom of his family's swimming pool, when he is huddling discontentedly in an underwater corner—literally as well as figuratively "underwater," "all wet," or "out of his depth"—while his twenty-first birthday party is being bulled along by his father up above. (Glass will often be used in the film, be it the glass of a scuba helmet, a window pane, a car windshield, or the fish tank in his room, as a barrier to suggest Benjamin's isolation or separation, entrapment, and even suffocation.) Indeed, particularly in such sequences as his welcome-home party—where the handheld camera stays close to Benjamin and pans with him as he weaves through the crowd, moving to another face only when he encounters it—it is as if Benjamin's narrow or tunnel-like or closed-off attention were controlling the camera's. The effect is balletic, in that Nichols here is seeking out quintessential rhythms, and quintessential states, in commonplace actions.

So much was this director seeking out such rhythms and states that he gave his cinematographer, Robert Surtees, license to experiment with filming techniques, as when the latter shoots Benjamin at some distance running straight at the camera—a technique that makes him look as if he is getting nowhere even though he's running. (This effect is accomplished with a very long telephoto lens, which foreshortens distances in relation to the camera.) Even though Ben is running very fast as his character races to prevent Elaine's marriage to someone else, the effect of the shot is to make him appear to be furiously running in place, getting nowhere—which is exactly how he feels at this moment. In another scene, Benjamin is walking from the right side of the screen to the left, while everyone else in the scene is moving from left to right. In Western culture, people or things that move from left to right seem natural (think of the direction in which one reads words on a page), whereas those that move from right to left seem to be going the wrong way. Such a visual technique thus echoes one of the film's points: that, from a conventional point of view, Benjamin is going the wrong way and getting nowhere in life.

Along with visuals, Mike Nichols also understands sound. The device of overlapping sound is somewhat overused (beginning the dialogue of the next scene under the end of the present one), but in general this effect, much like the match cuts

(cutting from Ben lying on the raft in the family pool to him lying in the hotel bed), adds to the dissolution of clock time, creating a more subjective time connected with Benjamin's drifting, "timeless" consciousness. And Nichols' use of nonverbal sound does a good deal to fix subliminally the cultural as well as temporal locus: for instance, a jet plane swooshes overhead—unremarked—as the married woman precipitously invites Benjamin into her house for the first time.

The musical soundtrack, in the case of this film, combines the nonverbal with the verbal, as it consists of folk-rock songs sung and played by Paul Simon and Art Garfunkel.7 The lyrics, it's true, deal a bit too easily with such matters as God, angst, the "sound of silence," and social change, but at least they deal with these matters rather than just tugging at our heartstrings or otherwise cueing us emotionally, as most movie music does. Moreover, Simon and Garfunkel's tunes are typical of the musical environment in which Benjamin, and Elaine, live; this is the music that, in 1967, they themselves would have been listening to on records or the radio, and that some young men are in fact listening to on a car radio in the parking lot of the hamburger joint.

I want now to make much of Mike Nichols' ability to direct actors, a factor generally overlooked in appraising film directors—many of whom, unlike Nichols, did not begin, let alone remain, in the theater. (Nichols' began his stage career as a comic performer, and his subsequent Broadway directing credits include Neil Simon's Barefoot in the Park [1963], Trevor Griffiths' Comedians [1976], Tom Stoppard's The Real Thing [1984], Ariel Dorfman's Death and the Maiden [1992], Anton Chekhov's The Seagull [2001], and Arthur Miller's Death of a Salesman [2012].) Some famous directors—Alfred Hitchcock, for example—can do little with actors; they get only what the actor can supply on his own. Sometimes—again like Hitchcock—these directors do not even seem to be aware of bad performances: think only of Tippi Hedren in The Birds (1963) and Marnie (1964) and of almost all the principals in Topaze (1969). Nichols, by contrast, helped the otherwise histrionic Anne Bancroft to a quiet, strong portrayal of the mistress, who is bitter and pitiful beneath her predatory exterior (as suggested by her leopard-themed or animal-print wardrobe). With acuteness he cast Elizabeth Wilson, a sensitive comedienne, as Benjamin's mother. And from the very pretty Katharine Ross, Benjamin's girl, he got a performance like none she had ever given before or has given since: of sweetness, dignity, and a compassion that is simply engulfing. Even the actor playing Ben's father, William Daniels, whose WASP (white Anglo-Saxon Protestant) caricature is a staple item in Stanley Donen's Two for the Road (1967), is helped by Nichols to give that caricature new life here.

In the leading role, Nichols had the sense and the courage to cast Dustin Hoffman, unknown (to the screen) at the time, physically slight, and unhandsome, and to surround him with the blue-eyed, blonde-haired adonises associated with southern California—one of whom you might have expected to see in the part of Benjamin himself. (Webb's novel says that Ben is 5'11" or so, and, in addition to being a track star and head of the debating club at college, he's a WASP8—unlike the Jewish, and Jewish-appearing, Hoffman.) Hoffman's anti-heroic face in itself is a proof of change in American film of the late 1960s, for it is hard to imagine him in leading roles ten years earlier. How unimportant, how interesting this quickly becomes, because Hoffman, when well directed, is one of the best actors of his generation: subtle, vital, and accurate. Certainly he is the best American film comedian (comic actor, not jokester of the kind embodied by Robin Williams or Steve Martin) since Jack Lemmon, and, as theatergoers discovered before he entered film, Hoffman has a much wider range than Lemmon, appearing in the 1960s in plays as different as Samuel Beckett's Endgame (1957), Brendan Behan's The Quare Fellow (1954), Bertolt Brecht's In the Jungle of Cities (1923), Murray Schisgal's Jimmy Shine (1968), and Ronald Ribman's Journey of the Fifth Horse (1966)—to be followed later by Hoffman's performances in films as varied as Madigan's Millions (1968), Little Big Man (1970), Tootsie (1982), Wag the Dog (1997), Perfume (2006), and Boychoir (2014).

With palpable tact and lovely understanding, Nichols and Hoffman and Ross—all three—show us how this boy and girl fall into a new kind of love: a love based on recognition of identical loneliness on their side of the generation gap, a gap that irrefutably existed despite the fact that it was often exploited in the politics and pop culture of the day. When Elaine's father is, understandably, enraged at the news of his wife's affair with his prospective son-in-law and hustles the girl off into another, "safe" marriage (to a medical student named Carl Smith), Benjamin's almost insane refusal to let her go is his refusal to let go of the one reality he has found in a world that otherwise exists, for him, behind a pane of glass. The filmic metaphors of the chase after the girl—the endless driving, the jumping in and out of his sports car, even his eventual running out of gas—do have some slapstick about them, making The Graduate rise close to the surface of mere physicality. But at least the urgency never fails: the urgency of a young generation's belief—still amply manifested all around us—in the value of romantic love in an arid world.

At the wedding, when Benjamin finds it—and of course it is in an ultra-modern church, in Santa Barbara—there is a dubious hint of crucifixion as he flings his outspread arms against the (literal) pane of glass that separates him from Elaine, and thus from his very life. But this symbolism is redeemed a minute later when, with the girl, Ben grabs a large cross, swings it savagely if not sacrilegiously to stave off pursuers, then jams it through the handles of the front doors to lock the crowd in behind them. The pair jump onto a passing bus (she is still in her wedding dress) and sit in the very back, as the aged, uncomprehending passengers turn and stare at them, dumbfounded. Benjamin and Elaine sit next to each other, breathing hard, not even laughing, just happy—and the film ends.

Nothing is solved—none of the things that bother Benjamin, in any event—by this ending, by the fact of their being together; in fact, one could say that their troubles have only begun, because Elaine is legally married to another man: Carl Smith. (In addition, her parents are divorcing; one can be fairly sure that the law firm of Braddock and Robinson will be splitting up as well; Ben has yet to face his parents about any of these matters; and neither Ben nor Elaine has a source of income.) But, for Benjamin, nothing would be worth solving without her. We know that, and she knows that, and all of us feel very, very good about it. The chase and last-minute rescue (to repeat, just after the ceremony is finished) are contrivances, to be sure, but they are contrivances tending toward truth, not falsity, which may be one definition of good art.

Nichols played to his strength in The Graduate, which is comedy; with all its touching moments and its essential seriousness, this is a very funny picture. To some viewers, a comedy about a young man and his father's partner's wife immediately seems adventurous, while a comedy about a young man and a girl automatically gets shoved into a pigeonhole. We have only to remember (and to me it is unforgettable), however, that what is separating these young lovers is not a broken date or a trivial quarrel but a deep taboo in our society. For me, therefore, the end proof of the film's depth is the climax in the church, with Dustin Hoffman (even more moving the more times I see him) screaming Elaine's name from behind the glass wall. A light romance? I don't think so. This is a naked, final, dramatic cry to the girl to free herself of the meaningless taboo, to join him in trying to find some possible new and better truth by which to live.

Some elements of slickness and shininess in this widescreen color film are disturbing, it has to be said. I disliked Nichols' recurrent affection for the splatter of headlights and sunspots on his lens, as well as his weakness for a slightly heavy irony through objects. (The camera holds on a third-rate painting of a clown after Mrs. Robinson walks out of the shot, not the first such painting we see in the film. When Elaine leaves Benjamin in front of the monkey cage at the San Francisco zoo, the camera, too luckily, catches the sign on the cage—Do Not Tease—and then cuts to a few shots of the animals themselves just to make sure we know that a monkey has been made of Ben.) And a couple of times Nichols puts his camera in places that merely make us aware of his cleverness in putting it there: inside an empty hotel-room closet, for example, looking out past the hangers. Additionally, there are some really egregious gags or gag lines: "Are you here for an affair, sir?"9 the hotel clerk asks the confused Benjamin in the lobby.

Other considerable charges were made against The Graduate at the time and have been repeated through the years. Some complained that neither Benjamin nor his parents seem aware that

his behavior is not exactly unusual for a college student in the late 1960s10; there is no reference—by California parents—to "Berkeley" behavior or dropouts or hippies. I agree that this is a slight omission—the landlord of Ben's Berkeley rooming house does ask him if he is one of those "outside agitators"11—and it touches on the credibility of the environment Nichols wants to create: what's missing somewhat is an objective correlative for Ben's confusion, anomie, even paralysis in the material, imperialist world of mid-twentieth-century American capitalism. (Such a correlative is missing from Webb's novel as well, which strains, like the film, to make Ben's alienation and depression a response to the social scene: to the corrupt mores, bankrupt consumerism, and mindless conformity of contemporary American society. But, to be fair, the book was published in 1963, before the political turmoil that began in 1965 with the race riots in the Watts section of Los Angeles, the assassination of Malcolm X in Harlem, the public harassment by police of homosexuals gathering on the streets of San Francisco, and Lyndon Johnson's escalation of U. S. military involvement in the Vietnam War.)

Still others objected that, precisely, there was no mention of the Vietnam War then raging12; but if there had been "mention" of it, in a film about domestic problems that would persist long after the end of the Vietnam conflict, The Graduate would have been accused of tokenism. Additional critics argued that Benjamin was too "straight," that a film about a radical would have been more significant.13 On this point I certainly disagree: what interested me in Benjamin was precisely that he is "straight" and that it doesn't protect him: the bottom falls out for him anyway. There would have been less drama, and not necessarily any more social truth, in having these events occur to a member of SDS, the student group that during this era organized "teach-ins," anti-war demonstrations, and other political activities across the United States in the name of creating a more democratic society.

Related to this, some have said that The Graduate is not about real change but about a little rebellious excursion that ends with happy mating and conformity.14 I don't find such an assertion supported in the film. There is a happy ending, but, as noted, it is a qualified one: Benjamin's smile on the bus gradually turns into an enigmatic, neutral expression as he gazes ahead, not looking at Elaine; and Elaine, after lovingly looking at Ben, notices the expression on his face and turns away with a similar one on hers. (In a 1970 interview, Nichols said, "When I saw those rushes [of the ending] I thought: 'That's the end of the picture. They don't know what the hell to do, or think, or to say to each other'."15)

Despite the defects, then, The Graduate bears the imprint of a filmmaker, alive, hungry, and properly ambitious—a whole filmmaker, warts and all. This is a very different imprint from that of a number of Nichols' highly praised, cagy, compromised American contemporaries in the 1960s and 1970s. The defects here show that he is not entirely sure of himself, that he is still feeling his way toward a style of his own. And the kind of cleverness or artiness (sometimes becoming grandiloquence) found in The Graduate did plague Nichols in his other early films, but it more or less stopped with Carnal Knowledge (1971)—ironically, his last genuinely important picture. His subsequent, far more commercial movies—among them Working Girl (1988), Regarding Henry (1991), The Birdcage (1996), and What Planet Are You From? (2000)—stopped taking the risks that sometimes result in artistic flaw and proved that he had always been only a good director who looked for things, other people's things, to do, not an auteur-like filmmaker who had things he wanted to do because he himself had something to say.

Still, what's important is not Nichols' subsequently revealed shortcomings or the shortcomings of The Graduate itself, but the extraordinary basic talent that the man showed in this film: humane, deft, exuberant. All the talents involved in The Graduate make it soar brightly above many other pictures made during the period, and since, and make it, by virtue of its cinematic skill, thematic intent, and sheer connection with its audience, what I called it at the start of this essay: a visible marker, or milestone, in American movie history. Milestones do not guarantee that everything after them will be better (the New American Cinema, after all, quickly became old course when some personal films—the fuddlers, fashion-mongers, or arty fakers—didn't make money, just as the French New Wave ebbed quickly when so many

of those pictures lost money); nonetheless, they are ineradicable.

Box-office receipts themselves neither prove nor disprove anything about ineradicability, let alone quality, but they do prove something about immediacy; and the financial facts about The Graduate at the time of its release are staggering. As of January 7, 1970, the first and second movies on Variety's list of "All-Time Box-Office Champs" (rated by distributors' receipts from the United States and Canada) were The Sound of Music (1965) and Gone With the Wind (1939), with $72 and $71 million respectively.16 Third was The Graduate, with $43 million. Third place in only two years, compared with the longer periods that the first two pictures had been in release. (With its receipts adjusted for inflation, The Graduate was still number 22 on the same list as of July 4, 2016, behind the likes of Avatar [2009] and Titanic [1997], the new number one and two17—but, I'm sad to say, with few pictures of artistic quality anywhere else on the list of 500 that I examined.) Consider, too—which even those who dislike The Graduate probably would not deny—the difference in ambition between this film and the only two movies up to 1970 to attract bigger audiences, and then the impact of Nichols' picture becomes all the more staggering.

If, as some believe, Michelangelo Antonioni's Blow-Up (1966) was instrumental in attracting young Europeans to film in the late sixties,18 the equivalent American landmark was Mike Nichols' The Graduate, whose romantic tale continues to attract "graduates" today (in an America whose social fabric is unraveling for different reasons, but whose politics is as contentious as ever, on the national as well as the international level). This was the film that attracted me, that's for sure. I saw it alone on a spring evening in 1968 (shortly after I myself had temporarily dropped out of college and was facing the military draft), stayed up all night thinking about how wonderfully different it was compared to all the other American movies I'd seen, then promptly saw the picture again the next day—with my girlfriend. I've been re-seeing The Graduate, and reflecting on it, ever since.

Notes

1 See, for example, Jerzy Toeplitz, Hollywood and After: The Changing Face of Movies in America (Chicago: Henry Regnery, 1974); Diane Jacobs, Hollywood Renaissance. (Cranbury, New Jersey: A. S. Barnes, 1977); and Axel Madsen, The New Hollywood (New York: Thomas Y. Crowell, 1975).

2 Charles Webb, The Graduate (New York: New American Library, 1963).

3 Stanley Kauffmann, Figures of Light: Film Criticism and Comment (New York: Harper & Row, 1971), 38.

4 Clifford Terry, "Charles Webb—Not a Household Word," Chicago Tribune, 25 May 1969, Section 5: 10.

5 Charles Webb, Letter to the Editor, The New Republic, 158.18 (4 May 1968): 40.

6 Stanley Kauffmann, Figures of Light: Film Criticism and Comment (New York: Harper & Row, 1971), 44.

7 "The Sounds of Silence," "April Come She Will," "Scarborough Fair/Canticle," "Mrs. Robinson," "The Singleman Party Foxtrot," "Sunporch Cha-Cha-Cha," "On the Strip," "The Folks," "A Great Effect," "The Big Bright Green Pleasure Machine," and "Whew."

8 Sam Kashner, "Here's to You, Mr. Nichols: The Making of The Graduate." Vanity Fair, 25 February 2008. Accessed 4 July 2016 at

http://www.vanityfair.com/news/2008/03/graduate200803

9 Buck Henry, The Graduate: Final Draft of the Script, 29 March 1967. Accessed 4 July 2016 at

http://www.imsdb.com/scripts/Graduate,-The.html

and

http://www.lc.ncu.edu.tw/learneng/script/TheGraduate.pdf

10 See Kathleen Carroll in the New York Daily News of 22 December 1967, as well as Roger Ebert in the Chicago Sun-Times of 26 December 1967.

11 Buck Henry, The Graduate: Final Draft of the Script, 29 March 1967. Accessed 4 July 2016 at

http://www.imsdb.com/scripts/Graduate,-The.html

and

http://www.lc.ncu.edu.tw/learneng/script/TheGraduate.pdf

12 See Bosley Crowther, "Tales Out of School: The Graduate," The New York Times (22 December 1967): 44; see also A. D. Murphy in Variety of 17 December 1967.

13 See John Simon, "The Graduate," in Simon's Movies into Film: Film Criticism, 1967-1970 (New York: Dial Press, 1971), 103-106; see also Pauline Kael, "The Graduate," in Kael's Going Steady: Film Writings, 1968-1969 (London: Marion Boyars, 1970), 124-127.

14 See Andrew Sarris, "The Graduate, " Village Voice, 13.11 (28 December 1967): 33; see also Hollis Alpert, "The Graduate Makes Out," Saturday Review, 6 (July 1968): 14-15, 32.

15 Joseph Gelmis, "Mile Nichols Talks about The Graduate," in Gelmis's The Film Director as Superstar (London: Secker & Warburg, 1970), 289.

16 "All-Time Box-Office Champs," Variety, 7 January 1970: 25.

17 Source: Box Office Mojo, an IMDb (Internet Movie Database) company. Accessed 4 July 2016 at

http://www.boxofficemojo.com/alltime/adjusted.htm

18 See Roy Huss's introduction to his edited volume Focus on Blow-Up (Englewood Cliffs, New Jersey: Prentice-Hall, 1971), 1-6.

Bibliography

Adler, Renata. "A Brilliant Breakdown: The Graduate." The New York Times (11 February 1968), Section 2: 1, 13.

Bapis, Elaine M. "The Graduate: Representing a Generation." In Bapis's Camera and

Action: American Film as Agent of Social Change, 1965-1975. Jefferson, North Carolina: McFarland, 2008. 41-60.

Beuka, Robert. "Just One Word . . . 'Plastics': Suburban Malaise, Masculinity, and Oedipal Drive in The Graduate." Journal of Popular Film and Television, 28.1 (Spring 2000): 12-21.

Birkvad, Søren. "Hollywood Sin, Scandinavian Virtue: The 1967 Revolt of I Am Curious Yellow and The Graduate." Film International, 9.2 (2011): 42-54.

Biskind, Peter. Easy Riders, Raging Bulls: How the Sex, Drugs, and Rock 'n' Roll Generation Saved Hollywood. New York: Simon and Schuster, 1998.

Cardullo, Bert. "Look Back in Bemusement: The New American Cinema, 1965-1970." Cambridge Quarterly, 37.4 (December 2008): 375-386.

Celeste, Reni. "The Sound of Silence: Film Music and Lament." Quarterly Review of Film and Video, 22.2 (April 2005): 113-124.

Clooney, Nick. "The Graduate." In Clooney's The Movies that Changed Us. New York: Atria, 2002. 65-78.

Coles, Robert. "Bonnie and Clyde & The Graduate: Hollywood's New Social Criticism." Society, 5.6 (May 1968): 15-21.

Cooley, Aaron. "Reviving Reification: Education, Indoctrination, and Anxiety in The

Graduate." Educational Studies: Journal of the American Educational Studies Association, 45.4 (July-August 2009): 358-376.

Costanzo, William V. "The Graduate." In Costanzo's Reading the Movies: Twelve Great Films on Video and How to Teach Them. Urbana, Illinois: National Council of Teachers of English, 1992. 113-120.

Fairchild, B. H. "'Plastics': The Graduate as Film and Novel." Studies in American Humor, 4.3 (Fall 1985): 133-141.

Foley, M. W. "Turning Thirty with The Graduate." America, 137 (13 August 1977): 78-80.

Geller, Bob. "Dear Benjamin: Dissecting Mike Nichols' The Graduate." English Journal, 58.3 (March 1969): 423-425.

Georgakas, Dan. "From Words to Images: An Interview with Buck Henry." Cineaste, 27.1 (Winter 2001): 4-10.

Gitre, Edward J. K. "A Failure to Communicate: Benjamin Braddock and the Aims of Education." Hedgehog Review, 12 (Spring 2010): 63-74.

"The Graduate." Monthly Film Bulletin, 35.408/409 (1968): 131.

Grindon, Leger. "Counter Conventions and Cultural Change in The Graduate (1967)." In Grindon's The Hollywood Romantic Comedy: Conventions, History, Controversies. Malden, Massachusetts: Wiley-Blackwell, 2011. 139-149.

Harris, Mark. "The Graduate." In Harris's Pictures at a Revolution: Five Movies and the Birth of the New Hollywood. New York: Penguin Press, 2008. Also published as Scenes From a Revolution: The Birth of the New Hollywood. Edinburgh, U.K.: Canongate, 2008. 47-51ff.

Hill, Geoffrey. "The Graduate: The Terrible Mother from the Black Lagoon." In Hill's Illuminating Shadows: The Mythic Power of Film. Boston: Shambhala, 1992. 194-211.

Kashner, Sam. "Here's to You, Mr. Nichols: The Making of The Graduate." Vanity Fair, no. 571 (March 2008): 418-432.

Knobloch, Susan. "The Graduate as Rock 'n' Roll Film." USC Spectator, 17.2 (1997): 60-73.

Laffey, Sheila A. The Bildungsfilm or the "Coming of Age" Film as Seen in The Graduate, You're a Big Boy Now, and Girlfriends. Ann Arbor, Michigan: UMI Research Press, 1983.

Lewis, Jon, ed. The New American Cinema. Durham, North Carolina: Duke University Press, 1998.

Lyman, Rick. "Ron Howard on The Graduate." In Lyman's Watching Movies: The Biggest Names in Cinema Talk about the Films That Matter Most. New York: Times Books, 2003. Chapter 3.

Man, Glenn. "1967-1968, The Wonder Year, Part II: The Graduate and 2001: A Space Odyssey." In Man's Radical Visions: American Film Renaissance, 1967-1976. Westport, Connecticut: Greenwood Press, 1994. 33-67.

Metz, Walter. "Consuming The Graduate." In Metz's Engaging Film Criticism: Film History and Contemporary American Cinema. New York: Peter Lang, 2004. 107-128.

Mitchell, Robert. "The Graduate." In Magill's Survey of Cinema. Vol. 2. Ed. Frank N. Magill. Englewood Cliffs, New Jersey: Salem Press, 1980. 667-671.

Morgenstern, Joseph. "A Boy's Best Friend: The Graduate." Newsweek (1 January 1968): 63.

O'Steen, Bobbie. "Comedy: The Graduate." In O'Steen's The Invisible Cut: How Editors Make Movie Magic. Studio City, California: Michael Wiese, 2009. 92-122.

Pizzello, Stephen. "The Graduate." American Cinematographer, 81 (April 2000): 18ff.

Rollin, Betty. "Mike Nichols: Wizard of Wit." Look, 32 (2 April 1968): 71-74.

Rosenbaum, Jonathan. "Bridge Over Troubled Water: The Graduate." Chicago Reader, 26.25 (27 March-2 April 1997): Entry 1, "Movies."

Samuels, Charles Thomas, ed. "The Graduate." In Samuels' A Casebook on Film. New York: Van Nostrand Reinhold, 1970. 141-173ff. (Includes reviews of The Graduate by Stanley Kauffmann of The New Republic, Edgar Z. Friedenberg of The New York Review of Books, Stephen Farber of Film Quarterly, and Jacob Brackman of The New Yorker.)

Sarris, Andrew. "After The Graduate." American Film: A Journal of the Film and Television Arts, 3.9 (July-August 1978): 32-37.

Schmidt, Matthew P. "Identity Crisis: The Graduate." In Schmidt's Coming of Age in American Cinema: Modern Youth Films as Genre. Ann Arbor, Michigan: UMI Research Press, 2002. 30-35.

Schuth, H. Wayne. "The Graduate." In Schuth's Mike Nichols. Boston: Twayne, 1978. 45-64.

Sluyter, Dean. "The Graduate (1967): Whaddaya Got?" In Sluyter's Cinema Nirvana: Enlightenment Lessons From the Movies. New York: Three Rivers Press, 2005. 67-80.

Starfield, Penny. "Duality in The Graduate." Caliban, 32 (1995): 89-102.

Stevens, Kyle. "The Graduate and the Subversion of Silence." In Stevens' Mike Nichols: Sex, Language, and the Reinvention of Psychological Realism. New York: Oxford University Press, 2015. 85-112.

Van Gelder, Peter. "The Graduate." In Van Gelder's That's Hollywood: A Behind-the-Scenes Look at 60 of the Greatest Films Ever Made. New York: HarperPerennial, 1990. Entry 29.

Whitehead, J. W. Appraising The Graduate: The Mike Nichols Classic and Its Impact in Hollywood. Jefferson, North Carolina: McFarland, 2011.

Whitehead, J. W. "'This Afternoon's Feature Attraction': The Graduate (1967)." In Whitehead's Mike Nichols and the Cinema of Transformation. Jefferson, North Carolina: McFarland, 2014. 36-51.

Williams, Linda Ruth. "The Graduate." In Contemporary American Cinema. Ed. Linda Ruth Williams and Michael Hammond. London: Open University Press, 2006. 101-103.

Wood, Naaman Keith. "Genre Mixing in The Graduate, Chinatown, and Taxi Driver." In Wood's Musical Ellipses: Theoretical and Critical Perspectives on Music and Film. Ann Arbor, Michigan: UMI Research Press, 2002. 43-51.

Zeitlin, David. "The Graduate." Life, 63.21 (24 November 1967): 111-115.

About the Author:

For twenty years, from 1987 to 2007, **R. J. Cardullo** was the regular film critic for the Hudson Review in New York. He is the author or editor of a number of books, including Theater of the Avant-Garde, 1890-1950, What Is Dramaturgy?, and In Search of Cinema: Writings on International Film Art. He is also the chief American translator of the film criticism of the Frenchman André Bazin. Cardullo took his master's and doctoral degrees from Yale University and received his B.A. from the University of Florida. He taught for four decades at the University of Michigan, Colgate, and New York University, as well as abroad.

THE LION
Lowell Jaeger

The Giant Octopus

An octopus
— almost entirely squishy soft tissue —
can squeeze into impossibly small spaces,
a factoid offered by the marine biologist
as an almost plausible explanation
how the coastal aquarium's favorite attraction
had slipped the bonds of its keepers.

Must have discovered how to nudge the lid
of its glass confinement
enough to probe one tentacle
for a determined toehold in open air.

Must have hid like a rumpled dishrag
in a dark corner
outside the night custodian's view.

Must have heard the ocean
in the drain pipe
and slithered through.

A story worth telling, says the marine biologist.
Funny, how people are so convincingly disappointed
the aquarium's only giant octopus
has gone AWOL, he says.

Even more curious, is how this story
makes even grumpy people smile, something
in us cheering a desperate primitive instinct
doing as it must
to find its way home.

The Lion

While huffing my way up switchbacks
of a treeless rocky trail, I've sensed
the presence of something watching.
I've stopped, held still in the empty terrain,
looked up and down and around and saw

nothing. And mocked myself, the spinal
electricity of my imaginary fears.
Laughed aloud and whistled my way
onward, reasoning my good vision
would clarify all there is to reveal.

But I've been uncertain of my sight
since, some years back, my wife and I
visited a zoo. Stood in front of
the mountain lion's den. Pressed our faces
between the bars. And waited for the lion.

The lion who wasn't there. Who wasn't there
until he twitched his long tail as if
to wake us. As if he'd been a rock till now,
staring right at us with the plainness
of a rock's eye, seeing all we see and more.

Squirrels

One summer, God knows why, squirrels
multiplied to plague us. Squirrels darting like rats
into and out of the woodpile — impossible
to calculate an accurate census since they all look
pretty much the same. An army of squirrels commandeering
the crawlspace beneath our rooms. We heard them

chewing and chittering in the floor joists while we paused
on the sofa with our dinner trays downstairs, watching TV.
Squirrels gnawing and loosening pinecones, dropping them
— heavy as hardballs — crashing and banging on the barn's tin roof
earlier even than the robins burst forth early dawn
with their simpleminded songs of praise and wonder. Whole afternoons

we surveilled a squirrel team of demolition experts escaping
to their bunkers in the brambles beyond our lawn,
their jowls stuffed with cotton candy-colored
muffs of fiberglass insulation they'd salvaged
from inside our bedroom walls. Bad-ass squirrels

who commenced with alarming boldness to chide us
if we dare walk too near their frenzied burglaries. Resentful squirrels
who'd scold us for not signing over the deed and simply surrendering
our digs to accommodate their rapidly expanding appetites.
Our dog and cats mewling plaintively, impounded,
lunging at porch screens as squirrels preened and teased them.

Truly, these were a breed of cocksure squirrels, so at home
with their providence they began to parade in the roses
with the pageantry of Caesar's empire. As if
there were no stopping them. As if
they'd forgotten the hardships of generations previous
and less fortunate.

As if they could ignore the shadows of hawks and ospreys
patrolling the open meadow. And, not long before
October's first cruel frost, the entire tribe
had vanished. As if it were perfectly natural.
As if, in some strange logic, it all transpired to proffer us
something to witness, something to think about.

Popeye

Oh, Popeye, how could it be easy to overlook
your sad estate so many years?
Your slapped-together scrapwood
shack, everyday diet of table waste,
unless we forgot, water bowl
with water in it or sometimes not.

We'd pack off to school with you
barking after us from down the block.
And howling to greet us late afternoons
as we skipped up the walk,
glanced your way and sailed on past.

The stink! The flies! You lunged
the radius of your rusted chain
when we knocked a foul ball nearby
and argued who should hold his nose
and go fetch it. Where swarms of gnats
breathed vapors of piss and piles of poo.

Never let us forget your face that day
you collapsed on useless legs and lay
smiling up at us. Nothing we can do
but let him die, Dad shook his head.
It's worms, he said. And raised his shovel up
to mercifully bash your head.

The Snail Trail

of dried silver spittle
glistens on a rock pathway
climbing the hillside
behind my house.

I've lunged forward
and sweat my chores
up and down that pathway
with armloads of whatever
projects compelled me.

But the snail spoor
moves in slow circles.
As if he's lost his compass.
Headed nowhere.

He belly-slides in the dark.
Everything delicious.
Each pebble. Every green blade.
Worth going over.

Wherever he's to be
is not far off. He's certain of that.
And confident
he'll discover
whatever he finds.

About the Author:

As founding editor of Many Voices Press, **Lowell Jaeger** compiled New Poets of the American West, an anthology of poets from 11 Western states. His seventh collection of poems, Or Maybe I Drift Off Alone, was published by Shabda Press in 2016. He is the recipient of fellowships from the National Endowment for the Arts and the Montana Arts Council and winner of the Grolier Poetry Peace Prize. Most recently Jaeger was awarded the Montana Governor's Humanities Award for his work in promoting thoughtful civic discourse.

DESPERATE SEEKER
Gary Beck

Technical Progress

In low-tech times
the mentally ill
listened to messages
on transistor radios.
Hi-tech times
allow conversation
on the cellphone,
a subtle effort
to appear normal.

Misstep

For thousands of years
man's biggest challenge
was a steady food supply,
energy exerted
to feed family.
Then profit reared its head
awakening the insecure
to paths of acquisition,
unsated hunger for more
controlling interaction,
erasing tribal ties
with mediums of exchange
at the expense of others.

Bird Brains

Hungry urban birds
flock to feeders
placed to attract them,
but have trouble eating
when they can't figure out
how the feeder works.

Call to Arms

Soldiers do their duty
fight, bleed, die
for love of country,
rarely knowing why,
believing their leaders
won't throw away their lives
for greed, power, stupidity.
They go to foreign lands,
kill who they're told to kill
and many become unfit
for the rigors of combat
nurtured on tv couches,
computer game joysticks,
unprepared mentally
for fanatic opponents
born to hardship,
raised in third world poverty
to view life differently
than young Americans
nurtured on Facebook, Twitter,
the illusion of freedom,
their harshest upbringing easy
compared to their enemies
whose religious dogma
devalues the individual,
rewards in the afterlife,
as long as they never give up
until American leaders
recognize their failure,
bring our men and women home
to an unwelcoming land.

Outdoors

Summer brings the homeless
to city parks
seeking security,
relaxation
the same need as others
for comfort from concrete,
unsightly, unmenacing,
unlike the mentally ill
raving, cursing, threatening,
blighting the oasis
for nervous neighbors.

About the Author:

Gary Beck spent most of his life as a theater director. He has 12 published chapbooks and 3 accepted, 11 published poetry collections, 5 accepted for publication. He has 3 novels and 2 accepted for publication. 1 short story collection and 1 accepted for publication. He lives in NYC.

Vulgate

Happiness is embodied
in the cat, a stray or a
neighbor's pet, that crept
in from the balcony,
knocked the lowest
hanging ball from the
Christmas tree, batted
it across the carpet
without breaking it, lost
interest, tilted its
head back and, taking
me for Jerome, (I was
reading at my desk in
nothing but a towel)
did its best to sprout a
tawny mane. I love
Genesis. Like me, it is
inconsistent and mysterious.
Like me, it is the echo of
ancient psychologies and
fallacies stitched together.
Its beasts make me think
of the fox puppet my
grandmother sewed from
corduroy and felt. The
seams are like my scars
which I like to feel with
my fingers, imagining they
are the stitches on a purse
which hides coins
struck from the first
sunless day's light. At the
brewpub, I loosen its mouth
and pour primordial
dimes on the bar. The
clatter catches your attention.

WINTER'S TALE
Timothy Robbins

Wichita

7 miles above Wichita,
19 years from Julie saying,
"If he breaks your heart,
he's dead meat." And me
thinking, "Who eats
my heart, eats lean meat."
How to convert years to
miles? The equation is longer
than the route from doubt to
faith and back. What about
the conversion from lousy
boyfriend to poem fodder?
19 years over Kansas, wondering
how low we'd have to dip
to drag impalpable dark across
wheat, to harvest/behead
the crop with our wings.
Having screwed me once, Tyler
gave my belly a gym tap.
My navel was neat as an
isolated grain. Words in the
plane are tight as my form pressed
to the curving wall. Why did I
never notice before? Julie's the
stuff of jet fighters.

One Summer in Bloomington

On the front porch swing, keeping time
mid-air, Brent sings The Tennessee Stud.
The Tennessee Mare shudders in my withers,
Boone's Farm is passed around, and Zot
square dances on the empty cans.
At the attic window Tim releases a stream,
amber unseen in the dark, pooling in the grass
with a calming plash. He wakes as night
shivers into day. A woman who wandered
in from the street is riding him Western style.
I crouch in chiggers outside a room
where two guys talk of eating pussy.
Ever since they were boys they've longed to eat pussy.
I picture them lifting their faces from half disks
of melon, pinkish water dripping from their chins.
Robin adopts a dumpster cat.
At night, nourishing its fleas,
it scratches for a teat in my hair.
The cross-dresser (one of the pussy-eaters)
filches chloroform from the Chem lab —
passes out with the glass stopper like a diamond in his palm.
"Dead meat in a skirt," the others laugh.
Then they pass out too. The kitten kisses the abandoned rag,
goes berserk and is prophetically blind
for two weeks. Natalie and I hike to the quarries.
I brush her hair. She brushes mine.
We strip and lay clothes and limbs
on the rocks to sun. She shows and explains
her anatomy much as my father once tried
to elucidate the Impala's engine.
Across a quarry wall a townie has painted
in momentous letters SATAN'S BATHTUB.
Cain's Cathedral is more like it — rocks that were
rejected, rocks that long to burrow back into darkness,
their saint, a boy who, diving to the bottom,
wedged his head between two blocks,
releasing blood that rose like smoke
through contaminated water.
She was not beautiful, but it was Tim's duty to love her.
I was not a woman, but it was his duty to love me.
I try to remember being inside Suzanne.

I remember the blacklight and waiting on the floor
while she inserted an IUD. The blue dim,
her posture, her pallor taunted the poster of Picasso's
Old Guitarist taped to the wall.
I remember the honed edge of her pelvis, the nicotine
on her lips, the uncertain shape of her breasts, their
disturbing shiftiness, like faces in dreams or
groceries in the trunk. The spasm was
instantaneous, unworthy of the word spasm.
She must have felt even less
than that tickle and loss in my groin.
I remember thinking later how gentle life would be
if that's all there was to it.
(It was Ted, Robin and the Tennessee Stud
at the top of the stairs when Ted sighed,
"I'd kill for a blow job."
And I thought, "No need to be rash.")
I used to say it took days to prepare
to drop acid. I was as strict as a Catholic
when it comes to communion,
reading Ginsberg and Eckhart and fasting beforehand.
We retreated to winter woods,
vaguely evoking a mini ice age,
squatted in a teepee and waited for the white man's
senseless re-ordering of the senses,
like spring coming, like leaves appearing.
Seeing no difference between evergreens laden
with snow and orange trees heavy with fruit,
we plucked and ate. The handsome pussy-eater and I
wandered off together and lay on a ridge,
lulled by swaying branches, pantheists at a strip show,
for once excited by the same nakedness.

Winter's Tale

The snow is clean, dinted in
few places. Too few, some would
say. He calls himself Cory.
It's the usual story insofar as it
features a Trojan that hinders
circulation, unusual in that
he'll stay all night, if I give him
a lift after breakfast. His middle
and index fingers are like a
child that goes naked wherever
it wants. My head flops on
a broken neck.

At the Probation and Parole
Division everyone's been
waiting too long: a white kid
doing his best to spread the flu,
two black men who seem to know
each other and a third black guy
who comes in s tamping snow off
his boots (they seem to know him
too), a heavyset white guy in
overalls with heavy metal in his ears,
a woman dandling a plump pink
bag on her knees. Cory leans close,
(our heads on the pillow for two
hours' sleep) mutters his real
name, says, "If I'm not back in
30 go to the window and ask what's
wrong." "40," I think, "then I
make my escape."

He's freeing the car from
a snowbank with a swagger
that says I had nothing to
fear from thugs at the jailhouse.
Four hours later his voice on
the phone wears the same
assurance. His father has barred
him from the prison of home.
He thinks I'll be his next warden.

Ways

1.
He tried to be blind.
A sleep-mask appeared temple to temple.
The right lobe asked the left lobe,
"Is it time to get up?"
"Not yet."
He lifted the left side of the mask,
opened his left eye just enough
to see the red numbers on the clock.

2.
I've come all the way from Sodom
I wrote before I went there.

I thought installing The Joy of Gay Sex
on my dorm room shelf would bring luck

that would embarrass Simon Peter's
haul (Brent in a black fishnet tank-top

pulling the taut net to the boat).
Grandfather of many waters.

What Muir said of lordly chickens
I say of poems that find themselves

"discussing the wonder in charming
chatter." The way to a city burning

not from judgment but from passion:
Never tire of taming his cowlick,

of pulling the beloved comb from his
rounded pocket (what fatuous fools

love combs?) and sailing it
like a grad's cap into the very sun

that worried Ben Franklin.

3.
The phlebotomist hurt my vein.
I call her the Bruiser.
The phlebotomist hurt my vein.
I call her the Bruiser.
She's mad at me because
I am both beggar and chooser.

My mother came to visit.
She pushed my man to tears.
My mother came to visit.
She pushed my man to tears
He's never forgiven what
he's kept hushed all these years.

About the Author:

Tim Robbins teaches ESL and does freelance translation in Wisconsin. He has a BA in French and an MA in Applied Linguistics from Indiana University. He has been a regular contributor to "Hanging Loose" since 1978. His poems have also appeared appeared in "Three New Poets," "The James White Review," "Slant," "Main Street Rag," "Two Thirds North," "The Pinyon Review," "Wisconsin Review," and others.His collection of poems "Denny's Arbor Vitae: Poetic Memoirs" was published by Adelaide Books in 2017.

BRAVO OU MANSO
Pierre Sotér

Too good

Full Moon

Too good, too near and often too,
seldom happens and never here,
and when things seem white, and green, and blue,
there's black somewhere, and also fear.
Too nice, too sweet and good smelling too,
in truth and faith I've never seen,
maybe I stumbled and it went through
the warps of time behind a screen.
And too much light into our eyes
in torrid brightness will drown the view,
reveal old secrets and leak all whys,
and leave us naked, in darkness too.

For too much of anything is, too,
more than we need, more than we can chew.

October third, two thousand seventeen,
the air is fresh and clean, the Moon is full,
I look at it, I'd like to fill its pull
while I see it's light as I've never seen.
Maybe I did, but I can't remember.
Never mind, now the Moon is very bright,
and to its beauty, its mysterious might,
this one more time I'll have to surrender.
And even the brightest stars are flirting,
trying to catch the attention of the Moon,
tonight I'm shaken, and I won't sleep soon,
I'll praise the Moon till the day is breaking.

October fourth, two thousand seventeen,
a night as nice as this there has never been.

Bravo ou manso

Fosse eu um grande pinheiro, bravo ou manso,
lançava longos ramos até poder chegar
a cada fonte em cada monte, a cada lugar
a que não cheguei e ainda não alcanço.
E com as raízes furava terra abaixo
até conseguir ver o centro deste mundo,
se é oco ou não, frio ou quente, quão profundo,
saber quando daqui sair o que mais deixo.
E com as minhas finas folhas forrava a terra,
e com uma pinha anunciava cada flor,
e fazia sombra onde houvesse mais ardor,
e contemplava como a vida se descerra.

Bravo ou manso, pinheiro, ave ou marinheiro,
com ou sem sorte correria o mundo inteiro.

Flocos de neve

Desafiam calmamente a gravidade,
não esperam que as suas leis inverta,
e descem, sobem, sem direcção certa,
e poisam suavemente na cidade.
E toda a cobertura é coberta,
cada pedra, cada ramo e todo o chão,
as horas deixam de ser o que são,
abrandam, tornam curva cada recta.
São águas de brancura e fresquidão,
cristais de estelar geometria,
milagres de física e alquimia
que acertam o bater do coração.

E podem mais do que pode a razão,
que espera, até deseja esperar em vão.

About the Author:

Pierre Sotér is the pen name of a well-established Portuguese author. After thirty years of successful professional life and intensive soul-searching, he now dedicates his time to poetry and philosophy. The DAWN is the first book in the Book Series "Poems and Thoughts of Pierre Sotér." Pierre writes in Portuguese, English, and French.

FORGIVENESS WEARS NO CROWN
by Richard Weaver

Winter Solstice: A Sermon

The moon shifts its fixed position.
What it has done for whatever reason
its shadows are left behind
and a question remains:
should math determine
what rises unfathomed?
Beyond number? Past silence?
Meantime, the moon sings
an aria swollen like the belly
of an orphaned cloud.
Another star dies. Music
rinses from the disturbed river.
Yellow moon unhinging.
An old prayer rising up,
bobbing to the surface.
It wavers between time past
and time to come, taking time
to laugh at itself. Left alone
the stars blink goodnight
as startled fish mouth novenas
and water diminishes
Light contemplates
its overdue death.

Forgiveness wears no crown as it unearths the old moon

The perfume of blood.
An earthen hand signing
in an unknown language.
Blue chasing orange
and green red. Translation.
Testimony. An unmoving whole
risen fallen folding
into itself before the rain
a lone bird calling the listening
gray white haunting black
lifting out in still life
where mountains are the point
where color blindly seeks
to be heard (its source?).
Praise falls diffidently to seize
to live in contrast and refrain.
All talking in shadowless
dense but radiant light.

Prophecy with sea salt

Blood-stars realign themselves
as two-headed geese flee eastward.
They know to never look directly
at a cyclops owl. Or the myopic moon.

Orion with his lyre and black mirror
marvels as the ochre light of his skin
becomes a blue silence. And asks
of no one, who could not see
this new ruined world
and not wish for blindness?

Will we all go cave-mad
after staring down
the blood-stained sun?
Or drop sadness like a coin
into the long black echoing
silence of a dry cistern?

Who wouldn't wake the night
to say the sun is a beggar
that shines as it stains,
and discolors what the past honors
in the fierce horrors of dawn?

An aged light will shift
across a world disfigured
by your godless absence;
its honey-combed light
fixed in diminishing chords.

Nearer than the desert of night,
neither heaven nor hell,
rain or wind, born dead when you died.

All flesh is grass, all life compost

When no color glows

in this wounded world

in a place where no light

lives long and all flesh

is revealed and cries out,

but remains unheard,

where water stutters

and the mountain's heart

stills, mortal in its way,

the red wind has no choice

except to mourn

another bloodied dawn.

Another bloodless day.

Witnessing

"Failing to comprehend, after hearing,
they learn like the deaf. The saying
is their witness, absent while present."
-- Heraclitus

There is no cloud
like the present
to urge a swarm of bees
towards night-green light.
After all, the soul
first melts in fallen fruit.
The river swells
wide, swollen fat
like a cow's undissected heart.
Wind offers its lurid dream
of stones languishing, and joy
knows they can never be
strangers. One prefers
the narrowed strait, and the other
red sky forever rinsing red.

Adrift in the blue wind
he listens and lends an ear
to covenant, each part
a purer blue animal.
In the juniper's pulse
he makes his nest,
crowned with stars. Rain

he calls his friend, and swears
each mortal note is a reminder,
a sacred refrain, as the early moon
advances dreamlike on the unbridled
mouth, and blood falls
like fermented pomegranate seeds
falls drunkenly in the wilderness.
Solitude breeds freedom in the lindens
as light loses its race
and an oyster disgorges
a crescent-shaped pearl.

About the Author:

Richard Weaver lives in Baltimore's Inner Harbor where he volunteers at the Maryland Book Bank, and acts as the Archivist-at-large for a Jesuit College founded in 1830. He also acts as a seasonal snow-flake counter, unofficially.

Poems published here are from a book-length series based in part on the art, correspondence, writing, and life of the German Expressionist painter Franz Marc (1880-1916). More particularly, they focus on the time between the years 1912 and 1916. Marc and Wassily Kandinsky co-founded the Blue Rider movement. Marc died near Verdun, France on March 4 1916. Poems from the same collection have appeared in 2River View, Gingerbread House, Clade Song, Conjunctions (web), Aberration Labyrinth, & Twisted Vine Leaves.

BARE HYMN

Seth Jani

Mountain Pass

I erased myself so I could learn
The inner life of things.
This river has a name,
But it's not the one we give it.
The grass blades are silent
But they voice the summer wind.
I believe there are meridians
That brush the edges of the light
And become the ground
For something new.
We awake in other worlds
With only a faint taste
Left from this one.
Is it mustard seed or wine?
The powerful distance between friends?
We come to a mountain
With a door built into the stone.
On the other side we don't remember.
We emerge repeating
"There's only this, only this."

Unfinished Business

Unfinished business
Rises-up from the radial point of sleep
Into the world of waking.
How can we correct
The transgressions of dreams?
Retract the unconscious violence
In those glittering nocturnal worlds?
Does the good we do here, or there,
Plant seeds in all the gradients
Of awareness?

After a lifetime
Of trying to be lighter,
Easier on the heart,
Does the universe gain
Even a particle of radiance
When we return to no one
On this rain soaked earth?

The Landscapist

The white butterfly comes through
And says, "No Problem."

It's been happening all day,
The shadows crosshatched,
The sun contending with rain,
And still, these dismissive wings.
I walk with two hands open
Not holding on to a single thing.

Water pours through my fingers
But the heart is always full.
Its golden cisterns reflect
The constant passage.

Even the city is there, windblown,
Full of beautiful refuse.
There is something wildly bright
That illuminates us even in sleep,

Even in death with its backroom exit.
The landscape is present in all seasons,
Bending the light branches,
Not caring where you place
Those heavy stones.

Bare Hymn

I rise-up, Saint Francis,
Into the simplicity of night,
The field and industry
Of joy.
We have been burdened
For so long,
And the animals come
With such lightness,
Such timidity in their steps.
See that hand reaching out
And grazing the world of innocence?
What does it bring back?

In the place where the mower doesn't go
There is a hard presence.
The white stones stand by it.
All it takes is a close eye,
An ear titled to the wind.
All it takes is absolute stillness.
The water in the garden
Fills with reflections.
A small wing nests
Inside the light.

Fossils

The blue ferns trailing all day
The silence of the sun itself,
Holding the darkness like a key.
I lay under them, shrunk to my
Proper size,
My medial, clockwork being.
It's not about religion
But simple awe,
The river that moves deep fossils
Into the child's searching hands.
Those dragonflies continue to exist
And they land on the ancestral stones.
Years from now, will someone feel
The light exactly as we do?
The whole summer miraculously present
Before vanishing through the rain?

About the Author:

Seth Jani currently resides in Seattle, WA and is the founder of Seven CirclePress (www.sevencirclepress.com). His own work has been published widely in such places as The Chiron Review, Pretty Owl Poetry, El Portal, The Hamilton Stone Review, Hawai`i Pacific Review, VAYAVYA, Gingerbread House, Gravel and Zetetic: A Record of Unusual Inquiry. More about him and his work can be found at www.sethjani.com.

Mark Young

Transcript

Back from an hour-long walk. Not much traffic.

Small city, no light pollution. No moon. Sky full of stars.

No recent rain. No frogs. Instead, cicadas.

Flying foxes flap leatherly from trees inches above our heads.

Change of diet. Too early for fruit. Nectar in season.

Talking whilst walking. Conversational avenues.

Different from solitary walks where you go out looking for poems.

Windchimes somewhere though not much breeze.

Train noises. A lifelong constant.

Geckoes on the front porch. I yearn for mountains.

A line from Ada Lovelace (2)

The way he ties his ties way
too long is a science of itself,
like hoisin sauce or miso. Do
I need to spell out my grand-

father spends a lot of his
time comparing brands in the
grocery store he goes to every
Saturday? He's getting old;

so to simplify his tasks, I've
added a little bit of code
& a few dedicated function
buttons to his Zimmer frame.

Where is Juárez

Strange shit goes on
in the bars of
Juárez. Some-
thing to do with the
architecture. So many
corners & temporal
anomalies to hide
within. & even without
concealment there
is always a tension
waiting for the next
word to make its
way out from behind
the plastic curtains
that the women
drape serape-like
around their bodies.

A Poem of Our Climate

Music from
across the street
    hangs in the
night air. Per-
cussive, piano
sounds perhaps;
    & I am put in
mind of the poetry
of Wallace Stevens.
    Clavier, Peter
Quince at—ob-
viously, but just
the first few lines
remembered. &
    moving on The
Blue Guitar, a-
gain music, again
the first few lines,
once more about
another person. A
    sad summation
of a poet's work,
    fat books rendered
into flat pegs from
which fall all
too easily other
folk & forms.

In the environs of the Palais des Tuileries

".....on the sundial of your life."
Robert Desnos: To the Mysterious Woman

A late
afternoon
point of
co-
incidence

this bench
in the
Botanical Gardens
shared
with Desnos
& Diogenes

neither there
when I arrived

but putting
a wide-
trunked tree
between me
& the sun

& moving
as its shadow
tracks the time

I recall
     the one
& refute
     the other.

About the Author:

Mark Young's most recent books are Ley Lines & bricolage, both from gradient books of Finland, The Chorus of the Sphinxes, from Moria Books in Chicago, & some more strange meteorites, from Meritage & i.e. Press, California / New York. A limited edition chapbook, A Few Geographies, was recently released by One Sentence Poems as the initial offering in their new range.

ENAMORED

Susie Gharib

Dolphins

Far from surly fish they dart
Into the invisible pinnacles of our sphere
To woo the air.

Playful, they court with ship and sail,
A blue-born date
With every mariner that navigates.

Of a chivalric bent, they chart the deeps,
Chaperoning galleys across the seas,
A heraldic feat.

Eloquence

He soaks his words in l'eau d'or.
Like floundering false teeth they grin to all.
Picks each matutinally with a pair of tongs,
To dry on a Mackintosh piece of cloth.

He sharpens each verb with metaphysical steel.
Cross-breeds his nouns with French and Greek.
Semi-starves his adjectives on a slimming diet,
Dilutes his preps to curb down their riots.

Enamored

His room was the size of an anchorite's
No matter where I sat
I had to confront his green-blue eyes,
The Smokey's looks
The muscular height
Of a man in the prime of life
So erudite.

He told me he was passive and so was I
But my verbal warfare represented me otherwise,
I was incapable of hurting a fly,
Or inflicting upon an enemy the atrocity of a frown.

Convivial we grew over the subject of multilingual bells
And 'gibbous' was a phase of the moon, he guessed,
Words that are still redolent with his breath.

I always marvel which one of his charms
More captivates his audience's hearts
The aesthetic façade
Or the brilliant mind.

When he goes mountaineering over Scottish heights
I arduously climb the cliffs of strife,
Hoping that peaks entail respite.

About the Author:

Susie Gharib is a graduate of the University of Strathclyde (Glasgow, Scotland) with a Ph.D. Her doctoral thesis, entitled Stylistic and Thematic Reassessment of The Trespasser, is a critical study of the work of D.H. Lawrence. Since 1996, she has been lecturing in Syria. She self-published four collections of poetry (My Love in Red, The Alpine Glow, Resonate and Kareem) and a collection of short stories (Bare Blades). She is a lover of Nature and enjoys swimming.

ORIGAMI AND SWEATERS

Kennie Romero

Yextla, 1970

Once upon a time
Year 1970, in a Mexican
village tucked in the folds
of corn and poppy fields,
abuelito threatened a witch
for putting incantations on abuelita
who laid in bed near oblivion's curtain of the dead
because there was no more milk to sell to the witch.
In the house next to the village's pharmacy, abuelito visited an herbalist

Herbs to put in abuelita's porridge, abuelito put on a brave face he told papa, and confronted the witch. Now, in the US Atlantic Coast, say you'll kill them papa tells me like your abuelito did. Converse politely about the witch's hands and feet left on the ritual site, about the deformed chickens and pigs you've seen, and how you wouldn't mind cutting off chicken heads and scalping a pig's skin, the fun it would be.
Fin.

Origami and Sweaters

Fold 5-inch square paper into flowers in the
school's library. In between the creases of the
paper,   read   about

that   day   in   autumn,
5   centuries   and   a   half   ago.
How   I   would   have   given
the   32,   000   sweaters
I   don't   own,   to   Jews
in   Lower   Bavaria.
Protest to the duchy,

Liberate   the   ache   in   their   bones
and   warm   it   in   front   of   firestones.

Now   I   know
it   must   have   been   cold,
Wonder   if   Jews
slept   in   the   streets
and cover themselves
with dry leaves.

About the Author:

Kenia Romero currently resides in South Carolina, USA. Romero enjoys reading prose and poetry by minority writers, watching Mexican Golden Age of Cinema films, and painting in her spare time. She is a senior at South Carolina Governor school for the Arts and Humanities.

SUMMER NIGHTS

Jacquelyne Nemeth

Alaska

Don't say you love me. You don't love me if you don't know that my favorite smell is when it rains in mid august and you go outside at 4am and inhale. You don't love me if you haven't seen me at my worst, when I'm crying so hard that I can't breathe. Don't say you know me if you don't know why I can't eat popcorn at a movie theatre. You don't know me until you've seen me at my most vulnerable side, when I'm sound asleep. You don't love me if the sound of my laugh doesn't make you smile. You don't love me until you know why I hate the color Purple but love Lavender. You can't love me if you don't know why I can't sleep unless it's light outside. You can't fully know me if you don't know that New York is my favorite state and that I'm terrified of Alaska. You don't know why rainy days are my favorite, and you don't know why I love Orchids. You don't love me. You don't even know me.

Counting Stars

I can't tell you how many times I cried for him. I lost track when I started bleeding for him. I took a shot for every time I thought of him. Every thought was like a star in the sky- impossible to keep track of without getting lost. Before I knew it, it had me feeling exactly what I wanted to feel: nothing. I'd wake up in the morning and it was the same routine. Not a day goes by where I don't wish that I looked him hard in the face and said the words that have been itching, burning, clawing at my heart for years. It's not easy to stop loving someone when they've woven themselves into your heart. You can't help it, you don't know you're falling until you've hit the ground. How do you cope in the aftermath when they're still woven in, but they've left? I wanted to cut him out, it was the only way. I can't tell you how many times I tried.

Summer Nights

He falls back into me but

he never stays

He's like each season- staying for a while, warming me, making everything beautiful, giving me the chills, and then leaving me cold

Seasons stay for a little while, and then you wait for Summer to come back around to bring you that warmth

But what do I do during the other 3 seasons?

I mourn Summer, I miss it

I miss him

I will wait through Autumn, and another cold winter

Spring will creep up on me, as I wait and hope he comes back

Summer has always been my favorite season

I miss it the second it leaves, and when it comes back, I can't get enough

I've always loved it, I've always loved him

Balanced

I can't remember his favorite color. I forgot what he likes to eat for breakfast. I don't know his sister's middle name or what he wore to his dad's funeral. I do remember the feeling of his skin against mine in late June. I still get that feeling in my stomach, the feeling I got when I first saw him. I can still feel my heart racing the way it did when he sat next to me in the car. I have his voice memorized. My favorite song is his voice singing to me at 1 am while we were driving in the middle of nowhere. I remember the spark that went through my entire body like a wave of electric when he first looked at me, really looked at me. He looked at me with purpose. Feeling his heartbeat with my hand on his chest is the best part of him that I've ever touched. All this time has passed but I can still feel the warm summer air hitting us when we walked outside hand in hand. There's one thing about him that could never slip my mind. I see it in his face, I hear it in his voice. I feel it on his chest and I feel it in his kiss. It balances me out when I've been thrown into a hurricane and tossed around. My favorite memory, the best feeling.

I remember how much I love him.

Blonde

I loved my hair blonde until some unworthy

mean

cold

man

said he liked it better black

"I think you look better when it is black, you look beautiful."

I dyed it black without question, never once hesitated

I loved him without ever hesitating

Never caring for myself

Never making sure I could swim before I jumped in the deep end

I couldn't even catch myself when I was falling

I look better without him

I look beautiful

Over two decades and I didn't feel free until he left and my hair was

blonde

About the Author:

In author's own words: "My name is **Jacquelyne Nemeth. I** have 24 years of spit and vinegar pent up. It comes out in poems and stories. My words are like seeds. I bury them, and after the right care, they grow. I'm a garden of words now. Thank you for reading the flowers that bloom."

BOHEMIAN BANKER

Thomas Locicero

Blame

There are events that cannot be wished away.
How often is a coroner unsure?
Or the detective knocking on your front door
late at night—is he sure of what he will say?
Good news does not come early in the morning.
The startle of the doorbell is our warning.
First whispers, then the inevitable shout.
One of us blames God and the other blames doubt.

Failing to Revive My Mother

Who among the sane looks to be heroic
and longs for the occasion to give his
breath to one who is not his lover? Who
claims to find glory in reviving the dead?
And if the dead is stubborn and finds glory
in death? Death is the living's last achievement
and she will not be robbed of it. I saw her
chest rise and fall. Is not that the evidence
of life? But I was breathing for two. When I
stopped breathing to perform compressions, she
ceased breathing. In war, soldiers are heroic
in defeat. Such a peace is not found in sons.

Bohemian Banker

for T.S. Eliot

You boast of virtuosity,
yet find yourself in dubious alleys
dressed like a banker so as not to
play the part of a poet or of a
bohemian because you are not Pound,
the drum of your heart distracting,
the women there a curiosity,
and you hear yourself wondering
with a faraway echoing voice
somewhere inside you, in the hollow
in which the soul resides, that deep
recess, if they would they want you
if you were poor. You are enamored
with the lowly, buoyant in your hope
that they could be besotted
with you, too. You sense that you
have yet to live your life,
but still choose to live it slowly,
convinced you are saving yourself
for something holier than flesh.
If they knew who you were,
if they heard your words, you would be
a deity among them. They would cry,
Divinity. But you know who you are:
a sinner like the lot of them, you
who would dare not barter what was earned
or gifted for a pound of flesh, you
who would be disappointed if the women
showed you any marks of virtuosity.

Liar

Because he did not want to be found wanting,
the stories of his successes still falling
from the lips of his siblings, who believed, and
because he did not want to be seen ailing,
the body in the photographs he sent them
younger than his actual years, his waist slim,
his back straight, his forearms veiny and thick,
he simply said he would be backpacking
in Europe, the lie rich people tell when
their children were really in drug rehab
at Betty Ford, all the while wondering
why any of them would want to visit
him after he refused to share any
of his imaginary wealth with them,
even as they begged, and, though he feared to die
alone, it was a better alternative
to disappointing them as he had when
he was young and spoke irritating words
about dreams while—and this was his great sin—
he was awake, in the hot afternoon,
boasting about the great man he would become,
without a drop of sweat on his body.

Subterranean Blues

I cannot discern the voice in the speaker,
but in the moments when I turn away
from you and glimpse again into the real world,
I see it is almost time for me to
get off. I am loneliest above ground.
I reach for you, but not with the intentions
of the perverts who press up against you
and who plot to ride when it is standing room
only. I do not know what it is I touch.
Do you not resist because, like me, you care,
or because, like me, you have stopped caring?

About the Author:

Thomas Locicero is an award-winning poet, short story writer, and essayist, as well as a playwright and monologist. His work has appeared in Roanoke Review, Boston Literary Magazine, The Long Island Quarterly, Riverrun, Omnibus Arts & Literature Anthology, A&U: America's AIDS Magazine and Beginnings, among other literary periodicals. Originally from East Islip, Long Island, Thomas resides with his wife, Lil, and their sons, Sam and Ben, in Broken Arrow, Oklahoma.

blog address is https://thomaslocicero.wordpress.com/

Facebook: https://m.facebook.com/thomas.locicero.3

Twitter: @ThomasLocicero

THE FORREST

Omar Alexandre

you can look and you can touch

a guy gave me head today
and my next door neighbor saw us

his fingers gripped
tightly unto my thighs

i felt the top of his head
touch my stomach
it was sweaty

his lips wrapped around my dick
and his tongue going in circles

i left the blinds open and i honestly don't care

the president once again proved today why he isn't fit to lead

but no one honestly gives a shit

so i play an LCD Soundsystem record
on a Wednesday evening

and i dance and keep dancing

and wonder why the girl
in my poems doesn't want to fuck me

i'm bored and lonely
but mostly bored and lonely
so i prepare the table and make
peanut butter and jelly sandwiches
for uninvited guests

an aubade courting insanity

its 3:09 in the morning and i have a sudden urge to drown in your chaos
i hear the wind calling out your cries

an aubade courting insanity

it's 3:10 in the morning and i have a sudden urge to dance with your waves
an early morning sortie into your catastrophic nothingness

your blank page shines brightly
and it's indomitable

so i relinquish all fight
for you make me tenuous

it's 4 in the morning and this perennial urge won't go away

The Forrest

this magic place
which holds life and laughter
under blue skies,
amongst fractured minds,
rainy afternoons,
and its tenderly sad unknowns
i find a world
which burns brightly
like floating dancers in pointe shoes
giving air to the sorrows
heard through a lonely man's instrument

They Cray

She told me her vagina is like Christmas in a taco shop

So I reached for my Wenger Swiss Army Knife, ripped my chest open and instantly gave her my heart

We're in a relationship now but not really

She does her thing and I do mine

i.e. she drinks mojitos all day and trains her cat to murder her next door neighbor's rooster because it doesn't have any concept of time and when the neighbor shows up with the dead rooster and accuses her cat she'll respond, "well maybe you shouldn't have food as fucking pets!"

I write her poems and tell her how much I've missed her

She says she only misses flip phones

I tell her I suffer from anxiety so she lets me touch her boobs for fifteen minutes

Then we drift and go back to doing our own thing

i.e. She drinks more mojitos and reads Simone de Beauvoir's 'Le Deuxième Sexe' and texts me in the middle of the night to tell me, "He bled for our sins but I bleed every month, tell me who's the real motherfucking Jesus?!"

I lay in bed disoriented and confused staring at my bright white screen and simply text back, "down?"

She replies, "sure."

untitled

I died a long time ago on the eastern coast
abducted from silence and placed in the middle of a five pm traffic
surrounded by apes pretending to know
what they're doing behind a steering wheel

time advances and the months get marked off
the crows take turns ripping into my flesh
and I allow my bones to rot for a simple yet incoherent pleasure

the wild man with a sad face who has been pushed away to the outskirts sees the sky mourn and writes
a song about it

And the girl that never texted back and dreams of becoming a star
comes to her senses and rides off to the desert searching for a lost promise
a dirty lost treasure

I come back from the dead after hearing the sad man's song and being rescued by the girl

And I find transparency within all the trash
and fall deeply in love

About the Author:

Omar Alexandre lives in Miami, Florida. He is an aspiring writer/filmmaker who recently completed his first short film and one of his music videos will be screened during the 16th annual Miami Short Film Festival. His poems have been published in In Between Hangovers, Your One Phone Call, and Juste Milieu. Follow him on Instagram @alexandre88.

FIVE CITY POETS FROM A CENTURY AGO
by William Ruleman

THE CITY'S GOD

By Georg Heym

He squats on a block of houses, black in mood.
The winds have settled, surly, round his brow.
He sees, enraged, how in far solitude
The last houses scatter in lands of field and plow.

With evening's advent, Baal's red belly glowers.
Around him, all the greatest cities kneel.
Cathedral bells from seas of gloomy towers
Peal before him with enormous zeal.

The music of the millions thunders through
The streets like Corybants' loud revelries.
Like fragrant incense vapors, waxing blue,
Smoke climbs to him from sundry factories.

In his eyebrows swells the thunderstorm.
Night benumbs the darkling evening's pyre.
Swirling clouds, like hissing vultures, form
Inside his hair, which stands on end with ire.

He strikes his fleshy fist out in the dark
And shakes it. Flaming oceans navigate
A street. Their smoke laps up their final spark
And keeps on rolling till the day dawns, late.

DER GOTT DER STADT

Georg Heym

Auf einem Häuserblocke sitzt er breit.
Die Winde lagern schwarz um seine Stirn.
Er schaut voll Wut, wo fern in Einsamkeit
Die letzten Häuser in das Land verirrn.

Vom Abend glänzt der rote Bauch dem Baal,
Die großen Städte knien um ihn her.
Der Kirchenglocken ungeheure Zahl
Wogt auf zu ihm aus schwarzer Türme Meer.

Wie Korybanten-Tanz dröhnt die Musik
Der Millionen durch die Straßen laut.
Der Schlote Rauch, die Wolken der Fabrik
Ziehn auf zu ihm, wie Duft von Weihrauch blaut.

Das Wetter schwelt in seinen Augenbrauen.
Der dunkle Abend wird in Nacht betäubt.
Die Stürme flattern, die wie Geier schauen
Von seinem Haupthaar, das im Zorne sträubt.

Er streckt ins Dunkel seine Fleischerfaust.
Er schüttelt sie. Ein Meer von Feuer jagt
Durch eine Straße. Und der Glutqualm braust
Und frißt sie auf, bis spät der Morgen tagt.

EVENING ON THE CANAL
By Paul Boldt

The riders take their white
Pathways to the town,
Whose dusty yellow light
Spews evening's blue with down.

The lindens, mourning, bow
And mingle, pair by pair;
The birches, grayer now,
Loom, overgrown with hair.

The gas begins to whistle,
Gently come to bloom
As if a giant thistle
Had sprayed with dust the flume.

The waves wax nickel. All
The channel's vessels freeze
Aglow, coiled in the shawl
Of evening's icy breeze.

ABEND AM KANAL
Paul Boldt

In weißen Wegen ziehn
Die Reiter in die Stadt,
Die lichtergelb bespien
Den blauen Abend hat.

Die Linden haben Trauer,
und ineinander lehnen,
Vom Haar bewachsen, grauer
Die Birkenmagdalenen.

Das Gas beginnt zu fisteln,
Sehr zart sich zu belauben,
Als blühten große Disteln,
Die auf das Wasser stauben.

Die Wellen werden nickeln.
Die Kähne im Kanal
Frieren beglänzt und wickeln
Sich in der Winde Shawl.

BIG CITY

By Alfons Petzold

Glaring posters smear their gaudy phrases on
The rout of trucks and people rushing everywhere.
The steely elephants of autos loom and drone;
Scaffolds, rails, and blocks of stones all flare and blare.

The granite cubes of streets and squares and alleyways—
Like silver insect eyes—bedazzle, daze, and stun,
While up on high, the wicked telegraph-wire-nests' blaze
Sprays and sparkles, spitting spite up at the sun.

Show windows shine like caves torn open, spill
Their treasures' gleam on hearts and brains of passersby.
"Forward!" roars the growling city's hammering will:
"Forward!" all cry. No eye sees the sky.

GROßSTADT

(Alfons Petzold)

Plakate schmettern ihre buntfarbigen Phrasen
in das Gewühle der Menschen und Wagen hinein.
Die Stahlelephanten der Automobile rasen
alles tönt: Gerüste, Schienen, verblocktes Gestein.

Die granitenen Würfel der Gassen, Straßen und Plätze
silbrig, wie Augen eines Insektes glühn
indes in der Höhe die Telegraphendrahtnetze
bös funkeln und Trotz in die Sonne sprühn.

Schauläden prunken, gleich aufgerissenen Höhlen,
schütten den Glanz ihrer Schätze in Hirn und Herz.
Vorwärts! Dröhnt es aus dem Knattern und Gröhlen
Vorwärts! schreit alles, kein Auge blickt himmelwärts.

ON MY WAY

By Hedwig Lachmann

I roam all through the massive town. A gloomy
Veil of fall mist hovers round its defenses;
The day's work buzzes, roars before my senses;
Hundreds of humans rush their way on by me.

I know them not. Who are these many? Do they
Bear in their breasts a loss like mine? And do
Their hearts, unknown to me, perhaps bleed too—
In ways my own strange heartbeat could not say?

The mist is dripping. And we wander on.
From you to me, no flashes of meaning flare.
And when we toss a word out on the air,
It dies in the wind, unheeded and unknown.

UNTERWEGS

(Hedwig Lachmann)

Ich wandre in der grossen Stadt. Ein trüber
Herbstnebelschleier flattert um die Zinnen,
Das Tagwerk schwirrt und braust vor meinen Sinnen,
Und tausend Menschen gehn an mir vorüber.

Ich kenn sie nicht. Wer sind die Vielen? Tragen
Sie in der Brust ein Los wie meins? Und blutet
Ihr Herz vielleicht, von mir so unvermutet,
Als ihnen fremd ist meines Herzens Schlagen?

Der Nebel tropft. Wir alle wandern, wandern.
Von dir zu mir erhellt kein Blitz die Tiefen.
Und wenn wir uns das Wort entgegenriefen –
Es stirbt im Wind und keiner weiss vom andern.

THE STREET
By Ernst Wilhelm Lotz

On violet mists swim lights of vivid bright
And burning gold. You dive right in, wade on
A-spin and blind in seas of faces right
Up close and panting, pale. You sink. And are alone.

Just you. You feel your hands to check and now
You know you dream. The dream drifts up all white.
You see the steep walls of the street somehow
Adorned with strange and glaring realms of varied light.

Your ears are shut. Your eyes alone can sense.
The street shows crosswise through the sky-forest-scapes.
The boughs of stars, whose streaming spans are immense,
Deceive with gestures of gods and sundry animal shapes.

You yourself are a star. You resound. And you can hear
Yourself ring through the All. You swim around
Through dreams of dear light sound that lure and charm
And make you take them for some other pleasant sound.

Where is the sun, which binds you in its ring?
Gone now. Too late for that. You stay the course.
Around your train of fire twirls, sharpening,
A glowing tail. Storm forth, a comet now, full force!

DIE STRASSE

(Ernst Wilhelm Lotz)

Auf violetten Dünsten schwimmen Lichter
Von brennend hohem Gelb. Du tauchst hinein,
Gewirbelt blindlings in ein Meer Gesichter,
Blaß, atmend nah. Versinkst. Und bist allein.

Nur du. Zum Prüfen fühlst du deine Hände
Und weißt, du träumst. Der Traum steigt weiß empor.
Vor dir erkennst du steile Straßenwände,
Behängt mit seltsam hellem Lichterflor.

Dein Ohr ist zu. Nur deine Augen fühlen.
Quer zeigt die Straße durch den Sternenwald.
Die Sternenzweige, die vorüberspühlen,
Bildtäuschen Göttergesten und manche Tiergestalt.

Du selbst ein Stern. Du tönst. Dich kannst du hören
Hinklingen durch das All. Du träumst und schwimmst
In Töne-Träumen, die dich leuchtend schön betören,
Daß du sie für den andern Wohllaut nimmst.

Wo ist die Sonne, die dich zirkelnd bindet?
Versäumt. Du steuerst fort. Es ist zu spät.
Um deine Feuerbahn nachschleifend windet
Sich hell ein Schweif. – Stürm glühend fort, Komet!

BIOGRAPHICAL NOTES:

About the Translator:

Georg Heym (1887-1912), one of the most famous of the German Expressionist poets, is best known for his strange depictions of modern Berlin and nightmarish visions of cultural collapse, which foreshadow the horrors of the First World War. His poetic output before his accidental death by drowning at the age of 24 was amazing.

Paul Boldt (1885-1921), one of the German Expressionist poets, was given to frolicsome and sometimes bawdy depictions of life, love, and sex in Berlin during the years preceding the First World War. Though drafted into the army, he was discharged in 1916, being declared psychologically unfit to serve. He died at the age of 35 from complications resulting from hernia surgery.

Alfons Petzold (1882-1923), a native of Vienna, was well known for his prose and verse during his lifetime, but since then, he has suffered neglect. He wrote of the working classes from which he emerged, the modern city, but also of nature during a life plagued by ill health and often poverty.

Hedwig Lachmann (1865-1918) lived in various cities, including Budapest and Berlin. She also translated many authors, notably Edgar Allan Poe and Oscar Wilde, into German. She was married to the German revolutionary Gustav Landau, who published her collected poems in book form after her death from pneumonia in her 53rd year.

Ernst Wilhelm Lotz (1890-1914) is most often associated with Dresden, where he wrote many of his best poems. Though he shared with his fellow German Expressionist poets the desire for an energetic spiritual transformation of the staid society of his youth, his poetic career was cut short when he died in battle in France in 1914.

William Ruleman is Professor of English at Tennessee Wesleyan University. His most recent books include his translations of Hermann Hesse's verse up to 1902, entitled Early Poems (Cedar Springs Books, 2017) and of Stefan Zweig's unfinished novel Clarissa (Ariadne Press, also 2017).

ABOUT PATIENCE
Glen Sorestad

Crow Ruckus

As we near one of the crescent condos, the black racket
grows in intensity. Since it's Sunday morning, I am
inclined to think it a crow-devised invocation, akin
to the urgent clamor of a church bell, though crows

have a wary intelligence that may well preclude
theological considerations. We watch more crows
passing overhead, their singular focus the same rooftop,
same apparent purpose, and as we near, we see them

Homing in like pigeons to an apartment-top cote.
We count twenty-five, a murder of crows, indeed.
The summoned corvid mob strut back and forth
atop the shingled pitch of the dwelling, shouting

what sound like imprecations at someone, though
the source of agitation or distress is not apparent.
I begin to see these coal-feathered declaimers as
parliamentarians, voicing their constituent concerns

to the head of state in daily question period, before
lifting off and returning from whence they came,
to resume the more germane consideration of feeding
fledglings with more nutrition than politics.

About Patience

The way morning sun splashes
pond reeds with light and pries
into the dense bulrushes, as if
to probe their depths, tells me
this is a good day to stop,
just stand here and be alert.

The Sora is a shy bird, a wader
of marshy shorelines, smaller
and rounder than a robin.

I do not wait long
before a slight flickering
near the base of the reeds
signals its presence as it
scampers and scurries,
back and forth, feeding
on whatever delicacies Soras
find in the pond shallows.
Dart and bend, repeat –
its modus operandi.
There for the briefest of moments.
Then gone.

One-sided Conversation

A lone Waxwing is perched on an upper arm
of the small green ash. I stop. Drab grey
is usually uninviting, but early sun-slants
can enliven even the muted slate tones.

A jaunty Blue Jay arrives, picks a seat
on the same ash, a few feet from the other
and begins to prattle, as jays will,
with neither provocation nor invitation.

Whatever the jay may ask or demand,
the waxwing remains mum, while the jay
flits, branch to branch, seeking, but not finding;
interrogating, but receiving no confession.

Frustrated by its companion's unwillingness
to divulge a single morsel of useful news,
the jay utters a few derogatory squawks,
flaps off to find more receptive listeners.

About the Author:

Glen Sorestad is a well known poet from Saskatoon whose poems have appeared all over North America and many other parts of the world. His poetry has appeared in over 60 anthologies and textbooks and have been translated into eight languages. His latest poetry book was jointly authored with Jim Harris; Water and Rock appeared this year from LCM Press in New Mexico.

MAPLE SAP AND SKIN HUNGER

by Adrian Slonaker

Discovery in the Stacks

A tawny art textbook last loaned
forty-five years earlier
sat like a hardcover wallflower in
the vastness of the university library.
A tired grunt of graphite trailing into nothingness,
the borrower's scribbled signature elicited voiceless questions:
Who possessed that signature?
Had it outlived him-
or her?
What had become of the cryptic signer
during decades of war,
disease,
and dance crazes?
Multiple marriages,
companions,
kids,
parakeets?
Had the erstwhile student aged
with reflective resignation
or battled biology with
dime-store miracle creams or costly lifts?
Not wanting some future reader
to harbor the same wonderings about me,
I shut the cover as I'd close a clam shell,
shoved the volume back on its shelf,
and slipped out to the snack bar.

"Palak Paneer, Protection and Pregnant Pauses"

Sheltered by the shade of an awful shingled awning,
I swatted away a secret more dismal
than the leaden clouds eavesdropping on us:
I craved your toenail clippings in my sink.
Raindrops slalomed down your supersized nose, but
the wetness of you is nothing new to me;
I watched the water whirl over your contours
when we showered together this morning
in that dodgy dormitory where we'd punctuated
the musty dreariness with delighted yelps-
unlike the sullen silence of this Sunday afternoon
with hurried helpings of curry and swigs of soda.
Conversation was scarce, at least the velar and uvular kind.
Why talk when a look can protect you?
Even with scattered sleep, you're still stunning-
made up like a mod masterpiece in brooding blacks and grays,
preened where appropriate, carelessly scuffed where irresistible.
I focus on your fabrics because anything further would
excise the candy core from our fun sin compromisos.

Maple Sap and Skin Hunger

King crimson maple tree branches
dangling behind my back
behind your back,
sap speckling the park bench, rivaling this afternoon's raindrops.
How long has the King reigned here?
Thirty years? Fifty years?

Will you beautify my life for as long as this tree has beautified this spot?
It's pointless to conjecture.
Why dwell on the unknowable
when the knowable is all too real
and all too sublime:
that elusive sating of mind hunger
and skin hunger.

Poets propose that you touch my soul.
Scientists say you switch on my brain's pleasure center.
Poetry or science,
press your thigh closer to mine
as leather meets velvet.

About the Author:

Adrian Slonaker works as a copywriter and copy editor in Lancaster, Pennsylvania, USA. He holds a Master of Arts degree in interdisciplinary humanities from California State University-Dominguez Hills. Adrian's poetry has appeared in Amaryllis, The Mackinac, Eunoia Review, Aberration Labyrinth, Nixes Mate Review and others.

SOMEONE ELSE

Jean Berrett

Words like forever or never are not enough.
The tiny animal who left tracks in patches of snow
over a quarter mile of rolling pasture and grain fields,
who lives, who lived, somewhere near the marsh sink
that divides the gigantic range.

Broken cornstalks in silent rows are watching
the swoop of an owl
over tiny footsteps
or are listening to the terrible roar of killer
cars and trucks on Highway 29.
He, too, was beloved.

ANALYSIS OF LIGHT IN PATUXENT PARK

What was that short, thick-bodied bird
that all at once flew, fluttering and splashing,
up from the Little Patuxent?

Night will come down differently
in spite of the traffic that crosses
the bridge, in spite of
the shouting, "Hey man, ya got some? Ya gettin' some?"

Pickerel weed in the small wind beside me.
The beaver who forgets
he is my drowned father
sleeps under dead fallen oaks
in the deep muddy bank on the other side.
He will not slow down until dawn.

So lightly the river carries its leaving.
Another night as though to answer
an asking beyond belief.

JON AT EIGHTEEN

In your eighteenth year you are
as fragile as October ice
that lies and lifts on Cramer Lake.
You turn away, angry and afraid.

When I see you like that, I want to give you
something measureless
and full of light.

Listen.

I have no mother, no father.
But I have driven alone all night
and watched the setting moon dissolve
mammoth and orange
into the black sea of Nebraska.

I have walked nights at the ocean
listening to jagged cliffs
who answer the unanswerable Pacific:
be silent and resist.

My son, I am giving shape
to another arriving dark.
My son, there is a wind when it passes,
it is nothing but the wind.

About the Author:

Jean Berrett has been publishing poetry since 1973, after she took a Creative Writing-Poetry course offered by University of Wisconsin-Madison. The instructor told her that he thought she was the best poet in the class and he encouraged her to begin submitting poems to magazines. She obtained her BA at University of Wisconsin-Madison and her MFA in Creative Writing-Poetry from Eastern Washington University, and she taught English at College of Menomonee Nation. Since she first started publishing, she has published 89 poems. Other publications include translations from Virgil and Lucretius and also three stories and two book reviews. She has two sons and seven grandchildren.

EMPTY HOLLOW HEARTS

George Gad Economou

all you've ever needed
was to get out of the rain;
silent moments in the storm,
stars making grand promises
to empty walls.

from far away a laughter soft,
moans from the uninhabited bed.
cold streets, no light,
sauntering into the darkness,
praying to listen to the oncoming train just on time to
jump.

on the window falls the rain,
slow,
there's nowhere to go.

so many years
of empty embraces,
cold replacements sleeping under
a blanket made of snow during
better years.

there's nothing but the broken needle;
squirting rotten blood and traces of junk
that once used to warm the soul.
snowing outside, children lost in avalanches.

cries of early morning,
gintears in every tall glass emptied.
there have been too many broken promises
to drown in just a single bourbon bottle.

failing at the game called life,
once more to square one;
one step forth means three backwards.
it's alright; there's a god somewhere
currently sitting on a golden throne,
laughing his ass off at the miseries below.

it's alright; the monkeys dance in street corners,
angels hide in the darkest alleys,
patiently waiting for you to arrive.
we tried, more than once,
to uncover the mysteries,
we kept on failing till we gave up
and discovered the greatest gift for the racing mind.

always gintears in empty bourbon bottles,
searching for meaning in all the places
that shouldn't be; from afar the Bar calls.
trying to run, chained
to the cold ground.

fears in the sky,
nightingales unable anymore to sing,
bluebirds that refuse to fly.
where do we go, where were we?
you were then only for a second,
too much lost time.

there was nothing then,
there's nothing now.
nor will it ever be anything but nothing.
hence, let's go.
walk the line, chop the line;
a new shooting gallery.
more walls to stain.

the bottles are getting here fast,
are emptied even faster;
it's all we could ever have wanted.
all our hearts ever truly desired.
it's all gone; perished into the devastating flames
of the bombs.

we cried only once;
that fateful night.
the tears never stopped flooding ever since,
filling empty bottles and I've still got
something
to drink.

Gentle Winds Blow the Dust

brace, brace
the silent movements of the sea;

as the industrial wings take off,
glide, glide along
the empty seashells and
the raised towns.

burn through the ground,
drill a hole
right through
the ghastly walls,
the dead confines
of a wooden coffin abandoned
to mold.

run, run,
along the seashore,
feel the waves,
embrace the seagulls diving
and
roll, roll the dice,
bring forth the deuces,
abandon all hope

as you walk up the staircase.
follow, follow the marble,
listen to the music from broken speakers,
hear the words,
brace the silent movements of the sea.

surf along the waves,
reach, reach for the island
in the middle of nowhere.

bring back the fire,
stolen from a mage of a
time no one remembers.

long forgotten miracles;
empty shells, bombings
in the streets.
take cover, hide,
hide.

and the moon has risen,
red, like wine
or blood;
the empty voices of ghosts
wandering lost
somewhere in the distance.
forget, fight,
fight.
fight;
the needle on the ground,
the glass-pipe buried
inside deaf, muted walls.

forgive, forgive;
darling of old times,
yesteryears' grand love.
can you still hear me?
break, break through the ceiling,
come, come through
the unholy hole.
illegitimate claims,
bring back our lost daughter
from the alleys;
somewhere far away,
laughter's heard.

listen, listen,
to the dead silence of the grave
night.
go, go.
nothing left.
leave, leave.
and brace,
brace,
the undying silence
of the dark ocean of
tomorrow.

Gentle Winds Blow the Dust

brace, brace
the silent movements of the sea;

as the industrial wings take off,
glide, glide along
the empty seashells and
the raised towns.

burn through the ground,
drill a hole
right through
the ghastly walls,
the dead confines
of a wooden coffin abandoned
to mold.

run, run,
along the seashore,
feel the waves,
embrace the seagulls diving
and
roll, roll the dice,
bring forth the deuces,
abandon all hope

as you walk up the staircase.
follow, follow the marble,
listen to the music from broken speakers,
hear the words,
brace the silent movements of the sea.

surf along the waves,
reach, reach for the island
in the middle of nowhere.

bring back the fire,
stolen from a mage of a
time no one remembers.

long forgotten miracles;
empty shells, bombings
in the streets.
take cover, hide,
hide.

and the moon has risen,
red, like wine
or blood;

the empty voices of ghosts
wandering lost
somewhere in the distance.

forget, fight,
fight.
fight;
the needle on the ground,
the glass-pipe buried
inside deaf, muted walls.

forgive, forgive;
darling of old times,
yesteryears' grand love.
can you still hear me?
break, break through the ceiling,
come, come through
the unholy hole.

illegitimate claims,
bring back our lost daughter
from the alleys;
somewhere far away,
laughter's heard.

listen, listen,
to the dead silence of the grave
night.

go, go.
nothing left.

leave, leave.
and brace,
brace,
the undying silence
of the dark ocean of
tomorrow.

About the Author:

George Gad Economou, a professional drinker
born in Athens, Greece in 1990, has recently finished his Master's degree in Science Studies at
Aarhus University and is currently living in Athens,
sending out CV's to any job ad he comes across.

BEAR MARKET

Francisco Mejia

IF AUSTEN WERE GOD

Let's sanctify the antipodal sisters
magnetizing the world they call mine,

and the orbitless cataclysms they outlaw.
Canonize them while still alive,

when freshly glazed in beatification.
Endorse these diametric siblings

diagonally opposed. Swoon
to their counterpoint polarities, and

swim the euphony between their arctic
and antarctic. Reward the dearth

of redundancies, nature's reluctance to coin
the same woman twice. Minted in one womb,

I am that nation amenable to both currencies.

BEAR MARKET

A word is worth the world in weight.
This word whose solitude
plunders the skies

so every star flames out
inside a poem
impossible to swap for bread.

The outsized world does not
shelter a sole word. Instead
it hoards trillions.

Every minute.

Just see that plenitude
burdening the earth: a polysyllabic

hyperinflation
incapable of buying us

a shard of divinity.

TRAJECTORY TO LOMBARDI'S, 1905

King Darius' armies baked your ancestors upon their shields,
mouths reeking of cheese while suppressing
Babylonian revolts
and Nebuchadnezzar III.

Did Celaeno not foretell
the blood guilt
of Aeneas and his men,
guilt driving them to gnaw the edges of the tables
prefiguring you?

Back when Gaeta was a southern dog of
Byzantium
tied to the slack leash of suzerainty
and hunting shade in the afternoons of eastern empires...

your name first yeasted in a Latin manuscript,
10th century vintage
and leaking odors of herbs,
hops & garlic,
double-syllabled and modest,
fragrant with threats of future franchises &

listing instructions for a taxed tenant –

a duodecim for the bishop every Christmas
                    & another duodecim every Easter Sunday

The fabrication of your archetype's origin
nourished the neon of later centuries:

flashing diaphanous fables
of tricolor ingredients
and visiting queens:

signals clarifying the death of myths behind
crepuscular eyes.

ALCHEMY

What kind of freak
am I,
to savor the unwashed
backside of
"I love you,"
like a connoisseur
of the disposable diapers
my incontinent abuela wears?

What type of aberrancy
am I,
to mine
every fecal lode
I suspect
the eons have cultivated in
"You're the most beautiful
man I've ever had?"

What genus of demon
am I,
to yearn
for the decay
of last night's
caresses,
like the amassment of putrescent
fruit under
the pear tree
no longer flanking
my childhood
home?

What brand of fiend
am I,
to invert every
compliment you give, their
gassy innards
hanging loose &
dripping...
dripping...
            dripping...
all over the floor I
never
help you clean?

What size of monster
am I,
to pupate your
turquoise gaze
in my head,
butterflying it
into a disgust
that mutates my ego
like the richest
tumor
oncology has never seen?

No, wait. I mean
metamorphosis in reverse here,
caterpillaring
                    back
            back
back
from that hideous
imago curtaining
your sleep,
down to the larva
intrepid enough
to have burrowed
in your bowels,
and you so
unaware
of the ecstatic
parasite living
inside you.

About the Author:

Francisco Mejia is originally from New York but moved to Europe permanently when he was 25. He eventually settled in Slovakia. He has been living there for 15 years as a translator and English teacher, with his Slovak wife and four children.

LEAVE

Katie Predick

The Physics of Loss

I thought of you today
in the grocery store.
It is strawberry season and a bounty of bright red fruit
was piled in the cooler.
And I am back in that afternoon we went berry picking,
a golden nostalgia relative to the present
blue-cast flourescent lights.
You drag along an empty bucket as tall as your chubby knees,
but shove every berry straight into your mouth.
I can see the red juice pooling in your dimples.
How could anyone resist
all that sweetness?

Physicists assume relativity as a given,
a theory, by which they mean a truth. That
speed controls our experience of time.
That all of us are walking around
with our internal clocks ticking
at different rates.

And I think of my brother, your uncle –
the one who bought you that book about mathematics for infants, because
it is never too early to start
learning these things.
How he runs and runs, every day along the lake shore
and even marathons sometimes.
How many seconds more than me has he lived these past six years
by going so much faster?

But they also disagree,
the physicists, about whether time
is inherent to the universe or
whether we construct it with our minds.
They say time may not exist
at all, that everything could be present
all at once; our brains just need time
to deal with change.

So right here, in the produce section,
I try to overpower my reality with desire.
Stop my time right now,
in this moment,
and keep the sweet ripeness
of these berries intact forever.
Or even
bend it backward to the moment
they were plucked
from the vine.

Leave

Leave:
Go away from.
Allow to remain.

Ripples in water,
footprints in snow,
lingering perfume,
halo of light
after you stare at the sun.
Nostalgia,
which sprouts wooden
childhood memories
into full bloom.

That summer afternoon
scented of cut grass
you crawled beneath branches
fat with summer leaves and
discovered a private
pocket of green.
In that sun striated hideout

you listened to wind hushing
between leafy bushes,
to voices whispering
between teeth.
"...time to put her to sleep...
too much pain too walk...
too tired to wag her tail...long life...
...tell the girls..."
It was not until later you understood
this was a different kind
of bedtime.

Leaves are named
for their transience;
harbingers of spring
and an inevitable fall.

Do trees celebrate each spring green bud
and mourn every yellowed fallen leaf?
Do they become increasingly hardened
every autumn?

Perhaps they can simply observe fleeting seasons
with the wisdom
of weathered creatures.

Your puppy's wet black nose
turns every stone,
roots through compacted dirt
exposing fine white roots and the tracks of earthworms and beetles;
churns up all manner of rotting things wafting sweet decay.
Leave it.
Leave it.
Leave it.
Good dog.

Leave hope intact.
Leave your past and your troubles behind.
Leave the page unturned.
Leave the kettle on.
Leave well enough
alone.
Leave out the obscenities. Leave out the milk.
Leave it to chance.
Leave the scene of the crime; leave a broken window.
Leave the sugar
out of the pie.
Leave the leaves on the sidewalk.
Leave your mark.

The root of all this ambiguity
perhaps based in
the push-pull of wanting everything
to stay the same
and everything to change,
probably Latin.

Everything you ever lost
and everything that remains
in one tidy syllable.

About the Author:

Katie Predick is a student in the Master Class at the Writers Studio, Tucson. She was born amid a Chicago snowstorm and began thawing a decade ago in the Sonoran desert. She lives in Tucson with her husband and three children.

LUNAE LUMEN

Sara Pridmore Bailey

Vix Satis

The world is made of broken pieces:
Broken bodies, broken minds,
Broken spirits, broken dreams.
Collect all the pieces.
Take your time
Putting it all back together.
The cracks will always be there.
Some wounds never heal.
Cracks make us who we are?
Who we are – no, what we are –
Is damaged,
Some of us beyond all repair.
Can a butterfly fly with broken wings?
Can a bird with a broken neck sing?
But hell, broken is the norm around here
So smoke 'em if you got 'em
And have a shot on me.
Wear your scars like a smile
And pretend you're happy to survive.
Pretend every breath doesn't hurt
And every heartbeat isn't agony.

Scavenger

In the fall, my daughter
Cracks acorns open with pliers,
Searching fervently for a grub,
Hoping to find one nestled there,
Plump, soft bodied, and pale.
As she cradles its dingy white body
In her palm, she does not care
What it will become –
A June bug, a dung beetle, a chafer –
She thinks only of what it is now,
Engrossed in her efforts, she casts
Empty acorn husks aside,
Squealing with glee when she hits pay dirt.
She gathers a few grubs together,
Names them, forces them to be a family…
"This one is the daddy…"
She talks to them, wags them around,
Wallows them to death,
Then discards their broken bodies.
As she moves on to fruitlessly forage
For frogs, I think to myself that
No grub was ever so loved.

Drive

The sky is the softest shade of grey,
Not stern or stoic, but sympathetic.
The leaves turn their flaming faces away,
Muting themselves out of consideration.
The sky sheds tears for me,
Droplets that patter softly against my windshield.
My soul is untethered.
I am without purpose or plan or path,
A shadow, a shade, a shame.
My eyes meet my own in the rearview mirror.
Seized by sadness, a spasm of a sorrowful smile
Slips across my lips.
I am but a floret
Floating, falling, fearing failure.
I drive to escape the inescapable.
I know who I am, who I've been.
I drive to find out who I'm meant to be.

Intectus

You wanted to see me naked
So here I am, laid bare,
Bleeding my thoughts and feelings
Across the page in ink
Made blotted and blurry by tears.
I opened a vein for you
And look at what spilled out –
The ugly truth of an exposed soul
Scarred with sin, with shame, with sorrow,
Nursing wounded pride.
Feast your eyes on my flaws,
On my innate inadequacy.
Drink in my imperfections.
This is the me unaltered.
My anger, my pain, my jealousy
Are all on display.
Was this what you had in mind?

Lunae Lumen

It's just me and the moon again.
As I sit on the steps in a puddle of cold light,
The darkness of night surrounds me;
It feels thick and heavy and dangerous
As it presses in. I hide out here with
My loneliness. The winter moon,
So far away and frosty; the prickle of
The cold night air; the smooth, bitter
Taste of a cigarette; and the nicotine that
Permeates my pores – these are the comforts
That I cling to. Alone in a world full of people,
Thoughts crowd into my head, so I escape
Outside where the cold quiets my mind.

About the Author:

Sara Bailey received her B.A. in Writing and Rhetoric from the University of Central Arkansas and her MFA in Creative Writing with an emphasis in fiction from Murray State University. The majority of her writing is fiction or poetry, but she has also tried her hand at nonfiction and screenwriting. Her work has been published in New Madrid and Torrid Literature Journal, and her poetry will be included in the fall edition of Big Muddy.

GOLEM

Leslie Philibert

Lemons for Klara

for Klara Grünzweig 1957-2016

drops of river or ice patches;
all of this without your notice
      but tough and half eternal

the lemon tree grows
      cool and silent;
      this makes you remain.

Golem

unholy earth, dark with stein,
unformed loam at birth;
a worded child of mud,

fingernail skinned blacklack eyes,
peek out of a ball of wet slam;
a groundling that waves like a black branch

across the sleeping fields,
see a shadow under the cold grass,
near in sight under a crust of frost.

Tower of the Blue Horses

(after Franz Marc)

Four of stained glass and stars
all leftglance beyond ratio or air,
thin as tissue but strong

as a pastel visa; fated curves
guide your hand, voices drag you
into mud and steal the day.

A Night in Tenerife

the sea the skin of a wet dog,
black the beach; a ruined church,
the coastal lights a string of lesser ways;
we are as empty as a dropped shell
pulled across the ebb, a ripple of salt:

and as the night gets deeper
a dragon breathes like the tide:
no mistake, the dark needs its hours.

After Reading The Bell Jar

curl up like black paper,
burning like a moth;
a glove turned inside out;

trapped too under a house,
a circle hidden and musty,
fragile under steps;

let us escape the carrying,
legions of white coats,
corridors as long as life.

About the Author:

Leslie Philibert is a London-born poet and social worker living in Germany. He studied English Literature in Ireland. He has published poems in a number of magazines in the US and UK and has also translated for South German theatre groups. He is married with two children.

SOME NIGHTS

Dianne Moritz

SIX

Teasing the dog
Back behind
The chicken yard
To distract myself
From loneliness,
Stench of the farm,
Uncle's mongrel seized
My thin wrist and bit.
My cries were smothered
In boozy serves-you-rights,
While blood spilled,
Staining my summer smock.
Aunie brought me milk
Straight from a cow.
I ran to the rusty sink,
Spit it out as Mother's
Hand slapped me hard.
I raced outside.

The slam of the screen
Still echoes....

SOME NIGHTS

She stumbled in,
Reeking, slurring
As fear flamed
In your belly, face
Flushed red and angry.
She slept, finally,
Passed out on the
Bathroom floor,
Small squares marking
Her cheek in the morning.
She said she craved
The flat coolness.

Some years later,
You would understand
When a bed sent you
Spinning, orbiting rooms,
Your head exploding.
You, too, found comfort
On cold, stone floors.
Nothing else could ground you.

About the Author:

Dianne Moritz grew up in Iowa and graduated from the University of Iowa. She studied poetry writing with the Iowa Writer's Workshop (correspondence classes) in the 1990's. She has published many poems for adults in various national poetry journals.

She is a frequent contributor to Highlights children's magazines. Her picture book, 1, 2, 3 BY THE SEA, was on the "best book list of 2014" compiled by Bank Street College in New York City.

EVOLUTION

Eduardo Escalante

Evolution

During the slow rollover of the morning,
I order the garden plants.
In my hands, several seeds.
I hear the groaning of the earth,
need to clear its throat, lacks water.
Everything grows dense, gathering light.
Gravity and time are working,
a leaf expecting to be born into the next inexorable instant,
sometimes with a somewhat musical impulse,
others, exhausting some emotional threads.
Fragrance in the air.
Everything with its own small moon, its tides
and longings.
Atoms of alive dust in the air.
Perhaps only a wind knows earth.
The wind touches flowers, something growth or dies away.
Listen and look.
A sparkling set of conversions of things surrounds me.
In the afternoon, a butterfly plays on the ground,
Diagonals are in harmony with the pleated lines
of the sky. The patterns of the earth and sky combine.
The same conjunction spiral of how old
shows its renewal.

Lies are here.

Disturbs the streets,
lies come slipping
Leaning on the dead weight of
      the moon.

Air without colors.
It's not just words,
not drunken dreams.
The eye bites and leaves the other
        in the dead water.

Lies are rolling on the steep
slopes of the black nights.
When silence,
danger is imminently devastating.
They tear us without
even acting.

Life does not train people to
dearly love the truth
......the slight
degrees where truth
go missing

Lies will remain the mud
splattering all over,
you will be trapped
if leaning and kneeling there
for a long time.

.

About the Author:

Eduardo Escalante is a writer and researcher living in Valparaíso, Chile; he publishes regularly in Hispanic Reviews (Signum Nous, Ariadna, Nagari, Espacio Luke, Lakuma Pusaki, among others); and reviews in English (StlylusLit, Writer Resits, Spillwords, Slamchop and in Gramma Poetry).

A BAG OF HANDS

Mather Schneider

A BAG OF HANDS

Jalisco, Mexico. In a black plastic bag
they found them:

12 severed hands
removed from their owners, for thievery, por rateros,

and put in this bag, the kind of bag
you put beer in from Osco, filled with ice

but no ice for these hands, rancid, rotting
in the heat, flies, dried blood.

I've always hated my hands, small, red, wrinkly,
old man hands.

When I was in 3rd grade I looked
at my classmates' hands and mine

were different. Ugly, deformed. Self-loathing.
Most of all I envied dark smooth hands,

Indian hands. I thought
they were beautiful. And now 50

years later I'm a taxi driver and I see this bag of hands
they found in Mexico

as a punishment
and a warning.

For 3 days I've been looking at these hands.
I think of that Sherwood Anderson story I read long ago

about the man whose hands got him into trouble
when he only wanted to love. That's when

I wanted to be a writer. So many things to do
with these guilty hands, but writing seemed

a good thing. And people say:
you should take that bag

of hands and craft a novel around it, make
money, entertain people, quit this

stupid job.
I don't know. It's real,

that's the problem, this black
plastic bag full of severed hands.

I've stolen things. Hasn't everybody?
One time when I was young I was too sick for school

and I was home alone, in bed,
and a man broke into our house

and came into my bedroom, looking for loot.
I woke up and said, "Who are you?" He ran

stomping up the stairs, I heard the door
slam and his truck tires throw gravel out

of our driveway. The police asked if I
could recognize the man and I drew a picture of him

and they used the picture to convict him. He lived
a few miles away. I drew a picture of him

with my hands and everybody
said I was a real good artist.

Nobody likes to have their house broken into.
Nobody wants to work hard for things

and then have someone come along and steal them.
I just hope

it was the right man.
Now I am old and have grown

into my old man's hands, but I still don't
like them, these hands on the steering wheel

of this taxi cab, arthritic, ticking.
I keep looking at everyone's

hands now, my passengers' hands.
Some of them have scars

on their wrists. Some of them are grotesque,
worse than mine. Some of them

don't work well, they tremble.
Some of them are beautiful and smooth

as buckeyes. Some of them are so calloused they cut
you when you shake them. Some of them cup

the sunlight.
Imagine the hands

that held the thieves down, the hands that raised
the machete, the hands

that fell. Pretension
is a fog on the brain. The poets

scribble, the novelists invent.
Hand shadows, hand puppets,

hands of time, hands of God. A clock
without hands. Why

couldn't that black plastic bag
have had a six pack of beer in it instead?

I remember when my wife first took my hand
walking in our old Tucson barrio.

My wife is Mexican
and she has lovely hands, hands that lifted

a barbed wire fence on the border, hands that turn
burgers to feed her father

back home. What would I not take
from this world to give to her? I ask myself

as I write these words with my numb hands.
Nothing? The truth is

I don't know.
When you're looking

at a black plastic bag full of severed hands
you don't know what to think. Your mind stumbles

and claws at the air.

About the Author:

BREATHE THE DAMP

The Mexican hospital
is hot   a long thin tube of light

sputters over the doctor's bald head   a polished
stone   an x-ray hangs on the wall

a skeleton buried within it   a ship
sits frozen

in a bottle on his desk
that my wife and I can see under

to his animal-skin shoes   the floor chewed
by the wheels

of his chair   a yellow stain in the corner
of the ceiling   what horrors are happening

upstairs?   I'm dizzy and seasick
at the thought of my angel's urine

in a little cup   the cups for the water dispenser
full of dust and spiders   her knees swell red and hot

as roasted agave hearts   molten tequila
sears each minute's throat   my poor Lupita

trembles on the doctor's table   Why are you nervous?
he asks her   it's only Death

preparing his needles   his poison smile
like a fishing hook   bone ready to give

birth to fire   brave Chiquita
crippled at 43   twitching in pain she thinks of the baby

she could never have
cries and squeezes my hand

while the doctor injects her
as if to kill bugs in a wainscoting   later that night

we lay in bed in the little house
in Hermosillo   sweaty and sticky as flypaper   lightning

starts in the south   slices the Sonoran sky
like the soft underside

of a wrist   rain
tramples the tin roof   scrambles for cracks   hail

like gravel on a coffin lid and a vile
merciless wind like the Devil

blowing out his birthday candles   the lights
go black   the blades

of the fan come poised   everywhere is a doorway   we open the window
lie there sprayed by saltless tears   side by side

hand in hand   breathe the damp   curling sulfur
of a ghastly wish

About the Author:

Mather Schneider was born in 1970 in Peoria, Illinois. He lived in Washington state for many years and now lives in Tucson. His poetry and prose have appeared in the small presses since 1994 in places such as River Styx, Nimrod, Hanging Loose, Pank and Rosebud. He has 4 full length books available on Amazon including the July 2017 release of Prickly by New York Quarterly Press. He recently won runner up in the 2017 Rattle poetry chapbook competition.

STEVEN PELCMAN

author of a poetry collection **like water to STONE**

" *Many poets can scratch words onto paper, but they lack the painter's eye that turns those words into images that rise from the page to take our breath away. Mr. Pelcman is what we might call a verbal cinematographer. His words often arrive with familiar experiences, causing us to nod our heads as we watch them unfold quietly, gently before us. And then, without warning, he delivers a sledgehammer's blow that slams an event before us--one that we don't deserve to share--and it hangs in memory like a fishhook in the mind's eye. A poet whose body and soul carry the baggage of his years with dignity and grace, Steven Pelcman's poetry has already made its mark. It will be read far into the future.*"

(Dan Masterson, Award Winning Poet)

ALM: Tell us a bit about yourself, about Steven Pelcman, a poet, and how many poems you have written.

My parents emigrated to the USA after the WW2 and they didn't know English so I spent a great deal of time alone as I tried to learn the language mostly because I didn't speak English till I went to public school. Due to the lack of help at home I wound up not doing well but I spent a lot of time alone often reading the World Book Encyclopedia which nurtured my curiosity. This resulted in creating a great sense of self-discovery and a desire to do well in English and to put thoughts onto paper. Over time it also meant that I discovered the beauty of the language and so I started writing when I was around 11 or 12. Eventually it led me to enter a writing program at college where I studied with a Professor who taught me the power of an image, of sound and movement and an appreciation for the written word. It made me want to be a writer and after leaving New York for New Orleans and then later on to LA to try and get work in the tv and film industry all the while writing poetry. Everyone knows how much of "life" took place in the 1960s and 1970s and as full of conflict and challenges it may have presented to us, it was also a great time for creativity in film, music, poetry and so on. That inspired so many, me included.

ALM: Do you remember what was your first ever poem about and when did you write it?

As a matter of fact, I do. It was early on in public school and it was a poem titled, "A Gentle Rain" and the teacher of my class promised I would get it published if I changed the title to "The Gentle Rain" which I refused to do, ha, have stood my ground ever since.

ALM: Why do you write poetry? How about writing a prose?

Because I need to. There is something in a person's heart and soul that says, "This is who and what I am." I guess many never discover that but I did. I needed to live out my imagination and emotions and I sought answers to questions I didn't even fully comprehend at that time. I write prose as well; short stories, film scripts, novels and like with the poetry I make every effort to get them published or sold as well.

ALM: What is the title of your latest poem and what inspired it?

The last poem written and published was a re-write of a poem I had worked on a while ago titled, A Small World, which is in my poetry collection, "like water to STONE" recently published by Adelaide Books. It was inspired by my mother or rather remembering a time with my mother. I envisioned her and I walking out into the garden and for whatever reason I felt the years that had passed, the sense of aging and the futures we all face and I showed some comparisons to nature, time and so on. For me it is a gentle, moving piece of remembering my mother when she was young and I guess when I was too. Popshot recently published the poem as well.

ALM: How long it did it take you to write your latest poem and how fast do you write?.

I often take notes about what I observe and feel and at times it takes a few hours but the initial writing may go fast but it is the editing process and repeating a poem aloud hundreds of times as I review it that takes time. I need to feel that every sense of the poem is in place, that there is logic and the beauty and is the story that I need to get onto the page before it is finished.

ALM: Do you have any unusual writing habits?

No, not really other than I rarely stop until I feel it is a finished product unless tiredness brings me to stopping before I am finished.

ALM: Is it poetry or writing the only form of artistic expression that you utilize, or there is more to Steven Pelcman than just poetry?

I love taking pictures and put a lot of creativity into that and the cover of "like water to STONE" is one of my photos. I believe the sense of image on the page is similar to what I try to capture with photography.

ALM: What authors or poets have influenced you?

I enjoy the work of many poets but some of my favorites are Mary Oliver, James Dickey, Mark Strand, Some Sexton and Plath, William Carlos Williams, Roethke, Miller Williams and my Profs work, Dan Masterson to name a few.

ALM: As an author and poet what are you working on now?

I recently finished a novel that I think will fly and I am beginning work on a new short story.

ALM: In your opinion, what is the best way when it comes to promoting poetry? Did you ever think about the profile of your readers? What do you think – who reads Steven Pelcman?

The best way to promote poetry is to read it; give readings, watch videos because poetry is often captivating when read aloud by a good reader but of course in today's world all marketing promotion is online, via podcasts and so on. I do think of the readers but I write on what I think works for me, what moves me and I hope the reader will feel and think and see what I do. As to who reads my work; I hope anyone that cares about a story. No one loves everything written by anyone but I do hope there are some pieces that matter and make people enjoy the work.

ALM: Do you have any advice for new poets/ authors?

It may sound corny but for me I would say, believe in your heart and intellect, believe in how you feel when you observe or experience something or when you listen to the experiences of others and out it onto paper or of course, a word page and write. Write and never give up till you are satisfied. Learning the technical aspects comes later and learning the pain of revision, the time and the dedication comes to us all, if you truly want to write. Never give up if writing is who you are.

ALM: What is the best advice you have ever heard?

Coming out of one of my first workshops having brought a poem of about 50 lines and being told that, "You have got 3 great lines to work with", was devastating and funny at the same time. The best advice is to listen to your heart. If it tells you to go on then go on.

ALM: What are you reading now?

I'm presently reading SPQR A History of Ancient Rome by Mary Beard and Death of The Poets By Paul Farley and Michael Symmons Roberts.

ALM: Who are your favorite authors and poets, and what are your favorite books ever?

Some of my favorite poets are the same ones that influenced me but other than poetry I am a Lincoln admirer and so some of my favorite books are on Lincoln: Gore Vidal's, Lincoln, Team of Rivals by Doris Kearns Goodwin, Lincoln's Boys by Joshua Zeitz or some great bios such as Boswell's The Life of Samuel Johnson, The Education of Henry Adams by Adams, and many historical novels and work by Robert Harris, Joseph Ellis or David McCullough and I love a good western so I read up on the old west; Custer and Earp and so on. I love history and Rome or Egypt, USA; France and so on have such great histories so I enjoy those a lot.

ALM: What do you deem the most relevant about your writing?

The image is central to my work and my work must tell a story, one full of thought and emotion, observation and realism and the desire to often make what is hard or cruel or rough, gentle and still see all sides to the moment.

ALM: What is next after "like water to STONE." Are we going to see something new on the bookshelves by Steven Pelcman?

In today's publishing world not everything published goes to bookshelves but I believe so, a modern western novel put out by Outlaws Publishing seems to be on the horizon.

Since the beginning of time mankind has created, experimented, investigated, explored, lived and died and time has passed and the world undergoes change all the time yet some things remain constant: creators of the written word and what those words must offer outlive everything. We can read what Cicero experienced in Rome, what Lincoln felt about slavery, how Anne Sexton thought about her father and it is for the writer to record the history of time, the pain of men's souls, the lust and happiness, the bitterness of war and the desire for freedom which cries out onto the pages of the author, the poet, the novelist, the historian, the song writer, the educator, the shopkeeper or the waitress, the dentist, the tech writer or copywriter or the University Professor; we all have one thing we share; to write about who and what we are and were. It's the main way to remember we were alive.

ALM: Thank you, Steven. Good luck with your future projects.

LIKE WATER TO STONE
by Steven Pelcman

Paperback: 152 pages

Publisher: Adelaide Books (October 6, 2017)

Language: English

ISBN-10: 0999214896

ISBN-13: 978-0999214893

Product Dimensions: 6 x 0.4 x 9 inches

" Many poets can scratch words onto paper, but they lack the painter's eye that turns those words into images that rise from the page to take our breath away. Mr. Pelcman is what we might call a verbal cinematographer. His words often arrive with familiar experiences, causing us to nod our heads as we watch them unfold quietly, gently before us. And then, without warning, he delivers a sledgehammer's blow that slams an event before us--one that we don't deserve to share--and it hangs in memory like a fishhook in the mind's eye. A poet whose body and soul carry the baggage of his years with dignity and grace, Steven Pelcman's poetry has already made its mark. It will be read far into the future."

(Dan Masterson, Award Winning Poet)

Steven Pelcman is an American educator, film producer and published author who has been residing in Germany for over 19 years. Mr. Pelcman's poetry and short stories have been published in many magazines including The Windsor Review, The Innisfree Poetry Journal, Fourth River magazine, River Oak Review, Poetry Salzburg Review, Tulane Review, The Baltimore Review, The Warwick Review, The Cape Rock magazine, The Greensboro Review, enskyment.org, Iodine Poetry Journal, Rockhurst Review magazine and numerous others. He was nominated for the 2012 Pushcart Prize.

http://stevenpelcman.blogspot.de

STEALING: LIFE IN AMERICA
by Michelle Cacho-Negrete

Paperback: 208 pages

Publisher: Adelaide Books (October 12, 2017)

Language: English

ISBN-10: 0999516418

ISBN-13: 978-0999516416

Product Dimensions: 6 x 0.5 x 9 inches

In this beautifully crafted, incisive collection, readers will admire Michelle Cacho Negrete's determination and fierce desire to transcend her early Brooklyn ghetto roots--particularly her sense of herself as a displaced outsider. What's also impressive about Stealing is not only how candid and open the author is, but how vividly she describes this complex human struggle. **- Michael Steinberg -Author, Still Pitching, 2003 ForeWord Magazine/Independent Press Memoir of the Year**

"Michelle writes with grace and clear-eyed, un-sentimental vision." **Sy Safransky, Editor, Sun Magazine**

"Cacho-Negrete champions the poor, the marginalized...Throughout this profound, compelling collection, she preserves the vanishing past with a hard-hitting yet lush remembrance." **Lee Hope Betcher, Editor Solstice Literary Magazine, author Horse fever.**

"With crisp, confident prose, Michelle explores the intricacies of our world in essays simultaneously unique and universal. A book to be read many times." **Barry Lyga - Best Selling New York Times author**

"The America we face in these timely essays is often poor, frequently unjust, sometimes heartbreaking – and always illuminated by the author's fearless truths, keen insights, and fighting spirit." **Krista Bremer – prize winner lecturer and author of My Tender Struggle.**

"Here is the power of the written word: Alone in his room, the reader feels a strengthened connection to all of humanity." **Gin Mackey, Author of DISAPPEAR OUR DEAD and SUDDENLY SPYING**

"These stories grab hold and won't let you go. They will change you." Anne B. Gass, lecturer, author - Voting Down The Rose

"Although these are separate essays, they are linked by these consistent themes and form in themselves an engrossing and beautifully-written memoir." **Jenny Doughty - President, Maine Poets Society, author—Sending Bette Davis to The Plumber**

ANDERS M. SVENNING

VERDANT GROUNDS, SUBTLE BOUNDARIES
by Anders M. Svenning

Paperback: 190 pages

Publisher: Adelaide Books (October 6, 2017)

Language: English

ISBN-10: 099951640X

ISBN-13: 978-0999516409

Product Dimensions: 6 x 0.5 x 9 inches

"In Columbus" takes the reader through an out-of-synch, or un-chronological journey through Timmy's childhood. The small sections are like vignettes on their own and when put together they create a miasma of human consternation.

"Planes" takes the reader along with pilot Davis Parker as he, while navigating through planes of thought, redefines fatherhood. He, too, is contending with the possibility of enlightening his adopted daughter, Lillian "Bird" Parker.

"The Beauty in Bereavement" takes the reader along with Judy Tremont as she, following the recent loss of her husband, apprehends the beauty in bereavement. Judy Tremont is an aging woman in a world which is quite changed. The recollections of her husband, Augustus Tremont, and of her son, Franklin Tremont, intermittent and entwined in the narration with dreams she has been having since her husband's death provokes thoughts pertaining to turn of the century philosophy, turn of the century familial dynamics, and music.

"Equal Men" takes the reader along with protagonist Richard Louis on a defining day in his life—the day he retires and the day his son, in his eyes, atolls.

Anders M. Svenning was born in New York. He started writing with seriousness at the age of nineteen and has now been published in many literary magazines throughout the United States and abroad. Some of the most recent include Dark Gothic Magazine, Adelaide Literary Magazine, and Degenerate Literature. He is the author of Nonpareil (Tule Fog Press), 50 States Poetry (Pansophic Press), and has a collection of short stories forthcoming, titled Verdant Grounds, Subtle Boundaries (Adelaide Books). The Phrenologist (Wapshott Press), a novella, is also forthcoming piece by Anders M. Svenning. Anders M. Svenning lives in Palm City, Florida.

THEY is a groundbreaking work that will prove to be lifesaving for those in the LGBT community and enlightening and liberating to others.

In this novel we met Tamar from the Hebrew Bible. Tamar lives as a hermit in the desert, is content with her life and is happily barren. She is attached to her pet camel. Her aversion to goat sacrifices becomes so strong that it prompts her to become a vegetarian. Tamar has a twin sister Tabitha who becomes pregnant after seducing a young muscular shepherd. Tamar plots with Tabitha to trick Judah (a patriarch from the Bible) into believing that the baby is his so that she can have status in society rather than being burnt at the stake. Tabitha gives birth to twins. Tamar becomes attached to the children (born intersex), who call her auntie, and follows their line of intersex twins.

Janet Mason is an award-winning creative writer, teacher, marketing professional and blogger for The Huffington Post. Her book, Tea Leaves, a memoir of mothers and daughters, published by Bella Books in 2012, was chosen by the American Library Association for its 2013 Over the Rainbow List. Tea Leaves also received a Goldie Award. She is the author of three poetry books.

THEY: A BIBLICAL TALE OF SECRET GENDERS
by Janet Mason

Paperback: 300 pages

Publisher: Adelaide Books (November 2017)

Language: English

ISBN-10: 0-9995164-3-4

ISBN-13: 978-0-9995164-3-0

Product Dimensions: 6 x 0.7 x 9 inches

SURRENDER LANGUAGE explores two different coming of age stories. The first of which is that of Dr. Neal Basilla, a European history professor at Hunting's Bridge College who has found himself struggling with severe Parkinson's disease following the recent death of his wife, Tess. Alone and in his last semester of professorship this cynical, slightly bitter, Vietnam vet is wracked with his past memories and thoughts of his dwindling future. The second, intertwining coming of age story is of Denny Helling a senior in college, who is about to graduate and enter into the 'real world'. This young man notices Dr. Basilla's discomfort and manages to step into his life as a friend and confidant. Denny is a quirky but shy inspiring actor who is far different than the aging, cynical professor. They do have something in common however. Denny's sister Bridget is suffering from stage four cervical cancer; once a budding dancer who had nailed a contract at a major ballet, she is now very weak and spends her days painting birds. Denny helps Dr. Neal come to terms with his illness, and his past. Dr. Neal's rough tone, and rich past can connect with any age, especially an adult crowd, both young and old.

Nina Wilson is a graduate of Coe College in Cedar Rapids Iowa. She lives in Indianola Iowa with her family. She loves history, especially early English history, photography, traveling, fishing, and camping. Surrender Language is her first published book.

SURRENDER LANGUAGE
by Nina Wilson

Paperback: 270 pages

Publisher: Adelaide Books (November 2017)

Language: English

ISBN-10: 0-9995164-5-0

ISBN-13: 978-0-9995164-5-4

Product Dimensions: 6 x 0.7 x 9 inches

LIVING AMONG STRANGERS
by Richard Schmitt

Paperback: 230 pages

Publisher: Adelaide Books (November 2017)

Language: English

ISBN-10: 0-9995164-2-6

ISBN-13: 978-0-9995164-2-3

Product Dimensions:6 x 0.5 x 9 inches

"Reading Living Among Strangers is like watching a series of Beckett plays recast in the percussive, irreverent voice of a writer who takes nothing for granted, who follows the possibilities inherent in language and in everyday human failings. Here are characters estranged from the world: unparented kids walking the train trestle, a widowed mother whose pack of daughters push her toward assisted living, an alcoholic trying to give up drink by questioning the very root of desire. It is in the characters' estrangement that the reader finds kinship. As with the manicured Floridian lawns of Bahia Vista Estates in the title story, in this collection, "[t]here are rumors, things under the surface, things man-made and not." Richard Schmitt is a writer who digs beneath the surface to yield up beauty in the coarse, wisdom in the baffled." (Jessie van Eerden , the author of a novel Glorybound)

"Richard Schmitt is a storyteller. His stories seem not to start so much as startle, drawing us into a world that might feel familiar, but that we've never seen quite this way. Like one of his narrators, he knows to ignore the map, point his nose, and go. The magic is in his sentences, which at their best are sleek and strange and urgent, surprising and illuminating." (Peter Turchi, the author of A Muse and A Maze)

Richard Schmitt is the author of The Aerialist, a novel (Harcourt, 2000), and has published fiction and nonfiction in Arts & Letters, Cimarron Review, Gettysburg Review, Gulf Coast, North American Review, Puerto del Sol, and other places. His story, "Leaving Venice, Florida," won 1st Prize in The Mississippi Review story contest. He has been anthologized in New Stories of the South: The Year's Best 1999 and The Best American Essays, 2013.

"There was a sub that day in freshman Latin class at St. Aloysius High in suburban San Antonio, Texas, so all hell had broken loose. Spitballs were flying, there were arm wrestling matches on desks, a trash can basketball game had broken out in a corner. Desks were rearranged for impromptu conference groups.

The sub was a painfully-thin, prematurely-balding man who lost control of the class immediately. His protruding Adam's Apple bobbed up and down spasmodically. The underarms of his starched white discount store dress shirt were soaked in perspiration, his shiny black polyester slacks were hiked up high over white sports socks and brown tasseled loafers. His name was Mr. Waldo, the name itself the inspiration for put-downs and derision. I felt sorry for Mr. Waldo. I pitied him. I identified with him. He was somebody who was never going to command respect or command an audience. He had a wife and young child, he had told us, and I felt sorry for them, too. You could only hope they would be blinded to what a dufus their husband and father was."

THE LATIN SUB, IMPURE THOUGHTS AND ONE MAN'S DEFINITION OF MORTAL SIN
by Steven McBrearty

Paperback: 220 pages

Publisher: Adelaide Books (November 2017)

Language: English

ISBN-10: 0-9995164-4-2

ISBN-13: 978-0-9995164-4-7

Product Dimensions: 6 x 0.5 x 9 inches

Steven McBrearty grew up in San Antonio, Texas, in one of those big, rollicking Catholic families so common in the 1960s. On any given day, there might be games of pitch and catch in the hallway or tackle football in the back bedroom. He moved to Austin to attend the University of Texas and has lived in Austin ever since. He has published more than 35 short stories, humor pieces, and non-fiction articles and has received several honors for his writing. His story collection, "Christmas Day on a City Bus," was published in 2011 by McKinney Press. He has two grown children and four lovely grandchildren.

EMOTIONS / EMOÇÕES
by Pierre Sotér

Series: Poems and Thoughts by Pierre Sotér

Paperback: 174 pages

Publisher: Adelaide Books (Fall 2017)

Language: English and Portuguese

ISBN-10: 0-9992148-5-3

ISBN-13: 978-0-9992148-5-5

Product Dimensions: 6 x 0.4 x 9 inches

With reason, we go beyond what we can sense. With emotions, we go beyond what we can reason. If, and only if, we take the time to listen to our deep states of mind, to our divine instincts, and then have the courage to follow them. And bring our souls with us wherever we go, whenever we come back.

We have a word for this: Emotions. But not enough words to explain it. We will never have enough words for such a task. Therefore, possibly, the only way to expose our emotions is through poetry.

In poetry each word can, in mysterious ways, by combining with other words, in mysterious ways, allow us to travel through our emotions, and make it possible for new emotions, sometimes unknown, to take over our souls and minds. That's what the words in this book are trying to do, in their own emotional way. Like in the simple words of love, in which there is love and there is more. There are emotions.

EMOTIONS is a poetry book written in two languages. English and Portuguese. All poems are original, for it is not possible to translate a poem without losing the emotions that are embedded in the words. Two people may share emotions, but they will never be exactly the same. Likewise, for words.

"Quando uma luz brilha sózinha
e à minha volta não há ninguém,
fico a pensar numa que eu tinha,
se afinal é essa luz alguém."

"In this life that is so brief,
we can only make it stronger
by making moments massive
till they can't move any longer."

Pierre Sotér is the pen name of a well-established Portuguese author. After thirty years of successful professional life and intensive soul-searching, he now dedicates his time to poetry and philosophy. The EMOTIONS is the third book in the Book Series "Poems and Thoughts of Pierre Sotér." Pierre writes in Portuguese, English, and French.

ART & PHOTOGRAPHY

NAZARÉ

Photography by A.F. Nikolic

Photos by A.F. Nikolic could be seen in our online gallery at:

http://photography.adelaidemagazine.org

The earliest settlements were in Pederneira and in Sítio, above the beach. They provided the inhabitants with refuge against raids by Viking, later French, English and Dutch pirates, that lasted until as late as the beginning of the 19th century.

According to the Legend of Nazaré, the town derives its name from a small wooden statue of the Virgin Mary, a Black Madonna, brought by a monk in the 4th century from Nazareth, Holy Land, to a monastery near the city of Mérida, Spain. The statue was brought to its current place in 711 by another monk, Romano, accompanied by Roderic, the last Visigoth king of today's Portugal. After their arrival at the seaside they decided to become hermits. The monk lived and died in a small natural grotto, on top of a cliff above the sea. After his death and according to the monk's wishes, the king buried him in the grotto. Roderic left the statue of the Black Madonna in the grotto on an altar.

The first church in Sítio was built over the grotto to commemorate a miraculous intervention in 1182 by the Virgin Mary, which saved the life of the 12th-century Portuguese knight Dom Fuas Roupinho (possibly a Knight Templar) while he was hunting deer one morning in a dense fog. This episode is usually referred to as the Legend of Nazaré. In memory of the miracle he had a chapel (Capela da Memória) built over the small grotto, where the miraculous statue had been left by king Roderic after the monk's death. Beside the chapel, on a rocky outcrop 110 meters above the Atlantic, one can still see the mark made in the rock by one of the hooves of Dom Fuas' horse. This Church of Nazareth, high on the rocky outcrop over Pederneira bay, was noted as a landmark in sailors' manuals. (Source:Wikipedia)

ACEITAMOS SUBMISSÓES

Convite a todos os autores independentes: Vamos tornar esta revista um sucesso!

Looking for contributors and guest editors.

A Adelaide Magazine é uma publicação internacional independente publicada trimestralmente em inglês e português, de momento, à procura de submissões.

Pretendemos publicar ficção, não-ficção e poesia excepcionais assim como promover os escritores que publicamos, ajudando os autores novos e emergentes a atingir uma audiência literária mais vasta. Na Adelaide Magazine, os autores podem promover o seu livro de modo grátis, listando o seu livro na página dedicada a Novos Títulos, submeter uma entrevista e uma crítica literária, e ainda oferecer os seus serviços de escrita, edição, design e tradução assim como outros serviços na área da edição, gratuitamente, na secção de Anúncios Classificados

We are accepting fiction, nonfiction, poetry, book reviews, interviews, event announcements, artwork and photography.

Check our submission guidelines at:

http://adelaidemagazine.org/submit.html

Esta é uma revista literária de autores independentes para autores independentes! Seja parte do nosso sucesso! Seja um dos editores convidados desta edição!

In our magazine you can promote your book for free, list your book on the new titles page, submit an interview or book review, and place an ad for free on our classifieds page, offering your writing, editing, design, translation, or other publishing services. You can be a guest editor for the issue!

Check out our website and don't be shy to send us your work. This is a literary magazine by indie authors for indie authors!

http://adelaidemagazine.org